PALIMPSEST

A Man's Life in San Francisco

By Charles A. Fracchia

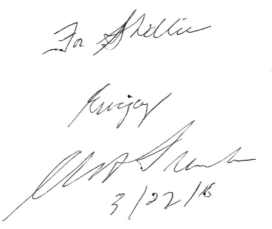

For Stella

enjoy

Chip Fracchia

3/22/18

pa-limp-sest, n. writing material (as a parchment or tablet) used two or three times after earlier writing has been erased.

CHAPTER 1

Frank Molinari looked over at his dozing companion as the airplane banked over Santa Barbara on its way from San Francisco to San Diego. He had known Chris Martini for almost fifty years, since they began St. Aloysius High School, and now they were on their way to the funeral of one of their closest friends and classmates. It was hard to believe that the vigorous, ebullient, brilliant Bob Franco was dead of cancer in his mid-60s.

It was even harder to believe that a band of friends (Italian Americans, Irish Americans, German Americans, mostly) who had gravitated toward one another in a Catholic high school in post-World War II San Francisco had now lost one of their group to a painful death.

Frank lay back in his seat, gazed vaguely out the window, and watched the surf of the blue Pacific gently crash on the white sand beaches of one of California's oldest cities.

What plans, what excitement, what a sense of never-ending life they had had in those high school years. These plans and this sense of excitement had extended for probably two decades after they graduated from St. Aloysius.

And what now? Frank bitterly reflected on his divorce, on the fact that his career in investment management had not brought him the riches or the satisfaction that he had expected when he joined Blakesley and Montgomery after law school, that all his four children were now married, and that he was growing old.

How had all this happened? What difference did it make? It had happened. The cramped airplane seat made his body feel stiff—a sign, he felt, of the deterioration of his body. He had felt this decline for some time. His delight in sexual encounters with his second wife had become a perfunctory, unsatisfactory, occasional copulation. Time had run out: he would never become an investment magnate, would never become one of the city's "movers and shakers." Perhaps he had expected too much. Maybe he had been too ambitious. Maybe life had realistically assessed his talents, and luck had not been on his side. But it was no use dwelling on these melancholy thoughts.

His old friend, Chris, contentedly sleeping next to him, was not bothered by such disappointments. He was blissfully happy in his first marriage, had raised two daughters who had done very well in their careers, and had been an executive in the same company for thirty-five years. He had numerous friends and never expressed any discontent with his life.

"What's down there, Los Angeles?" asked an awakened Chris. "Thank God we don't live there. Look, it's like an endless suburb."

There it was—the typical San Francisco response to Los Angeles—a city without culture, a city where it was impossible to get a good meal, a horrible urban sprawl intersected by ugly, impassible freeways, a city whose inhabitants had no elegance.

Frank knew better. He had spent some time in Los Angeles during his career as an investment advisor. Yes, he preferred the small physical space of San Francisco; it reminded him of Paris or Florence. And he appreciated the last vestiges of elegance that could still be seen in the city. But, Los Angeles' creation of wealth, its raw energy, its ability to efficiently create and organize civic enterprises had brought to the City of the Queen of Angels wonderful restaurants, museums, superb music.

"Yes, we should be in San Diego pretty soon," Frank replied.

"I'll bet Catherine is pretty broken up."

"I don't know. She's had a long time to get used to it. She's a pretty stoic person."

"Still, they've been married for thirty-five years, and I think they had a pretty good marriage."

"Do you think so?" Frank queried. "I don't think Bob had much energy or time for anyone but himself. I loved him to death, but he had the biggest ego I've ever seen."

Bob Franco had been an academic who loved to talk about his ideas. He hadn't been content to write and teach, but had sought a wider stage: appointments to governmental commissions, for example, where he found new pulpits for the never ceasing expounding of his opinions.

"I know, but I think they really loved each other. She certainly seemed to adore him. We all overlooked his eccentricities."

"I'm not saying they didn't love each other. I just don't think that Bob had much room in his life for anyone but himself. Remember when we would see him after a long absence? He'd just start pouring out his ideas, not once stopping to ask us how we were or letting us say anything about ourselves."

Chris laughed. "It's amazing that we've been friends for so long. Well, I liked him, despite his faults."

"That's the very nature of friendships," Frank responded. We're going to the funeral of a man we've known and liked for almost fifty years and whose faults we've known for that length of time."

Chris turned in his seat and looked directly at him. "You're sounding very philosophical. How's everything going in your life? You and Paula seem to be very much in love. Business is going well for you. You're doing a lot of traveling."

"I'm very happy you feel that way. Yeah, everything seems to be going great. I've got a great marriage. I haven't made all the money I thought I'd make, but I'm comfortable. And I'll never run the company. The children all seem pretty well situated. And I am enjoying having some more time and money to travel. But you know, something still seems to be missing."

Chris smiled dismissively. "You're getting old."

"Aren't we all? But don't you ever feel something is missing in your life, even with all the good things that have happened to you? Something's not quite right?"

"I can't say that I do. I have a terrific marriage. My kids are doing well. The company has done better than I ever expected. I've got leisure to read and play tennis. I'm not as keen as you are to go hopping around the world. What more do I want? My health is good. I like life. You've always been more demanding of life than I've been."

"You're a lucky man, Christopher Michael Martini. You will live the rest of your life and go to your death a happy person. You've found nirvana."

"I haven't found nirvana, but I admit I live a pretty contented life."

"I'll have to find your secret," Frank responded. "I can't seem to shake this feeling that something's missing, that I should have done better in life, that I should have accomplished more, that...I don't know."

The two of them had shared such confidences for almost half a century. Their friendship was marked by a frequent opening of their innermost thoughts. They certainly joked and engaged in light chatter and gossip about people they knew. But neither of them ever held back his innermost thoughts from the other.

"You should get off those morose thoughts," Chris earnestly implored his friend. "They're unhealthy. Plus, do they do you any good? OKAY, so you haven't gotten everything out of life that you expected in your twenties, but who has? And now you get a couple of arthritic pains and you think you're about to die. You've had a lot of disappointments, but you've got a lot of wonderful things in your life, as well. Sure, your first marriage went bust, but you've had great relationships since then. You've got a terrific wife, nice children. Lots of friends. Lots of interests. What's missing?"

Frank looked at his friend. He didn't feel like delving any more into his sense of deficiency. Despite their closeness, Chris and he looked at life—*felt life* would perhaps be more accurate—very differently.

"I guess you're right," he replied to his friend. And he tried to get these thoughts out of his mind. The two lapsed into silence, staring into space as the airplane slid into the San Diego airport.

Saints Cyril and Methodius Catholic Church in San Diego was filled for the 11 o'clock "mass of the resurrection," which was being accorded Robert Leo Franco. Bob had come from a large family, had been a popular teacher at this university, and had had numerous political connections from his days serving on various governmental commissions. Representatives from these facets of his life were now present as three priests greeted his casket at the main entrance to the church and processed before it to the sanctuary. Frank could see the requisite mask of solemn sorrow on the faces in the church; the feeling of relief among those present that it was not they who lay in the box draped with a white piece of cloth was almost palpable.

The mass continued in its cheerless, talky fashion. Mass of the resurrection, thought Frank, why don't they just call it a funeral mass and keep the old black vestments? He despised the liturgical changes that had become dominant in the Roman Catholic Church since the end of the Second Vatican Council in the mid-1960s.

When the mass was over, the body in its wooden coffin was incensed, and the priests, pallbearers, and mortuary attendants somberly walked the length of the church, followed by the family and the hundreds of others who had known Bob Franco.

In the bright sunshine outside the church, as Franco's remains were being placed in the hearse for his internment at Holy Angels Cemetery, small knots of the mourners gathered, uttering brief platitudes of sorrow to members of the family and then shifting to more congenial conversations with those they knew. "What a shame...so young...happy that he didn't have to suffer any longer" were the obligatory openings to such conversations, uttered with the mournful solemnity expected of the professional undertakers. And, then, with graceful elision, the mourners took up the cares of the living.

Frank and Chris stood together, trying to determine where to go. Their decision was made for them by the sudden appearance of Jack and Cynthia Sherman. Jack had been their classmate at St. Aloysius—a classmate whom Frank had detested during their four years there and continued to detest some decades later. Perpetually suave, a successful trial attorney in San Francisco, Jack had progressed through life as if he were a favorite of the Almighty. Although Frank couldn't stand him—and suspected that the feeling was reciprocated—they were polite and friendly whenever they met in San Francisco's small world of social acquaintances.

"I didn't expect to see you here," Jack commenced with a broad smile. "I thought you'd be too busy with all those clients. Can't believe that Bob is gone. Good mind. Good football player at St. Aloysius. Hey, Chris, how's the golf game? Are you going to the AT&T? Cynthia and I just rented a house at Pebble. Can't believe the price—$10,000 for a week."

"No, I'm not going this year," Chris answered.

Jack turned to Frank. "I'm really surprised to see you here. You're always so busy."

Frank flashed a bland smile. "Nothing would have kept me away. Bob was one of my closest friends."

"Sure, I know," said Jack. "All you bookworms stuck together. But Bob was a first-string fullback, as well."

Sherman's memory of his athletic inability and his interest in reading rankled Frank.

Cynthia sensed Frank's discomfort and sought to bring the conversation to a more equitable plane. "It's so great that all you guys from St. Aloysius are still such great friends," she interjected. "Jack and I haven't seen much of you two in the last year. How are Monica and Paula—they're not here, are they?"

"No, they couldn't make it," Chris said.

"Oh, what a shame. I thought we three girls might have gone shopping after the funeral."

His wife, Cynthia Sherman, was a perfect consort for Jack. They met at college. Cynthia Donohue was considered one of the prettiest girls at San Francisco College for Women—a Catholic women's college taught by the Madames of the Sacred Heart, a religious order of nuns known for teaching girls and women from the Catholic upper classes.

Even at sixty, Cynthia Sherman looked stunning. Elegantly dressed and perfectly coiffed, she had a presence that her wealthy Irish-American background and sixteen years of schooling by the Madams had honed to the smoothness of marble. Congenial, poised, sure of herself, Cynthia sought to live life without pain, to smooth every difficulty from the lives of her family and friends. Her background and her perfection annoyed Frank. His working-class background still loomed large for him, and his doubts and disappointments served as a counterpoint to her assuredness.

When Jack, Chris, and he were at St. Ignatius College, he had seen Cynthia as an unattainable goddess, a remote Madonna. She had given him an occasional smile at mixers, when the boys' school or the girls' school hosted dances, but he always knew that Cynthia had considered him a clod.

"I'm afraid you're going to have to go shopping by yourself, honey," Jack said to his wife. "And don't spend me into the poor-house."

Jack made a great deal of money and didn't mind his wife's taste for expensive clothes, jewelry, and antiques; but he frequently cast his wife in the role of a shopaholic with the implication that he couldn't afford her extravagances. She had often heard Jack's line about "spending him into the poor-house." She just flashed him a vacuous smile and turned to Frank and Chris.

"You know, all three of us couples should really get together sometime soon. We haven't for a very long time. There's a benefit coming up next month for the Convent of Mercy, you know, the homeless shelter for battered women. Well, I'm on the board and I'm trying to pull some tables together. Why don't you get four tickets for the dinner? We'll have a delightful time."

"Why don't you call Paula when you get back to San Francisco? She keeps our social calendar," Frank retorted, hoping that she would forget this sudden impulse to get together. Wasn't that just like Cynthia—pretending that she wanted to see them socially just to hustle some benefit tickets for one of her charities.

The truth was that Cynthia and Jack no more wanted to see Chris and him and their wives than they wanted to see the Shermans. They had socialized for a few years after Jack finished law school and Frank and Chris finished graduate school. It was the obligatory round robin of young married couples that had known each other in school having dinner together every couple of months. Unlike the present, Frank thought, when it seemed that every young couple ate out at a restaurant. When they were in their twenties, it was a rotating sit-down dinner on a Saturday night, trotting out wedding china and silver, trying out new recipes.

But things had changed. Both Frank and Chris and their wives considered the Shermans pretentious bores. And the Shermans, Frank knew, felt that they had far outstripped them socially and economically. Jack made millions of dollars suing companies for product liability and sat on a number of prestigious boards of directors. Besides her penchant for shopping, Cynthia sat on the boards of several charitable groups.

When the Shermans traveled, it was always in the most luxurious style: the Ritz in Paris, the Danieli in Venice, and the Medici-Hassler in Rome. And the restaurants in which they ate during their rambles also had to be well known and expensive. They could only share their delight in these hotels and restaurants with friends who similarly had large amounts of money.

"The hearse is ready to go," Chris remarked. "We better get into our cars and follow it to the cemetery."

"We'll see you at the reception afterward," Frank said to the Shermans, as he and Chris headed toward their rental car.

"Let's try to avoid them at the reception," Frank said quietly once they had gotten to the car. "I can't stand them."

Chris smiled. "You still haven't gotten over the Madonna of Lone Mountain," he teased. "You're pissed that she wound up with Jack rather than you."

"Sure, right, really someone I would have wanted to marry. Let's face it, she's a phony, and if there is anyone who could bankrupt Jack, it would be she."

"Well, you weren't so down on her thirty-five years ago. I can still remember your wistful yearning for her as if it were yesterday."

"Yeah, well, I came to see the light. Marrying her would have been worse than my marriage to Claudia."

Frank lay back in silence as Chris drove through San Diego's sun-drenched streets. He thought of Claudia, his first wife. Mentioning her name to Chris had triggered a flood of memories.

It had been twenty-five years since they divorced. It took a few years for them to resolve the hard feelings, the pain, and the recriminations of their separation. But time had healed their bitterness, and they now enjoyed a comfortable and harmonious relationship. They chatted about their four children and their grandchildren and occasionally reminisced about their life together.

He had entered the marriage with great excitement and hope. Their sexual inexperience had not seemed a barrier, for both of them were virgins when they married. They had done all the things that young married couples aspiring to upper-middle-class life did: attended the opera, symphony, theatre, cocktail and dinner parties, symposia at St. Ignatius College, and made occasional excursions to the Napa Valley or Carmel.

Frank understood what had gone wrong in their relationship and in their marriage. The woman he had married, whom he had met when she was a junior at Stanford, had either not been the same person he had fallen in love with, or she had changed. They shared few interests, and she had become increasingly unpleasant. She had little interest in sexual experimentation, while he had become more fascinated with the spectrum of sexual pleasures. And for this he had looked elsewhere.

It wasn't too long after they were married that he began to shut her out of his life, to isolate her from his innermost thoughts. This had only served to make them both increasingly unhappy. Divorce was out of the question. Good Catholics didn't get divorces. There had never been a divorce in either of their families. And the plague of divorce that started in the 1980s hadn't yet begun. So, shackled to each other, and increasingly miserable, they stumbled through being together.

She had ended it, stung by their constant arguing and irate at his flaunting his infidelities. She demanded a divorce; he was relieved. He was in a psychological trough and in financial difficulties. Let the whole house come tumbling down on my head, he thought.

Within a week he had moved in with Chris and Monica. He felt somewhat bewildered and his heart ached that he wasn't living with his children.

"We're here. Were you asleep?" Chris interrupted his reverie.

"No, not really. I was just daydreaming."

"Lusting after the lovely Cynthia?" Chris laughed.

"You and Cynthia," Frank came back at his friend. "I'm beginning to believe it's you who had the hots for her."

"Let's not change the historical record now. Who's the one who traced out the route of where you were going to have dinner on that one date she allowed you?"

"Okay, okay, I admit that in college and grad school I thought she was the pinnacle of womanly perfection. She was beautiful, she was bright, she was poised, she was a great conversationalist, and she was from a socially prominent family. What can I tell you? But, you can see what she's become—a rich snob."

"Well, that's not surprising, since she's been married to Jack all these years."

"That's no excuse. I remember how bright and engaging she was in college. One night several of us were sitting around a table up in the coffee room at Lone Mountain and she was talking about a class she was taking on some aspect of Thomist philosophy. You should have heard how eloquent she was. I was trembling with delight."

"Erotic delight, no doubt. But that was a long time ago," Chris conclusively said.

They parked the car and walked into the clubhouse of the La Jolla Golf and Country Club. Once more, small groups of those attending the funeral were standing about. Waiters were serving cocktails; and the more festive surroundings of the clubhouse, coupled with the alcohol people had begun to swallow, lessened the nervous solemnity that had been so evident earlier.

Catherine Franco, Bob's widow, walked up to them. "Frank. Chris. Thank you so much for coming down for Bob's funeral. I'm sorry that I didn't think to call you to be pallbearers, but there's been so much to do during these past few days."

She looked beautiful in a chic black dress with a simple strand of pearls around her neck. Frank had always admired Catherine Sullivan Franco. She had a regal poise. He had never been erotically attracted to her, for despite her beauty, there had always been something faintly sexless about her. She carried her intellectual attainments lightly, and could be described with the old phrase, "There's a real lady." But there was an air of detachment about her that her rippling laughter and illuminating smile could not hide.

"How are you doing, Catherine? I know this is a tough time for you," said Frank, gazing at her intently. They had known each other for many years. There was no need for the shibboleths of condolences and the banalities that accompany death.

"Oh, you know, I'm doing okay. Bob had been fighting for his life for so long...I've had plenty of time to get used to his death. Still, now that it's happened, I'm somewhat in shock."

Chris grasped her hand and gave her a kiss on the cheek. "And that shock isn't going to go away right away. We love you. Don't hesitate to let us know if we can do anything."

A sweet smile spread over her face as she took one of each of their hands into hers, nodded, and walked over to another knot of Bob's friends.

The two friends looked at her silently. "There is one classy gal," said Chris.

"No doubt about it," Frank simply replied, not wishing to share some of his reservations about the widow Franco.

Frank and Chris maneuvered to a table far from where the Shermans were sitting. They introduced themselves to their luncheon companions. One was a Jesuit priest to whom Bob had turned about a year before his death to reconcile him to the Church—a church that he had not tired of reviling nearly to the end of his life. The others were academics from the university where Bob had taught.

Frank and Chris went through the process of finding out how each of them had known Bob, and, once having established their individual places in the firmament of his life, went on to offer their own personal experiences and vignettes. This was, after all, the purpose of funeral obsequies, Frank thought—to remember the dead person's life.

A slight wave of boredom came over Frank. Dissecting his dead friend's life had now turned into the pleasant, light conversation that fills the hours of strangers who are placed into one another's company.

"How are you doing, Frank?" A hand flapped on his shoulder. He saw a look of recognition on Chris' face, and Frank looked up to see Terry Donohue, another high school classmate.

"Hey, Terry, it's been too long," said Frank. "I didn't see you at the funeral. Were you hiding in the confessional?"

Frank got up to shake hands with his old friend, while Terry and Chris waved to each other. Frank was pleased to see Terry, whose face, with its boyish good looks, was wreathed in smiles. The silvery laughter was his trademark reaction to Frank's query about "hiding in the confessional."

"I only got here now. I had an early morning operation to perform in the city and grabbed a plane as soon as it was finished."

"The patient sill alive?" Frank joked.

"As much as one of your clients after they've seen your fees," Donohue laughed.

Both men laughed. They had been good friends in high school and college, and had continued that friendship when one had gone to medical school and the other to graduate business school.

"That's some rotten luck about Bob," Terry began. "The old "C" doesn't spare anyone—rich or poor, bright or dumb."

"It's hard to imagine him dead." Frank shook his head in wonderment. "He was such a force of nature. I can't believe he isn't going to walk into this room, slap us all on the back, and spend hours deluging us with one of his monologues."

"How's Catherine taking it?" Terry asked.

"Well, you know, this thing wasn't sudden. She had months to get used to the fact that he was dying. She seems pretty much in control."

"She always seems in control. She's the most 'in control' woman I've very seen. But she was a great wife...kept Bob within some orbit of saneness. On the other hand, I didn't see a lot of passion in their relationship."

"I see you're not just satisfied with operating on people's backs, but you want to open up their personalities, as well. You never saw much passion because I don't think Catherine is a passionate person and Bob was too much into himself to be passionate."

Terry put his arm around Frank. "You know, Frank, you should have become a psychiatrist."

The two men laughed, each fully conscious of being in the presence of a longtime trusted friend. Their conversation unfolded almost in shorthand, their mutual pleasure in each other's company a given in their lives.

Chris had disengaged himself from the table to join his two friends.

"Hey, Terry, glad you finally got here. We couldn't have put Bob to rest without you."

"I'm sorry I had to miss the funeral, but I did want to come down and offer my condolences to Catherine and the kids."

"Do you want something to eat? The food's pretty good," Chris inquired.

"No, thanks. When are you two going back home?"

"Our flight leaves in three hours," Frank said, looking at his watch. "What about you?"

"Not until five, but let me call and see if I can change it to the one you're on."

"Yeah, it will be great to catch up on the airplane," said Chris. "We haven't seen each other in six months."

"Let me tell you, at our age nothing much changes in six months," Terry laughed, feeling somewhat guilty that he hadn't called Chris for lunch or a golf game, or had his wife invite him and Monica to dinner. "What's new in my life? I carve up a certain amount of backs each month, play golf at the club once or twice a week, make love to my wife maybe once a month, go out maybe once a week to some boring dinner party, and occasionally get a phone call from one of my kids."

There was an undercurrent of bitterness in Terry's voice, Frank thought. Or was it disappointment? Terry generally kept his conversation fairly light and optimistic. Anyone speaking to him rarely saw any angst in the statements of Terence O'Brien Donohue. Was something going on within him to change his optimism?

While Frank's antennae were twitching at this unusual revelation, Chris countered with his usual bonhomie. "That's the nature of being in your early 60s. You feel you want to retire because you see the energy and enthusiasm these young guys have, but you aren't ready to do it. The routines of life have become comfortable, so you don't want to change them. You can only get your pecker up about once a month, so that's the time you have sex with your wife. And you're terribly depressed because you know your window of opportunity in life is shrinking."

"My God, I'm surrounded by psychiatrists," Terry laughed. "Let me go make a telephone call and see if I can get on your flight. Then I can put my seat back and discuss my fear of dying with you guys."

Frank had noticed a click in Terry's eyes as Chris was talking. The mask over Terry's emotions had been pulled down. There must be something gnawing at Terry, Frank thought. Maybe it was the same thing that was gnawing at him. But Frank also knew that Terry detested showing any personal vulnerability. Open displays of emotion were not part of his calculus. Frank realized that Terry's brief statement showed more dissatisfaction than he wanted his friends to see.

"What do you think?" Chris asked Frank after their friend had left to make his telephone call. "Terry seems less than pleased with life. Pretty unusual for him."

"He's like all of us—except for you—beginning to notice that we're getting older."

"Are you going on about 'something missing in my life' again?"

"No, I'm not. But all of us, all our friends, are getting older. And they're noticing that some friends are getting pains, or dying, like Bob, noticing that our gut is getting bigger, and it's more work to get a hard-on. It's jut that you exist in a Pollyanna state, maintaining that you're not any different than you were thirty or forty years ago."

"I'm not being a Pollyanna. I just don't see what good comes from bellyaching about some twinge in your knee, or the fact that you don't feel like working the same hours you did in your twenties. That's just life. You've got to accept it, or you're going to drive yourself crazy."

"But sometimes don't you lament it? Aren't there times when you wonder where the last forty years have gone? How fast time is going by? How you don't feel the same excitement now you did as a teenager, or in your twenties? How sex is no longer the explosion it was years ago?"

Frank surprised himself at the vehemence of his machine-gun questions to Chris. God, something must really be going on inside me, he thought.

"Frank, if I let those kinds of things worry me, I'd be taking a dive off the Golden Gate Bridge."

"Okay, okay, I can't sell you on angst. Let's go say goodbye to Catherine and the kids and get out to the airport."

They saw Felicity and Raymond Franco, who were in their early twenties. They wore the look of not comprehending death that one sees on the young: sorry that their father was dead, but too shy to appear to be mourning. Both Frank and Chris kissed Felicity and shook Raymond's hand, uttered the usual, conventional banalities of condolences. Both told Bob's orphaned children to call on them if they needed anything, and invited them to visit San Francisco. All four knew that such calls and visits would never happen. Bob's children just wanted to get on with their lives; they didn't want any extraneous relationships with friends of their dead father.

"Here comes Terry," Chris noticed as they began to look around for Catherine Franco.

"Today's my lucky day, guys," said the affable Terry. "I'll have your company on the flight to San Francisco. Plenty of time for us to catch up."

There was no trace of his earlier outburst of introspection. Terry Donohue had recovered his controlled composure.

The trio of friends ambled up to various members of Bob Franco's family, strewing words of sympathy in what seemed to be a series of stylized formulas. Just before leaving, they encountered Catherine. Terry became their spokesperson.

"Catherine, if there's anything, and I mean anything, any of us can do for you, or help you with, please call us. You know how close we were to

Bob and how much we love you."

Catherine Franco looked up at her husband's friend and smiled wanly. "Thank you, Terry. And thank you, Chris and Frank. I can't tell you how much your friendship means to me at this time. I was so happy to see the three of you here at the funeral. I'll see you when I go up to San Francisco. Have a safe trip home."

The three friends found themselves backing away, as if from a regal presence. Catherine Franco had that impact on people. Despite Frank's reservations about her, she awed him. He could tell that she had the same effect on his two companions.

They headed for the door to the parking lot to retrieve their rental car. Frank turned for a last survey of the gathering. His eyes stopped for an instant on Cynthia Sherman, who was intently gazing at him. He looked away and then quickly back at her. Cynthia gave a brief wave and smiled.

CHAPTER 2

The party was at its peak when Frank and Paula walked into the stately Edwardian house in San Francisco's Pacific Heights. The crowd was young—in their 20s and 30s—reflecting the 29-year-old host's age. David Kendall was a multi-millionaire software entrepreneur who had recently sold his company to a computer conglomerate for $600 million. The young set who were now drinking wine and munching on hors d'oeuvres in his house were mostly those employed in some aspect of the world of technology, which had come to dominate the San Francisco Bay Area.

"Frank, how is it that we're invited here?" Paula asked.

"Dave's a client and he likes me. I think he feels that I can keep him in touch with the older generation."

"You're only in your early 60s," she laughed.

"Yeah, but to these people, everyone over 40 is antediluvian."

"How did he happen to become a client?"

"His mother was a client, and when Dave started to make all this money she convinced him that he should take a small chunk and invest it with me. She said to me, 'Make sure they're all conservative investments.' I think she figures that if his fortune evaporates, at least this small amount will be left."

"How much did he give you to invest?"

"A mere ten million dollars."

Paula chuckled, rolled her eyes, and took another sip from her glass of champagne.

"Frankie, boy, how are you doing?" David Kendall had appeared to greet his new guests.

"Great, Dave. Let me introduce you to my wife, Paula. Paula, Dave Kendall."

These proprieties observed, Kendall began to categorize the other guests, trying to identify some whom the Molinaris might find interesting to speak to.

"We'll do just fine, Dave. I'm sure many of your guests will want to hear about the olden days."

Kendall smiled at him, relieved that they would not feel isolated in a crowd of young, successful computer business people.

"All right, but start over there with Barbara Kingman. I think she went to the same school as you. Nice to have met you, Paula."

For all his faults, Frank thought, David Kendall is not an insufferable jerk. Modest enough about his achievements, polite in his demeanor, and caring about others, David Kendall was the kind of person that Frank liked. He had virtually no education—education as Frank defined it—even though he had gone to Stanford. He had been laser-focused on technology since he had been in high school. And everything that David had done since then had been with one objective: to master an area of technology that would create great wealth for him. And by the age of 30 he had accomplished his dream.

Barbara Kingman had gone to St. Ignatius College and to its law school. She was one of the few at the party not directly involved in computers. She was an attorney—an expert in intellectual property and much sought after by tech companies.

"Hello, my name is Frank Molinari and this is my wife, Paula. Dave told me to come up and say hello because he thought you had gone to St. Ignatius College."

"I did," she responded in a perky way. "I graduated in 1988." She vigorously pumped both Frank's and Paula's hands.

"That was way before my time," Frank smiled. "Just kidding. Class of '59."

"My father graduated about then. Joe Kingman. Did you know him?"

"Can't say that I did," Frank responded. "Did he board or commute?"

"Commuted. My grandparents lived a few blocks away."

"I didn't know a lot of the commuters. They tended to be in for classes and then left. We boarders had a lot of time to spend together."

"I love your hair," Paula interjected. "Where do you have it done?"

Why did women always comment on other women's hair-dos? Frank wondered. He was always mystified by the female train of thought.

"Oh, thanks. I go to the Paradise Salon downtown. Tony does my hair."

More handsome than beautiful, dressed in a somewhat mannish way with black slacks, a tie drooping down the front of her blouse, and a tailored red jacket, Barbara Kingman was tall, self-assured, and bright. Even the banal conversation they had had could not dim her powerful intellect. In her mid to late-30s, Barbara Kingman was a highly compensated partner in the firm of Summerfield, Sloane, Marx, and Privitelli—one of the largest and most prestigious law firms in San Francisco.

But, Frank thought, she seems to be missing something—a husband and family? He decided to probe.

"Do you live in the city, Barbara?" Frank inquired.

"Yes, over on Jackson and Steiner. How about you?"

"Oh, we're virtually neighbors," said Paula. We're at Pacific and Scott."

"We love Pacific Heights," Frank broke in, determined to turn the conversation into a direction that would satisfy his curiosity. "It's quiet, pretty safe, and convenient." He hated himself for this moronic conversation. If Paula hadn't been there—and he worried about the possible jealousy—he could have been more direct, charming, sympathetically inquisitive.

"I've lived there for five years, and I like it a lot, too."

"Where did you live before?" Frank asked, seeking to establish a chronological structure.

"After law school I clerked in D.C. and then practiced in New York. I moved here about five years ago."

"What do you do when you're not practicing law?" Frank continued to press his queries, presuming that Barbara Kingman would consider them just polite conversation.

"Work is pretty demanding. I don't have a lot of time or energy left over. But I've just joined the Junior League, and that takes some time. I go to the symphony occasionally, read…you know, the usual."

Thank God, she's not one of those multiple-athletic women you see all over, Frank thought. They run, ski, hike, bicycle. One got exhausted just listening to them reel off their activities.

Frank attempted another reconnaissance. "What, no social life?"

Paula shot him an annoyed glance. Barbara smiled, "An occasional date, I guess, but men aren't always eager to commit to women who are on partner-track in law firms. They're not always available."

"It's their loss," said Paula, eager to end the conversation. "It's fine for men to work until midnight six nights a week. But if a woman does it, it's weird."

Barbara Kingman smiled but said nothing. Clearly, she would have preferred spending many hours at Summersfield, Sloane, Marx, and Privitelli and making partner and also having a boyfriend or a husband. Barbara wanted it all.

A signal that the conversation had ended came with a thwack on his back. Frank turned around to see a beaming Jeff Krueger.

"Haven't seen you in ages," boomed Krueger. "Hi, Paula."

Frank introduced his old friend to Barbara Kingman, who took the interruption as an opportunity to escape Frank's probing.

Frank and Jeff had been classmates at both St. Aloysius High School and St. Ignatius College. Both had taken their Catholicism seriously as boys and as men; they both had strong intellectual interests; but, despite similarities in outlook and backgrounds, they had never developed a strong friendship.

Jeff was a product of ethnic melding in San Francisco. His mother was Italian; his grandmother was Irish. His father's family had come from Germany. His desire for economic security and social prestige drove him to the rigorous world of math and science and into medical school. Since then he had become a successful cardiologist. But his recent divorce had disoriented and distressed him, as his search for a perfect world had been derailed.

"What brings you here?" Frank asked, somewhat surprised to see his straight-laced classmate at such a young gathering.

"Kendall's a patient of mine."

"He must be going through his Christmas card list. I'm here because he's a client."

Tanya Devereaux had made contact with Paula, and since Frank despised the young socialite, he guided Jeff a few feet away to continue their conversation outside the ambit of his wife and Tanya.

"I hate that bitch," Frank began with a nod toward Tanya. "She's as phony as a three-dollar bill. Ever since she got half of Bill Devereaux's estate, one would think she's Marie Antoinette instead of some tramp Bill picked up in a strip joint."

"There are many ways of becoming successful in life," Jeff said with a benign smile. "Sometimes it's better to be lucky than smart."

Jeff did not like to say unkind things about people. One of his goals was to avoid confrontation; another was to safeguard himself from the harsh judgments of others.

"You are being even more charitable than usual tonight, Jeff. That's one of your problems: you're always such a nice guy."

Frank had said this in a wry way, but he also realized that Jeff's penchant for always playing it safe was what had kept their friendship from deepening over the years. Frank hated playing it safe. He had a spectrum of strong opinions, and usually did not hesitate to express them. It was one of the reasons so many people disliked him.

"It's not about being 'a nice guy,'" Jeff responded. "It's about living and letting live. You've always driven yourself crazy because people don't meet your expectations. But there's nothing you can do about the way people are. They are what they are. All you're doing is making yourself cynical and cranky."

Frank pursed his lips. Jeff ended his mild reproof. His realization that Jeff had made a correct assessment of his character hadn't made the exchange any more pleasant.

"How are you doing after the divorce?"

Frank was entering into troubled waters, he knew. Jeff and Mary Krueger had been married for thirty-five years, had raised three children, now all grown, and had seemed like a happy couple. Then, one day Mary, who to all appearances had been a happy, dutiful doctor's wife, told her husband that she wanted a divorce. When pressed for reasons by her shocked husband, she told him that she had been bored for years, that she felt stifled and as if she were drowning, dying.

A stunned, uncomprehending Jeff had tried everything he could to change her mind, but Mary was adamant. Only later did Jeff find out that Mary's recognition of her unhappiness had been sparked by a feminist psychologist whom she had been seeing. Mary subsequently went back to school and married one of her professors, a widower. Jeff had been devastated.

Jeff was silent for a moment. The pause in the two classmates' dialogue allowed the buzzing hum of multiple conversations, the yelps of laughter, and staccato of brief introductions to flood Frank's consciousness.

"It stinks," Jeff stated simply. "Thirty-five years of marriage ended. A world we'd made together ended. The dreams we shared for after I retired ended."

It was unusual to see Jeff this passionate. He rarely let his emotions surface. Frank could see that his question had penetrated Jeff's usual placid demeanor.

"Isn't it time for a new world, for new dreams? It looks like you're here alone. Why didn't you bring a date?"

Jeff became pale. His vivid green eyes flashed. Frank could see that he had aroused volcanic emotions in Jeff.

"I've had so many dates I feel like I'll shoot myself if I have to ask another woman out. It's hour after hour of boring conversation. You ask all the right questions to get to know someone, and sometimes they even ask you questions about yourself. I know I'm not young, but every woman I ask out seems old enough to be my mother. You know, wrinkles, gray hair, and sagging bodies. It was one thing to see Mary get older, but who wants to go out on a date with someone who's old?

"And then you get caught up in sixty years of their neuroses. Their antagonism towards ex-husbands if they're divorced, what saints their husbands were if they're widowed. They either hate or adore their children, and their grandchildren are always perfect and gifted. They've got odd hobbies they want you to get involved in, like ballroom dancing. They want you to say nice, romantic things to them and take them to romantic dinners and on romantic trips. I can't stand it. I'd rather be alone."

Jeff stopped his tirade, surprised at his own outburst. Frank was stunned at the intensity of his classmate's feelings, and sympathized with his unhappiness.

"I didn't realize it was so bad out there in the singles world," Frank stammered, not quite knowing what to say. "I can't believe that out there in this whole Bay Area there isn't someone whose company you might enjoy and who might be an excellent companion for you. After all, you're a successful doctor, you're well-educated, you're interesting, you're…"

"That's what I thought when I finally realized that Mary was gone. But in four years I haven't found that person. The truth is that I haven't got enough money to attract a trophy wife, and, if I did, I wouldn't want one. And when I go out with someone who's substantially younger than I, it's like going out with some alien from Mars.

"I dated someone a while back who as in her 30s, cute, graduated from Wellesley, had a good job. What did she want to do? Go out to these all-night dance clubs and dance to music that sounds as if it was piped in from Dante's Inferno. She wanted to hike the Sierras, go camping, ride bicycles all day, and backpack. I told her that my idea of backpacking was having to carry my own luggage to my hotel room."

"I know it's been tough for you, and I can understand the frustration and the boredom you have to undergo; but you're too bright and too talented not to attract someone whom you'll find compatible. I'll cast about for someone you'll be smitten by."

"Yeah, fat chance."

Frank wanted to escape the conversation. It was going nowhere and was all too familiar. He remembered the fifteen years after he and Claudia had split up. If it weren't for the sex at the end of a date, he would have lost his mind as a result of the inconsequential chatter that he'd had to listen to.

"Let me get us another drink," said Frank. "It will help to drown our sorrows."

"What sorrows do you have?"

"Oh, you know, the usual. Aches and pains. Getting my pecker to function. Trying to decide whether I have enough money to retire. Wondering what my life has been about. Contemplating whether anyone will remember me after I'm gone. You know, things like that."

"I can't believe you," Jeff said with a smile. "Why is it you're always torturing yourself? You've done it since we were in high school."

The two men arrived at the bar, which had been set up in a solarium next to David Kendall's living room. The usual, young, unflappable bartender looked at them and asked, "What's your pleasure, gentlemen?"

Frank got a refill of his glass of chardonnay, while Jeff asked for another glass of single malt whiskey.

"You know, Jeff, I can't answer that. It's been a condition I've been aware of since I was a kid. I think it's probably a condition I inherited from my parents, particularly my mother. And it's a condition that seems to be getting worse as I get older. I'll probably go to my grave with it."

It was unusual for Frank to be so open with Jeff, and he decided to stop his spontaneous revelations. He was accommodated by the appearance of his wife and Tanya Devereaux wanting them to refresh their drinks.

"Well, don't say hello, Mr. Fancy Pants," said Tanya.

Jeff had wandered away before Frank had an opportunity to introduce him to Tanya. Part of the waltz of cocktail parties.

"Hello, Tanya. You were engaged in conversation with my wife, and I was talking with my old friend Jeff. You know I wouldn't not say hello to you."

"I'm not so sure of that. You know, there are times when I think you don't like me."

Frank had never let on to Tanya that he didn't like her. But he remembered

Paula's admonition that people knew instinctively if someone does not care for them, even if the distaste is not directly stated. And the truth was that, while he disliked Tanya—her shallowness, her social climbing, and her self-assuredness—he was also attracted to her. He had often fantasized about having sex with her. He had been occasionally tempted to act on his desires, but each time had decided not to complicate his life.

"You're imagining things, Tanya. Who could help but like you? In fact, who could help but adore you?"

"Let's not use the trowel now. I like flattery, but not when it is probably insincere."

"Come on, you know I'm not insincere. You're good-looking, you're charming, and you're smart. What's not to like?"

Frank felt he had to cover his dislike of the ubiquitous Tanya Devereaux. She was always with people; she didn't hesitate to gossip; and Frank didn't want her to bad-mouth him to those who were clients, potential clients, or people who could be useful to him.

"Frank, I don't know about you. I feel that what you say and what you think don't always match up. But I'm willing to take you at your word at this time."

It was Tanya's warning shot across his bow. She was no fool, and she realized that she could harm Frank.

"Thanks," Frank responded with a smile. "I can assure you that I won't disappoint you."

Tanya flashed one of her I'll-cut-off-your-nuts-if-you-do smiles and Paula wore a weary but relieved look that said, "Let's get out of here."

But Frank wasn't ready to depart. He enjoyed parties like this. He liked observing the good-looking young women, their responses to the Lotharios who fluttered around them trying to impress them, the charged sexual energy fueled by alcohol. It was a voyeur's pleasure. But age and marriage had reduced him to a mere onlooker.

"Oh, there's Jim Foley. I better go over and say hello." It was Frank's way of extricating himself from Tanya and Paula and extending his participation in the party.

Jim Foley was another high school and college classmate. He was a doctor, happily married with a large family, one of those individuals whose life actually seemed to work out. Jim and Frank hadn't been particularly close in their eight years of being in school together, but they shared the siege mentality of ethnic Catholics.

Jim was talking with two men whom Frank didn't know when he walked over to him. Jim introduced him to his two companions, who took the opportunity to depart for another corner of the room.

"I hope I didn't intrude on some deep, philosophic conversation," Frank asked in a bantering fashion.

"No," Jim responded with a smile. "George is a patient. Sam is his law partner. Just cocktail party chit-chat."

"I can never figure out why these affairs are always so...so shallow."

"Well, you know, people come to cocktail parties to escape the serious. Most of the people here work hard, they're struggling to pay their children's tuitions, and they're wondering when they'll be able to retire. They don't want to discuss anything heavy."

"I don't think most of the people here have children. And they believe that retirement is an eternity away. However, I'm sure they certainly work hard."

"But that's my point," Jim continued. "Here's an opportunity to connect both with strangers and people you know. Why not talk about topics you generally don't discuss? Why not engage in polite chit-chat? You're always the inquisitive philosopher, Frank. You should just relax and have fun."

Frank sighed. He could tell that he wasn't going to get Jim engaged in a serious conversation on why so few people ever had serious conversations about important topics, especially at cocktail parties.

He was about ready to move on, but when he saw Paula approach and greet Jim, he knew by her look that his time at Dave's party had come to an end.

"Frank, I think it's time for us to go. I'm tired."

The tone was peremptory. He knew that to reject her demand could only be done at his peril; and he assented.

Goodbyes were said to those they knew and to their host. Within a few minutes they were in Paula's BMW headed home.

"What got into you tonight, Frank?" asked Paula with weary resignation. "You were like a bull in a china shop—asking rude questions, prying into peoples' lives. Can't you just go to a social gathering and have fun like other people?"

Frank knew from Paula's tone of irritation that she had not had a good time and was annoyed with him for what she considered his eccentric behavior at such affairs. He decided to try to deflect her annoyance.

"We've been married a long time, love, and you know I've never been able to float through life like other people. I always have this urge to get beneath the surface of things and people."

"Well, maybe it's time to get rid of your urges. You always sound ridiculous when we're out."

"A person's got to do what he's got to do," Frank responded. Not much deflection here. Paula lapsed into a purse-lipped silence.

The garage door opened to the touch of the car's remote garage-opener, and Frank and Paula wearily walked up the stairs of their Pacific Heights home, going immediately into their bedroom. Both brushed their teeth, and while Paula attended to whatever pre-bed rituals she did each evening, Frank slowly undressed and tossed his suit onto the rocking chair in the bedroom.

He picked up the novel he was reading, not feeling sufficiently sleepy to turn out the light. Paula was undressing. Frank watched her over the top of his book, no longer interested in what he was reading.

Unlike Frank's dumping of his clothes on the chair, Paula methodically removed each article of clothing and placed it in its appropriate place. Her skirt went onto a hanger in the closet, her blouse into a bin for the dry cleaner, her underwear into the laundry hamper. Frank had always admired Paula's meticulous ways, even though he never sought to imitate them.

Paula's unconscious striptease infused an erotic charge throughout Frank's body. He watched with delight, his penis stiffening, as she glided into bed. Although in her late 40s Paula had a curvaceous, yet lithe, body that continued to arouse him. He extended his left arm to embrace her.

There was none of the eagerly passionate trembling that would have marked such a beginning embrace in the years of their courtship or during the early years of their marriage. Paula turned partly to Frank and kissed him. Frank returned the kiss and pulled her closer to him. They continued to face each other and kissed for a few minutes. Then Paula reached for Frank's penis and began to stroke it gently.

He reciprocated by reaching for her vulva, separating out her clitoris and rubbing it between his thumb and forefinger. Both murmured a purring delight.

Paula shifted onto her back and pulled Frank on top of her. Her practiced fingers guided Frank's penis into her vagina. A spasm of pleasure flowed into his groin; but he suddenly realized that his penis had become flaccid. Almost with desperation in trying to seize the anticipated pleasure, Frank raised his body in an attempt to create the piston-like movement that he had enjoyed so many times in his life. But his now limp penis would not respond, and fell out of Paula's vagina.

This had been happening more and more to Frank during the past few months, and disappointment mingled with anxiety as he rolled over onto his back.

"Well, it's not going to happen tonight, dear," proclaimed Paula as she reached to turn off her bed light.

"Good night, sweetheart. Sleep well," intoned Frank as his fingers reached up to his light switch.

CHAPTER 3

Frank tossed on the queen-size bed. He had slept fitfully after the aborted sexual intromission. Dreams punctuated his semi-consciousness. It was almost as if he were viewing a videotape of the history of his sexuality.

There was little Joyce Pallin from the third grade. What was he...eight or nine years old? He vaguely remembered some "liking" of his classmate.

And then there was Deborah McIntyre—the "love of his life" from the fifth through the eighth grade. They never had a date, nor did he ever tell her that he had a crush on her. He thought about her constantly—this was just about the time that his hormones were kicking in—but his extraordinary shyness around girls and his dislike of his looks, especially his over-sized nose, never allowed him to ask to take her to a movie or even go on a walk with him.

Once, when he had a student body office in the seventh or eighth grade, he did go to a school dance, where he danced once with her. And one time one of Deborah's friends had invited him to a party at her house, where they had played "spin the bottle" and he had kissed her. He had entered paradise, but it was a brief paradise.

Into Frank's subconscious came the feelings of yearning for this beloved creature that had marked these years. In his mind's eye he was forever hugging and kissing her—his inchoate ideas about human sexuality didn't allow much more contact than that.

His dreams were flickers of memories: listening to Vaughn Monroe's "There, I've Said It Again" on the portable radio that dangled from the handle-bars of his bicycle as one night he was returning from collecting the monthly fees from the customers to whom he delivered the *San Francisco News*, the numbing sense of melancholy that he felt because he could not declare his love to Deborah and hug and kiss her, the excruciating world of his erotic imagination that would seize him in the moments before sleep would come while he lay on his bed in his darkened bedroom listening to "Music Till Dawn" on his radio.

The fact that he and Deborah went to different high schools ensured that his yearnings would diminish. He and Deborah would continue to see each other occasionally during those four years, but someone else would take her place as the goddess of his waking dreams: Sandra Cavagnaro, one year older than he and the daughter of close friends of his parents. Sandra, aloof and untouchable, became the center of his yearnings as he listened to the romantic and maudlin music played on The Lucky Strike Hit Parade.

Frank was now wide awake, lying on his back, listening to Paula's soft, regular breathing. He sought to replay the dream memories in his now more conscious mind. Where did the shyness with girls come from? He certainly was not a shy person. Was it because he felt he had a vocation to the priesthood? Or was it because he thought he might be ugly and therefore unattractive to girls?

Whatever deficiencies he may have felt in his teens certainly disappeared in his late 20s. Frank thought of his many sexual conquests, of the women with whom he had had thoroughly enjoyable relationships. He wondered if his newfound self-confidence had come out of desperation or maturity. Did he realize that his mind and personality might have made up for what he felt was his physical unattractiveness?

The imagery of these objects of his yearnings and the questions they raised made Frank aware of another, more importunate memory: that of the intense emotions that buffeted him so often during those years, the years that began before he was an adolescent, that continued throughout his adolescent years, and began to lose their intensity during his mid-to-late 20s.

Frank looked at the clock next to his gently slumbering wife: 4 a.m. Annoyed at his inability to sleep, to rid himself of these semi-conscious dreams, he plumped his pillow and turned himself into another position. No sleep came.

The dream kaleidoscope began again. This time, the erotic chronology shifted to San Mateo, twenty miles south of San Francisco, where his parents had built a home and moved in the early 1950s.

Thrilled to be out of the working-class district and the too-small house he had grown up in, Frank delighted in his new surroundings—the sun-splashed suburb and the large ranch-style house that was his new home. He enjoyed the summer job at Myers' Drugstore, where he was the delivery boy, allowing him to explore his new community and those surrounding it—Burlingame, Hillsborough, Belmont—in the green van in which he made his deliveries.

There he was entering an estate in Hillsborough, the home of a bank president, where, beside a swimming pool situated in a large expanse of lawn, sat a girl about his age. Her youthful, curvaceous, tanned body was attired in a bikini. A beautiful face looked quizzically at him. Frank stared at her budding, pubescent body glistening in the sunshine with aching admiration and desire. Finally he was able to stutter, "I...I...have a prescription delivery." She languidly lifted her hand from the book she was holding, and Frank placed the package in it. Not another word was spoken. Do such goddesses exist? Frank asked himself as he drove through the open wrought-iron gate. The memory of the goddess would never leave him.

"Stop moving," an irritated Paula muttered. "I can't sleep with all your shifting around."

"Sorry. I can't sleep."

"Get up and get yourself some hot milk and honey."

Unwilling to leave the bed, Frank held himself rigidly, desperate for some restful sleep.

Instead, the image sequences continued. He was at a party at a home in the Los Altos hills filled with students from a toney girls' school in Menlo Park, the Convent of the Sacred Heart. All the girls were beautiful, all had the curvaceous bodies of well-fed, well-exercised girls in their teens; all were smiling and self-confident. They laughed at his jokes and pronouncements, but he never thought that he could ask one out for a date, these scions of the Peninsula upper classes.

Now the scene shifted to a mixer dance at Notre Dame High School in Belmont—one of those ritual social gatherings by which Catholic boys and girls attending single-sex high schools could meet one another. There he met two more goddesses, their faces indistinct in the dream. He couldn't remember one girl's name; the other he did: Pamela Neville. But he did remember the impact they had on him. Their beauty, their bodies, their smiling good humor; the light russet hair at the nape of their necks; their silvery laughter at his boisterous conversation. Once more he ached for them; once more he realized that they were out of his reach. Frank Molinari always knew that he wasn't good-looking. And that he certainly wasn't "cool." And his access to the family car was severely limited.

That was the end. Frank was relieved. Now he could sleep. He gingerly changed his position. Sleepiness closed his eyes. He sank into a drowsy unconsciousness. And then the alarm rang.

CHAPTER 4

There was a crowd at Sam's. The old dilapidated restaurant, which dated from the 1860s, had not been painted in decades. And its wisecracking, septuagenarian waiters in their old-fashioned black coats had been serving customers since the last paint job. Nor had the menu changed. Frank wondered if the menu had ever been changed: salads, chops, and, most notably, fish.

Frank saw his luncheon companion at the bar and walked over to him.

"Francis Molinari, you old rogue," declared Christopher Francis Xavier Fermoyle.

"Christopher, good to see you."

It was never "Chris." Anyone meeting the six-foot-two-inch, handsome, muscular Fermoyle knew it bordered on the blasphemous to address him by the shortened name.

"We have a booth, old friend," said Christopher as he led Frank into the long aisle, which featured a now-vanished aspect of old, San Francisco restaurants: curtained booths, each with a buzzer to summon a waiter.

Frank smiled at Christopher's ability to be seated while scores of expectant patrons waited for tables—and to obtain a booth for only two. Frank was amused, but not surprised; Christopher Fermoyle's charm, wit, and larger-than-life presence could inveigle even the flintiest maître d' to accommodate him.

"Let's see," Christopher told the waiter who came to take their drink orders, "let's have a bottle of Far Niente Chardonnay. My friend here doesn't have much work to do this afternoon, and I never work. Give us about fifteen minutes to decide on what to eat, even though both of us know what we want."

Christopher flashed one of his light-up-the-room smiles, and the waiter left to get the wine.

"So, Francis, tell me what you have been up to since we last saw each other long ago, too long ago."

It had actually only been a couple weeks since the two had last met, but Frank began to marshal some summary of his life during this time. He and Christopher Francis Xavier Fermoyle, the name his card proclaimed, went to college together and remained friends after they graduated. They had become friends as a result of their common intellectual and literary interests, drawn together because both were eccentric, although Christopher had no equal in eccentricity, and by their interest in Roman Catholicism. Both had enjoyed each other's company for more than forty years.

Fermoyle, a never-married bachelor, had retained much of this eccentricity. He dressed like an English barrister, claimed he was Thomas Merton's illegitimate son, albeit not very seriously, and around old friends such as Frank, he conversed long and volubly about an endless variety of exotic subjects.

They had been together in the small classes of Latin and Greek at St. Ignatius College, and Christopher continued to pepper his conversation with tags from the two classical languages.

His affluent lifestyle—membership in several prestigious San Francisco clubs, the Jaguar he drove, the elegant apartment in the Brocklebank atop Nob Hill, the fact that he had never in this life had to work—was due to being the only child of parents who were in their late-40s when he was conceived and who died as he was finishing college, leaving him a substantial legacy of stocks and real estate.

Christopher's father was Irish, a successful attorney who remained part of San Francisco's Irish ascendancy of upper-middle-class professionals and businessmen who had been socially and economically well ahead of most of the city's population for two or more generations. His mother was an Italian whose parents had acquired substantial real estate holdings, which she had passed on to her only child. She had attended San Francisco's Convent of the Sacred Heart and Stanford University.

The wealth that descended to Christopher at an early age had confirmed his desire for a life of well-bred, intellectual leisure. "Work is for those who have no other option," he had declared jocularly at his college graduation; and he steadfastly held to this declaration, even though he had been offered jobs that had not required much work.

"What have I been up to since we last met a couple of weeks ago?" Frank wanted to make certain that his friend knew the exact amount of time that had elapsed since they had last seen each other. "I went to Bob Franco's funeral in San Diego. Sad. I've been to a few cocktail parties. Surprised that I haven't seen you at any of them. Work's going on the same as usual. Kids are fine. Marriage is going along well. You know, the same boring routine."

Christopher looked at him intently and then lifted his right eyebrow. Frank had never known anyone who could raise an eyebrow as high as Christopher could. He waited for a pronouncement.

"Why is it, dear Francis, that it always takes me halfway through a lunch before I can get anything from you more than a string of platitudes and a jejune listing of a few of your recent activities? Do you not realize that time is precious? Who cares if you went to a few cocktail parties or to Bob Franco's funeral? Tell me about the state of your soul! What profound insights have you had? What of significance have you been reading?"

Christopher reached up to make certain that his perfectly tied Windsor knot on his Hermes tie hadn't come undone as a result of his tirade. Satisfied, he brushed some imaginary crumbs from his apricot-color Turnbull and Asher shirt.

It struck Frank that Christopher had never really liked Bob Franco. Their personalities were too large to inhabit any contiguous space. Thus, rather than responding with sympathy to Frank's statement that he had gone to the funeral, he dismissed any interest in hearing about it.

"It always takes me longer to get to the important things than it does you," Frank improvised, grateful that the waiter had arrived with the wine.

"Excellent," Christopher pronounced. "And, now, Carlo, please bring me the sand dabs in exactly twenty minutes and the Sam's Salad for my friend. Vinaigrette dressing."

Frank smiled and nodded. There wasn't a time that the two had come to Sam's when they hadn't ordered the same items: sand dabs for Christopher and a salad of shrimp, crab, tomatoes, and avocados on a bed of hearts of romaine lettuce for himself. Did this say something about their lives? Frank wondered.

"Very well, let's begin the process gradually. First, let me ask how you're feeling about your life these days. The last time we spoke you said that you felt that you were a failure and that you were about to die."

"I think you're exaggerating what I said, but, yes, those sorts of thoughts are still flickering in my mind."

"Ah, how powerful are the dreams of youth," Christopher pointed out. "From the time I've known you, you've constructed a utopian universe that you'd inhabit. The universe changed, of course. First, you were going to save souls, as a great Jesuit scholar or as a missionary. Then you were going to be a financial magnate. And now that you perceive yourself a failure on these counts, you need new dreams."

There was one thing about Christopher, Frank realized. Beneath the old-fashioned conversational style, beneath the "out-there" personality, and beneath the Latin tags, he cut through the bullshit that filled most conversations.

"What new dreams come to us at this time of life? And what do we do about them even if we dream them?" Christopher continued. "You're a student of religion and theology, Frank. Why don't you reach out to an Asian religion? Become a Sannyasin. This is the time of life when Hindus and Buddhists tell us that we leave the householder state and go into the forest and become an ascetic, detaching ourselves from earthly concerns and possession."

"Right, I can see Paula and me wandering in a forest."

"The Hindus and the Buddhists tell us that the husband can either go alone or with his wife."

"Get serious, Christopher." Frank's voice contained some annoyance. "If I did anything even approaching that—like going to Mexico or Guatemala to help the poor there in some way—I'd be locked up as a crazy."

"You flatter yourself, Francis. Many people, after they retire, do exactly that; and they're looked up to, not locked up. But you'd rather spend your remaining years on earth lamenting what might have been. Francis, I expected more…well…heroic, behavior from you."

"I guess I'm not feeling very heroic these days. Yes, I am lamenting my failures. And, yes, I am lamenting my increasing old age. But I can't just give up my life to wear a loin cloth and go wandering in some goddamn forest."

"Then you turn your back on the most sublime teachings of all the major religions. Jesus told us to be poor. The Hindu sages and the Buddha told us to leave all earthly desires and goods when our children were grown and await death in a detached state. You're trying to fly in the face of all this wisdom. And you're going to be dead anyway, but you'll die in this tortured state. Ah, what a long purgatory for you."

Frank never knew if his friend was truly serious in their conversations. Was he trying to convey some deep-felt thoughts? Was he trying to jolly him out of his depressed thoughts by expressing some outrageous ideas? Or was he simply having fun? Frank didn't know, but he did know he wanted to change the topic.

"So, what have you been up to since we last met a couple of weeks ago?"

"I see that you are uncomfortable with my Socratic attempts to make you look at your life more clearly," said Christopher, as he held his knife and fork over the sand dabs that had just been delivered. "Well, you can lead a horse to water. What did you ask me? Ah, yes, about how I have spent the last couple weeks.

"Well, I suppose that I have spent them very much as I have spent the last forty years...trying to enjoy life, trying to improve my mind, trying to save my soul.

"Specifically, I have lunched with someone each day since we last met. Dined out, let's see, five times. Gone to mass each day. Read the breviary each day. Swum at the P.U. four times. Visited three or four art galleries. Saw the new show of medieval miniatures at the Legion of Honor. Spent four hours each week attending to business. Read two more Trollope novels, and am now galloping through *Kristin Lavransdatter*, which I haven't read since the two of us read it in college. I think that about does it. Oh, no, I forgot that I spent two or three hours visiting Marianne in the hospital."

"Marianne's in the hospital?"

Frank pretty much knew how Christopher spent his days, but he always enjoyed hearing him recite the rather strange catalog. But he was concerned about their mutual friend.

Marianne Cadwalader O'Brien had been a beautiful and intellectual college student at San Francisco College for Women—a short distance from St. Ignatius College. Run by an aristocratic order of nuns mostly for the daughters of wealthy Catholics, the school had a reputation for attracting young women who were both good looking and bright. And the seminars in philosophy, literature, and theology—which were taught by some of the most engaging Catholic lay teachers of the time and by some of the best-educated nuns—brought forth a pious, intellectual group of women who all seemed to be unattainable to the scions of working-class students who attended St. Ignatius. Marianne was one of the most beautiful, pious, intellectual—and one of the most unattainable—of the college's graduates.

Frank and Christopher had met Marianne when all three were sophomores. She had come down the hill to St. Ignatius to try out for a part in a play, and had gotten a small part. The intimacy of a theatrical production had thrown the three of them into a thespian-infused friendship. Over innumerable cups of coffee they would discuss Kierkegaard's ideas, the novels of Evelyn Waugh and Graham Greene, aspects of neo-Thomism. After the play had run its course, the three of them would occasionally go to a movie together—almost always one of the depressing foreign ones at the Clay or the Vogue.

But neither Christopher nor Frank ever had a true date with Marianne. Both of them always assumed that she was not interested in them in that way. All three frequently got together for coffee and to discuss ideas or books, exchange some gossip, or go to an occasional movie, but they never expected that romance would emerge from their companionship.

"She's been in for a week," Christopher responded. She's not feeling well, but the doctors can't figure out what's wrong. But she seems to be in good spirits."

"What hospital is she in? I'll have to go see her."

"St. Francis. Fourth floor. I'm sure she'd like a visit from you."

Frank felt a twinge of guilt. He hadn't kept up with Marianne much after graduation from St. Ignatius. For a couple years they met fairly regularly, but Frank had been on the lookout for a romantic liaison, and soon their visits dwindled to one or two a year. Eventually Marianne married a good-looking attorney from the Peninsula. Mark had come from an upper-class family, pursued a variety of intellectual interests, and was, like Marianne, an ardent Catholic.

This was the marriage that Frank had always expected Marianne to make. Soon they lost track of each other, until many years later she called him to say that she was divorcing. By that time Frank was himself divorced. They had a brief affair. The sex was good—he couldn't believe that he was fucking this Madonna from his college days—but neither of them sustained the new relationship. Soon the old distance that had separated them since college returned.

"Tell me, Christopher, when we were at St. Ignatius or in the years afterward did you ever think of Marianne as a possible girlfriend...or maybe even of marrying her? I recall that you continued to see her for several years after we graduated."

"No, never. In grammar school I realized that I liked girls—and then women—but I could never visualize myself as having a girlfriend or as being married. This has allowed me to lead a life of singular selfishness, which I hold dear.

"I don't think I'm selfish in the conventional use of that word; but, aside from commitments and loyalties to friends such as yourself and some commitment to the community, I am beholden to nobody but to myself and God. And God doesn't ask me to empty the dishwasher or to switch the clothes from the washing machine to the dryer.

"No, I was—and am—very fond of Marianne. I continue to enjoy her company, but not once have I looked at her with romantic eyes.

"There are several other women with whom I have similar relationships. I know that a number of my acquaintances think I'm gay, but I'm not, as you know. I just long ago sensed that I was not meant to be in a committed relationship with a woman.

"As I said, I love women, and I generally enjoy their company more than that of men, present company excluded. They reveal more of themselves. They discuss things that most men feel is sissy stuff. They don't bore me with a lot of machismo crap or discuss their golf games with me. But a girlfriend or a wife? No, my friend."

"That's one of the most enchanting aspects of your life, your freedom from such entanglements."

"I don't think not being married—or being married for that matter—means that one is free. Certainly, your freedom is not impinged on by being married to Paula. Oh, yes, you've got to do some things together, you've got to make some compromises, and you occasionally have to adjust your temperament, but I don't think of you as not being free. On the other hand, I see single men and women all the time who are not free. Freedom is something that one has to choose and to maintain. One can be free in a prison or in a Soviet Siberian concentration camp; and one can be not free with no visible constraints, with all the money in the world, and with no ties to anyone."

"Christopher, you're the only person I know who can respond to a vagrant idea with a philosophical disquisition." Frank smiled and returned to his abundant salad.

The two were silent for a few moments, as they ate their lunch and drank the superb wine that Christopher had ordered.

Frank put down his fork and looked at Christopher. "Are you happy?" he asked directly.

Christopher paused and smiled. "Oh, boy, here we go. And you objected to my earlier philosophical disquisition. How many times in the past half-century have you and I asked that question of each other? And I wonder now whether you're asking me about the state of my being or whether you're wondering whether you're happy. So, tell me, what is it? I need to know so that I don't spin my wheels answering a question that wasn't asked."

"I'm sorry, Christopher, I guess I did ask the question because I'm feeling unhappy these days."

"Aha, I knew it. Well, let's start with the question you asked: Am I happy? Then, we'll get to the subject of your unhappiness.

"I must admit that I don't know what happiness means. There are days when I get up and my heart is singing, so to speak. Let's say that the sun is shining, my devotions have gone well, and going to mass filled me with consolation...well, I'm on top of the world and feeling what most people would call happy.

"But is happiness dependent on good weather, a well digested meal, a good night's sleep, a pleasant sexual encounter, or even a good book? I don't think so.

"There are days when I get up and can tell there isn't a proper balance of whatever there is inside me. For no reason I am feeling grouchy, out of sorts, or depressed. Am I thus unhappy? I don't think so.

"So I look at my life, and I say to myself, I live exactly the life I want to live. I have plenty of money to do everything I want to do without having to work for it. I stimulate my mind and I nurture my soul. I stand in reverence of God. My health is good. I have wonderful friends. And yet there is something missing, something that keeps me from being happy, knowing that something is missing. You and I know what's missing. We've known it virtually all our lives. What we're missing is union with God in heaven, when true happiness will be ours."

"My God, Christopher, I can't believe that you still talk like that. You sound like you're reciting the Baltimore Catechism. I mean, I realize you're right, but it's not as naturally in my consciousness as it is in yours."

"That's because you're busy about many things, my friend. Let me recommend daily mass and reading the breviary, as we both used to do so many years ago, as a starter. Then you've got your business to attend to, the organizations you're involved in, and thoughts about nookie with Paula. At least you've reduced this pursuit to one person. As I said to you earlier, clear the decks, simplify your life. You'll be much more content. You see, I haven't used the word happy."

The waiter appeared to clear their plates, returning a short time later with coffee.

"Now, tell me about what's making you so unhappy," Christopher asked Frank with genuine solicitude in his voice.

"Well, I guess you've put it pretty much in perspective, as you usually do. I think I can best describe what I call my unhappiness as recognition of my ebbing as a human being. I have aches and pains I've never had before. I have less energy. As you've discovered already, I am feeling depressed about what I consider the failures of my life. I don't have the zest and the exuberance I had in my teens and twenties, even my thirties. You know, when the whites were whiter and the blues bluer, when the sap was running high in my veins. Most of the time I can't even get it up with Paula when I want to have sex. I hate it."

Christopher pursed his lips and looked at Frank with evident sympathy. Frank looked down at his coffee during the ensuing quiet. They could hear the sound of dice being rolled at the bar.

"Well, Francis, that sounds pretty unhappy...or discontented, I should say. I'm sorry."

"Oh, forget it," Frank responded. " I guess I just got carried away, and you were the recipient of my discontent."

"That's what friends are for: to serve as sounding boards for one another's joys and sorrows. None of us can make it better for the other, but perhaps we can help provide some understanding, some balm for the aching soul.

"Look, Francis, you and I are the same age. I am going through the same decline of human faculties as you. Since I don't engage in sexual activity, I'm not bothered by the dysfunctional penis. And, since I never dreamed of the glories you did, being content pretty much to live my life as I found it, I'm not sorrowing about what might have been. I think that what you call unhappiness is simply your failure to adjust to the circumstances all human beings face as they get older: a decline in one's physical and mental faculties, the sap not running very vigorously, and the knowledge that you'll soon be quitting this earth."

"How is this so easy for you and so hard for me?"

"I think a good amount of that adjustment is due to temperament. I never reached as high as you did, even though I believe that if you'd achieved everything you tried to accomplish we'd still be having this conversation.

You remember the Peggy Lee song, 'Is That All There Is?'

"And I also believe what I told you rather extravagantly earlier in our lunch: that you've got to know when to give up, when to detach yourself from all your running around, to get spiritually ready for the end of your life."

"But I'm not ready for the end. I feel as if I've just begun," Frank exclaimed, so loudly that four men in the booth across the aisle turned their heads toward him. He lowered his voice. "God damnit. I spent so long trying to get it together that finally when I do, I start breaking down."

"I hear your cry, Francis, and I sympathize with our plight. But nothing is going to set back the clock for you. *Forsan et haec olim meminisse juvabit.* Nothing is going to bring back any of those sixty-plus years that have gone by for you. This is when philosophy and religion have to kick in. Try starting with Cicero's *De Senectute.*"

"Fuck religion and philosophy. Just when I started to get laid, I started getting old. Just when I started recovering from my financial debacle, it's too late to get a really major career going. And you ask me to be philosophical?"

Christopher didn't respond. His hands were folded together, as if in prayer, with their tips resting against his lips. He seemed lost in thought.

Frank felt somewhat embarrassed by his outburst. There weren't many who would engage him in conversation on this obsession of his. Christopher was one of the few. But he saw that he was pushing even his patience. He suddenly felt as if he had been whining.

"I'm sorry, Christopher, I didn't mean to unload all my shit on you. Listen. It's a beautiful day. Let's go outside and think happy thoughts."

Christopher still didn't respond. He seemed lost in thought. Finally, he placed his hands, palms down, on either side of the remaining silverware at his place at the table, looked at Frank directly, and said in almost a whisper, "Francis, I will increase my prayers for you."

He pushed the buzzer for the waiter, who came bearing the bill. Christopher put the amount of the tip on it, signed it, and thanked the waiter with his usual urbanity and charm.

The two men walked out into the bright midday sunshine. Both instinctively looked up at the clear blue sky.

"I love it when the city gets like this," said Frank.

"Yes, this is lovely—and unusual. Maybe I'll go home, get in some shorts, and stretch out in Huntington Park."

"Watch out, people will think you're an aging fag."

"What do I care what people think? Do I owe them anything?" Christopher snapped.

"Christopher, thanks for lunch. I really appreciate your patience in listening to me. I'll get over whatever this mood is. You're a real pal."

"There's no need to thank me. As they say, that's what friends are for. But I do want you to know that I meant everything I said at lunch—analysis, diagnosis, and advice."

"Okay, I think I'll take the cable car up the hill. Call me."

Frank decided to stay for a few minutes in front of the dun-colored building that housed Sam's. He alternated between looking at the resplendent sun-splayed sky and at the post-luncheon parade of people returning to their offices, going shopping, or completing the multiplicity of chores that are necessary in the business district.

Then he saw her, languidly walking up Bush Street, with a shopping bag in each hand.

Startled, Frank gazed at her. Then she saw him. Their eyes locked. She smiled and called out, "Frank."

He quickly walked over to her. "Vanessa, what a surprise. What a treat to see you."

CHAPTER 5

Frank and Vanessa Walker embraced each other in front of Sam's. Vanessa gave out a tiny giggle. Both stood back to look at each other. It had been three—no, maybe four—years since they had last seen each other. Frank gazed at Vanessa. There were a few more wrinkles around the eyes, but these past few years had been good to her. Her dark-complected good looks were unchanged; a smart suit covered what he had known from long experience was a stunning, curvaceous body.

"What, we don't see each other for a few years and then, wham; we bump into each other on the street. Amazing." Frank was trying to contain both embarrassment and excitement at seeing his former lover.

"Well, you know, San Francisco's a small town. Sooner or later we were going to bump into each other," Vanessa responded.

"Yeah, well, I guess we lost touch, and the years do go by. Looks like you were shopping."

"I needed a few things, so I thought I'd take the day off, go to the stores. I had lunch with my friend Wendy. I've got a few more things to get, and then it's home."

"Listen, Vanessa, I've got an idea." Frank tried not to sound too eager. "I've got a few things to do at the office. Why don't we meet in the late afternoon for drinks? I'd love to catch up."

Vanessa's smile disappeared. Her lips formed a pout, and she seemed suddenly to be deep in thought. Frank began to feel foolish about his proposal.

"That would be great." A smile eclipsed the pout. "I've still got about two hours of shopping still to do. How about 4:00 or 4:30?"

"Perfect, let's say 4:30 at the Compass Rose. I'll meet you under the clock. Just kidding. Whoever gets there first snags a table."

They gave each other a brief, perfunctory hug and walked in opposite directions along Bush Street. Would she show up at the Compass Rose? Frank wondered. He was surprised at the disappointment he felt at the prospect that she might not. What was she feeling at this moment, about seeing him so unexpectedly, about sitting down for cocktails with him after all these years?

Frank was distracted when he entered the offices of Blakesley and Montgomery. Jessica, his secretary, smiled as he swung by her desk to go into his glass-sheathed office.

"Got lots of messages, Mr. M. Welcome back from lunch. How was the weirdo from the deep lagoon?"

"He told me to give you a big hug and kiss for him."

"Yuck!" Jessica retorted. "I'd rather be kissed and hugged by a chimp. Well, I mean that I wouldn't mind the hug and kiss from you, but I can do without the weirdo."

"Just kidding. Actually, your name didn't come up today, but I could tell he was secretly lusting for you."

Jessica had been Frank's secretary for more than a decade. She was sweet; she was competent; and she was devoted to him. But her life experience could not envisage the likes of a Christopher Fermoyle. She had called him pompous, a self-absorbed windbag, arrogant...and worse. This had led to a bantering between Frank and Jessica after any occasion when Jessica knew that he would be seeing Christopher.

Frank closed the door to his office and began to read the ten or so messages that had accumulated since he left for lunch. "Bob Turner. What does he want?" Frank wondered aloud. "Pamela. She must want something. I haven't spoken to her in a month." Frank felt a spasm of annoyance at his daughter.

He tossed the sheaf of messages down on his desk, sat in his chair, and swiveled to look out his window at the view of the bay. The sails of the boats floated like foam on the bay. He imagined the delight of those boat owners, out skimming the bay on such a sun-filled day. Large container ships headed for Oakland. San Francisco, which had once been one of the busiest ports in the world, had ceased to have any maritime activity. Modern ferries seemed to skip their way to Marin County. Frank remembered how he used to enjoy climbing on the old ferries going to Oakland until the late 1950s. He and his friends would often ride them over to Oakland and immediately back to San Francisco just for the pleasure of an inexpensive excursion, feeling the spray of the bay as a balm for the frustrations and longings of those student days.

As Frank gazed out the window, he lost sight of the bay and its marine activity. Instead, images of his long relationship with Vanessa ignited his imagination. They had met in New York about a year after he and Claudia had separated. He had gone to New York on a business trip, and had arranged to see his old friend Jonathan while there. Jonathan was amicably separated from his wife and had decided to take her along to a party to which both he and Frank had been invited. Vanessa was to meet Frank in the lobby of the Plaza Hotel. They would wait until Jonathan arrived and go on to the party.

When Vanessa walked into the lobby, there was an instantaneous attraction. The two of them chatted amicably, even flirted, until Jonathan arrived, when they walked to LaTerrere, where John Rothschild was hosting a party for some friends of his.

Frank and Vanessa found every opportunity to talk privately and to dance; and, as each moment went by, their physical passion for each other grew. Then a waiter handed Frank a note. It was from Jonathan, and it read, "Frank, please see that Vanessa gets home safely. I can't stand this loud music, and I'm getting a headache. I'll call you tomorrow."

He showed the note to Vanessa and asked, "Shall we go back to the Plaza for a nightcap?" She nodded eagerly in response, and within a few minutes they were walking hand-in-hand toward the hotel. Each had expectations that were met by the other's.

Frank and Vanessa slipped into the Oak Bar, ordered drinks, and continued to converse. It was Vanessa who said, "Why don't we go to your room?"

No sooner had the door to Frank's room closed than the two of them began to kiss, tongues darting, exploring every part of the other's mouth, arms entwined, hands and fingers eagerly exploring each other.

They were thus engaged for several minutes, until finally they tumbled onto the double bed. Their legs they added to the entwining, rolling on each other, first one on top, grinding genitalia on genitalia, then the other.

Clothes were shed. Frank's overcoat, then Vanessa's. Not stopping the frenzied kissing, Frank's dropped his three-piece suit to the floor, and Vanessa dropped her de Grezy suit. Bra, panties, Frank's underwear were then shucked.

Frank began to feel his penis harden as he thought back to that evening at the Plaza almost thirty years ago. The two had pulled back from the kissing and the hungry exploration of breasts and buttocks, and, still holding hands, looked at each other.

Vanessa was tall, with long dark hair, a massive, black pubic thatch, long, well-molded legs, large breasts, but not excessively so, a flat stomach, and well-rounded buttocks. The sight of Vanessa's body, splendid in its sun-tanned nakedness, increased his spasms of lust.

After their eyes had taken in each other's naked bodies, Frank pulled Vanessa close to him. They lay on their sides, facing each other, once more passionately kissing, their hands softly touching each other's inflamed bodies.

Frank began to kiss Vanessa's ears, throat, and shoulders, as she writhed and moaned with pleasure. He lifted himself to his knees and hunched over her, kissing her breasts, sucking her now-swollen nipples. Almost reluctant to leave her heaving breasts, Frank's lips made their way down to her flat stomach, along which his tongue languidly made spirals. His hand urged her thighs wider apart, and his mouth hovered over them.

Vanessa looked at him with surprise as he slowly licked and kissed her thighs and then moved his tongue into the tangle of her thick pubic hair. A spasm of pleasure shook her body as Frank's tongue and teeth found her clitoris and began to tease the engorged button of flesh. Her moans and screams of delight crackled in the room. She brought up his legs to straddle her torso, dug into his buttocks, and took his swollen penis into her mouth. Slowly, gently, but firmly she allowed the combinations of lips, tongue, and mouth to slither along his member. Then both simultaneously changed their positions. Frank straddled her and looked down on her flushed, expectant face.

"Come into me." she pleaded.

The command was instantly obeyed. Frank vowed that what was to come would last as long as possible, and he entered her slowly. Her vagina was tight, but wet. He could feel the hard, pink lozenge at the opening of her cavity.

The passion of their encounter put them into a different state of being. They kissed even more intensely as the rhythmical strokes of Frank's penis filled Vanessa's vagina. He alternated between probing her mouth with his tongue and kissing her cheeks and her throat. She met each of his strokes with a thrust of her own.

A barely audible gurgle that increased in intensity came from Vanessa's mouth. Her body stiffened, and then shuddered. The gurgle became a scream.

Frank lifted himself slightly, allowed himself one more long thrust deep inside of her, and then gave himself up to the waves of pleasure that swept through his body. He panted from the exertion. Sounds of no known language emitted from his mouth. A post-coital languor had begun to suffuse their bodies, as they lay intertwined.

The telephone buzzer interrupted Frank's reveries.

"Mr. M., it's your daughter, Pamela," Jessica announced.

"Okay, I'll take it." Frank was disappointed to be called out of his pleasant memories.

"Hi, sweetheart, how are you doing?"

"Hi, Dad. I'm calling because you were going to let me know about whether you'd be able to loan us the money for half the down payment on the house we're looking at."

"Pamela, I said I'd get back to you by the end of this week. It's only Tuesday."

"I know. I'm sorry, Dad. I guess I'm just anxious. Rick and I really love the house, and it's big enough for all the children we'll have."

Frank realized that his daughter was pulling out all the stops. He was pretty sure that he would lend her and his son-in-law the money but was annoyed that she was pressuring him. Paula had kept out of his decision making. She hadn't wanted to get involved in a decision that involved her stepdaughter. These relationships, she had told Frank, were always tenuous. Do whatever you think best, she had told him. But Frank had realized that if he turned down Pamela's request, his daughter and son-in-law would blame Paula anyway for his decision. Paula was right; relationships with stepchildren were tenuous.

"Pamela, why don't you call me on Thursday night? I'll give you my decision then. Now tell me how you and Rick are doing."

"We're fine, thanks. Rick's job is going well. It looks as if companies are buying computer software again. And Jennifer's a doll. She's really getting big."

"Bring her by sometime. Paula and I haven't seen her in more than two weeks."

"I will. Got to go now, Dad. Back to work. I'll talk with you on Thursday night."

Another conversation with Pamela, Frank thought, in which she would either want something or it would be a perfunctory call that she felt would meet her filial obligations. Ah, well, Frank reasoned, you can't control your children's lives or their relationship with you.

Frank would have liked to continue his earlier daydream, but the conversation with his daughter had brought him back to the practicalities of the afternoon.

He looked at his messages once again. He might as well start with Bob Turner. Bob had been complaining recently about the performance of his portfolio compared with that of various averages and mutual funds. Might as well get this unpleasantness out of the way.

"Bob? Frank Molinari. I'm returning your call." Frank stated dryly when his client picked up his direct line. "What can I do for you?"

"Frank, what's this about the feds and the states suing Microsoft? You've got a slug of that stock in my account. It's been going down like a rock in the ocean."

"Okay, let's go through this again, Bob." Frank hated these calls from malcontents who liked to flex any power they felt they had. "First, if you're going to second-guess every holding in your portfolio—or wonder why you're not holding a certain stock—you don't need an investment advisor. You can manage your own portfolio.

"Second, you've got pennies a share as a cost basis for your Microsoft. If we sold it, you'd have to pay umpteen dollars in capital gains taxes, far more than the stock has gone down.

"Third, these antitrust lawsuits will probably be settled soon, and Microsoft will not be unduly penalized. It's a great company."

"That may be, but it's not doing much for the overall return on my portfolio."

"Look, Bob, I've told you already: returns vary from year to year, and comparative returns are always different. One year one company or fund has a hot record; the next it's a dog. What counts is a long-term good return, and that's what we've given you."

Frank knew that Bob Turner was someone who would never be satisfied, who would always have to have the last word. He wasn't disappointed.

"Look, Frank, I've been generally satisfied in the past with how Blakesley and Montgomery has managed my account; but when my golfing buddies tell me about their rates of return, which are a lot higher than mine, I begin to wonder."

"Bob, what can I tell you? Maybe you should ask your golfing buddies to manage your portfolio." Frank chuckled to indicate that he was joking, but simultaneously wanted to indicate that he thought that Bob was a horse's ass.

"Yeah, right. Well, I just wanted to check in about this Microsoft thing. Let me know if there are any more developments."

"So, long, Bob."

Frank looked morosely at the sheaf of messages. Most were calls, he knew, similar to Bob Turner's. They were from clients who had turned over their assets to Blakesley and Montgomery to be managed, but who, when they read something negative about one of their holdings, heard about a stock that had done particularly well from a friend, or felt that their portfolio was not performing as well as some average, fund, or friend's they had heard about, would begin calling the firm and complaining.

For all that, Frank realized, it was amazing how few of the firm's clients ever left. Maybe this was just individuals' way of letting off steam. Who knew?

Frank began to return the calls, starting with those from the biggest complainers. Most of them were not available, either away from their offices or in meetings. The three he did reach were duplicates of Bob Turner. After many years, Frank knew how to handle such calls. You couldn't let them get to you, and you had to be detached as to whether they stayed with the firm or left it. Calls like these were just nuisances.

There was one message from a caller Frank didn't recognize. An answering machine picked up. "You have reached the office of James Silliman," a gravelly voice spoke. "Please leave a message."

It could be a referral from another client, Frank thought, but something inside him said that the call might be more portentous. He left his name and telephone number.

Frank did a quick appraisal of the stack of paper on his desk. Most of the matters in the folders were routine and could be taken care of tomorrow. He looked at his watch. He had forty-five minutes before his meeting with Vanessa. There was plenty of time to walk from his office to the St. Francis Hotel.

"Jessica, I'm gone for the rest of the day. Have a good evening."

"Mrs. M. called while you were on the phone. She said not to forget that you have a dinner engagement at the Harrises' house at 7:30."

"Will you call her back and tell her that I have a late appointment? I'll meet her at the Harrises' at 7:45."

Jessica nodded and waved goodbye as Frank strode to the elevators. Frank had forgotten about the dinner party at Midge and Bob Harris's house and realized that this would put a time limit on his visit with Vanessa.

Frank left the office building and walked down Montgomery Street. Each day he reflected on what used to be the principal street of San Francisco's financial district, "the Wall Street of the West." Beautiful, classical, two-story buildings on corners of the street had become nothing but deceptive façades for the first two stories of behemoth office buildings. A large 1920s office building had been transformed into a hotel. Bottom floors of buildings contained tacky retail stores. Montgomery was no longer the elegant street it had been when he first came to work there in the early 1960s.

He no longer recognized anyone as he walked down the street. Most of his contemporaries were dead or retired. He knew very few of the young men and women who worked in the now far-flung financial district. He noticed that the men and women who walked along Montgomery Street seemed to hold low-level jobs: that the "movers-and-shakers" now worked in the new high-rises east of Montgomery and even across Market Street.

The eating places that Frank had known in his early years in the financial district were mostly gone. A high-rise had replaced the building that held the Fly Trap with its charming small rooms for dining upstairs, as had Jack's, which had recently been gutted, its old San Francisco charm replaced by a pretentious exterior and an equally pretentious menu. The Iron Pot, the Iron Horse, Tadich's on Leidesdorff Street, where you didn't have to wait for an hour to have lunch, the El Prado on Union Square, where clients who worked at I. Magnin's would take him to lunch, Goldberg-Bowen's, and how many more? He couldn't remember how many restaurants no longer existed.

Now there were the fast food places, with food that bore no resemblance to something that one would want to eat, or else there were fashionable restaurants that call attention to themselves with exotic menus: the pumpkin gnocchi with raspberry vinegar.

On the other hand, most of the young people he knew working in the financial district didn't seem to eat lunch. They would gobble unfathomable concoctions of greens, bean sprouts, and yogurt while guzzling incredible quantities of bottled water at their desks. Or they would go out on their lunch hours to gyms and workout places and then come back to their desks to stuff greens, bean sprouts, and yogurt into their mouths.

As he turned off Montgomery Street onto Post, Frank continued his meditation on the changes he had witnessed during the past forty-some years that he had worked on Montgomery Street. Clothes, for one. Everyone had worn hats when he had first gone to work. Now, the only hats you saw were baseball caps worn backward. Ties and suits had almost disappeared; and casual attire, which generally appeared as if it had been snatched from the Salvation Army grab bag, was de rigeur.

Life had become uncivilized, Frank mused. He felt grumpy about the changes. He hated the monosyllabic exchanges that now passed for conversation. He was stunned that no one seemed interested in a discussion of ideas anymore. Unless it was to register how one did or did not enjoy a movie or to discuss a hike, a run, or a bicycle ride, the people he encountered who were younger than he—and everyone these days was younger than he—seemed incapable of talking about anything else.

The stores he encountered on Post Street added to his distaste. There was Gump's, which had moved to its new location a few years before. He remembered it as it was when he was a boy and a young man at its location across Post Street and a block nearer to Union Square. It was like Ali Baba's cave, with its treasures from Asia and its exquisite goods selected with impeccable taste from all around the world. Now it was like any other purveyor of household goods, like Cost Plus or Pottery Barn, no longer spoken of in hushed tones, no longer a "must" place to visit by tourists and other visitors to the city.

As Frank crossed Grant Avenue he looked across the street to where Gump's had been for as long as he could remember. The sign now said "Eddie Bauer." Although Frank had never stepped foot in the store, he knew it as a purveyor of casual clothes and suppliers for those whose lives revolved around thinking they lived outdoors, hiking, camping, and rock climbing.

There's the sign, there's the omen, Frank thought: an Eddie Bauer store where Gump's used to be.

At the corner of Post and Stockton Streets Frank looked up at the tall Hyatt Hotel that stood there and remembered the elegant but down-at-the-heels Prado Hotel that was on that corner for so many years. The hotel had contained a chic restaurant where many of San Francisco's wealthy matrons had dined. Where, he wondered, did socially conscious, wealthy matrons now lunch?

Frank's eyes moved from the Hyatt across Union Square to the elegant St. Francis Hotel, and, as he approached the hotel, his excitement about seeing Vanessa became palpable. He could feel his heart pumping, and he felt the light-headed excitement he had felt as a teenager on a date with a girl he believed would make out with him.

Frank strode up the stairs of the hotel's main entrance and stepped through the glass doors. He impatiently skipped up the stairs off the lobby to the Compass Rose, his eyes searching the rococo room with its columns and high ceilings. She was sitting, looking pensive, at a table overlooking Powell Street. Frank walked over to the table, trying to conceal his excitement.

"Vanessa, how great you could come."

She looked up and smiled at him. "It's always good to see you, Frank."

CHAPTER 6

Both Frank and Vanessa seemed to be somewhat ill at ease, even embarrassed, to be sitting across from each other. Their romance, which had lasted for several years, had been over for more than two decades. Vanessa had been living with a doctor for much of the time since their relationship had ended, and Frank had been married for the past seven years. But, as the two of them smiled at each other and groped their way toward conversation, both were aware of the passionate intensity of their romance.

Marriage was never an option for them, but the explosiveness of their sexuality had created a bond between them that could not be forgotten. It was not only the sex that tied them into such a strong togetherness: they explored life with an equally strong passion.

They had met at a time when they both were at a crossroad. Frank had just separated and was in the process of getting a divorce. Vanessa was separated from Jonathan, but they were attempting reconciliation—one that never occurred.

Both had been virgins when they married, and neither of their partners had brought any experience to the marriage bed. Their spouses both had a prudish sensibility that precluded any sexual experimentation. Frank had conducted some clandestine affairs, but these, aside from the excitement of novelty, had offered no permanent pleasure. Jonathan's affair with an intern in his office had led to his separation from Vanessa and to their eventual divorce.

When Frank and Vanessa had met that snowy January night at the Plaza Hotel, neither of them realized that they would sexually liberate each other and have a sometimes stormy but always exuberant relationship that would last for years.

There were a number of reasons why they chose not to marry. They were of different religions. Frank wanted to marry a Catholic, and there was no possibility that Vanessa would ever convert. Her family in New York disapproved of him. Their backgrounds were so different that Frank was like an alien in their midst. And Frank wanted more children if he married again. Vanessa did not. The subject of marriage never came up. They mostly were happy with the excitement they found being together.

"So, what have you been up to these past few years?" Frank inaugurated the conversation.

"Oh, you know, not much has changed. Josh and I are together still, and we have a very nice relationship. My interior design business has been going well. The girls are fine. We've been doing quite a bit of traveling...went to China last year and just got back from Russia a couple of weeks ago. How about you?"

Frank pursed his lips and thought for several seconds. He was struck by the stiffness of the conversation. He felt as if the two of them had just encountered each other at a high school reunion.

"Let's see...the last four years, hmm. The children all seem to be well. My marriage is going well. Business is good. You know, nothing much has changed. I see the same old friends; have made a few new ones. I'm getting older." Frank laughed.

"Are you happy?" Vanessa peered at him without a smile.

"I think I am as happy as I can be at this state in my life," Frank responded. "I'm not kidding about getting older. I feel my body, the aches and pains, a little more. I no longer believe that I'm going to do great things. And life is not as exciting as it was in the past. You know, 'the blues are not as blue, the whites are not as white.'"

Vanessa did not reply. Her face was serious. She turned away from him and looked out the window. Outside, visitors to San Francisco and residents of the city alike scurried along Powell Street. The sun was casting shadows as it dipped in the western sky. The Dewey Monument glistened in the declining light.

"That's the kind of thought that depresses me," Vanessa finally said. She turned from the scene outdoors and looked at Frank. "I remember it, too, when I was younger, and I felt the sap in me running so hard and so high. Oh, God, how good and how exciting it all felt during those days. I felt really alive."

Frank couldn't determine whether Vanessa was lamenting the days when they were lovers or bemoaning her loss of youth in generic terms. He found that he was still very much attracted to her, and he suddenly began to worry about what would happen if both of them became agreeable to resuming their physical intimacy. Was Vanessa signaling him that such a resumption, even if only once, was possible?

"Isn't it amazing," Frank began, "that when you're younger you think that those feelings will last forever, that fulfillment of your desires will lead to permanent happiness? You hope some terrible tragedy doesn't happen to you, but you have no preparation for the least dramatic decline; life becoming bland. Yet you can look back and, on some level, remember pulsating with excitement."

Vanessa smiled slightly and looked pensive. Frank had decided not to probe whether she was interested in an assignation then or later. It was too risky, he had decided. Vanessa was committed to a long-term relationship, and he was happily married. He had not been unfaithful to Paula and felt that to start being so would lead to unwanted troubles.

But he had indicated to Vanessa some ideas that correlated with those she had just expressed. His divorce had been a watershed for him. The agony of not being in a happy marriage involved in the day-to-day raising of his children was disastrous. The financial problems that had beset him after the divorce had deepened his depression. He had existed for a number of years in this trough of despondency. Vanessa had been a saving influence. But, when he had arisen from the trough, when a good life seemed to have been restored to him, he couldn't quite pull out of his depression. It seemed that these days nothing gave him pleasure.

Frank's doctor had given him some anti-depressants, but they hadn't worked. He felt that he was each day living a two-tiered life; on the outside he felt an almost zombie-like contentedness, yet he felt that he could peer into an inner being who was still depressed, feeling curiously disconnected from the outer being.

This dual life had gone on for some time. When he and Paula were married he gave up the anti-depressants. He had felt fine, but he also felt that he would never return to an earlier time—a time when he had felt life so much more intensely.

As if reading his thoughts, Vanessa reached over and put her hand on top of his, which was splayed over the champagne flute from which he was drinking.

"No matter what you do, those feelings of pulsating excitement will never return. They're gone forever." And she removed her hand.

"Well, that's pretty definitive," Frank laughed. "It sounds as if all that's left for us is death."

"No, although death is going to be our final act. What I'm saying is that we'll continue to lead happy, productive lives, but they'll never be as exciting as they were. You know what they say about 'salt losing its savor'? I think that's what happens to human beings as they get older. And the terrible thing is that we can still remember the excitement, when 'the blues were bluer and the whites were whiter,' as you put it. We remember, and we are sadder because our lives aren't that way anymore."

"Whoa, that's a pretty depressing thought, and it's exactly the thought that has been depressing me. It makes me feel that I'm on a downhill slope. I'm wondering if there's any solution for this situation, or if there comes a time when we just forget everything about the excitement of earlier years."

Vanessa was silent. She looked out the window again. Frank wondered how they had ever gotten to converse on this subject. He thought that their getting together might have been a flirtatious reminiscing about the days of their passionate love affair—and perhaps the expectation of something more—but neither of them had ventured into this territory. Instead, they had embarked on a serious assessment of life in their 60s.

Vanessa returned from her sojourn at looking at Powell Street and Union Square, flashed a broad smile and said, "We should probably change the subject before we get depressed. Tell me about your children…really they are no longer children, are they?"

Frank began the usual litany about his four children, but since Vanessa had known them well, he did not give the sanitized account.

"Well, they're grown now. There's not much you can do about these things. Do give them my love. They're wonderful kids."

"It's one of the big disappointments in my life—that my children didn't turn out the way I wanted them to."

"You can't blame yourself and you can't blame them," Vanessa responded. "They're separate human beings from you, and they're going to develop in their own ways."

Vanessa and he had always disagreed on childrearing. Frank was a believer in "tough-love" and an active molding of children; Vanessa was much more tolerant and permissive. Their differences sometimes would lead to quarrels, especially after her children misbehaved.

"We've always had our differences on raising children," Frank said with a smile. "We're not going to agree now."

"You'd be a lot better off if you didn't have such high expectations. The children would be better off, too."

"You know, I can't help it. I feel there are certain ways you behave in life, certain...well, just certain values..."

Frank was stuck. He couldn't articulate what he felt about how individuals should be. His "enlightened" friends called him "judgmental," and indeed he was. He had gotten this from his parents, who had most definite views on human deportment and had no trouble enunciating their judgments. They perhaps could have been described as rigid. They had raised him very strictly and with numerous injunctions on how to behave. He had pretty much gone along with them in his behavior, and had come to believe their ideas. His brother had "slipped the traces" and his youngest brother, in a different way, had ignored most of their parents' admonitions.

Frank sighed. He knew he was out of sync with the times, but he had always clung to these ideas of how people should lead their lives. He knew it was an old-fashioned, Italian immigrant, pre-Vatican II Catholic ensemble of values; but he also knew that these values were the bedrock of his being.

He looked intensely at Vanessa. "What is is, and nothing I say or do is going to change what is—not my children, not the world around me, not anything. But, knowing this, I am going to continue to enunciate what I believe or feel about people or events. And how's that?" he concluded with a laugh.

Vanessa smiled. She had known how stubborn and definitive he could be. Both of them knew that their conversation wasn't going any further, and both were pleased to move on to something else.

"How's Paula?" Vanessa began a new topic.

"She's terrific. She loves her work. We have a good time together. We like to travel. It's a good marriage, I'm happy to say. We're good companions. And Josh, I presume he's well and making people better."

"Josh is great and the relationship is great. I know a lot of people wonder why we don't get married, but I see no reason for us to get married. We have nothing to gain by doing so. In fact, from a tax point of view, it would cost us money. We have a good life together, and, at the same time we lead independent lives."

"Well, then there's no reason for you to get married," Frank mused. "You have a close relationship, you obviously aren't going to have any more children, and whatever deficiencies there are by not being married you can't obviate by legal contract."

"I think of Josh as my husband...I really do. But neither of us wants to get married."

"The two of you certainly do lead different lives than you used to," Frank said, smiling, "You do all sorts of outdoor activities. You go to resorts. Are you enjoying all this?"

"What's not to enjoy? I love spending time lying on the beach, lazing around, going out boating, and I'm thrilled that I'm back skiing. I work hard, and I'm very happy to be able to take time off and do these things."

"That's terrific. I'm still allergic to physical activity and do as little as I can. Well, that's not entirely true. I'm trying to get an aerobic walk in every day."

It was Frank's turn now to look out the window. How odd, this conversation, he thought. How strange that two people who had loved each other so intensely, had had such an exciting and passionate relationship for so long, would now be having such a banal conversation.

Their chatter contained some components of their former intimacy but was decidedly a let's-catch-up-after-all-these-years type of talk. And, although Frank had felt an emotional rush when he had first seen Vanessa on the street, he was now pleased that they were no longer together. But the memories of their relationship still had a powerful hold over him.

Vanessa brought him out of his reverie. "I think it's time for me to get home. Do give my best to Paula and do let's all get together for dinner sometime. We shouldn't let this much time go by."

"Absolutely not. Somehow the days turn into weeks, and the weeks into months...you know, life slips by. But it has been great bumping into you and getting a chance to catch up on our lives. Give me a minute and I'll walk out with you."

Frank jotted the tip on the credit card reckoning, signed it, and tore off his copy. Vanessa and he walked through the lobby and outside to Powell Street. It was early evening, and a chill had settled onto the city. Shoppers were rushing down the streets to their cars or to buses. Early diners strolled purposefully to restaurants. Others swirling around them were leaving shops or offices where they worked. Each face had a look that indicated a desire to let the evening bring relaxation.

"I've got to go back to my office building to get my car," Frank said. "Do you have your car here, or can I give you a ride home?"

"I'm at the Sutter-Stockton garage."

Frank reached over for her hand, looked at Vanessa, and then gave her an antiseptic hug and kissed her on both cheeks. "I've really enjoyed seeing you again, Vanessa. I'll give you a call for dinner."

Would he, he wondered?

CHAPTER 7

The Jaguar entered Highway 101 in the southeastern part of San Francisco. Frank had no real interest in cars, except for getting from one place to another. He had no mechanical knowledge and no interest in automobiles as status symbols. But when he saw the black Jaguar XKE as he was walking by British Motor Cars one day, he couldn't resist its sleek design. His aesthetic sense was suddenly ignited, and in an uncharacteristic moment of impulsiveness he went into the showroom and bought it. It had served him well, and he had had no problems with the car, which pleased him.

Frank had arisen later than usual today. The dinner party had gone on later than usual the previous evening, and since he had a mid-morning business appointment with a client, he decided not to go into the office before heading down the peninsula. He called Jessica to tell her that he wouldn't be in until mid-afternoon. After his meeting he would try to call on a couple of prospects for the firm's investment advisory services.

Cocktails with Vanessa the previous afternoon had unsettled him. He had felt threatened by the continued attraction he felt for her. Yet he was thankful that neither of them had made any approaches toward renewed sexual contact. The nature of their conversation had also distressed him. Thoughts and feelings that had been flickering within him for some time had come out. They had always been able to talk frankly to each other, to share ideas that Frank was usually not able to share with others. Vanessa and he had slipped into this openness without any effort. There had been in addition this banal so-what's-been-happening-to-you exchange that was understandable for two people who had once been intimate, but who hadn't seen each other for four years.

The towns of the peninsula began to slide by—Brisbane, South San Francisco, San Bruno, Millbrae. Impulsively, Frank decided to get off the freeway at Burlingame and head west and then south. He would travel to his appointment on El Camino Real for the rest of the route.

He felt nostalgic when he saw the familiar tall, gnarled eucalyptus trees planted along El Camino in Burlingame by John McLaren, the legendary superintendent of San Francisco's park system for fifty-six years. How many times had he passed by these sentinels? They had been there the multitudinous times he had gone to visit his parents after he moved out of their home when he got married. When he went to the peninsula for a date or a party, they had guided his way.

Frank tried to recollect the specific times these majestic trees had connected with a pleasurable event. There was the time in high school when he had driven to Hillsborough for a date with Pamela Neville. He had no idea where he had gotten the courage to ask her out on a date. Pamela was gorgeous, with a supple, curvaceous body. She was the cousin of a friend of his, and Frank had met her at his home. Shedding his usual reticence and shyness around girls, he had asked her for a date and she had responded positively. He had been thrilled, and intensely excited the entire week before the date.

That was fifty years ago. Frank remembered turning off El Camino to head into the wealthy, socially prominent enclave of Hillsborough, leaving the eucalyptus trees behind. Arriving at the magnificent Georgian mansion where Pamela lived, the excitement of a date with her that evening was enhanced by the lush gardens surrounding the house and the elegant house itself.

He had gone through the ritual of meeting her parents, chatting a bit with her father, one of a troika of top executives at Pacific Gas & Electric Company. Then the two of them left for their date, which had consisted of dinner at the Villa Chartier in San Mateo—a sign that he had extended his spending on a date—and then to see *Love Me Or Leave Me* with James Cagney and Doris Day at the movie theatre in San Carlos.

Frank had fantasized a drive to the hills behind San Carlos after the movie. But it had become clear during dinner that he lacked the nerve for such a suggestion, and that Pam would most likely have sniffed her pert nose at the invitation.

They talked pleasantly enough during dinner, but Frank could see that he was not sparking this beauty. They had friends in common, whom they discussed, but there was none of the flirtatious give and take that was a hallmark of dates where each present has erotic vibrations with the other.

After the movie he drove Pamela home. They spoke briefly at the door and said goodbye, and then he left. She hadn't offered her cheek or her lips for a kiss, and he hadn't thrust his head forward to kiss her. Nonetheless, the excitement of having had a date with her continued to pulsate within him, along with a deflating premonition that there would probably not be another date. There wasn't.

Driving through San Mateo, Frank snapped back to reality. His family had moved here after he finished high school. He had spent summers, Christmas vacations, and the occasional weekend when he was in college at his parents' home, and had enjoyed the quiet suburban life. There was a much different feel to the peninsula than there was to San Francisco. Even the girls and young women he had dated or whom he had met seemed different: more sensual, tanned, and voluptuous.

The combination of apartment houses and retail stores that characterized El Camino Real from Burlingame through Redwood City now changed to lush vegetative roadside displays as he neared Atherton.

Atherton was home to new money, largely. These were the venture capitalists, the investment bankers, the attorneys, and the owners of tech businesses who had made large amounts of money in recent years, after Silicon Valley became ground zero of the technological revolution. Huge fortunes had been made, both by those who had invented some new device and by those who provided money for these new companies or advised them in their legal affairs.

Frank and his firm had strenuously tried to develop business in the Silicon Valley. As the fortunes of the "old money" in San Francisco began to decline, the net worth of the "new money," mostly living in the suburbs south of the city, grew exponentially.

It was not a group that Frank relished doing business with. Most of the prospects for the services of his firm or those whom they advised were arrogant. They had made a great deal of money at very young ages and felt that they knew everything. Whereas the firm's old clients were content with the results they achieved on their portfolios, the newly wealthy were constantly second-guessing and trying to show their superiority by wishing to discuss the newest and most abstruse theories of risk management.

Frank pulled into the circular driveway of a huge modern house on Selby Lane in Atherton. The four-acre estate had once boasted a large,

Colonial-style house built there in the 1920s. That six-bedroom house had been torn down by Frank's client, Dolph Wickstrom, and replaced by the current mammoth mansion that contained a movie theatre, a bowling alley, and ten bedrooms.

The door was opened by a middle-aged Latino woman in a blue maid's dress with a short white apron over it. Uniforms for the help were mandatory in the Wickstrom household, but Dolph, who had just entered the atrium from his study, had on a pair of faded, torn Levi's, a ragged T-shirt, and dirty tennis shoes—an ensemble of clothing that was itself the uniform of newly minted money.

"Frank, welcome," Dolph greeted Frank. "How about a cup of coffee or tea?"

At Frank's assent, Dolph turned to the maid and said, "Two coffees, Blanca." He led the way into the nearby study and motioned Frank to sit down.

Adolphus Wickstrom III was from an affluent Connecticut family. He had gone to the Groton School and then to Stanford. Dolph had demonstrated an aptitude for the new technology while at Stanford and, after his third year there, had come to the conclusion that any further education would be a waste of his time. He left before getting his degree and went to work for a recently founded company in Mountain View, where he plunged into the life typical of Silicon Valley denizens: incessant work, often working throughout the night. After three years at Spectrum Factors, Dolph cashed in on his options and, at age 26, used the money to found Alpha Systems.

Dolph had realized that the big money to be made in the Silicon Valley would be harvested by those who started their own companies, became financed by venture capitalists, and then went public. He was the solo founder, although some stock was given to a few key employees who had joined Alpha early on.

The company prospered. Its growth was fueled by three rounds of venture capital financing, and, finally, when Merrill Lynch spearheaded the company's public offering a few years ago, Dolph found himself at age 32 worth $200 million.

A year before the public offering, when Dolph felt he could shake loose from the eighteen- to twenty-hour days he had been working seven days a week, he had married. Melissa Hapgood was a superb choice. She was a recent graduate of Stanford and worked in Alpha's marketing department. She also came from an affluent family. Dolph did not have to go far to meet and court her. She had all the credentials he was looking for. After six months, feeling the time had come to marry, he proposed and she accepted. They married three months later. A year later, they welcomed their first-born, Courtney Hapgood Wickstrom. The young family moved into the newly constructed house on Selby Lane.

Dolph sat on a sofa opposite Frank. "We might as well get down to business," he began, waiving all the amenities of chitchat. "I got your report on my portfolio. It shows an 11 percent return for the year. Now, mind you, I'm not complaining—it's a good return—but I did expect better. I thought that we should get together to discuss what might have gone wrong."

Frank stifled the desire to tell his client to "fuck off." Instead, he looked intently at Dolph and began the justification of his firm's management of Dolph's account.

"First of all, let me say that nothing 'went wrong.' Your return is 5 percent above the Dow's return and 2 percent above the NASDAQ's."

"Sure," Dolph countered, "but if I had wanted to approximate the returns of the averages I could have bought index funds and saved your commission."

Frank pursed his lips and again stifled his anger. "Five and two percent advantages over the averages are not 'approximating' them. Over the years, such differences total a lot of money. Most individuals are quite happy to beat the averages."

He noticed he had made a mistake in his presentation when he saw Dolph's eyebrows rise at the mention of "most individuals." Dolph would never consider himself one of "most individuals."

Frank continued. "To get down to specifics, one of the reasons your returns—and the returns of all our clients—weren't higher was that the portfolios were over-weighted in foreign stocks. We were right to do so, but we were early. Foreign securities began to pick up steam during the latter part of last year and have done quite well for the first two months of this year. If all goes as expected to the end of this quarter, you'll see your return outpace the averages by an even greater amount."

Blah, blah, blah, blah, Frank thought, annoyed with himself for what he considered to be toadying to his client. But Frank also knew that catering to the egos of the firm's clients was part of his job and that there would be consternation in his office if one of the firm's biggest clients decided to take a hike.

Dolph appeared to be thinking about what Frank had said, his hand rubbing his chin. "As I said," he began, "I certainly didn't mean to criticize your management of the portfolio or to indicate that I was dissatisfied with the return. But, having said that, I'd also like a somewhat higher return on my assets. You might mention that to those who make suggestions for the portfolio. I'm not adverse to higher risk for a higher return."

"I'll talk to the portfolio manager and the analysts about this, and I'm sure they'll respond. And, of course, all this depends on how the market fares this year."

Frank now yearned to escape from Dolph. He drank the last sip of coffee to suggest his departure. "Not adverse to higher risk for a higher return." What bullshit, Frank thought, and how often had he heard it. If there were some serious losses due to a higher risk profile in his portfolio, Dolph Wickstrom would be threatening a lawsuit. Frank suddenly felt a loathing for his job: being deferential to clients, listening to their everlasting and unreasonable complaints, realizing that not one of them was ever satisfied, no matter how well he did for them.

"Yeah, well, do the best you can," Dolph responded with a cold smile. "So, how have you been?"

"Oh, I've been fine. And how's your family?"

"Never better. Courtney's growing up a beauty and smart as a whip. Melissa's busy with a million volunteer activities. And I'm finally able to relax a bit."

"What are you doing now that you've retreated from such an intensive involvement with Alpha?"

"Well, I'm still chairman of the board, and that takes a lot of time. Then, Melissa's got me involved in some charitable boards, plus I'm on a couple of business boards. I play golf a twice a week, and—poof! —Before I know it, the week's gone."

There they are, Frank thought. The amiable banalities had come at the end. Dolph needed to exercise his ego, had done so, and now he managed a few pleasantries. At least he hadn't said that Courtney was a "gifted child."

"Sounds like a good life," Frank smiled. "Give my regards to Melissa."

"I will. She's playing tennis. It's good to keep active."

They shook hands at the door. Frank eased the Jaguar out of the driveway into Selby Lane. His next destination was one of the principal centers of money and power in the world: Sand Hill Road in Palo Alto.

As Frank drove through the manicured lawns and carefully pruned trees that surrounded the homes of the wealthy in Atherton, he thought about his next destination. He would call on a venture capitalist that he knew only slightly. Henry Simone had encouraged Frank to visit and talk about the firm's investment services whenever he was in the area.

Frank hoped that Henry would be able to see him, as Frank had enjoyed his company the few times they had encountered each other. Born in Brooklyn of an Italian father and a Lebanese mother, Simone had pulled himself out of the ghetto where he had grown up, majored in classics at Columbia University, and had gotten his M.B.A. at Harvard. He was a rarity in the world of finance: a true humanist and scholar and a tough, hard-charging businessman.

Sand Hill Road replicated the mansions of Atherton. Lawns, trees, and shrubs surrounded the buildings of the business complex where Simone's firm was located. Frank put the Jaguar in a parking place next to the complex and walked into its entrance. He noticed that not a single leaf was out of place.

"Frank, good to see you. How nice of you to stop by," Simone greeted him as he walked in the sumptuous but austere office. "Your timing couldn't be better. I've got some time to chat with you."

Even though Frank did not know Simone well, he had been impressed with his graciousness when they had met. There was little or none of the ego-driven personality that dominated the Silicon Valley complex of technology and finance.

They sat down facing each other on couches situated in a corner of the large office. Simone's secretary came in to inquire if they wished coffee or tea, but both declined.

"Henry, I always enjoy your company, and I'd love it if we could see more of each other socially. But this visit is to follow up on your kind invitation to discuss our investment advisory services with you," Frank began.

"Of course, that would be great. Let me tell you, first of all, that most of my assets are invested in the companies we finance. But I try to keep a portion of my capital in marketable securities. I've been pretty much managing these investments myself, but I've begun to think of having professional management. So, you see, your visit is timely."

"Great. I've already sent you the packet of information on our firm—its record, and so forth. I don't know if you've had a chance to read it..."

"Yes, I have. It's impressive, but so are a number of other firms. Tell me why should I place my money under your management."

It was a direct question that Frank had answered many times, and he proceeded to explain to Simone the methodology of the firm's investment philosophy that it had crafted many years ago.

"It's been the firm's philosophy that 'fear and greed' rule the market and that most institutions are uncomfortable investing in companies that are not well-known names. And we believe that these two situations create inefficiencies in the market.

"Thus, our investment strategy is to purchase large companies that are out of favor or have some temporary cloud over their heads...for example, when Apollo Group announced they were going to open more education centers and the stock went down, we bought them. And not too long ago we bought Alliance Capital when they were touched by the mutual fund scandal. We also buy well-managed companies that have a good business franchise—both value and growth companies—but have been overlooked by Wall Street.

"Now I know that other investment firms have a similar strategy, and I'm not going to denigrate them. And the truth is that you could go to a number of good firms. But our record is right up there with the best, and we've been able to beat the averages by a substantial margin year after year."

Henry Simone did not respond to Frank's pitch. He looked thoughtfully toward his desk, his swarthy handsome face in meditative repose. Frank had long ago learned not to interrupt these moments of silence. Simone at long last cleared his throat, and, looking at Frank, said, "You know, Frank, I think the time has come. I've been thinking about professional portfolio management for some time, and I think we can analyze these things to death. I like you, and I'm impressed with how well your firm has done. Let's do it. I've got about ten million dollars in cash and securities that we can use to start. Why don't you let me know what steps to follow to transfer these assets to you, and send me your contract for me to sign. I think that will do it."

A smile of pleasure spread over Frank's face. He always enjoyed the process of getting new business, but this was particularly delectable. Simone's quick decision was unexpected. It was a goodly amount of assets to begin their relationship. And he liked Simone as a person. He did not have the proclivity that so many wealthy individuals had of making one grovel when conferring a benefit.

"Henry, I'll take care of all that. I want to tell you how pleased I am that you have become a client of the firm. You'll, of course, get numerous reports on how your investments are doing; but I'm always available to answer any questions you have or to discuss anything you might want to talk about."

"Yes, yes, I think it will work out very well, and it will be a pleasure to work with you. Send me whatever papers I need to deal with and let me know what you need from me to transfer the cash and securities over to you."

"I'll do that. Thanks for your time and thanks for your confidence. You won't regret it."

The tall, dark-complected, and poised Simone stood and with a warm smile, held out his hand to Frank. "Thanks for coming by, Frank. I hope we'll see each other soon, when we can get a chance to become better acquainted."

"Absolutely," Frank rejoined, quite sincerely. "See you soon."

He smiled at the secretary as he left the office and walked out toward his car. It was midday, a typical day on the peninsula—warm, clear, blue skies, with just a hint of breeze. It was the kind of day that he had marveled at when his parents had moved the family to the peninsula when he was a teenager. Gone were San Francisco's perennial fog days and howling wind. So many years ago, he felt he'd been transported to the Garden of Eden.

As Frank approached his car in the parking lot, he noticed a Latino gardener leaning on his rake, observing him. Frank smiled and gave him a wave. The gardener responded with a smile and then resumed raking the leaves on a strip of lawn in front of the building Frank had just left.

What does he think about all this? Frank wondered. Here he is working all year for a pittance, surrounded by untold wealth. Do his friends tell him about the lavish displays of wealth at the houses of those who work in these buildings? Is his wife a blue-uniformed maid in one of those houses? Does he comprehend the lifestyles of those he works for? Frank mused, even I don't understand such wealth and its impact on the lives of those who have it, and I've been dealing with them for decades.

Frank gave a glance back at the gardener as the Jaguar nosed out of the parking lot. The gardener was rhythmically raking the lawn. He's probably happier than most of the people in that building, Frank thought. At least, I hope so.

Frank decided to drive home on Highway 280. West of Highway 101,

Highway 280 links San Francisco with San Jose. Sculpted through the lush lands between the suburban homes and development of San Mateo County and the communities along the Pacific Ocean, Highway 280 provides an untrafficked route through a beautiful landscape; Frank always enjoyed driving that road.

As he headed north, Frank slipped into the meditative trance that this drive often brought upon him. And, then, on the radio station he almost always listened to while driving—he loved the "oldies" they played on KABL—came the Four Aces singing, "Tell Me Why." From the first time he heard the harmonic lushness of this song, Frank had been deeply touched. Even now, when he heard it, the sounds of the song excited him.

Suddenly, his mind involuntarily flashed back to the spring of 1955. He had borrowed his parents' Oldsmobile to go to a party in Los Altos Hills—a wealthy community just south of where he was now driving. Frank had forgotten the name of the girl who had given the party or why he had been invited. Almost all the girls at the party attended the Convent of the Sacred Heart in Menlo Park and most of the young men were in college—Menlo College, Stanford, the University of Santa Clara.

Frank remembered how excited he had been that evening, surrounded by gorgeous girls, all from affluent homes, well-dressed and self-assured. He had attached himself to one of them. What was her name? Frank tried to remember. Ah, yes, Deborah Riley. Deborah's father was a well-known doctor, and she carried herself like a self-confident young mare. She had a bubbling sense of humor and a quick wit. Plus she was bright and had talked with Frank about literature. To top it all off, she was pretty, had smooth alabaster skin, and a great sense of style.

Frank and Deborah had found themselves talking and laughing on a stone bench just off the patio of the house where the party was when he heard "Tell Me Why" coming from the record player in the nearby living room.

His body shuddered with an erotic charge, and putting aside his characteristic shyness, he put his arms around Deborah and murmured, "I like you very much." He proceeded to kiss her on the lips. She responded to this kiss, and Frank was suffused with a joy and excitement he could barely contain.

As he pulled back from the embrace to look at Deborah, she smiled and said, "Why, we've just met and here you are, kissing me."

The joy and excitement vanished. Frank felt himself turn red with embarrassment. Had he offended her? Had he been too aggressive? He suddenly felt ashamed.

He tried to recoup by pointing to the nearly full moon and saying to her laughingly, "I guess the full moon made me lose my head."

There had been no other embrace, no more kisses. They sat together for another two hours, discussing a nineteenth-century Russian novel and some foreign movies they had recently seen, until Frank left. He didn't have the nerve to call her after the party.

It was forty-five years later when he reencountered her. Frank was shocked that she remembered the party and their brief encounter. "Why didn't you kiss me more?" she inquired. "I could have made out with you all night. It was very romantic, and I really liked you. And, then, you never called me."

What was wrong with me at that age? Frank asked himself. I can still remember how excited I was, how I would have loved to kiss her again and again, how I would have loved to date her. He sighed at the memory. As an adult, one never gets enough of those things one feels one didn't get in one's youth.

Frank felt somewhat glum at the memory. He decided to turn his thoughts elsewhere.

It was now mid-afternoon. It had been a productive day. He had effectively handled the discontent of one client and had gathered in a new client...for $10 million, no less. Frank decided not to go back to the office, but instead to visit Father Michael O'Sullivan at the Jesuit infirmary at St. Ignatius College. Even if he went straight to the office, it would be too late to do much work, he rationalized, and he had been putting off this visit for too long.

CHAPTER 8

Frank pulled the Jaguar into one of the parking lots at St. Ignatius College. The campus had greatly changed since he had been an undergraduate there many years before, but the familiar buildings still brought back warm memories of his years there.

The receptionist at the Jesuit residence directed him to the eighth floor, where the infirmary was located, and told him that she would call the nurse in charge to tell him that he was on his way to see Father O'Sullivan.

Father Michael O'Sullivan, S.J., had been a close friend and mentor when Frank was an undergraduate and for a number of years thereafter. Frank had been a raw youth from a working-class family. Father O'Sullivan had introduced him to a life that he had some inchoate inclinations for, but had not known how to actualize. As both the librarian for the college and the faculty head of a cultural group of undergraduates, O'Sullivan had taken Frank and a score of other students in whom he had noticed some promise under his wing and excited their passion for what was perhaps best described as "the finer things of life."

The student group was called the Special Events Committee and was responsible for putting on classical and jazz musical events, lectures, and events having to do with rare books. These events were often done in conjunction with the Friends of the St. Jerome Library, a group that aided the special collections department of the library.

In the process, Frank had become a book collector and was introduced to those involved in the book world—fine printers, bookbinders, and rare book dealers. O'Sullivan's charm and passion for the exotic world of fine printing had attracted many San Franciscans (a number of them wealthy alumni of the college) into his ambit. He had introduced these people to

Frank and other members of the Special Events Committee. These interests and involvements had stayed with Frank into adulthood, and his gratitude to O'Sullivan had remained.

Now, Father Michael O'Sullivan lay dying of cancer in the Jesuit infirmary at St. Ignatius College. The end of his productive career was now reduced to weeks or months. Memories of their excursions, their working together to enhance the cultural aspirations of the students, of the pleasant meetings with those who supported O'Sullivan's vision, flooded Frank's memory. As an undergraduate, Frank had helped organize lectures by the French philosopher Gabriel Marcel, the American Jesuit philosopher Walter Ong, and the celebrated English Jesuit Martin D'Arcy, as well as many other distinguished scholars. Through O'Sullivan he had met and become friends with numerous scholarly figures in the cultural world of San Francisco and with socially prominent residents of the city. Under O'Sullivan's mentoring, the scion of a working-class family had slowly been transformed into an urbane, culturally attuned young man, able to maneuver his way among the elite of San Francisco.

As Frank stepped out of the elevator into the quiet, austere infirmary, a pretty young woman came forward to greet him. "Hello, I'm Beth Richardson. I'm so pleased that you're here to see Father O'Sullivan. He'll be so happy to see you. He's feeling pretty well today."

"I'm happy to hear that," Frank responded to her cheerful greeting. "Are there any limitations on the time I can stay?"

"No, you'll be able to tell when he gets too tired."

Beth knocked on the door of a room that had Father O'Sullivan's name in a brass plate. She opened the door and said, "Father, you have a visitor."

The gaunt, emaciated man lying in the bed of the sparsely furnished room looked up. A broad smile appeared on his shrunken face. "Frank, you're here. What a wonderful surprise. Come in, come in."

Father O'Sullivan placed the rosary beads that were in his shriveled hand on the nightstand next to his bed and held his hand out to Frank. Embarrassed by his failure to have visited O'Sullivan sooner, Frank took the cold hand proffered to him and held it. "Father, I'm so happy to see you. How are you feeling?"

"Great, great. And so much the better now that you're here."

Beth pushed a chair for Frank to sit down next to the bed. "I'll leave the two of you to chat," she said, as she left the room.

"Frank, how have you been?" O'Sullivan began, his emaciated face beaming with pleasure as he looked at him.

"Fine, Father, I've been well. Things in my life have been going splendidly. I'm happily married. My work is going well. And just about everything else is working out well. How about yourself? How are you feeling?"

"Well, to be truthful, sometimes the pain is pretty terrific. They want to give me morphine for it, but I tell them to back off. I'd like to leave this earth as conscious as I can be."

Both men smiled. Beneath Father Michael O'Sullivan's urbane demeanor and distinguished accomplishments lay the austere Jesuit, the man for whom God's afflictions were to be more than accepted; they were to be cherished.

Frank tried to bring the situation to its best possible perspective. "I'm sure that in that consciousness you can look with pride on everything that you've done. You've built a fantastic library that has an excellent rare book collection. You've attracted a distinguished group of collectors and other lovers of the book arts to the college. And those symposia you've put on…"

"You know, Frank," O'Sullivan cut him off, "all that was fluff. This— being in this bed, dying—is the gold."

Frank looked at his mentor in amazement. But he soon recovered from the surprise he felt and realized that this was, in fact, the response of those truly attuned to Christian spirituality: the ability to participate in Christ's sufferings by welcoming suffering in one's own life as a sign of God's favor.

"It was pretty good fluff, though," Frank sincerely told the priest. "You were the instrument for changing the lives of a goodly number of individuals—and you created a great institution for St. Ignatius College."

"Thank you, Frank, that's very kind of you, but I did all that because my superiors gave me that job. A lot of people could have done what I did. But God has given me an opportunity to test my mettle, and I don't want to let Him down."

Father O'Sullivan was one of the few religious people who could talk in that way without sounding a false note. It was not the conversation of Montgomery Street, the mansions of Pacific Heights, or any other place Frank could think of, but, from Michael O'Sullivan, S.J., it sounded like everyday conversation.

"I want you to put in a good word for me when you see Him," Frank rejoined with a smile.

O'Sullivan smiled, but did not respond to Frank's quip. His face became serious, and his intense eyes, made more so by the wasting effects of his illness, bored into Frank. "How's your spiritual life, Frank?" he asked. "Are you still a faithful Catholic? Are you doing everything you can to love God?"

Frank was somewhat taken aback by O'Sullivan's questions. They're not questions one usually asks another. Even priests usually are generally not that blunt.

Frank thought for a moment. He decided to give an honest response to the query.

"I am certainly a practicing Catholic, Father. By that I mean I go to mass every Sunday and holy day of obligation, and I certainly follow and believe in the Church's teachings. But I feel I should be doing more. I'm behind in my Easter duties. And, despite all my efforts, I'm not praying as much as I should. And I always feel I should be doing more than I am for those less fortunate than myself."

"Frank, that's terrific. It's a sign that you're not spiritually dead, that you want to establish a closer relationship with God. Think about your sins, and then go to confession. If you want, we can do it here. You do so many things; you can train yourself to pray more. And you can do all your activities in a prayerful mode.

"Read the Gospels, and reflect on what Jesus asks of us...the Beatitudes and all of His injunctions to help those less fortunate. Once you really think about these things, there is no doubt you'll follow the right path."

How often had he heard such advice? Frank asked himself. Probably ever since he was a child. He had ingested it as a small boy in Catechism class, in Catholic schools, in the seminary, and in so many encounters in his life. And here was his dying mentor, telling him again. Was it truly as easy as O'Sullivan maintained? Frank hadn't found it so. He had made resolution upon resolution—say my morning and night prayers, give more of my income to charity, spend more time helping out the unfortunate—but he had never achieved the goals he sought. He had felt frustrated and disappointed that he couldn't fulfill his spiritual desires. Perhaps he needed to try another approach.

"You're right, Father, but I haven't found it as easy as you make it sound," Frank at last responded. "I've made countless resolutions, but I can't seem to get into the habit of regular prayer, regular confession, or a sustained approach to charity."

"You don't want this to be a habit, Frank. You want this to be a joyous outpouring of your life." The excited priest tried to lift himself as he spoke to Frank. "You want to do these things because you can't stand not doing them, because you're so filled with God that they become as much a part of your life as eating and sleeping."

Frank couldn't recall O'Sullivan ever having been this intense about spiritual subjects. Perhaps it was the imminence of his own death that was compressing his advice to those who came into contact with him on his deathbed.

"Father, I know that's the ideal, but I find that I'm not always so joyful, or so turned on. Sometimes, for example, going to mass is a slog. I just do it anyway."

"Prayer, Frank, prayer. Prayer lets you see more clearly; and once you achieve clarity, you can't help yourself from enthusiastically following Jesus's precepts in the Gospels."

Frank smiled at O'Sullivan's excited injunction to him. "Okay, Father, it's a deal. I'll really put some effort into praying more, but you've got to help me out by praying for me and my efforts."

"I pray for you all the time, Frank, and soon I'll be able to intercede personally with God, His Blessed Mother, and His angels and saints." A smile spread across O'Sullivan's face.

"Oh, Father, you're going to be with us for a long time more," Frank interposed. He felt uncomfortable acceding to the dying man's prediction of his looming death.

"Let's not kid, Frank. I can feel death coming. I can sense God calling me. And it's not going to be months or years, but weeks. I'm very happy about this. I've always believed that we were born to die, and that death would bring us to our reason for living: to be happy with God forever. And I'm ready for this transition: I've put myself entirely in the hands of God's mercy and have asked for the intercession of His Blessed Mother."

Frank was astounded by the priest's fervent statement of faith. He thought of his own fears about physical annihilation.

"Father, that is quite a tribute to your faith. I believe everything you say, but I'm still somewhat nervous about my life ending. I mean, everything you've known—life with its ups and downs, sensations, hopes and fears, pain and pleasure—all gone. Life snuffed out. Maybe it's not nervousness, maybe it's plain fear."

"Frank, Frank, how can you be fearful of leaving what was from the start only a temporary assignment, a twinkling of an eye, and going instead to an eternity of being, an eternity of being happy in so total a way that we can't comprehend this happiness."

"I believe that intellectually, Father. I was taught it from the time I was a baby. But, as I got older, I've had a hard time emotionally ingesting it. When I was a teenager, or in my twenties, let's say, death was an abstraction, something that would happen, but would happen an eternity away. Now I can count the years before it is probable that I will die. I see how rapidly the past ten, twenty, even thirty, years have gone by, and I think to myself that before I know it, in a twinkling of an eye, I will be dead. I will be gone from this earth."

"You're looking at this through the wrong prism, Frank. You shouldn't be looking at this as your being 'gone' or annihilated or will exist no more. Instead, you've got to see death as a transition to total life, to a fulfillment of your being, to a cessation of all the imperfections of this present life. Death is something that we should look forward to because it brings us to real life."

"But, Father, I know that's what we've been taught, and, as I said, I give intellectual assent to it, but, let's face it, there is no empirical proof for this. I am haunted by the thought, what if this isn't the case? What if I'm not going to heaven?"

"Frank, I've got to tell you that I'm a bit disappointed in you. Faith, Frank, faith. This is the nature of faith. Somehow you've not let your faith convince you, I mean really convince you, of these truths. And that is where prayer comes in, Frank. Pray to God to give you faith."

It was classic catechism teaching, Frank thought. He had always believed it. He believed it now. But, for the past ten years or so, the idea of death had loomed larger and more ominous in his mind. Fear of it had entered his world, as the serpent had entered the Garden of Eden. It didn't obsess him, but he thought about it often. It didn't depress him, but it made him uneasy. This exchange with his old friend, a priest a few steps from the grave, had allowed him to articulate his feelings. O'Sullivan's response to his feelings had reiterated what he had been taught, what he believed and wanted to believe, but they didn't assuage his fear, that fear of the unknown, that fear of his life being snuffed out without any larger explanation.

Frank noticed that O'Sullivan seemed tired. An occasional spasm of pain seemed to twitch across his face. It was time to go.

"I don't want to tire you out, Father," Frank said to him. "I'm afraid all this conversation is exhausting you."

"Not a bit. I've got nothing else to do, and I always enjoy seeing you. And I am able to exercise my priestly ministry by getting you to pray more and stop being afraid of death." A smile spread across O'Sullivan's pale features.

Frank looked sadly at the thin body lying beneath the light coverlet. "Father, let me ask you one more thing before I leave. What do you feel right now? You said you believe that you will not have much longer to live. What are your regrets about your life? What has given you pleasure? What do you feel about leaving life?"

"Boy, you leave the zingers till the end, don't you? God has given me a wonderful life. My parents were solid, working-class people who loved my sister and myself and gave us a good education and a wonderful Catholic upbringing. After high school I entered the Jesuits, and every day since I entered the novitiate more than sixty years ago I've thanked God that he gave me this vocation.

"The work God and my superiors gave me to do has been a blessing. I built and maintained a library. It wasn't easy, given the financial constraints the college had for many years. But I think we have an excellent undergraduate library and a superb rare book library.

"But what I think gave me the most pleasure was my association with young students such as yourself, who came to the college as such open books, if you'll pardon the pun, eager to be taught, eager to open up new worlds for yourself. And what a pleasure it was for me to show you a world that so many of you entered with passion. What a pleasure it was for me to introduce all of you to older men and women who would help you develop your interests and ideas.

"And, while I wasn't a missionary in China, or helping the poor in a ghetto or barrio, I felt that I was doing God's work, and that made me very happy.

"It's interesting how few regrets I have...I have the usual regrets about not being more talented, not having accomplished more, not being as good a person as I might have been, but I have come to see these as the imperfections of being a human being. Many times I've asked God to forgive me these imperfections, these sins. I have asked Him to make good my imperfections, to forgive me for my shortcomings.

"One can only do one's best. I have long given up lamenting my failures, those people I couldn't reach and lead to God. I did what I could; God must do the rest.

"And now I want to go to God. My desire is not just because I long to end the pain I've been living with for the past few years but because I always knew I was destined to go there.

"Frank, you expressed a fear of death. For me it's like the prospect of leaving a cold, snowy place knowing you're going to a tropical island where there are sandy beaches and warm sunshine. I know that's a crude analogy, but I use it to indicate that death is the fulfillment of life; it brings us to God.

"None of us knows what heaven is like or what 'being with God' is like, but I do know, at my deepest level, that going to God is what I was meant to do. I'm happy, Frank, happy."

The priest stopped, obviously fatigued. He looked at the ceiling somewhat vacantly, as if wishing to rip the curtain between this life and the next, wishing to peer into that life that he was so confident awaited him when his wasted body was put into the earth.

Frank knew that he needed to leave. "Father, I want to let you get some rest, and I need to get home. Thank you so much for your time and your good advice. I'll come back soon."

"Goodbye, Frank. Thank you for coming. Pray for me." He slowly lifted his arm. Frank took the bony hand and clutched it. He held the hand while they looked at each other. Then Frank laid the old priest's hand gently onto the bed and walked out of the room. In the minds of both men the thought came: would they ever see each other again?

Frank walked out into the waning afternoon sun. How beautiful San Francisco looked on such days! The air had a special, sparkling opaqueness about it. The buildings glimmered with a white and pastel glow. The blue of the sky was replicated by the blue of the waters of the bay and the ocean beyond.

Frank felt both excited and depressed. He couldn't analyze his feelings about the visit: he felt sadness at seeing his old friend and mentor dying and in pain; he was perplexed by O'Sullivan's calm acceptance of pain and the death that would come so soon; he was disturbed by the reflection of his own mortality.

"Hi, Frank, what brings you to your alma mater?"

"Hey, Dick, how are you?"

The two friends and classmates shook hands and greeted each other. Dick Mahoney and Frank had been close friends in college, both being intellectually curious and interested in the arts. After college Mahoney had gone to an Ivy League university and had gotten a Ph.D. in comparative literature. The two men had stayed in touch sporadically, but had not remained the close friends they had been in their undergraduate days.

"I'm fine," Mahoney replied to Frank's question. "Still trying to turn raw teenagers into scholars. So, what brings you here?"

"I've just been to see Father O'Sullivan, and we just finished a long talk on death."

"I went to see him a couple days ago." Mahoney, like Frank, had been one of O'Sullivan's disciples and friends. "It made me think about how long it's been since we were hauling chairs for some concert or lecture he'd come up with. It breaks my heart to see him so sick."

"Did he speak to you about your spiritual life?" Frank asked, smiling.

"Not this time, but he has in the past when I've gone to see him. I feel as if I'm in the presence of a dying saint when I'm with him. And what did he say about your spiritual life?"

"He told me to pray more and that God would give me greater faith," Frank replied in a joking matter.

"Well, there you have it. You've got your marching orders. What else did you discuss?"

"We talked a lot about death. That's a sore subject with me these days."

"Ah, you must have been in your element. Remember how fascinated with death and all its trappings you were in college? When we used to usher at the symphony I thought you were orgasming when we heard Verdi's *Requiem*. And when we served at funeral masses, you were ecstatic during the singing of the *Dies irae*.

"Well, that was then, and this is now. In those days I loved the abstraction of death and the magnificent music and art that dealt with it. But death itself was an eternity away. I could safely contemplate death without in any way feeling threatened by it. But, now, at my age, I'm beginning to feel the hot breath of death on my back."

"You have always been a dramatic individual, Frank. So what did Father O'Sullivan say?"

"He said that death would be the happiest moment of my life."

Both men laughed. They had been bantering, but both men recognized the seriousness of each other's concerns. They had frequently discussed serious topics in a wry, humorous way during their college days. But both Frank and Dick Mahoney knew that they were purposeful in delving into those topics that intellectual undergraduates feel are important to discuss during their college days: What is life about? What is my role in the cosmos? Where do I come from? Where am I going? What is the nature of the true, the good, and the beautiful?

"I'm sure he's right," Mahoney snickered. "But it's a shame you won't be there at death to experience the happiness."

"Very funny. Well, did you have any heavy conversations when you went to see him?"

"Always. I feel that he doesn't want to waste any time on idle chitchat at this point in his life. He's at death's door and in a lot of pain, and when he sees us he wants to compress what he feels are his final views. No more talks on the arts or abstract ideas. He is now focused on saving our souls. I guess death concentrates the mind."

"I guess. ...All I know is that part of me hated seeing him lying there, grimacing in pain, never asking for morphine, and the other part of me was thrilled just to be there talking with him. He's always been a sort of spiritual confessor to me."

"For a bunch of us. I'll be one sad person when he goes. He gave us a lot."

The sun had begun to set. A chill descended in the air. Frank looked at his watch. There was no social outing planned for that night, thank God, just a quiet night at home with Paula.

"Well, I should get going. Paula and I are having a quiet dinner at home tonight."

"How is Paula?" Mahoney inquired. "Give her my regards."

"She's fine. ...Her usual happy, feisty self. She asks about you often. How about you and I having lunch sometime soon?"

"Sure, that would be great. Give me a call."

"Can I lure you into the maw of mammon?"

"If you're buying, I'll hazard an expedition into the canyons of the financial district. Call me."

Frank was reluctant to depart from his friend. The warm glow of memory brought him back to their college days, when they would often sit up through the night discussing big ideas, often inveigling one of their favorite teachers to join them. The next day, zombie-like, they would stagger from one class to another, keeping awake by quaffing numerous cups of strong coffee.

Those were great days—those college days—Frank thought. The sap was running. Everything seemed possible.

Frank walked toward his car, but, upon noticing St. Ignatius Church, which had held such an important position in his life when he was an undergraduate, he decided to walk into the church.

The familiar gloom of the baroque interior always refreshed him. He walked along the side altars, genuflected in front of the tabernacle, and decided to do something he almost never did: he knelt in front of the altar dedicated to St. Aloysius, put two dollars in a metal receptacle, lit a candle, and whispered, "Dear Lord, Blessed Virgin Mary, and St. Aloysius, take care of Father O'Sullivan, take care of me."

CHAPTER 9

Frank's house was a two-story Italianate Victorian in San Francisco's Pacific Heights area. His divorce, many years before, had curtailed the grand lifestyle that had characterized life during his first marriage. But Paula had decorated this house in a pleasing way, and Frank found his home both comfortable and elegant.

This evening Paula and he would enjoy what in recent months had become an increasingly rare event—a night at home alone. Their social engagements with friends, business associates, or clients, or cultural events—had begun to consume their evenings. Frank had relished for a week knowing that nothing was on the calendar for this evening. And the satisfaction of having snagged a major new client gave the evening a special glow.

Paula had just arrived home when Frank came into the house after parking the Jaguar on the street. He had resisted the convenience of constructing a garage in the Victorian, insisting to Paula that it would mar the lines of the house.

"Hi, sweetie," Frank called upstairs. "We have a night at home alone. What are we going to do?"

"I'll be right down. I'm changing my clothes."

Frank put his briefcase in its accustomed place in the second parlor, took off his coat, and went into the kitchen to pour himself and Paula a glass of wine. He brought the two glasses into the front parlor and began to reflect on the day's events. Lots of memories, he said to himself, and lots of painful confrontations with himself.

His thoughts were interrupted by Paula's effervescent entrance. A welcoming smile on her face, she walked across the room, enfolded him in her arms, and gave him a long kiss.

"I can't believe we're finally at home alone," she smiled. "Let's go out for dinner."

He knew she was joshing. She had looked forward to this evening as much as he.

"Just kidding. I got us some salmon and string beans for dinner…and a salad. Just you and me, Babe."

The two of them sat down on the sofa to begin a domestic ritual that had been part of their lives since their courtship. They would drink two glasses of wine before dinner, sitting for an hour discussing the day's events or perhaps what had transpired with friends. It was Frank's favorite part of the day—on those increasingly rare days when they were home. He was never bored by their conversations, whether they lingered on trivialities or were dealing with major issues in their lives. And he enjoyed the break from dealing with clients or the other business responsibilities that dominated his life.

"Well, how was your day?" This was Frank's opening line whenever the two of them sat down for this evening conversation.

"It was fine. I finished Greta's house…finally, talked with someone Ann recommended, and then went to the studio for a few hours. Nothing out of the ordinary." Paula's concise account described her normal day: dealing with her interior design clients and spending some time at her ceramics studio, pursuing what had become an artistic passion. "How about you?"

Frank recounted his day, leaving out some of the memories and reflections that he had encountered on his business trip down the peninsula. She was delighted with his success at getting Henry Simone as a client, saddened by his sadness at seeing a dying Father O'Sullivan, and pleased that he ran into Dick Mahoney.

At fifty-two years of age, Paula was fifteen years younger than Frank. She had escaped the mental and physical morass of a middle-aged matron. Her youthful looks and tall willowy figure, combined with an effervescence that one usually associates with women in their twenties or thirties, gave her the appearance of a much younger woman.

Frank adored her. She had established a position in his life that no other person ever had, not even his mother. They quarreled occasionally, mostly over inconsequential matters, but quickly ended each dispute. Her vitality and her insistence on "growing" their relationship had captured his imagination, and their twenty-year marriage had been a happy one.

Their conversation rambled through the various topics that formed the staple of the pre-dinner get-togethers when they were home: bills to pay, friends' activities, their own thoughts and musings. They both reveled in their openness with each other at such times.

"I saw Dave McGee yesterday, by the way. I forgot to tell you last night." Frank began what he knew to be a difficult conversation. Dave McGee was a long-time friend and also his doctor.

"Did you get a check-up?"

"No, I went in to get some advice." Frank did not want to disclose his search for a diagnosis of his recurring abdominal pain.

"Advice? About what?"

"About the fact that I'm having such a tough time getting it up this past year."

His statement riveted her attention.

"What?" she exclaimed.

"Yeah, well I don't have to tell you that I've been having trouble getting an erection when we're going to have sex or during sex...and it's not only when I'm really tired or particularly stressed. I thought maybe Dave would have some ideas."

"What did he say? I just can't believe what I'm hearing."

"He gave me a prescription for Viagra. In fact, he gave me a handful of pills that he had on hand. I can take one tonight."

"Viagra!" Paula exclaimed. "You've got to take a pill to have sex? I can't believe this. You don't need pills to have sex."

Frank had anticipated Paula's expostulations. She hated pills, and wouldn't even take aspirin when she had a headache. The idea of taking medication to achieve penile erection, he could see, outraged her. He had thought about taking the Viagra surreptitiously, but had felt that such action would complicate his life. He would tell her. Her reaction—the frown, the pursed lips, and the hint of anger in her voice—was what he had expected.

"We haven't discussed this problem, except to maybe joke about it when it happens. But it's been bothering me. You've been to see your gynecologist about the vaginal dryness you've had since you began menopause, and she prescribed some remedies. I decided to ask Dave if there was anything that could be done in this situation."

"It's just because you're getting older. It's just...well, a natural process."

"I know that, but if there's something that will help, why not use it? You still have to be turned on for it to work, but Dave says it does help."

"I'm stunned. Whoever thought we'd ever have to use pills to have sex?"

"Who ever thought we would get old?"

"We're not old. Old is a state of mind."

If Paula had a crotchet, it was on the subject of age. She would become angry if you called her middle-aged, and to call oneself old was met with scorn. She herself would never take any steps to artificially change her appearance—no facelifts, eye enhancement, or other such cosmetic surgery—but she resisted any talk of being middle-aged or old.

"There's nothing shameful about my taking a pill if it's going to help us have sex. I told you—as if you haven't noticed—that even when I'm eager to have sex I can't sustain an erection. And, if I do have an erection, I lose it right after I enter you. Dave says this is common in men as they get older."

Paula did not immediately respond to Frank's defense of the drug. Her knitted brow indicated that she was processing the news her husband had given her. Finally her face softened. She had worked through whatever objections she had at first held.

"When do you have to take the pill?" she asked.

"From a half hour to an hour before sex." Frank responded. "But it's not automatic. You still have to have desires, and you still have to touch... you know, stuff like that."

"Well, whatever...I guess we can try it."

"Don't worry, I won't get hair on my palms or start howling at full moons."

They drifted off into other conversations. As they chatted, what was uppermost in Frank's mind was whether Paula and he could inaugurate the use of Viagara that evening. He was curious about how it would work.

Frank sat on the sofa musing after Paula got up to prepare dinner. He had been shocked and embarrassed by the sudden onslaught of the signs of age, most notably in the area of sexual performance. Paula and he had been intensely attracted to each other from the moment they met. Frank remembered with pleasure their active sexual life, both during their courtship and after they were married. They passionately lunged at each other whenever possible, not just after going to bed at night. He smiled as he recalled the times when one of them would visit the other, and they begin kissing and removing each other's clothes just inside the door. The sexual encounter would often take place on the floor by the front door. The mental vision of the two of them, panting and perspiring, lying on the floor entwined captivated him.

Is this truly the end? Frank wondered. Will those days, when I could have sex for hours, never return? He knew the answer, but what he knew displeased and depressed him.

"Frank, dinner is ready," Paula called from the kitchen, interrupting his reverie.

Frank walked to the dining room, which appeared prepared for an elegant dinner party. Paula had lit the candelabra, and the table was elegantly positioned with two placemats she had bought on a trip they had taken to Provence, set with crystal, china, and silverware atop them. Paula insisted that, even when just the two of them had dinner at home, they would sit down at the table as if it were an elegant dinner party.

This evening both of them seemed preoccupied as they sat down. Frank couldn't quite penetrate Paula's almost morose mood. He himself was trying to plumb his thoughts of that day, his visit with Father O'Sullivan and the onslaught of memories as he had driven to Atherton and Palo Alto. Each would make an occasional stab at conversation, but their attempts quickly died out.

"I'm going to go to my study to get some work done before a meeting I have tomorrow," Frank announced after they had finished dinner.

"Okay, I'm going to clean up in the kitchen and then go to bed and read. I'm tired tonight."

Was this a subtle suggestion that they try out the Viagra that evening? Frank wondered.

Frank heard Paula engaged in her chores in the kitchen while he made some preparations to transfer ten million of Henry Simone's assets to the firm and read through some materials before the next day's monthly meeting of the investment committee.

Paula finished her kitchen cleanup and went into the study to tell Frank that she was going to bed to read.

Frank looked at her. "Don't go to sleep," he told her. "I'm going to take my first Viagra."

"Oh, boy," she rejoined. "Watch out, San Francisco." Paula laughed lightly and left the study.

Frank opened the drawer in his desk, where he had put the envelope with the blue-green pills that Dave McGee had given him, and put one in his mouth. An antique glass pitcher with two glasses stood on his desk. He poured water from the pitcher into one of the glasses and pushed down the pill. Frank was curious about its effect, but after ingesting it he could determine no physiological changes.

He finished the work that he needed to accomplish before going to the office tomorrow and walked up the narrow steps of his Victorian home to the bedroom he and Paula had shared for the past twenty years. She looked at him curiously and smiled.

"Still no hair on my palms," Frank laughed, holding up his hands.

"No, but you've got some in your ears. You better get a haircut."

"What are you, my mother?"

"Better. I'm your wife."

Frank enjoyed such humorous exchanges with his wife. They amused him, and both of them cherished the repartee, which, even if not brilliant, let them exercise their sense of the whimsical.

After brushing his teeth and removing his clothes, Frank glided into their king-size bed.

"It's been a long day. I can't tell you how happy I am that we didn't have to go out tonight."

"I love these nights when we can come together at the end of our work days and just be alone." Paula put her arm around his shoulders.

They both adjusted their postures on the bed so that they faced each other. Frank reached out to hold and fondle one of her small but firm breasts. Frank was thrilled by Paula's still smooth skin — the result of her having stayed out of the sun when she was young and of innumerable applications of body lotion as she grew older.

She said it first, as usual. "I love you."

They gazed into each other's eyes. Frank responded, "I love you, too."

Their hands now began the explorations of each other's bodies that they had gotten to know so well during the past two decades. Their lips joined and their tongues darted in and out of their mouths. Their passion mounted, and their hands roamed more quickly as their caresses became intense. Moans of pleasure escaped.

The Viagara must be working, Frank thought, noticing the stiffening of his penis.

Frank's mouth now left Paula's. He bent it to her breasts, and flicked his tongue and teeth over the now-hardened nipples. Paula's hand now began to caress Frank's thighs, and his body twitched with pleasure.

Their bodies yearned for union, and Frank now moved from caressing Paula's buttocks to the light brown thatch of hair at the apex of her legs. Slightly separating her legs so as to relinquish access to the wet slit covered by the hair, and his fingers now began to probe for that hardened kernel of flesh and nerves which he knew gave such pleasure to Paula when he manipulated it with the tips of his fingers.

Her fingers had now found his penis, and they stroked its shaft, alternately flicking around its swollen head.

With a deft move, Paula gently pushed Frank over onto his back and straddled him. Looking somewhat dazed, Paula took his penis and began to use it to stimulate her clitoris. Frank eagerly cooperated by rocking his hips to synchronize with Paula's rhythmic jabbing of the small focal point of her pleasure.

Their rhythm increased in tempo. Paula released her hand from Frank's penis, and in his next thrust he found himself slithering up the warm, moist canal of her vagina. Paula shifted to allow him even greater penetration into her body and then began to lift herself in time with his increasingly eager strokes.

Paula shifted from her upper body upright position and bent over him so that her face was next to Frank's. She began kissing him passionately, while Frank responded eagerly to her kisses and continued the rapid thrusting into her.

After a few moments Frank and Paula rolled over so that he was on top of her. The piston-like strokes continued, until, throwing his head back, Frank uttered a long, drawn out moan of pleasure and felt his penis grow slack. Exhausted by his coital activity, Frank slumped forward into Paula's prone body and held her in his arms.

He realized that the cessation of their lovemaking was due, not to the releasing of orgasm, but to the ending of his erection. Their union had been pleasurable, but not orgasmic. At least the Viagra had worked to give him an erection, Frank thought…that's something.

As Frank and Paula lay dos-à-dos in their bedroom, illuminated only by two flickering candles, Frank's musings turned to his sexual performance. How had it happened, he wondered, that his sexual yearnings had become so infrequent? That his ability to sustain an erect penis so difficult? That the liberating orgasm had ended? Ah, the mystery of one's passage through life.

CHAPTER 10

Frank was sitting on his sofa in reverie when the buzzing on his speakerphone startled him.

"Frank, It's that Mr. Crofts calling. Remember? He called yesterday. He insists on speaking with you," answered Jessica.

"Okay, I'll take it."

Who in the hell is this? Frank wondered. He walked over to his desk and pressed the button on the telephone to receive the call on the speaker.

"Yes, this is Frank Molinari."

"Mr. Molinari, my name is Jason Crofts. I'd very much like to have a meeting with you."

"A meeting about what?" Frank inquired.

"The matter is most delicate," the caller responded, "and I do not wish to even hint at it on the telephone. I want to divulge what I have to say to you in person."

What the hell is this all about? Frank wondered. And what answer should I give him? He played for time while he considered his response.

"I must say that is a strange request. I've never had someone ask me for a meeting and not tell me what the meeting would be about."

"Mr. Molinari," the slightly gravelly voice at the other end of the telephone began, "I can assure you that you will want to hear what I have to say, and if I don't want to tell you the subject of my conversation with you over the telephone, it is only because the complexity of my revelation cannot be so neatly described in a telephone conversation."

Was this caller some sort of nut? Frank wondered. Well, why not? What could possibly happen? Frank realized that his curiosity was piqued. What could Mr. Crofts possibly have to say to him that was so complex and so mysterious?

"When next week would you like to come to my office?" Frank asked.

"Any time you have available would be fine with me."

Frank glanced at his calendar. That next week was filled with engagements, but he noticed that Thursday morning was available.

"How about Thursday of next week...say, 9 o'clock?"

"That would be fine."

"How much time do you think you'll need?"

"I think we should leave the duration of our meeting open-ended," responded Frank's caller.

"Very well. Next Thursday at 9 o'clock. Do you know where my office is?"

"Yes, I do. I'll see you then." And he was gone.

Frank was puzzled. What could this possibly be about? Should he see if he could check out the mysterious caller? Too much trouble. He would just wait until Thursday of the following week to see what the odd-sounding man had to say.

It was almost noon, Frank realized, as he glanced at the clock on his desk. Where did the morning go? He looked at his calendar and saw that he had a luncheon appointment at noon. "Chris Martini/VT" read the calendar memo. Great, thought Frank, it will be fun to sit and relax with Chris over lunch.

Jessica was not at her desk as he left. The elevator took him down the twenty floors to the lobby of the old Russ Building. Frank enjoyed the fact that the firm continued to operate in the dowdy old building on Montgomery Street. No move to a newer or more fashionable building. It proclaimed that the firm knew what it was and didn't need expensive, fancy offices in which to operate.

Frank looked up at the carvings around the entrance to the Russ Building. They don't build them like this any more, he thought. When it was built, the Russ Building had been, and had remained for some decades, the tallest and most prestigious office building in San Francisco. When he first arrived, Montgomery Street was "The Wall Street of the West," the capital of the West Coast's financial world. Virtually every financial firm had its headquarters on Montgomery Street—firms that now were part of a necrology. It always annoyed Frank that companies that had been around for decades—some for even more than 100 years—no longer existed: Sutro,

E. F. Hutton, J. Barth, Reynolds and Blyth. The list went on and on. Some had merged. Others had gone out of business. And Montgomery Street was no longer the premier street in the financial district; it seemed down-at-the-heels, displaced by numerous tall office buildings that had been built to the east of the formerly prestigious street.

The moldering buildings in the blocks east of Montgomery Street—many of them containing businesses dedicated to San Francisco's once thriving maritime industry—had been swept away for high-rise office buildings. And the expansion had leapt south of Market Street, an area behind the handsome headquarters of long-gone corporations—Southern Pacific and Matson among them. Those elegant old buildings had housed coffee companies, commercial printers, ship chandleries, and other small businesses that sustained themselves through San Francisco's connection with the ocean. All gone, Frank pondered, and gone within the last few decades of his own life.

Frank's musings about the changes in San Francisco's financial world came to an end as he turned onto Washington Street from Montgomery. There was the tallest building in San Francisco—the Transamerica Building—and there the financial district came to an abrupt end on Washington's north side. That once-derided triangular shaped building was now a San Francisco icon.

Immediately across Washington Street was a contrast—several square blocks of two-, three-, and four-story buildings dating from the nineteenth century. They had survived the fiery holocaust of 1906, and had been, over the years, used for many purposes: wholesale establishments, consulates of foreign countries, bars and saloons, strip joints, chocolate factories, and antique stores. Frank loved what was now called the Jackson Square area. He relished the small, brick buildings with their patina of age. He reveled in their history, paralleling that of the city he loved.

Frank especially enjoyed walking down the one-block street he had turned onto. It was named after A. P. Hotaling, a liquor distributor who had built two handsome buildings in about 1860. Flanking the street's northern end on Jackson Street, Hotaling Street, just a stone's throw from the skyscrapers of the financial district, reminded Frank of a different San Francisco—a city of characters, bright hopes, and limitless possibilities.

He opened the door of a squat, stone building with Quattrocento lamps flanking the entrance. The building housed a private club, the Villa Taverna, which had been founded in the 1950s by a group of Italophiles as an eating club. Frank had been a member for many years, and enjoyed its quiet elegance and superb food.

Chris was waiting for him. Both friends greeted each other with cheerful smiles and hearty hellos that signified their decades of close friendship. Sandro, the Villa Taverna's manager, welcomed Frank and led him and Chris to a table on a dais-like area in the back of the dining area.

Frank nodded and said hello to a few acquaintances as he walked to the table. He passed one table that caused him to narrow his eyes with distaste. Sitting at it was one of the self-proclaimed "leaders" of San Francisco society. Frank had encountered her from time to time at various social gatherings, and had found her arrogant and boring. He had laughed when she had told a newspaper interviewer that anyone from another area of the country who wished to enter San Francisco society needed to talk with her and another society doyen in order to do so.

She sat there at the table with three other women, her heavy Slavic features in their usual impenetrable mask. Frank had nicknamed her the "Serbian Slut" for her ability to have contracted marriages with a succession of men who had given her entry into both social circles and wealth after they had divorced or died.

"How the hell have you been?" Frank asked when he and Chris were seated. Chris smiled at Frank's exuberance. "I've been well," he answered. "How about you?" Chris Martini's mildness and equanimity always surprised Frank, even though they had been intimate friends for almost half a century.

"Oh, you know, the usual...not so much very new."

Frank smiled at their rather banal greetings. It had almost become a ritual. Within a short time after these stiff opening lines to their conversations, the two friends would be exchanging intimate confidences.

The two men ordered drinks and began to chat about some of the inconsequential matters in their lives. Gossip about mutual friends, city politics, members of their families. This part of their exchange always reminded Frank of runners' warm-up exercises. The topics were interesting enough in themselves, but both men knew they were but a prelude to the discussion of the more important issues in their lives.

After they had consumed two glasses of the house sauvignon blanc and ordered the fresh petrale, Frank and Chris recognized that the time had come for the more substantive part of their conversation. Frank began with his account of meeting with Father O'Sullivan.

Chris listened to Frank with a quiet solemnity. When Frank finished his summary, Chris smiled and looked directly at him.

"You're the only person I know who has such heavy conversations. You're still living the life of a teenager or someone in his twenties. You're still asking yourself, what's-it-all-about-Alfie questions. This is a time to relax and enjoy life. Why do you keep torturing yourself with ideas of death and other gloomy considerations? I mean, we all know we're going to die someday. But you're like a dog with a bone. You keep gnawing on it."

Frank noticed a note of exasperation in Chris's voice. Frank wondered if he was indeed boring his friends with these concerns. Had he become morbidly preoccupied with death? With the state of his soul? With his flailing attempts to revive the chiaroscuro of his earlier years?

He tried to deflect Chris's exasperation with some light-hearted banter. "I've always thought that the most important concerns, the most germane issues, were the transcendent ones...you know: Who am I? Where do I come from? Where am I going? What is my purpose here? What should we be concerned about? How my bridge game is going?"

"Don't get offended now," said Chris, noticing a note of impatience which had crept into Frank's tone of voice. "But during this past year you've become obsessed with death and dying and with recovering your 'lost youth.' I'm just trying to tell you to lighten up. You're driving yourself crazy."

Frank felt hurt. If he couldn't discuss these subjects with Chris, with whom could he discuss them? With Christopher Francis Xavier Fermoyle? With Father O'Sullivan?

"Well, I'm sorry that I can't discuss the prospects for the 49ers or the Giants for the coming years, because, frankly, I don't give a shit. What do you discuss when you get together with your other friends? A new shirt you've bought?"

"Now that's unfair," Chris responded. "Just because I'm telling you that your gloomy reflections on getting older and dying are getting, well, old, it doesn't mean that I'm a thoughtless philistine."

Frank said nothing. Both men glumly pushed the food around on their plates. After a few minutes, Chris broke the uncomfortable silence.

"Frank, you've got to appreciate the things you've got." He spoke softly. "You've got good health, lots of friends. You like what you do for a living, have lots of interests, a wonderful wife, and great kids. What could be better?

"Sure, at some point in the future you—and everybody else—will get sick and die. There's no surprise there. In the meantime, why don't you enjoy all the things you've got?"

Frank smiled. The tension between the two men had been broken, and Frank decided not to pursue his ideas. What good could it do to say that the litany of positive things in his life that Chris had just enumerated did not in any way lessen the truth that we're going to die or the implications of that truth? Chris clearly didn't want to hear his reflections on the subject. Frank decided that he would have to learn not to share such ruminations with this old friend.

"You're right. I've got a lot to be thankful for, and I do have a wonderful life. I'll just have to enjoy it more."

Chris didn't respond. Both men concentrated on finishing the food on their plates.

The waiter brought coffee. Chris and Frank stared gloomily into their cups.

"Well, how are the Giants and 49ers going to do this year?" Frank asked Chris with a smile.

Both men laughed loudly. Frank's total lack of interest in sports was widely known. The humorous query had succeeded in breaking the uncomfortable tension between them. They now felt at ease once again to chatter about the inconsequential matters that they shared.

The two of us have known each other for decades, thought Frank. We are intimate friends. There was no need to upset their long friendship with the insistence that Chris listen to his troubled meditations on life and death.

A warm feeling that the harsh feelings had evaporated swept over Frank, and, as they left the Villa Taverna and walked out into the afternoon sunlight, both men felt relief that they had retreated from a more serious confrontation. The cords of a deep friendship continued to bind them.

CHAPTER 11

The annual fete at the Fleishmans' was in full swing when Frank and Paula arrived. Most of the guests were already there. Their faces showed their delight at having been invited, for an invitation to the Fleishmans' annual party was a coveted prize for those who considered themselves part of San Francisco's social elite, as well as those who wished to join their ranks.

Frank appraised the scene with some cynicism as he entered the magnificent house on what had come to be called the Gold Coast. The Willis Polk-designed mansion had a center courtyard, similar to some Italian palazzos, surrounded by the rooms of the house on all three stories, allowing hundred of guests to be accommodated. From the back of the house one could enjoy sweeping views of the northern part of San Francisco, the bay, and the hills of Marin County.

Parties such as this one always created a sense of unease in Frank. There were probably 500 in the Fleishmans' house at the moment. Nothing had been stinted. Young valets took your car when you pulled up to the curb and brought it to you when you left. Maids took wraps and coats when you arrived and returned them to you when you departed. Squadrons of caterers brought any kind of beverage one desired—although the drinking of red wine was discouraged—and passed around an amplitude of hors d'oeuvres. No one even thought about what to have for dinner later. In a corner of the courtyard, a trio played smooth jazz.

Throughout the house, the 500 guests had arranged themselves in ever-shifting groups of from two to six in some sort of human molecular action, chattering away to one another about what Frank knew were myriad inconsequential subjects.

One of the first people to catch Frank's eye was Myra Delmonico, a former model who had encountered a very-married Frank Delmonico, a wealthy contractor and real estate developer, while she was vacationing in Hawaii and he was attending a business conference. Within four days Frank Delmonico was on a plane to San Francisco, determined to tell his wife that he was divorcing her.

Myra had entered San Francisco's social world with ease. Her pleasant manner and financial ability to entertain those who entertained her made her an asset to what had become an expanded society. Even if at times her fellow socialites raised an eyebrow or made a humorous comment about how tightly she clothed the ample curves of her body, Myra was considered part of the "in crowd."

She was now speaking in her animated and droll way with Mary and Carter Webster. Frank knew the Websters slightly; he knew they were old San Francisco money. They were quiet people, preferring small dinner parties and intimate bridge games. They were uncomfortable when they saw their names or photos in the social column of the newspaper. And they seemed uncomfortable talking with Myra Delmonico.

Myra, for her part, was quite subtle in looking over the shoulders of the Websters to see if someone more interesting or higher in the society pecking order had come into sight, at which point Myra would abandon them with a smile and a wave and move on to the next participant in her social *pas de deux*.

Frank and Paula now began their own minuet through the crowd, looking for someone they knew well enough to greet and speak with. Early in the course of any social occasion, Frank and Paula would become separated and traverse their own routes through the thickets of whatever party they were at and then reunite when they were ready to go home.

Frank had always wondered what the purpose was for such large parties, not only those thrown by the Fleishmans, but by others as well. A large amount of money and effort was expended. Hundreds of individuals in crowded spaces said a few inconsequential things to one another. Everyone smiled, whether or not they felt like doing so. They ate and drank, depending on which of the latest fashionable diet they were on.

After each of these parties, Frank asked himself why he had attended. His first answer was always that he was there to "show the flag" for the firm, to see if he could expose himself to individuals who might avail themselves of his firm's investment advisory services. But he knew that the real answer was that he enjoyed being there. The fact that he, from a working class background, had been invited gave him a subtle satisfaction. Another reason for his pleasure at these gatherings was that he enjoyed watching the guests and their interactions. It reminded him of the hours when as a boy he enjoyed watching strange creatures at the zoo or aquarium.

Frank spied Ted and Liz Fleishman holding court in front of the huge fireplace in the mammoth living room. He decided that this was an appropriate time for him to greet his hosts and to thank them for their invitation.

He threaded his way through the knots of chattering partygoers and reached the Fleishmans just as Mark and Clare Sanders had finished performing their ritual of greeting and gratitude. Frank smiled and said hello to the Sanderses, gave Liz Fleishman a kiss on her cheek, and thrust out a hand to Ted.

"Ted, Liz, you've done it again. What a fabulous party. Thanks so much for inviting Paula and me."

"Don't mention it. We're so happy that you could make it," Ted stiffly intoned. One could tell that these events were Liz's brainchild rather than Ted's. She flashed a smile as wide and dry as her native Texas.

"Frank, you have a wonderful time. We're absolutely thrilled that you both could come. I'm sure we'll see Paula later," she drawled.

"She's here, somewhere," Frank quickly answered. "We got separated in the crowd, but I'll find her...and she'll find you." All three grinned, and Frank made way for five individuals he didn't know.

Ted Fleishman was in his 60s. He had been a successful trial attorney in southern California, and some years earlier had been tapped to be the country's solicitor general. While in this office, his wife had died after a long, painful illness. Ted had resigned his post, and had moved...to Washington, D.C., to San Francisco. There he had joined the circuit of dinner parties, charity balls and auctions, and Napa outings that were the fare of the wealthy and socially prominent. At one of these gatherings he had met Liz Masterson. Within a couple of months, they were married. Almost instantaneously they were at the core of San Francisco society.

Liz had come to San Francisco in the 1960s from Texas. It was rumored that she was from a sharecropping family. Her beauty and vivacious personality caught the attention of a prosperous car dealer in Dallas, and they had married. The marriage ended in divorce, and Liz left Dallas for San Francisco, where she got a job as the secretary for the general manager of the city's parks and recreation department. While there, she had met one of the commissioners, Sam Skinner, a wealthy businessman from an old San Francisco family, and they had married. The sharecropper's daughter from Texas was no longer a secretary in San Francisco. She had been propelled into the midst of money and society exposure.

Skinner had died of alcoholism, and Liz subsequently married yet another wealthy, socially prominent businessman, who died a few years later of cancer. Shortly thereafter she met and married Ted Fleishman.

The accumulated wealth from her two deceased husbands, in addition to Ted Fleishman's considerable assets, had enabled Liz to construct a lavish lifestyle. In addition to the jewelry and couture clothes that she sported, the parties to which the city's hierarchy was invited, and elaborate trips abroad, Liz had her hand in virtually every society benefit given in San Francisco. The success of any such event was assured if Liz were the chairperson.

"Frank, my man, good to see you."

Frank looked behind him to see Tom Osterman, smiling and with his right hand outstretched.

"Tom, how have you been?" Frank had his hand pumped vigorously by the pink-cheeked society cosmetic surgeon.

"Never better, never better." Osterman responded. "And how about yourself?"

"Oh, I've been fine. Still slicing and dicing? You must have transformed most of the women here," Frank asked with a smile. He had a strong distaste for cosmetic surgery, maintaining that nature gave one an age-appropriate face and body.

"As long as the hand is steady, Frank, as long as the hand is steady. And, yes, as I look around, I did enhance the female pulchritude of most of these lovelies here."

Frank did not particularly care for Tom Osterman. The doctor was a loquacious dandy, dressed tonight in a red cashmere jacket and tailored black woolen pants. An ascot tucked into his custom-made shirt gave him the appearance of a boulevardier. He came across like a homosexual, but his twenty-year marriage to Lydia, a notorious social climber, seemed to belie this impression.

Frank could not bring himself to blatantly dislike Tom Osterman. Tom was once a client of the firm's but had withdrawn his assets a few years ago. "Too conservative," he said. He subsequently invested in a series of improbable schemes, including the search for a sunken treasure ship, which had lost him hundreds of thousands of dollars. Tom had every reason to hope that his hand remained steady.

Osterman's bland insouciance irritated Frank, but not enough to make Frank actually dislike him. His blatant superficiality was almost a caricature, and Frank had to admit that Osterman amused him. Despite the man's bland drivel and odious occupation, Tom Osterman made Frank smile.

Frank knew his conversation with the doctor would not last long. Tom Osterman was like a hummingbird at parties—in constant motion from one person to another.

"Planning any trips soon?" Frank inquired. The Ostermans frequently traveled to exotic spots with several other socially prominent San Franciscans in tow.

"Interesting that you should ask," Osterman responded. "Lydia and I have just been looking at the possibility of a trip to Ethiopia, Somalia, and Eritrea. Haven't been to that part of East Africa yet. The Wilsons and the McCrackens are thinking of joining us."

"Sounds interesting. I understand that Ethiopia has some wonderful Coptic art and architecture. I don't know anything about the other two places."

"Well, you should join us. The trip should be great fun. And it would give me a chance to convince your gorgeous wife to become even more gorgeous. Sam, Sam, how do you do. Frank, I'll see you later. Think about the trip."

Osterman had spotted another acquaintance. The meter had run out for his conversation with Frank, and Tom was onto the next. He left Frank smiling at the thought of traveling with the Ostermans and their entourage. Each trip was carefully chronicled in the *Nob Hill Gazette, Paper City*, or the society pages of the *Chronicle*. The couple and their companions traveled lavishly to exotic areas of the world where few others had ventured. They would go to Venice only for the feast of Christ the Redeemer, when "the marriage of Venice and the sea" would be re-enacted. Two weeks later you'd see the photos of Tom and Lydia and whomever had joined them smiling from a boat on the Grand Canal. But the standard cities visited by tourists—Paris, London, Rome, for example—were eschewed, unless there was some good reason to visit them. They cared little for what they saw in the places to which they traveled, except to provide some patter when they returned to report on the latest trip at the next few social gatherings.

The quartet was playing a rendition of "Blue Moon." The melody gave Frank a mellow feeling. There was Paula, he noticed, in animated conversation with Abel Gantner, a well-known columnist for the *Chronicle*. Frank decided to join them.

"Hi, sweetie, good to see you again," he joked to Paula. "Abel, how have you been?"

"I've been fine, Frank. Thanks for loaning me your wife. We've been having a great time chatting."

"Oh, what have you been talking about?"

Frank felt a twinge of jealousy and made an attempt to stifle it.

"You, my writing, Paula's work, city politics...and it's only been ten minutes," Gantner replied with a smile.

"Just think what we could cover in half an hour," Paula added.

"I'll talk about anything except city politics," Abel said. "The less I think about Snow White and the Eleven Dwarfs the better off I am."

"You don't seem to have trouble finding other topics other than 'silly hall' to write about." Frank replied.

"Well, I've got a different beat. I don't cover the local political news. I try to find local human-interest stories. I find it a much more interesting and fulfilling mandate."

"And much more interesting to read," added Paula.

Abel Gantner's articles in the *Chronicle* were long pieces on people, places, and events—more magazine essays than newspaper reporting. Both Frank and Paula enjoyed the glimpses into the unusual aspects of San Francisco life and behind-the-scenes presentations.

Frank liked Gantner. They met when he had interviewed Frank for an article he was researching. The two men had liked each other, found they had many interests in common, and had become friends...if not close friends, friendly enough to get together for an occasional lunch.

Abel Gantner was in his late 30s, but looked younger. He resembled a young Charles Lindbergh. He had never married and had the reputation of being a "bachelor-about-town." To Frank, one of Abel's most endearing characteristics was his unassuming manner. Most journalists Frank had encountered had a cocky attitude and displayed an arrogant streak. This was not so with Gantner. His almost shy, friendly manner, his warmth, and his charm combined to disarm those whom he interviewed and made him a pleasant companion and conversationalist.

There was an earnestness about Gantner that Frank liked. Gantner had a sincerity that set him apart. He seemed to be an engaged, and engaging, human being.

"I liked your piece the other day on behind-the-scenes at the strip club on Broadway," said Frank. "Pretty depressing."

"Not exactly glamorous lives those girls have," said Paula. Paula's compassion for the numerous women who worked at the few remaining strip clubs in North Beach was evident.

"It was a fascinating story to do," Abel said. "I had to put it in perspective. Every city has a section that has strip clubs, and they have been around for decades. What interested me is what motivates these young ladies to choose such unconventional work, what their days and evenings are like, and what happens to them when they leave this work. As you saw in the article, there are as many answers as there are women working in the clubs."

"I was amazed at the socio-economic spectrum of the women you interviewed," said Frank. One was from the projects in Hunter's Point. Another woman's father was a heart surgeon, and she was raised in Pacific Heights. What is a heart surgeon's daughter who went to fancy private schools doing taking off her clothes and simulating sex acts in a skuzzy dive in North Beach?"

Gantner, his brow furrowed, thought a moment.

"That's what fascinated me. Unfortunately, I didn't have the time to really probe their motivations. Some of their stories are easy to figure out. They come from extremely poor families in the projects, they were abused as children, they engaged in sex quite early, they are often pushed into stripping by the boyfriends, and they like the money. These women usually don't have the discipline to get an education or to work at a regular job.

"But the girls from upper-middle-class and wealthy families are the intriguing ones. They're primed for good careers and good marriages, children, comfortable lives…the whole thing. Yet they turn their backs on all that and gravitate to a life that is the antithesis of how they've been raised. I can speculate on how these women happen to start stripping or get into porn movies, but my speculations still don't provide explanations. We can talk about cold, distant parents. We can talk about rebellious teenagers, about bad company in school. We can even talk about abuse, but that's less common in the upper classes than in the lower classes. I just don't know."

The trio became silent for a moment. Paula broke the silence.

"It could also be a search for self-esteem on the part of young women without the discipline or the passion to find it elsewhere," Paula speculated. "You know, they come to love men staring at their faces and bodies and lusting after them."

"All these things are possible. Unfortunately, the *Chronicle* isn't willing to pay me to do years, or even months, of in-depth research, conducting psychological interviews with young women, their parents, teachers, and friends. If I could do this, I think I could set out a pattern of motivation."

"Ah, how many questions we all have," Frank interjected. "Will we ever get the answers?"

All three laughed. All knew of Frank's penchant for wanting answers to things that puzzled him: Why are there so many cars on Highway 101 during the middle of the day? How can people afford to buy houses in the San Francisco Bay Area? How can young people bear to listen to rap music?

The Fleishmans' party swirled around them, but the three of them were not eager to break up their conversation and join it. But, as an eight ball hits a cluster of three balls and sends them spinning, Ham Foster III accomplished this task.

"Abel, how the hell are you?" the burly politician bellowed. The 6'4" former restaurateur who had recently been elected to the board of supervisors weighed in at 250 pounds at least, but carried his bulk well. His dark blue suit, expensive Hermès tie, handkerchief fluffed out of his jacket pocket, and red carnation boutonniere in his lapel labeled Hamilton Foster III a dandy.

His blustering approach to Abel Gantner was vintage Foster. No word to Frank or Paula, Foster thrust his ample body between the Molinaris and Gantner and began spouting questions, his East Coast nasal twang underscoring his boisterous, almost bellicose, manner.

Frank would have enjoyed continuing this conversation with Abel Gantner, but he despised Foster.

"Abel, as always great to see you. I'll call you for lunch...or dinner. Paula always loves seeing you."

"Goodbye, Abel, I hope we'll see you soon," Paula added.

Abel Gantner gave them a warm smile and a wave, indicating that he would now be subjected to an unpleasant conversation with Foster.

Frank and Paul joined the ever-changing swirl of human constellations that formed in the large rooms of the Fleishmans' mansion. Frank observed the multiple handshakes, superficial hugs, and kisses in the proximity of cheeks…and then the move onto new sets of handshakes, hugs, and kisses. He heard a cacophony of what he had labeled "the party squeal"—a chatter of unnaturally high voices, breathlessly and rapidly spoken.

Frank took Paula's hand into his. She looked at him with surprise and smiled with pleasure.

"I can't believe this," she said, looking at Frank. "You're holding my hand during a party? Usually, you give me a pat and send me on my way."

"Well, tonight is different. I'd like you by my side tonight."

"Oh, Frank, you're so romantic," she teased.

"Always," he replied, looking around him to see if there were any of the surrounding partygoers with whom he would like to engage in conversation.

"Look, there are Jim and Brenda," Frank exclaimed to Paula, a broad smile of pleasant anticipation spreading across his face.

The Stellas were speaking with a woman whom Frank didn't know. As usual, Brenda was listening with a placid smile on her face while Jim spoke in a serious, animated way, hovering over his listener.

As Frank and Paula approached, Jim Stella noticed them. Breaking off his conversation and then ignoring the woman to whom he had been speaking, he called out, "Frank, Paula, come here. I want to talk with you."

While Brenda and Paula exchanged kisses, Jim Stella gave a perfunctory introduction to the woman with whom he had been speaking. Then he virtually dismissed her.

Frank smiled at Jim's impulsiveness. He knew that Jim had never been one to adhere to life's conventions, and here was yet another example of his unpredictable behavior.

James McGrane Stella was the product of an Italian-American father and an Irish-American mother—a typical alliance among Catholic families in the United States in the decades following World War I. But this alliance didn't hold: the couple divorced when Jim was a small boy. The divorce had plunged his mother and her two sons into poverty and his mother into emotional instability. Jim and his brother spent years in a Catholic orphanage and being raised by relatives.

Jim Stella was academically successful in high school, and this success had escalated at St. Ignatius College, where he had been in Frank's brother's class. He and Frank had met and become friends—a friendship that had lasted more than four decades.

After graduating from St. Ignatius, Jim had married, been an officer in the U.S. Army (the result of his R.O.T.C. training at St. Ignatius), and then pursued his Ph.D. in comparative literature at Yale. He taught at Yale for a few years before returning to San Francisco with Brenda and their two sons.

In San Francisco Jim had begun a career that incorporated his academic credentials in a most un-academic way. He cranked out one book after another, well researched and well written, that appealed to a general reading public. This literary output garnered him extensive critical praise. He eschewed the normal tenure-track academic appointment, and instead taught as an adjunct faculty member at several California colleges and universities, while at the same time, or at intervals, working as a librarian, a newspaper columnist, and a magazine editor.

As a result of such a varied career, Jim Stella had found himself to be a well-known personality in San Francisco, accepted in the world of academics and often a celebrity in the many venues in which he traveled.

Frank had long admired Jim's numerous talents: his scholarship, his vivid way of describing the immigrant Catholic world of San Francisco in which they had both grown up, the intensity with which he illuminated any topic he spoke about, his wit and humor.

There were few people whose company Frank enjoyed as much as Jim Stella's. Their conversations lifted him into a near-mystical state, and their times together were rollicking, good fun, and filled with soul-searching.

The 6'2" Jim Stella gave Frank a hearty handshake and looked pleased to see him.

"Jim, Paula and I are going to get a drink," Brenda intoned. "Don't the two of you get into any trouble."

"We'll be right here, doll. Don't you two get picked up by a couple of rich guys looking for trophy wives," Jim answered.

Paula and Brenda laughed softly and maneuvered themselves through the crowd toward the bar that had been set up in the capacious living room.

"How is the new book coming, Jim?"

"Oh, you know, fine, I guess. By now writing has become second nature. I think about what I want to write about; I research which I'm going to write about; and then I write it."

Frank laughed. "Just that easy, huh?"

"Well, I'm not saying it's easy. I get up at five in the morning and spend two hours writing, and in the afternoon I spend three hours doing research. I wouldn't call that easy; but I do it. It's become an indelible part of my life."

"Well, the results have been terrific," said an admiring Frank. "Your works will be definitive for decades to come."

Jim laughed. "You do exaggerate…always have. The books are okay, but I don't think they're going to be classics. But, who knows?"

"I saw Father O'Sullivan a couple days ago." Frank decided to relate the story of his trip to the peninsula and the visit to the man who had mentored both of them.

"No kidding? How is he doing? I need to get over to see him."

"He's in pain, and I don't think he has much longer to live. But his spirit is good, and he had enough energy to give me lots of spiritual advice. And we talked about death."

"Sounds like the same Father O'Sullivan. What did he have to say about death?"

Frank pondered for a moment. How could he summarize the conversation he had had with O'Sullivan?

"I confessed to him that as I've gotten older I've begun to have fears of death. He said to me, essentially, that death is the beginning of life. And he told me to pray. That's it in a nutshell."

"And have you begun to fear death?"

"Yes, I must admit I have. I've thought about death all my life. I was an altar boy at funerals at eight years old. I went to funerals with my parents—more funerals than I can count. In my family we talked—even joked—about death. Death cropped up constantly in the books we read and the movies we saw. I've always known about death intellectually, but in the last couple years I've gotten an emotional sense of death. And the idea of dying, of my physical presence here on earth being annihilated, has made me extremely uncomfortable."

"Hmm…I guess I haven't gotten there yet," Stella began, "and I don't know how I'll react when I'm finally faced with the reality of death, I mean, when I finally realize on a deep level, that yes, I'm going to die. I guess that realization can be pretty scary. What O'Sullivan said to you was pretty classic Catholicism. Did it help?"

"Well, it didn't have me skipping down the street, cheerfully saying, 'O, great, O, great, I'm going to die one of these days,' but, as we've always done with O'Sullivan's advice and dicta, I've certainly taken it to heart."

"It sounds as if you had some day."

"That was the end of a weird day. It began when I drove down the peninsula to see some clients. On the drive down, I was flooded with memories of the years when I lived down there. The excitement of adolescence came back to me with a vengeance."

"Never to come back, my friend, never to come back."

Jim's throaty laugh punctuated their conversation. Here was a person, Frank thought, who could understand his torments about trying to recreate those years of his teens and early twenties. Jim had had two tumultuous romances with young women who lived on the peninsula; one had ended, the other had resulted in his marriage to Brenda. Jim knew the rhythms of life there, could remember the sun-drenched summer days on Hillsborough and Atherton estates, the numerous heartfelt crushes that had consumed them.

"I can't tell you the memories I had as I drove down the El Camino," Frank resumed. "The day was warm and sunny, just as I remembered them years ago. I could remember, but I couldn't bring up those swirling feelings when you felt that you were 'in love' or, even, 'in like.' It was as if a wall had been built between then and now."

"I know," Jim answered, his hearty laugh now reduced to a chuckle, "I was flashing back the other day to when I was sixteen and went on a vacation to the Russian River. I was paddling in a canoe behind Debbie Riley. Debbie had on a two-piece bathing suit, and I remember staring at the tiny golden hairs that went down along the spine of her tanned back. I can remember feeling such a rush of emotion. I wanted to beach the canoe immediately and make out with her. In those days we never thought of doing more than making out."

"How well I remember," Frank responded. "In fact, I was so retarded in those days I could barely hope to make out. I can't figure out why I was so shy and retiring."

"Most of us were. I think there were a lot of reasons. Most of the girls we met were from a higher socio-economic strata. We were very much caught up in the Catholic guilt thing. We had pretty low self-esteem about our attractiveness to the opposite sex. There were a lot of factors. But I'm convinced that as an adult you can never get enough of those things you felt you missed in your youth."

"Wow, that's a statement that could have come from Greek mythology or the Greek tragedies, or even the Divine Comedy."

"No really, I believe it." Stella continued. "Our yearnings when we were young were never truly met when we got older. And, now, as old age begins to take its toll on us physically and emotionally, we know we'll never be able to fulfill those yearnings from yesteryear…it's a double whammy."

"My God, that's pretty depressing…and damn it all, we can't go back!" Frank responded with a smile.

"We're the lucky ones," Jim continued. "You went through your post-divorce days, banging everything in sight. Now you've got a terrific marriage. I've had a terrific marriage since I got out of St. Ignatius. But I realize that there is still a hole in my life, a yearning for those things I feel I missed when I was younger. We both have terrific careers. We've been very productive as adults. I still wonder why I wasn't as productive earlier in my life. So it obviously isn't just about sexual deprivation."

Out of the corner of his eye Frank caught sight of Emily Kornfeld approaching them. He instinctively knew that the delicious conversation with Jim Stella was over. He knew Emily only slightly—just well enough to know that she would feel no compunction about barging into this intimate conversation.

"Dr. Stella," she began, with a slight nod of acknowledgment to Frank. "You're just the man I wanted to see. I want to talk to you about your new book."

Emily Kornfeld was a good-looking, pushy woman, ill educated. She'd met Sam Kornfeld, a prominent venture capitalist, while he was on the rebound from his first marriage. Their marriage had provided the social standing and the money Emily required to reconstruct her life. A score of Pygmalions stood to her Galatea. These included cosmetic surgery, speech coaches, personal shoppers, mentors in social deportment, and—probably most important to her—a degree from Cal Berkeley and a law degree from Hastings Law School. Emily's transformation was now complete, and she fancied herself not only one of San Francisco's leading socialites, but also one of its leading intellectuals.

She inaugurated a monthly book luncheon, attended by her socialite friends, to hear authors talk about their latest book, after which she would lead the discussion. Society editors in the local newspapers soon began to portray her as some sort of eighteenth century French savant, presiding over a noted salon. What was, in Frank's mind, most in keeping with the great hostesses of eighteenth-century salons was her increasing arrogant hauteur. She would be better described as one of the grande horizontals of

La Belle Époque.

When Emily intruded into their conversation, Frank said, "Jim, I'll see you later." With a wink, he left his friend.

Frank looked around for Paula and Brenda, but they were nowhere to be seen. He threaded his way through the crowd toward the bar, not seeing anyone he knew well enough to begin a conversation.

Frank obtained a Campari and soda at the bar, fixed himself a few feet away, and silently contemplated the crowd around him. Across the room he spied the Serbian Slut holding court, her eyelids half closed, quietly presiding over a clique of several ladies. His eyes traveled around the room. It was filled with the familiar faces that one saw almost daily in the society pages of the *Chronicle*, or monthly in those of the *Nob Hill Gazette, Paper City,* or *7 x 7*.

Despite the still extensive chronicling of San Francisco's social set, the amorphous group continued to reel from the death of its high priest of chronicling—columnist Herb Caen.

For almost 60 years Caen's column had detailed the comings and goings of San Francisco's social elite. But his was not just a society column: he would write about shoeshine men and flower vendors as well as social or business movers and shakers. Caen's amalgam of clever reportage and wordsmithing was universally popular. It had forged the San Francisco Bay Area into a metropolitan village. One might not have known the magnates and the social swells—or the shoeshine men and flower vendors—that inhabited Caen's column, but one felt as if one did.

If he had been still alive, Caen would have been at the Fleishmans' party. Frank smiled at the thought of the balding columnist standing amid a swarm of admiring groupies, still somewhat arrogant in his late-seventies, throwing one quip after another to his admiring audience.

For all his fame and what had been perhaps a handsome salary, Caen had always remained the quintessential outsider. From what he described as a middle-class, but most likely penurious, family in Sacramento, and no college education, Caen had clawed his way to the fame he came to relish. Despite his sizeable income, his Pulitzer Prize, his notoriety, and his phalanxes of admirers, one always got a sense that in Caen's mind, he would always be the chronicler, not one of those he so cleverly wrote about. What would he have written about this party? Frank wondered.

"Hello, sport. Looks like you're wool-gathering."

The greeting and the clap on the back brought Frank out of his musings.

"Fred, good to see you. How've you been?"

"Never better," Fred Haines answered. "Never better."

The tall, burly Haines was smiling his usual bland smile. He and Frank had served on a couple of non-profit boards together many years before, and, ever since, Frank was the recipient of Haines' "hail-fellow-well-met" greeting and verbal bromides.

Haines was the scion of a pioneer San Francisco family that had once been quite wealthy, and had been educated in the tradition of the well-heeled and socially prominent: St. Paul's in New Hampshire for high school, Yale for college. The problem was that Haines' father hadn't done much to enhance the family fortune, nor had Haines. The days of his polo-playing grandfather and his yachting father were now only memories. Haines had held onto the family mansion in Pacific Heights, worked as a real estate agent for a prominent San Francisco firm (where he was known as one of the worst producers), and had just enough money to pay his bar bills at his clubs: the Bohemian, where he was a mainstay at the bar; the Pacific Union, where he played dominos while sipping a scotch and soda; the Burlingame, where he played his weekly round of golf; and the St. Francis Yacht Club, where he gazed longingly at the photos of his father and the long-vanished yacht.

Fred Haines continued to give the appearance of a socially superior man of means, but no one had ever witnessed him buying a drink or a meal for anyone else, and his name never appeared in a list of donors for any philanthropic group.

"I haven't seen you holding up your end of the bar at the club for a while," said Frank with a malicious grin. He had noticed that Haines had been posted for non-payment of his Bohemian Club bill.

"Yeah, well, I haven't had much time to get to the B.C. recently," Haines responded. "Been hanging out at the P.U. more. They've just had a dominoes tournament."

Fred Haines once more thumped Frank on the back.

"You stay out of trouble, sport."

"Goodbye, Fred, nice to see you," Frank lied.

This is what I hate about these gatherings, Frank thought. They are filled with exchanges such as this one with Fred Haines. Frank decided it was time to go.

Frank looked around for Paula but did not see her. He decided to prowl around until he found her.

The cacophony of the crowd began to annoy Frank. Each of the partygoers had assumed pleasant smiles and an animated demeanor that belied their usual personalities. Marissa Bingham, noted for her despicable behavior to the domestics in her house, to waiters, and to retail clerks, was standing next to Frank and discussing her recent trip in dull tones with a couple he didn't recognize. Several feet away Sandra Melops, known for being a malicious gossip, was beaming an angelic smile as she listened to the Bottoms telling her about the recent crush of Chardonnay grapes at their Napa Valley estate.

It was all such a fraud, Frank thought, and yet it intrigued him.

Paula waved to him across the room and began to walk over to him with a man whom Frank did not know. Frank stood in one of the few areas in the room that was not jammed with people and awaited her.

"Frank, this is Alden Capellini," announced Paula with a beaming smile, "and, Alden; this is my husband, Frank Molinari. Alden and I just met, and I thought the two of you should meet, too."

The two men shook hands and greeted each other. Paula often made introductions like this one at such parties; there was usually a reason why she would introduce him to someone she had met in her wanderings. What was the reason for this one? he wondered.

"Guess where Alden went to school?" Paula asked Frank.

"St. Ignatius," Frank replied with a smile.

Alden nodded with a smile.

"When did you graduate?" Frank asked.

"1980," Capellini responded. "And then on to law school."

"Ah, 1980, way before me," Frank joked.

The two laughed. Frank liked what he saw of Paula's new acquaintance. There was an openness about him that was rare at these parties. And there was a general "niceness" about him, Frank thought.

"How did someone with the last name of Capellini get the first name of Alden?" Frank inquired, smiling at such a waspy name given to an Italian surname.

"My mother was born in this country, but of immigrant parents," Capellini began. "When she was in grammar school, she read the quintessential Puritan romantic story about John Alden proposing to Priscilla as a surrogate for John Smith. Well, my mother thought this was the most splendid story ever, and, a couple of decades later, when I was born my parents decided to name me Alden."

"Love it," Frank responded, smiling. "I've heard tons of similar stories. I should publish a book of them sometime. ...So, you practice law?"

"Yes and no," Capellini answered. "I'm the CFO for a technology company in Silicon Valley, and while I'm involved in some corporate legal matters, I'm not really practicing law."

"Okay, Paula, now we can befriend him," Frank joked.

"Don't tell me you're not fond of attorneys," Capellini joined the humorous attack on lawyers. "Some of my best friends are attorneys."

"Only they sue you," Paula put in.

"What did you major in at St. Ignatius?" Frank inquired. He always found it interesting to probe with this question when he met someone. The answers often provided a basis for discovering mutual interests or gaining an insight into a person's character.

"History," Capellini answered.

"No kidding," Frank said. "So did I. But I won't ask you about your teachers. The ones I had I'm sure were gone by the time you got there."

"Let's see, who did I have? Who might have been there for a while? I had medieval history from Father Bill Strain and California history from Father John McShane."

"Sure, I had both of them. So you must have had them shortly before they retired."

"I guess so. Both were wonderful teachers."

"I got a very good education at St. Ignatius," Frank asserted. "The teachers were good. It was a solid classical education. The student body was diverse. And I still have close friends I met there."

Frank was suddenly and surprisingly flooded with nostalgic memories of his days at St. Ignatius College. Long hours of study followed by all-nighter bull sessions, watching the sun come up. He time-traveled to the days of hard-fought student elections and mad-cap pranks, of long hours spent in discussions with the younger teachers, still in the first fervor of their careers, taking the bus to North Beach during the beatnik era and having a full-course dinner at one of the Italian restaurants there for $1.25.

It was his golden age, Frank mused. He was out of his parents' home, and not subject to their regulations, yet he had none of the responsibilities of a job and family. What wonderful, carefree days.

"Did you know Father O'Sullivan?" Capellini broke into his reverie.

"Father O'Sullivan was one of my closest friends and one of the most important mentors in my life," Frank responded. "You knew him, too, I gather."

"He was the student advisor for some activities I was involved in," Capellini answered. "So I got to know him somewhat. He was really a special priest and human being. I am still motivated by some of the conversations we had. I'm only sorry that I didn't keep in touch with him after I graduated."

"He's still dispensing good advice. I went to see him in the infirmary the other day—he's dying of cancer—but he continues to be his old self."

"I'm sorry to hear about the cancer," said Capellini. "I should go by and reintroduce myself. I don't know why I didn't keep in touch...well, I do know. It was law school, business, a job that kept me working from twelve to fourteen hours a day, marriage, children. Who had time for anything else?"

"Is your wife here?" Paula inquired.

"No wife. I'm divorced...have been for five years."

"No kidding. How unusual for the Bay Area," Frank laughed. "What's the matter, can't you make a commitment?"

Capellini rubbed his chin thoughtfully. "I could, but she couldn't. She became a partner at the Bailey firm and then decided that the distractions of a husband and family would impair her career."

"You're raising your children?" Paula exclaimed.

"She couldn't go quite that far," Capellini explained. "She and I have them alternate weeks. We live close to each other, so there's no disruption as far as school goes."

Frank noticed pain in Capellini's eyes as he succinctly described the terms of his divorce and the co-custody of his children. The divorce and its outcome had not been easy for him—another casualty in the modern re-evaluation of gender roles.

"Divorce is always difficult when children are involved," said Frank. He disliked uttering such bromides, but nothing more meaningful came into his mind. "How old are they?"

"Michael is ten and Lucy is eight."

"Great ages," Paula added.

Capellini looked so distressed about his divorced situation that both Frank and Paula were uncomfortable, sorry that they had brought up the question of his marital status and then quipped about how common divorce had become. One could see that even after five years, Capellini's divorce was still tender and sore for him.

Frank nervously tried to change the subject. "I only know the company you're with by name. It hasn't gone public, has it?"

"No. The founders wanted to wait until the company shows a proven earnings stream. That happened this past year, so I think we'll have a public offering in a year or two. It should be a blockbuster. The company has done very well."

"Sounds like you'll be able to retire after the public offering," Frank said, smiling.

The pain seemed to disappear from Capellini's face. "No, I won't retire, but it will be very nice to have a big chunk of capital at my disposal. But, then, 'there's many a slip between cup and lip.'"

"I've always liked that quote," Paula chimed in.

"I can't imagine that you wouldn't have a very successful offering, unless something catastrophic were to happen," said Frank. "It's nice to anticipate becoming rich."

"Yeah, well, I've discovered that money can't buy you happiness." The sadness returned to Capellini's face.

"You'll have money and happiness," Paula rejoined. "You're going to find Ms. Right and live happily ever after."

Capellini smiled. "I hope that's true," he said.

Frank liked Capellini, and he could see that Paula did also. Perhaps they would have him to dinner some night and introduce him to one of the single women they knew. He could see that on this night, Alden Capellini was overwhelmed by the end of his domestic dreams five years before. Nothing could alleviate his sorrow and sadness at his divorce and his seeing his children only every other week.

"Alden, Paula and I would love to have you to dinner some night. Do you have a card?"

Capellini fished in his coat pocket and handed Frank a card.

"I'd love to see the two of you again," he said. "Hopefully, I'll be in a better mood than I am tonight. I don't know…being here alone…seeing couples all around me. I probably should have stayed home."

"Then we wouldn't have met you," said Paula. "We're glad you came, but we know these situations can be tough sometimes."

Frank looked lovingly at Paula. Her kindness was always evident, he thought. He could see that Capellini was pleased with her comment.

"Well, my dear, enough partying for tonight. Let's say goodnight to our hosts and go home. Alden, I really enjoyed meeting you. We'll call in a week or so to set up your coming to dinner."

The two men shook hands and the three broke up with exchanged pleasantries. Frank and Paula intruded upon the Fleishmans' circle and thanked them once again for inviting them to the party. Then they waited in front of the imposing mansion for the valets to return with their car.

"Poor Alden Capellini," Paula began their post-party analysis "Is he ever in pain."

"Some individuals can't get over the breakup of a marriage," Frank responded. "And in his case it was his wife who wanted out, not him. It's tough to have those dreams come apart."

"You and I both got through it."

"Yes, but both you and I wanted to get out of intolerable marriages. We were the ones that left. And I can tell you that it was hell not being present every day as the children were growing up."

"I got a sense that Alden's wife would probably have preferred having him take the kids full time."

Frank's long-held ire against parents who had children but allowed them to be raised by domestic help rose to the surface. He loathed the selfishness of high-powered individuals who preferred the long hours of work to achieve substantial power and money, but who had children as part of some package or from some list of necessary achievements and then abandoned them to others to be raised and nurtured.

"She probably never sees them during the time she's got them," Frank said. The housekeeper or nanny supervises them when they return from school, feeds them supper, and puts them to bed. She may see them when they wake up in the morning. But, I'll bet she works on the weekend. Some life for those kids."

The Jaguar slid up to the curb, and Frank slipped $5 to the attendant. He adjusted his seat and released the brake. The Jaguar noiselessly glided the ten blocks to their home.

"I'm glad to be home," Paula wearily said as they entered their home. "Those parties exhaust me."

CHAPTER 12

The telephone intercom on Frank's desk buzzed. "Yes, Jessica."

"Mr. Molinari, your 9 o'clock appointment, Mr. Crofts is here. He's a little bit early, and says he's happy to wait until 9," said Jessica, with the formality she assumed when announcing his appointments.

"No, go ahead, send him in."

Jessica ushered into his office a solemn-looking man of medium height, graying hair, not particularly distinguished features, who appeared to be in his fifties.

"Hello, I'm Frank Molinari, please sit down," Frank motioned his visitor to the couch in his office. Frank took the chair opposite.

"I'm Jason Crofts. Thank you for seeing me."

"Not at all. Can I get you some coffee?"

"No, no thank you. I'm fine."

Frank crossed his legs and looked at the man sitting across from him. There seemed to be some great sorrow burdening him. Why, Frank asked himself, had this man wanted to see him?

"Well, what can I do for you?" Frank asked, curious about Crofts.

"I'm a regular person, Mr. Molinari. Nothing fancy or special about me. I've worked for the post office for almost thirty years...a great job, I'm happy to have it. I'm a person of regular habits. I guess I lead a dull life. I certainly lead an ordered life."

What the hell is he leading up to? Frank wondered. Why is he here?

"I've been married for twenty-five years," Crofts continued. "I think I can say that I have been happily married...except for now."

Frank sat back in his chair, perplexed as to what Crofts was going to say.

"What I'm leading up to is that my life has been pretty content up to the past few months. About three months ago I found that my wife was having an affair with your wife. I asked my wife to stop it, but she said she couldn't and wouldn't."

Frank bolted upright in his chair. The blood drained from his face. His cognitive process stopped. All of his being was only conscious of this blow.

"What?" he shouted at Crofts.

"I'd like for you to get your wife to end the affair," Crofts went on in his quiet way. "It's wreaking havoc with my life. It's ruining my marriage. But I still don't want my marriage to end. Despite this, I love her. I don't know why she's fallen in love with another woman. I don't understand these things. All I know is that I'd like to have her back."

Frank couldn't respond. He stared at Crofts, trying to kick-start his thought processes, engulfed by the news he had just heard. He tried to speak, but only stuttering, incoherent noises came from his mouth.

"This is absurd," Frank finally stuttered. "My wife can't be having an affair, and certainly not with another woman. This is crazy. Where did you get this information?"

"From my wife, of course," Crofts responded. "And I can assure you it's true. I know a bit about you, Mr. Molinari...stuff that my wife heard about you from your wife."

Frank felt light-headed and immobilized. An impulse flickered through him to bolt out the door, drive to Paula's office, and confront her with the news, but his legs wouldn't move. He could only continue to stare at Crofts and struggle to breathe.

"Where do they meet? How often?" Frank spit out.

"I don't know all the details," Crofts answered. "But I know they've been together at my house...and at yours. And I know that they've gone away some weekends."

Frank, who had begun to slump in his chair, bolted upright. He remembered that during the past few months Paula had taken off by herself on two specific occasions...once to see friends in the Napa Valley, another time to see friends in Carmel. Or so she had told him. The realization that these two weekends had not been innocent trips visiting girlfriends in those two places, but assignations with a lover, further deflated Frank. Pain bubbled up throughout him, as if he were in a in a cauldron. He could no longer concentrate on Crofts' face; he could only stare vacantly into space.

He finally was able to inquire listlessly, "How did you happen to find out about this? Did your wife tell you?" Frank fought against the waves of nausea that came over him.

"She had been acting funny...unusual...for some time. I just knew that there had to be something going on with her, but I didn't know what. Then she went off for those weekends, something she never does. And, so, one day I confronted her, and she told me all about the affair she was having. She said that she wanted to stay married to me, but that she wasn't going to end the affair."

Frank covered his eyes with his hand. His head was throbbing, and he couldn't arrange his thoughts in any logical sequence. He felt as he did when he was a boy in the Fun House at Playland-by-the-Beach, listening to a cacophony of noise and watching a kaleidoscope of flashing lights. How could this have happened? he kept asking himself.

He looked up to see Crofts intently watching him.

"Are you absolutely certain it's my wife?" Frank asked.

"I got your full description from my wife," Crofts replied with assurance. I even got the low-down on your kids...their names...what they do. I checked out the information. There isn't a chance in hell that this could not be the wife of Frank Molinari."

Frank took a few deep breaths to calm himself. Hot flashes alternated with chills as he tried to think about this situation.

"Well, what would you like me to do?" Frank asked his voice barely audible.

"I'd like to have you make your wife stop having this affair...to not see my wife again."

"And if she refuses? Your wife hasn't said that she's willing to end this affair."

"This is a phase," Crofts pleaded. "Marta's not a lesbian, and I'm certain that she's been faithful to me all these years...up till now. I don't want to say your wife seduced her...I don't know...but I think that you can make your wife stop this affair."

"This isn't the old days," Frank responded somewhat impatiently. "These days wives pretty much do what they want to do. And they generally don't consult their husbands about their affairs."

"You mean you won't tell your wife to stop this affair?" Crofts demanded. Crofts' obtuseness annoyed Frank. Within the last few minutes his world had come smashing down on him. He'd learned that his wife was having a lesbian affair, and now this oaf is telling him to order an independent-minded woman such as Paula to give up a love affair. What age was the man living in?

"Mr. Crofts, you must admit that the news you're giving me is pretty shocking and upsetting...and surprising. In fact, I can barely think. As soon as you leave, I am going to see my wife and get some explanation of all this. I have no other plans...just to talk with my wife. What happens after that I don't know. ...And, now, Mr. Crofts, as you can well imagine, I need to get along with my day."

"I understand, Mr. Molinari, I'll be going now. But, please, please, tell your wife to give Marta back to me."

There were tears beginning in Crofts' eyes, and Frank regretted the way he had just spoken to him. He should have been more compassionate. What did this ordinary, hardworking man know of lesbian affairs between married women or feminist theories emanating from academia? He was a poor, hurt man, yearning for his wife to again be faithful to him.

Frank doggedly got up and stretched out his hand to Crofts. "I can't say this has been a pleasant encounter, Mr. Crofts, but thank you for coming. I pray this will all work out for everybody."

"Thanks for seeing me, Mr. Molinari," Crofts mumbled, and then walked out the door.

Frank pulled on his coat and walked to his secretary's desk. "Jessica, cancel any appointments I have this morning. I'll be back after lunch."

Jessica looked up at Frank's pale, stony face with concern. "Frank, is everything okay?"

Frank didn't answer but swept past her out of Blakesley and Montgomery's offices and to the bank of elevators. He felt as if there were two Frank Molinaris: one a pained, animal-like person, and the other a dulled mind watching the other Frank Molinari.

Upon reaching the Jaguar, Frank heaved himself into the car and steered it out of the garage. He noticed nothing of the familiar streets as he drove out of the financial district into the South of Market area toward the foot of Potrero Hill. He had no trouble finding a parking place in front of the rehabilitated brick industrial building that housed a variety of interior design, fabric, and lighting firms.

Frank ran up two flights of steps to his wife's office. No one was in the office except Paula, who was on the telephone. Talking with her lover? Frank bitterly wondered. She looked surprised to see him, and held up a finger to indicate that her call would be shortly terminated. Frank slumped down in a chair in front of Paula's desk.

"That would be great. Okay, I'll wait to hear from you...fine...good, I'll talk with you tomorrow...goodbye." Paula hung up the phone and turned to Frank.

"Well, this is quite a surprise," she said, looking with concern at Frank. "You look like you've been hit with a sledgehammer. What's the matter?"

Frank looked up at Paula. "Sit down, I'd like to talk with you," he intoned.

Paula automatically sat down. "What on earth is going on?"

"A man came to see me today," Frank began. "Guess why he came to see me? He tells me that my wife is having an affair with his wife, and that he wants me to stop it."

The blood drained from Paula's face and she bolted up from her chair. "What?" she yelled. "What are you saying?"

"That's what he told me. And he seemed to know about me...about the children...facts that he could only have gotten from someone close to me."

"And you think that I've been having an affair with this man's wife?" Paula asked with incredulity.

"That's what I am here for: to ask you," Frank answered. "And, yes, I do feel as if I've been hit by a sledgehammer."

Paula's face hardened. Her hands curled up into fists. Her lips were pressed together. She looked at her husband with anger.

"You are a fucking asshole," she hissed. "I've never been unfaithful to you in our marriage...not with a man, not with a woman, not with an animal. What kind of trust can you have if you would believe some man's tale about me having an affair?"

Frank, surprised at his wife's use of profanity, words he had heard from her only once or twice since they had known each other, looked intently at her. Paula had never lied to him. She had made a fetish out of honesty and integrity, refusing even to tell the occasional "white lie" to harmlessly ease some uncomfortable situation. Frank felt that air was being pumped into his body.

"You're telling me that you haven't had an affair with this man's wife —he said her name was Marta?" Frank asked. He began to feel that this was all some big mistake and that he could breathe and live again. Hope surged up in him.

"Are you crazy?" Paula's visible anger at her husband poured forth. "I don't know anyone named Marta, and right now I wish I didn't even know you."

Frank felt engulfed by light. He could not have been more ecstatic if he were hearing church bells pealing and Verdi's *Requiem* performed. As deflated and pained as he had felt a few moments ago, he now felt equally resurrected and elated. He leapt up from the chair in which he was seated and bounded around Paula's desk to embrace her.

Paula averted his embrace. Her eyes continued to blaze in anger. "Get away from me. You come barreling in here, accusing me of having a lesbian affair, and then you want to hug and kiss me. No, thank you."

Frank didn't press his surge of wishing physical contact with his wife. She would, in time, forgive him his accusation and forget his momentary doubting of her. His mind now began to work on the puzzle of who this woman might be who was having an affair with Crofts' wife. He sat down again in the chair he had formerly occupied, ignoring Paula's glowering looks, his brow furrowed.

"Who can it be?" he asked aloud. "Who could know so much about me and the kids?"

"Frank, I am stunned that you would think that I'd have an affair, that I'd be unfaithful to you. And, have you ever seen me romantically interested in women?"

Frank was eager to placate his wife. Her simple denial instantaneously convinced him that Paula had not been the woman having the affair with Crofts' wife. Her anger at his mistrust was justified.

"Sweetheart, I'm really sorry. Please...please forgive me. You can't imagine how blown away I was this morning when this man came into my office and tells me to stop my wife having an affair with his wife. And then he offers what sounded to me like proof that this was the case. I freaked out. I couldn't think. I just felt this numbness...pain."

Paula's demeanor softened. There was a growing look of sympathy as she looked at her husband slumped in the chair facing her desk.

"I don't understand," she began. "This man said his wife is having an affair with your wife. And, again, how did he think it was me?"

"Apparently, his wife shared with him information about me, about the kids, that could only have been known by you. He said he had done his homework, that he had checked out the information, and that the only person it could have been was you. I can't figure it out."

"This is too bizarre. This is either a gigantic mistake or someone is impersonating me. But, why would someone do that?"

Frank didn't answer immediately. He simultaneously was relishing the relief he was feeling that Paula was not having an affair and trying to solve the puzzle of why Crofts was so convinced that she had stolen his wife's affections. No resolution was forthcoming. He found it preposterous that someone would deliberately impersonate his wife in an affair. And who could know so much about him and his family?

"I guess that the only way that I'm going to get to the bottom of this is to call Crofts and ask him some specific questions. I've got to figure out what's going on."

"Why didn't you do that when he was in your office?" Paula asked with sarcasm.

"Because none of my thought processes were working after he told me that my wife was having an affair with his wife and offered what seemed to be proof that this was so. That's why."

Frank stood up and began to roll his neck in an arc to relieve the tension he had begun to feel there. The stress of his morning conversation had manifested itself in a painful constriction of his neck and shoulders. He decided to head back to his office and from there launch his investigation.

"Okay, Sweetheart, I'm going to get out of your hair and get back to the office. I'm going to get to the bottom of this. And, again, I'm really sorry. I know I should have known better, but my normal thought process closed down, I guess, at the shock of hearing what I heard. I love you."

This time Paula did not resist his embrace and his long kiss.

As Frank piloted the black Jaguar back to the financial district, he felt as if a judge had given him a reprieve from a death sentence. Although he fancied himself as a person who could survive any catastrophe in his life, he felt that any abortion of his marriage might just put him over the edge. Theirs had been a passionate courtship and marriage. And he valued her presence in his life more than he could admit.

He felt abashed that he had doubted Paula's faithfulness. His instincts should have clearly told him that Crofts' revelations were not about his wife; but the shock of those revelations, combined with the knowledge Crofts had about him and his children seemed to have given his charges the appearance of truth.

"You're back early, Mr. M.," Jessica said, looking with continuing concern at her boss as he strode by her desk. "Everything okay?"

"It is now," Frank answered. "Thank you for asking."

Frank entered his office and closed the door. He needed to clear up the mystery of who was having the affair with Crofts' wife: otherwise, he would not be able to function. Where was he to begin? The obvious place was to call Crofts and ask him some more specific questions about the identity of his wife's lover.

Frank opened the door of his office and called out to his secretary. "Jessica, could you give me the telephone number of Jason Crofts, the man who came to see me this morning? Thanks."

Frank went back into his office and began to pace. Jessica brought him the desired telephone number, and then left the office, closing the door behind her. He sat at his desk and dialed the number. After several rings, Crofts answered the telephone.

"Hello." The man sounded dispirited.

"Hello, Mr. Crofts. This is Frank Molinari."

There was surprised silence. After several seconds, Crofts responded. "Ah, Mr. Molinari." And that was all.

"The reason I'm calling," Frank began, "is that I've confronted my wife with the news you gave me, and she denies having an affair with your wife. My wife has never once lied to me, and I believe her. But the extraordinary nature of our conversation today compels me to find out who is having the affair with your wife, and I would like your help in finding out who this woman might be."

Once again there was silence at the other end of the phone for several seconds.

"As I told you this morning, Mr. Molinari, I have checked out the information my wife gave me. It can't be anyone else but your wife."

Crofts sounded mournful. It was obvious how much pain his domestic problem was causing him.

"I know what you said, and I'm sure that you have checked out the information you got. But, I also know my wife, and I know she's not the one who's having the affair. This whole thing, however, touches me closely enough that I want to find out who is having this affair with your wife.

"I know that this is an unusual request, but is it possible that I could talk with your wife to straighten this out?"

Silence again.

"I don't know, Mr. Molinari. I didn't tell Marta that I was coming to see you. She'll be upset if she finds out I did."

"Well, Mr. Crofts, I was pretty upset by what you had to say this morning, and my wife was pretty upset by my bursting into her office and accusing her of having an affair. You've been upset by your wife's affair. It's time she joined the crowd."

Frank was becoming annoyed by his involvement in this mess; but he was determined to uncover the identity of the person who seemed to know so much about him and his family. Silence again at the other end of the line. It was obvious that Crofts' wife's affair had taken Crofts out of the comfortable rhythms of his life. He was thrashing around in those new circumstances, unsure of what to do.

"Come on, Mr. Crofts, your wife may initially be surprised by the fact that you've been to see me, but she'll be flattered that you love her enough to fight for her."

Once again the response was momentary silence.

Hesitatingly, Crofts finally murmured the telephone number. "She's a secretary in an architectural firm downtown. Tell her that I'm sorry, but I was going out of my mind."

"Thank you, Mr. Crofts. I'll get to the bottom of this. Thanks for your help."

"Goodbye," Crofts intoned.

Frank instantly dialed the number that he had been given.

"Hello, Joshua Galvin's office. May I help you?" The voice was a cheerful one.

"Marta Crofts?"

"Yes, this is she."

"My name is Frank Molinari," Frank began, wondering where his conversation was going to go. He heard an audible gasp at the other end of the telephone. "If you have a little time today, I'd like to have a cup of coffee with you and clear up a few things. I'd be most appreciative."

A pause.

"Mrs. Crofts?"

"Yes, yes, I'm here. I'm just...a little surprised. How did you get my number?"

"Your husband gave it to me."

Yet another pause.

"I was going to take lunch today at 1 o'clock," Marta Crofts finally responded. "Why don't we meet for coffee at Paoli's Chop House on Battery Street? Do you know it?"

"Yes, I know it. I'll see you there at one. How will I recognize you?"

"I have on a bright yellow dress and I'm blonde," she answered.

"Okay, and I have on a blue suit and a bright red tie. See you in a bit."

What an odd way to spend the day, Frank thought as he replaced the telephone. I had no idea when I got up this morning that these strange events were going to unfold.

Frank looked at the clock on his desk and saw that he had forty minutes until his rendezvous. It would take him only ten minutes to walk to Paoli's Chop House. He felt too wired to do any work for the intervening half hour. And he wasn't in the mood for one of his colleagues to walk into his office to discuss some matter. He decided to take a leisurely walk until his appointment.

"Jessica, I'm going out. I'll be back no later than 2:30."

His secretary looked up at him with a concerned look, but made no inquiry.

"I promise I'll get back to work when I return," Frank laughed. "Don't worry, it's nothing serious."

Frank emerged onto Montgomery Street and contemplated where he should walk. This was an unusual experience. His leaving the office most often had a purpose: to go to lunch, to meet with a client or prospective client, to attend a meeting, to go home. He couldn't remember the last time he had simply gone out for a stroll in the financial district.

Frank decided to wander down Montgomery Street in the general direction of Paoli's Chop House. Strolling for a block, he spied Wells Fargo Bank's headquarters at California and Montgomery Streets. He had worked for Wells Fargo once, he mused. Not here, but just as it was merging with American Trust, in a building at the juncture of Post, Montgomery, and Market Streets. The post-1906 building had long been torn down and a modern skyscraper put up in its place.

His free-associating led him to decide to walk into Wells Fargo's history museum to pass some time. Although he had been there many times, Frank never tired of looking at the exhibits. Wells Fargo had begun in San Francisco in 1852 and was the oldest bank in the West. It was amazing that it had survived all the changes that had taken place during the past century and a half.

Frank smiled as he walked by the bank's logo—the red stagecoach that dominated the museum's space. He thought he would look at one of his favorite paintings of San Francisco and walked up to the mezzanine level, where he was greeted by the bright green, red, and white painting of tents on Telegraph Hill during the Gold Rush, with the red-roofed Fremont Hotel at the base of the hill.

Frank loved this painting, its simplicity, its colors, and its effective depiction of an aspect of the Gold Rush in San Francisco. After gazing at it for several minutes, he returned to the ground floor to view a temporary collection telling the story of the Pacific Mail Steamship Company. After looking at the last painting in the exhibit, he looked at his watch: it was time to meet Marta Crofts.

He noticed her through the window of Paoli's Chop House. The bright yellow dress provided instantaneous identification. She was probably a few years on the other side of fifty, attractive, and faux blond. Frank noticed that she appeared to be nervous.

"Mrs. Crofts?" Frank asked.

"Yes, I'm Marta Crofts."

Frank put out his hand and shook hers. "Hi, Frank Molinari. Why don't we get a booth?"

He signaled the maître d', who led them to a booth and seated them.

"Would you like to have lunch?" Frank asked his companion.

"No, just coffee," she said.

Frank nodded. His stomach was still churning, and the thought of swallowing food made him feel nauseated. Under the guise of signaling for a waiter to bring them coffee, he looked at Marta Crofts. Frank's penchant for reconstructing individuals' lives from his interpretation of their appearance or from a few shards of their conversation came into play.

Marta Crofts looked, in Frank's estimation, like a woman who had expected much more out of life than she had gotten. This affair—with whomever—was probably her rebellion against her fate in life, an attempt to ward off the thought that she would die in the same, disappointed state of being as that in which she lived.

Frank gave the waiter the unwelcome news that they would be having only coffee, and then turned his attention to Marta Crofts.

"May I call you Marta?" he asked her.

"Sure."

"Marta, let me tell you why we're here. Your husband came to see me in my office today to tell me you were having an affair with my wife. He asked me to try to have my wife stop the affair. He told me a number of things about me and my children that would only have been known by someone close to me. Just a short while ago I confronted my wife, who never lies to me. She denied having any affair.

"Now, Marta, I don't want to get involved in your relationship with your husband or in any way to pass judgment on you, but I would like to find out who knows so much about me."

Marta Crofts had lowered her eyes during Frank's questioning. A blush covered her face. She looked confused, embarrassed. Her eyes were glistening, as if tears could start flowing at any moment.

She fought to control her emotions, and then looked up at Frank.

"Oh, Mr. Molinari..."

"Frank, please."

"Frank, I'm so sorry that you had to get involved in this thing between Jason and myself. I apologize that he bothered you this morning."

"It was understandable," Frank assured her. "Any man who discovers that his wife is having an affair after many years of marriage—whether that affair is lesbian or heterosexual—is going to be upset."

"This...err, situation of my having a lesbian affair has shattered Jason's universe. I feel badly...he's a kind, sweet man. But I fell in love, and I don't want to go back to the same hum-drum existence that I've lived for so many years."

How many times had those sentiments been expressed in the past few decades? Frank wondered. The liberation of women had been accompanied by a tsunami of shattered commitments. Lives that had previously seemed tenable now seemed intolerable. Frank thought that the logo for the women's movement should be the image of Oliver Twist in the workhouse, holding up his bowl and asking, "Can I have some more, sir?"

"Now, Marta, we've got to get down to whom you're having this affair with. Your husband is convinced that it's my wife. My wife denies it, and I believe her. And, so, who is this mysterious person who knows so much about my family?"

"Oh, Mr. ...Frank, I'm not having an affair with your wife. I'm having an affair with your ex-wife."

Frank dropped the spoon he was using to stir his coffee. A spasm of shocked surprise jolted through his body. The reality of Claudia, his former wife and the mother of his children, having a lesbian affair stunned him. Do the children know? he wondered. So this explained the mystery of how Marta Crofts' lover knew so much about him and his children.

The shock and surprise of Marta's revelation began to subside. Frank had long realized that Claudia was lonely and had been unable to maintain a satisfying relationship with a man. This was her response—an entry into the world of lesbianism.

"Well, that is a surprise," Frank began after a long silence. "How did you and Claudia happen to meet?"

"I'm so happy you're not angry, Frank. And I'm sorry that Jason made you think it was your present wife. You must have been upset."

"To say the least."

"Claudia and I met at our hairdresser's. We got to talking while we were waiting for our stylists and decided to have a cup of coffee after our hair was done. We enjoyed each other's company so much that we decided to get together for dinner. And the rest is history. My only regret is how much this hurts Jason."

Frank digested Marta's brief account of how she and Claudia had met and begun their affair. Now that it was all out, it was not difficult to comprehend. Marta worked at a dead-end job and was married to a kind, but dull, man. The dreary sameness of their life together had begun to pall. Claudia was lonely and very much wanted companionship. Both decided that their relationship would have a sexual component, and there they were.

"I'm not a marriage counselor, but I will urge you to consider your husband in all of this. He's in great pain. We don't have to discuss this, but just let me say that I feel sorry for him. He's a very nice man."

Marta Crofts looked sad. "I know, Frank. It breaks my heart. I don't know what's going to happen. What I would like to happen is for us to stay married and for me to continue in my relationship with Claudia."

"Hard to imagine, but anything is possible," Frank responded. "And now it's time for me to get back to the office. Thanks so much for your time and for clearing up this mystery."

"I very much enjoyed meeting you, Frank, after hearing so much about you. Claudia speaks very highly of you. And I'm sorry for all the pain this has caused you."

Frank put money down on the table to pay for their coffee and reached out his hand to shake Marta's. "It was a pleasure to meet you. And…good luck."

Frank realized that Claudia would soon know that Marta and he had met. He would call her as soon as he got to the office. He would keep Marta's revelation from Paula until they were both home that evening.

Jessica looked relieved to see Frank smiling as he strode by her desk. Frank decided he would take her to lunch in the next couple days to explain to her what had been going on. He appreciated her concern and loyalty, and didn't want to worry her unnecessarily.

Frank closed his office door, sat at his desk, and dialed Claudia's telephone number. He didn't know what he was going to say, but he felt that he needed to say something. He didn't want to let his newfound knowledge sit unacknowledged.

Claudia answered the telephone with a crisp, "Hello."

"Hi, Claudia, Frank here."

There was a bit of a pause, but Frank did not get a sense that Claudia was surprised to hear his voice. They spoke often, usually about matters having to do with the children. Their old conflicts and their harshness toward each another had evaporated, and in their place had arisen a practical relationship, perhaps even a friendship, based on the welfare of their children.

"Haven't talked with you in a while. How are you doing?"

"I'm fine. How about yourself?"

"Oh, I'm okay," Claudia responded. Frank could hear in her voice her wondering why he was calling.

"The reason for my call," Frank began, tentatively, "is that I got a real scare today. A man whom I had never heard of came into my office and told me that my wife was breaking up his marriage by having an affair with his wife, and he wanted me to stop my wife from continuing the affair. He knew so much about me and our children that I was convinced that he was right.

"Well, I got out of him his wife's name and telephone number, and I just had coffee with Marta Crofts, who was able to clear up that it was not my wife, but my ex-wife, that she was having the affair with. It's been quite a day...and it's not even half over."

There was no response...just a thick silence. Then, Claudia said, "You met Marta?"

"Yes, I met Marta. I had to find out whom she was having the affair with who knew so much about my family and myself. Paula told me that it wasn't she, and Paula never lies. I had to clear up the mystery."

"Well, I guess the news is out. Yes, I'm a lesbian. And I met Marta, and we fell in love."

"That's great, but her husband isn't too keen on the idea." His statement had an acerbic edge to it.

"That marriage has been dead for years," Claudia asserted. There was a feisty quality in her voice. "Marta deserves to come alive and have a fulfilling life."

"I don't want to get involved in other people's marriages, but I must say that I felt very sorry for Marta's husband. He looked as if he'd been punched in the stomach."

"He'll get over it," Claudia shot back. "Marta's not going to leave him."

"You're pretty compassionate. The poor man is suffering, and you're saying he'll get over it."

Frank could see that their conversation was beginning to follow a pattern that had existed from the time they were married, and which had intensified after their divorce—a back-and-forth sniping at each other. He didn't want their conversation to descend to this level.

"What is this...your Catholic thing about homosexuality?" There was almost a snarl in Claudia's voice.

"No, it's not my Catholic thing at all. What you want to do with your life and with whom you want to have relationships are entirely up to you. All I said was that Marta's husband was having a hard time with her not being faithful to him. But, let me also say that what Marta does is no concern of mine, either."

"You sounded very judgmental," Claudia responded.

Frank felt as if one of his teeth had broken off and that he was in excruciating pain from the exposed nerves. He had such a reaction whenever he heard the word "judgmental." It had become the mantra of this "I'm OK, you're OK" world that he now inhabited. What, Frank had wondered so often, is wrong with judgments? He took a deep breath in order to conceal his irritation from Claudia. No use antagonizing her over matters that were none of his business.

"I'm not judging anyone. And I guess Marta and her husband will work things out...or they won't. Do the kids know?"

"No, and I'd like to be the one to tell them."

"That's fine. My lips are sealed."

"Please keep them that way. This is nothing I'm ashamed of, and I've never been happier in my life. But I just want to let the children know in my own way."

"No problem. I wonder what their reaction will be."

Claudia's response was testy. "I guess it will be what most people's response is...disapproval. That's because for centuries people have been taught that homosexuality has been wrong, and homosexuals have been persecuted. All this religious crap has convinced people that being gay is the equivalent of being sick."

"Be prepared for some surprised people as word gets out," Frank warned his ex-wife. "For all this time you've been known as a heterosexual woman with four children. Some are going to be amazed that you're a lesbian."

"I don't care. People are going to have to accept me for who I am, or not at all. After all, human beings can change."

Frank felt some compassion for his former spouse. It was true that she was expressing her sexual "awakening" with the same unthinking impulsiveness as she had lived much of her life. She and Marta Crofts had come together as two lonely, dissatisfied women who expressed delight in each other's company in a sexual way. But Frank knew that Claudia would face hostility by some, merriment by others, ostracism by many, and the severing of social relationships by still others. The children would be loyal to their mother, but unhappy about her choice.

Frank's compassion was tempered by his annoyance at Claudia's truculence in defending her sexual preference and her utilization of New Age shibboleths in her defense. She had undergone every New Age therapy in the 1970s and 1980s, and her language was now peppered by the lingo of EST, Esalen, and other modern consciousness movements. This New Age lingua franca grated on Frank's nerves.

"All I want to do is to warn you that your decision may not be warmly accepted by a lot of people you know, so I wouldn't go around blabbing that you've come out of the closet at last. Believe me, everyone will find out soon enough."

"I'm not going to stay in the closet," Claudia retorted somewhat angrily. "I don't care what people think. It's my life. I'm just not going to hide my true feelings because I'm afraid of what people will think."

Frank sighed. Prudence was never one of Claudia's strong virtues. It was time to end their telephone conversation, Frank thought. To continue it would only lead to an argument. And, after all, Claudia was right: it was her life.

"I just want you to know that I'm with you, no matter what." Frank began the disengagement of their conversation with an ironic opening. "And I'm sure that the children will be, too. You'll have plenty of support."

"Thank you," Claudia said simply. "I appreciate that." The anger had abated.

"I'm going to have to get back to work. This has been quite a day. I'm exhausted. I'll talk with you later, Claudia."

"Goodbye, Frank. Thanks for your support."

"Take care, Claudia."

As Frank put down the telephone he felt warmly towards his ex-wife. Despite her harshness, her imprudence, and what sometimes seemed like shocking callousness, she was a good and generous soul. The months ahead would be very difficult for her.

His next sensation was to feel the exhaustion and tension in his body. Frank could not remember a day in which he had been on an emotional roller coaster such as he had been today. It would never occur to him to go to a fitness place to work out the kinks he felt in his neck and shoulders. He thought about taking a long walk or going home to take a nap, but he felt guilty about the work he had to do and the sheaf of messages that were probably awaiting him.

Frank didn't feel like returning telephone calls, so he decided to start looking at the reports on his desk—a task that he had begun what now seemed eons ago. He stared at them, sightlessly, his mind still reeling from the day's events.

It occurred to him that he should probably call Paula to give her the latest news. He dialed her work number, and she answered after the first ring.

"Hi, Sweetheart," Frank began in a cheery manner. "The mystery has been solved."

"Oh?" Paula responded. Her curiosity had been piqued.

"I had coffee with Marta Crofts, and guess who is having the affair with her?"

"Frank, for Christ's sake, just tell me. I'm not in the mood for guessing games."

Frank realized that his wife was still angry about his accusation and lack of trust. He would have to tread gingerly.

"Okay, okay. It's Claudia."

"My God, your ex-wife?" Paula exclaimed.

"None other. That's why the mystery woman knew so much about the children and me. I was stunned." Frank did not add that he was also relieved.

"I can't believe that she's a lesbian."

The amazement in Paula's voice was palpable, and Frank realized that this was a harbinger of the reaction of those who knew Claudia when they would hear the news.

"Who can?" Frank responded. "Particularly her ex-husband. But once you know it's true—and I still don't know if this is just a phase—you can understand it. Well, whatever ..."

"Frank, let me say one thing."

"Yeah, honey, what is it?"

"Never, ever, again accuse me of having an affair."

"That's a promise, Sweetheart. See you tonight. Love you."

CHAPTER 13

I t was noon, and Frank was cutting his favorite sourdough bread from the Boudin Bakery and matching it with the cold cuts. He looked at the choice of salami, prosciutto, coppa, and zampino he had purchased at Molinari's in North Beach a couple days before, and wondered why his delight in eating these today did not equal the enthusiasm he had had for them during most of his life.

He thought back to the days when his mother would give him $2 (or $5 on high feasts like Christmas and Easter) to go to the local Italian delicatessen to purchase the cold cuts for a Sunday dinner or a gathering of his family's friends. He remembered what a large parcel of cold cuts he would take back to his home for $2. For $5 he would return with a dazzling package.

Now, he thought, $5 would give him three or four slices of one kind of cold cut and a couple of smells, as he would joke with Paula.

What annoyed Frank as he folded a piece of prosciutto on a thin slice of the Boudin French bread was that he no longer craved or relished eating these cold cuts as he did during the first four or five decades of his life. Sure, he still liked wolfing down a slice of French bread topped with one of his favorite meats, but it no longer dazzled him. He could remember as a boy gobbling up several of these sandwiches with a greedy eagerness that his parents would notice, and which he would describe with delight.

When he was married to Claudia he would frequently go to the kitchen three or four hours after dinner and indulge in a few of those French-bread-and-cold-cut delights. And in the years of his post-first marriage bachelorhood, one of Frank's favorite pleasures after love-making with one of his myriad sexual partners from those days was to munch French bread, dry Monterey jack cheese, and cold cuts in his kitchen.

And, now, the thrill was gone. That highly treasured gustatory delight no longer provided him a compelling pleasure. What had happened? What transformed such an all-encompassing treat into an ordinary eating experience? Had his taste buds changed? Was there a connection between his getting older and the diminution of his pleasure in eating cold cuts?

His thoughts were leading him to his constant preoccupation with his diminished sexual prowess, his diminished emotional response to many of life's pleasures, and to his reduced excitement when Paula walked into the kitchen.

It was unusual that they were in San Francisco this weekend. For most weekends they went to their modest ranch near Healdsburg in Sonoma County. They both enjoyed the respite from their busy complex lives in San Francisco in the bucolic, relaxed atmosphere of their Healdsburg retreat. But, this week, the fortieth wedding anniversary of their friends the Lo Prestis was a compelling reason for them to stay in the city. The party would be held on the next day—Sunday—at the Bohemian Club, and he and Paula had decided that their friendship with Michelle and Dan was important enough for them to stay in San Francisco for the anniversary party.

"You didn't wait for me to have lunch?" Paula questioned as she saw Frank fumbling with the cold cuts.

"You seemed very preoccupied with your fabrics," Frank responded. "And I know when you get going, such mundane things as lunch don't have any importance."

"All you have to do is to say you're ready to have lunch, and I'll be there."

"Yeah, an hour later."

"Don't get smart. If you said that we're ready to eat and had lunch on the table, I'd be more prompt. But you generally announce that lunch is on and when I come in you ask me to make it."

Frank hated these arguments. He realized that there were merits to both their positions. Yes, he did want her to make lunch on those days they spent together. And, yet, on those days when, if he wanted lunch, he would have to prepare it himself, Paula could be a half hour late partaking of it.

He realized that these minor battles in their lives would never cease. The days of his parents—or even those of his first marriage—would never come back. His mother and his grandmother (his father's mother who had lived with his family since his parents were married) had always catered to his father. Of course, the trade-off was the responsibility for the household and the family's security. Frank's father brought in the paycheck; the women and children had been taken care of financially. The women had the responsibility for meals, the care of the household, shopping, preparing meals, and childcare. Frank still held this arrangement in high esteem.

But Paula could never be weaned from her interior design business, which was successful, and she would never trade this lucrative, satisfying business that gave her financial independence for a life that centered on taking care of his needs.

And, yet, Paula did take care of his needs. She prepared most of the meals for them. She took care of the upkeep of the house. And she was the principal architect of its aesthetic presentation.

These disagreements, Frank told himself, were the price of having an independent wife, and having an independent wife insured that he would live in a sort of dynamic tension that he liked.

Frank cut some bread from the Boudin sourdough loaf and sliced some cheese for Paula and himself. He completed the lunch by pouring each of them a glass of sauvignon blanc. The two sat down at the round glass table in the kitchen and began to eat their simple meal.

"We haven't had much alone time in the past few weeks," Paula announced after taking a sip of wine. "There's been something almost every night, either a party to go to, a musical event, or some business thing."

"Those are the rhythms of life. Thank God we've got Healdsburg to go to most weekends. It gives us a chance to catch up."

"It's great, but it's not the same as coming home and relaxing alone together after a day at work," Paula countered.

"We can cut down accepting dinner parties or fundraiser events, not go to so many concerts, and try to cut down evening business appointments." Frank wondered where Paula was going with this discontent. She was as ready as he to accept a dinner invitation from friends, to hear the symphony or some musical concert, and to meet with a client.

"Some of these things I think we can do during the day," Paula continued.

"That's true. We probably could," Frank proceeded cautiously. "If you feel that we should be home together more, I will become more conscious about not scheduling things in the evening."

Paula was silent. Frank tried to fathom her intent in this conversation. After all, she was often scheduling dinner dates with girlfriends, evenings at the ballet, or even solo excursions to the movies. What was behind this plea for more evenings at home alone?

"I don't want us to become just roommates," she began again. "We both lead full, busy lives. Neither of us depends on the other for entertainment. I love the fact that both of us like to lead independent lives. But we are married."

"And married means spending more time alone together?" Frank joked.

A look of annoyance passed over Paula's face. Perhaps he shouldn't have been so jocular, Frank thought.

"You make a joke about everything," Paula said. There was an edge in her voice. "What I am saying is that a couple needs times to be alone together in order to become increasingly intimate. Otherwise, as I said, we might as well be roommates. We go to some events together. Others we don't. We might as well be two strangers sharing a house. And one day one says to another, 'I'm going to move into another house with a new roommate.'"

Frank furrowed his brow and looked at Paula, who had turned her head to look at a lithograph hanging on their kitchen wall. This was not a random conversation on Paula's part. Her comments were coming from some deep recess of her being. What was behind it? He decided to avoid any subtle attempts to fathom the specifics of Paula's discontent, but instead to apply a frontal approach.

"So, what's the problem? 'Another house. Another roommate.' What's this all about? I know you've got some specific complaint in your mind."

Paula hesitated for a moment. "I feel as if you and I are drifting apart," she began. Here it comes, Frank said to himself. "We have a good time together. We get along pretty well...we rarely argue..."

"And there's something wrong with that?" Frank interrupted.

"No, but it's not enough," Paula continued. "Don't forget, this is a marriage. Whenever we do spend time together, I don't feel you're really there. You always seem so...so abstracted, so far away. You never hold my hand. You never just spontaneously kiss me or touch me. We only really embrace when it's a prelude to sex. And you never, ever say nice and romantic things to me. That's what's missing from our marriage."

Jesus, so here's the indictment, Frank thought. He studiously worded a quick response and made every attempt to stifle his misogynistic streak, which was never far from the surface of his emotions. What is it that women want? he asked himself once again. Can't they be satisfied with a happy and contented life? No, it's always got to be something more, something that they feel they don't have…and then they'll drive everyone crazy complaining about what's missing in their lives.

But Frank wasn't in the mood for an argument. What can I do to get her off my back, he wondered. And how serious is this? He gave thought to his response and immediately concluded that a hostile or sarcastic reply would lead to a bitter argument. Nor could he dismiss Paula's distress as nonsense.

"I don't get it," Frank began. "I think we have a wonderful marriage. Everyone who knows us thinks so, too. We get along, we have fun together, and we enjoy each other's company. We love each other. Most people would be thrilled to have this kind of marriage. And now you're grousing that it's not enough."

"It's not enough. All sorts of people can live in friendship and civility. But a marriage is something more. It needs romance. You never bring me flowers or little gifts. You never spontaneously kiss me or touch me…unless it's before having sex. You never say sweet things to me. That's the stuff of romance. That's what keeps a marriage healthy and alive."

What did God have in mind when he made marriage between men and women? Frank asked himself. It was like joining together two species, each unable to comprehend the other. It wasn't enough that he loved Paula and that they had a pleasant and fulfilling relationship; now the marriage had to be defined by flowers and small gifts, saying sweet things, and the requisite number of kisses and touches. He fought not to utter some harsh rejoinders.

"I have a feeling that if each day I said several sweet things to you, touched you, brought you flowers and small gifts—every day, mind you— and kissed you several times each day, it still wouldn't be enough."

"Try me," said Paula with a smile.

The smile helped to suppress Frank's annoyance with his wife's romantic expectations. "Tell me what's really going on with you that I'm suddenly presented with this list of my deficiencies as a husband."

"Nothing else is going on. But I've become increasingly upset by your lack of loving acts and words. It's fine to say that we love each other and enjoy each other's company, but each of us can say that about our friends. A marriage takes more."

"Why is it that men never make these demands?"

"That's a good question. Why, indeed?"

"I just don't feel that our marriage needs to be evaluated by how often

I bring you flowers or whisper sweet nothings into your ear. It's a good marriage because we love each other, we support each other, and we enjoy each other's company. Do you think our mothers were disgruntled because your father or my father didn't buy them flowers or didn't kiss them all the time?"

"We'll never know, and, besides, we pride ourselves on being more enlightened than our parents and wanting to grow our love more than they were capable of doing."

Frank took a swallow of wine and bit into his sandwich. Paula did the same. They chewed their food in silence.

There was no doubt in Frank's mind that Paula was serious about what she considered the defects in their relationship. He realized that he would have to try to remedy what she considered his romantic deficiencies, even though he considered them bunk.

It was not that he considered such actions—kissing, the occasional intimate touch, the compliment, and the bringing of flowers or gifts—to be wrong. On the contrary, he thought them fine. But it never occurred to him to do any of them. Much of their time together he spent being preoccupied—about work, mostly. It had never been in his nature to say sweet nothings or to buy flowers. Somehow it just wasn't who he was.

And now he knew he was going to be sucked into this vortex of romance and that he would promise to be more attentive to these things. Couldn't she just let him be in peace? It was just one more goddamn thing he had to worry about, to keep in his mind. One would think that at his age he could expect some tranquility in his life instead of going around worrying about buying flowers, kissing, touching, and saying sweet things that always sounded dumb.

"I always want to make you happy, and if you think those things would bring romance into your life and make you happy, then I can try to do them," Frank conceded.

"Our life! Our life! Not my life," Paula insisted with a vehemence that surprised Frank. "We're a couple. You want to do these things because they're spontaneous signs of your love for me, and I do them because I love you. Doing them shouldn't be a chore."

"Well, they're a chore for me!" Frank shot back. "This is a woman's thing. It may come naturally to you, but it sure as hell doesn't to me. Maybe I can grow into it; but, even if I did, you would still be complaining that it's not enough."

Frank's resolve not to let their discussion become a full-blown argument had dissolved. He had been looking at Paula as he had been speaking and saw her look turn into one of mingled anger and hurt.

"That's not true, and you know it," she retorted. "I've done everything I could to enhance this marriage and to make our love grow. Look at all the things I do for you. I do occasionally bring you small gifts. I do give you spontaneous kisses and hugs. And none of this is a burden for me. And it's not just because I'm a woman. Men have romance in their hearts, too."

Frank knew that to pursue his thoughts on this matter would be to precipitate a heated argument between them, which would then lead to a period of coolness. He wasn't in the mood for such a scenario; it took too much energy. What he would do is to placate her and hope that this romantic phase would pass with time.

"Okay, okay, you know what I'll do? It's time for the red-dot-on-the-watch approach."

Paula looked at him and smiled. "And I know that once you get started, you'll wonder why you haven't been doing it all along."

Putting a red dot on the face of one's watch had been a behavior modification device that Paula had brought to their relationship from one of her California New Age experiences. You put a red dot on your watch, and every time you look at it, it reminds you to fulfill whatever your resolve was for that time period.

Actually, Frank had used a similar device many years before during his stint as a Jesuit novice. A wire with a number of beads was pinned in the inside of one's cassock. Let's say that you wished to affirm something or you wished to get rid of some habit. You would determine what you needed to do, and for each time you did it you pulled one bead from one side of the wire to the other. You could thus measure your progress at the end of the day—or week, or month—by keeping track of the number of beads you had pulled.

Frank got up from the kitchen table and walked over to one of the drawers next to the kitchen sink. He rifled through the drawer until he found a supply of red dots. He pulled one triumphantly from the cards that held them, and walked over to Paula.

"Will you please place this on my watch, my dear?" he asked.

"With pleasure," Paula responded. She stuck the red dot in the middle of his watch's face, and then kissed him on the cheek. "And may you become a romantic," she said.

"Let's not get carried away," Frank said, laughing. "You might not like the transformed Frank Molinari."

"You want to bet? I like the present Frank Molinari, but I'd like him a lot more if he would bring more romance to our relationship."

"Okay, okay, okay. I get the point, and here's the red dot to prove that I get your point. And here's my opening romantic move."

Frank bent down and gave Paula a kiss on her lips, simultaneously touching her breast. "See, two for the price of one."

"Funny. I said you should be romantic, not a jerk," Paula said, tossing her head.

"I think I'm going to go out for an aerobic walk," Frank announced. "Then I'll come home, take a shower, and do some work."

"I can't believe we don't have an engagement tonight," Paula said. "Just the two of us together and alone."

"A romantic evening together," Frank laughingly commented. "My favorite way to spend time. And there's no one I would rather spend time alone with than you. See, there's a sweet nothing. Give me a point for romance."

Paula playfully pushed him out of the kitchen. "Go take your walk."

Frank quickly changed his clothes, gave Paula a goodbye kiss, walked down the steps of his home, and began the purposeful stride that characterized his aerobic walk.

His path was always the same: west on Washington Street to Presidio Terrace, where he would loop around, and then head east along Clay Street to Alta Plaza Park, where he would walk along the perimeter of the park and take in the splendid views of San Francisco before striding back home. It took fifty minutes, and he enjoyed the exercise.

The walk gave Frank a chance to have a "monkey mind," chattering and hopping from one idea to another. Despite the many times he had seen the houses, he was always delighted when he saw some architectural detail he hadn't noticed before. His memory would bring out some anecdotes about people he knew or had known who lived in the houses he passed. It gave him a strong sense of the passing of time. There were people who had been in his life and were now dead. There were those whom he no longer saw. There were even those whom he no longer cared for...or they him. *Mutatis mutandis*, Frank thought.

Sometimes his mind would wander to some book he was reading, some abstract idea that had come into his head, or some new addition to one of his collections. The time he spent always passed quickly, and in what seemed like an instant he was walking up the stairs of his home.

As he was making his loop of Alta Plaza Park, Frank looked up to see the strapping figure of Christopher Fermoyle, looking at him with an ironic smile.

"Taking care of the exigencies of the body, Francis? *Mens sana in corpore sano*," intoned his friend.

Christopher was holding his two King Charles spaniels—Gog and Magog—on leashes, and was dressed in what Frank thought typical Fermoyle fashion: gray woolen slacks, a blue Brooks Brothers blazer, and a violet ascot tucked into a white Oxford shirt.

"Christopher, what brings you to Pacific Heights from the sacred precincts of Nob Hill?" Frank was surprised to see his friend walking his dogs so far from where he lived.

"I thought I would experience the dog-walking habits of another enclave of privilege and observe the habits of a geographically diverse group of canine lovers. I notice a much younger crowd here than on Nob Hill."

"Lots of singles live in this area," Frank responded to Christopher's whimsy. "I don't see how they can afford the rents or the prices of houses."

"Young people will sacrifice much to establish good addresses. They think doing so gives them a 'leg up' in the marriage and job markets. That way, they believe, they can duplicate the upward mobility of their upper-middle-class parents and grandparents."

The King Charles spaniels looked at Christopher as he spoke, quizzical expressions on their faces. They've gotten used to their master's eccentricities, Frank mused.

"And how is the 'Last Gentleman in San Francisco'?" Frank asked.

"Peeved with you," Fermoyle answered, a disapproving frown registering on his face. "When we lunched last week, you said you would be in contact with Marianne, and, you unfeeling, uncaring, naughty boy, you haven't done so."

Frank felt a spasm of guilt and embarrassment. He had totally forgotten about his resolution to see Marianne in the hospital. His mind had been filled with other things, but he still felt guilty about not going to see her.

"Is she still in the hospital?" he inquired.

"She went home yesterday, but she's still weak from this mysterious malady. I know she would very much enjoy seeing you...why, I don't know. You're such a faithless friend."

"I'm really sorry I didn't call her immediately, but it's been a crazy week." Frank didn't feel inclined to discuss the particulars of the past week with his friend. "I'll call her as soon as I get home. I'm sorry to hear that she's been ill."

"I'm afraid that she's not in very good spirits. Perhaps you'll be able to lift them. Maybe the memories of when the two of you had sexual congress with bring smiles to her face."

Frank smiled. His friend's expressions had charmed him for almost fifty years, and his whimsicalities still had the power to amuse him. Christopher Fermoyle would always be one of the great pleasures of his life.

"Either that or she may suffer a relapse," Frank joked.

"Don't be so modest, Francis. I'm sure that your Italian exuberance made you a most delicious swordsman.

"But, on to other things. Are you still suffering from your crisis on discovering that you are mortal?"

"It's been a crazy week since we've lunched," Frank answered. "I've been too preoccupied to focus on my crisis. Perhaps it's passed."

"Oh, it will be back, I can assure you. It will indeed be back. Everyone has to face contemplation of the inevitability of death and the fear it brings. However, there are few who are as forthright as yourself in discussing those fears."

"When I feel like another discussion I'll call you for lunch."

"Do so, Francis, do so. I enjoy conversations on the fears of personal annihilation."

"Ah, Christopher," Frank said laughing. "Deep down, you are a lugubrious sort."

"Not at all. Not at all, dear friend. But I do believe that the best conversations are about death and its impact on our lives. As we get older and death's reality becomes clearer to us, we are faced with that basic question: will death mean our ceasing to exist in any way or does it mean entrance into everlasting life? You and I are now engaged in answering that question for ourselves."

Frank was eager to end the conversation on death. Christopher could go on and on, he thought. He would try to switch it to one of Christopher's current manias: the antics of local politicians.

"Well, on to another subject," Frank proclaimed. "Are you still actively following local politics?"

Christopher Fermoyle looked grim and pulled himself up to his full height. "Those rogues," he pronounced magisterially. "Those rogues should be taken out and shot like dogs. Never have a group of legislators been such a disgrace—never in the history of mankind."

"So you don't have an opinion?" Frank inquired laughingly.

The joke did not stop Christopher's stream of indignant invectives. "Fools. Petulant children. Communists. And the fact that the voters allow these buffoons to stay in office is a permanent stain on the collective soul of this city. It is incredible that this so-called board of supervisors isn't horsewhipped or tar-and-feathered out of this city!"

Frank knew that Christopher despised most of the sitting members of the board for being too liberal and for their childish antics when their pet projects or ideas were opposed or voted down. But, Frank knew, it was the board of supervisors' increasing tendency to approve restrictions on the owners of income property that made Christopher apoplectic. He felt his rights were being infringed upon by a group of ideologically bankrupt politicians out to advance utopian causes by lessening the value of his assets. Christopher was but one of many real estate owners—perhaps the most articulate one—who detested what he was considered to be a permanent majority of renting helotry in San Francisco.

Christopher was almost purple-faced after delivering his harangue. Frank noticed that he was even trembling in indignation. Frank made no immediate response to Christopher's outburst, but instead looked around the lawns of Alta Plaza Park. It was filled with dogs and their owners — mostly young, but with a sprinkling of older residents of the area. Many had met while allowing their dogs to scamper about and had become friends... at least for the time they were in the park. Most people—strangers to one another—talked amiably in a brief spasm of neighborhood conviviality.

The scene brought Frank back to his youth, when everybody in the neighborhood knew one another. They did not necessarily like their neighbors, but they all knew one another. No dog-walking venue was needed to know your neighbors. You knew them from the time you were a child. You played with the children who were around your age. You ran errands for the elderly in the neighborhood. When your mother was sick, one of the ladies in the neighborhood would come over to do the wash and hang it out on the clothesline. Another would bring over supper for the family.

Now, it seemed to Frank, most residents of a neighborhood did not stay very long, did not grow up there, and triangulated between their houses or apartments to work to some social engagement. The neighborhood was only a geographical backdrop to their lives.

Oh, well, Frank thought. It's a start to have these scores of Pacific Heights residents cheerfully engaging in conversation because their dogs' leashes tangled together or for whatever reason. And, Frank smilingly thought, there was probably no one else in the park discussing death or inventives on the San Francisco Board of Supervisors.

"Well, Francis, I should be getting the pooches home," Christopher answered. "What are you and the Lovely One doing this weekend? I'm surprised to see that you're not in Healdsburg."

"A friend of Paula's is having a big anniversary party tomorrow tonight, which is why we aren't in the country. Tomorrow is free, though, and I think I'll see if I can visit Marianne then."

"That's a splendid idea, Francis," Christopher responded. "She would be pleased to see you."

"I'll call her when I get home."

Frank and Christopher said goodbye, and Frank walked the remaining blocks to his house. Paula was arranging some flowers as he walked in. He noticed the red dot. Frank walked over to Paula, put his arms around her, and kissed her.

"You look gorgeous, Sweetheart," he told her.

CHAPTER 14

Marianne looked wan, certainly older than when he had first met her almost a half century before, but she still had a captivating smile and still had the élan that had made her such a compelling presence in his life and the lives of a number of his contemporaries so many years ago.

Frank had called her shortly after getting home from his aerobic walk the day before. Now they were sitting together in a glass-covered addition to her house in Seacliff. Both seemed somewhat uncomfortable. Was it because they had had an affair some years before, Frank asked himself, or was it because they saw in themselves faded and unrealized dreams?

"I'm glad that you're feeling better," Frank said after they were seated in the solarium, "but I can't believe the doctors don't know what's wrong with you."

"We never think that medicine has any limitations until we ourselves are faced with these limitations. Sometimes I think that I'd rather know that I was dying of something, than not know what my illness is…even if it is not life threatening."

"Hopefully, whatever it is that you have will go away just as mysteriously as it appeared," Frank said.

"You and I both. It's a drag to be sick."

Marianne sat looking at Frank. He was amazed at how well preserved she looked. Her face was still the perfect oval shape. It had not puffed up, as faces tend to do as one gets older. Her doe-like, almond-shaped brown eyes still had a sparkle. And she was still trim. Age, Frank thought, had treated her kindly.

"I'm sorry that I haven't kept in touch, Marianne," said Frank, pleased that she had not launched into a long disquisition on what her doctors had said, what her stay in the hospital had been like, and other myriad self-preoccupied details that sick people heaped upon their listeners.

"I haven't been so good at that either, Frank. What is it about getting older? It seems we never have time or energy for anything. When we were in college it seemed like we were able to do everything. I took eighteen units each semester, had lots of time to spend with friends, did a number of extracurricular activities, went to mixers and other parties, and often could stay up all night."

Frank smiled at Marianne's accurate reminiscences. "I guess that's why they call it old age," he responded. "Life contracts."

"What an awful thought. Who would have thought, back in college, that we'd be sitting here lamenting the shortcomings of advancing old age?"

"In those days we thought we'd never die," Frank said. "Oh, sure, we knew it intellectually, but not emotionally. Life stretched out before us like an infinite plain, full of hope and promises, of perpetual youth and health."

Marianne giggled. She held out her hand to hold Frank's. "You always put things so well," she told him. "And you were always such a romantic. You certainly have done well with your life; and getting older has been kind to you."

"You're being kind, as you always were. I can't begin to tell you—you know a lot of them already—how many disappointments I've had in my life...and, you know, what we were just talking about...our dreams and hopes in college, our exuberance, our limitless vitality. And now I sit here, hoping I don't get senile."

"Remember when we read about 'the ages of man'?" Marianne answered him. "It was an accurate description of what happens to us as we go through life."

"When I read it last, I grasped the concept in my mind. But I never emotionally experienced its reality, as I do now."

"There's no escaping it, Frank. I sat for days in the hospital, wondering 'How did I get here?' I used to be as healthy as a horse. I could push my body as much as I wanted. And here I was sick in the hospital, with no one knowing what's wrong with me. It really depressed me."

"Christopher told me you were pretty 'down.'"

"He has been terrific," Marianne said. "No one could have been more caring."

"Christopher Fermoyle is great," said Frank, feeling guilty again about not visiting Marianne while she was in the hospital. "Beneath that crusty, eccentric exterior, there is a kind, generous person."

"He seems to be so lonely," Marianne said, concern in her voice. "There's nobody in my life at the moment, but I was married for a number of years. But, Christopher...well, he's always been alone."

"Being alone doesn't necessarily mean being lonely, Marianne. I think Christopher realized early on that his inclinations and personality would not thrive—or even mesh well—with a mate, and he decided to live life independently. He's structured his life so that he can do pretty much what he wants when he wants. He has tons of friends—or, I should say acquaintances—and an adequate number of friends. He's got his clubs..."

"I don't think of those as substitutes for having one intimate, committed relationship."

"Can you see Christopher in one intimate, committed relationship?" Frank asked.

"Sure...well, maybe not," Marianne laughed. "It would be a very unusual person who could live with Christopher, I admit."

"I still see him often," Frank continued, "although we don't visit each other as much as we used to. But the rhythms of his life are totally unsuitable to a relationship of the kind you describe. Can you imagine Christopher whispering 'sweet nothings' to a wife? No, I think his life is full, and I think he's very happy with it."

"Maybe you're right, Frank. Of all the people I still see, he's the most unchanged. Oh, sure, he looks older, but I can close my eyes and still see the Christopher Fermoyle of our college days."

"That's what comes with a life without care. Not that I think there's anything wrong with that," Frank laughed. "Think about it. Christopher's health has been excellent. He's always lived without economic want, and, as it turned out, his parents' deaths, just as he was getting out of school, have allowed him to lead a comfortable life without having to work. He never had the cares of a family. And he's been able to live just the kind of life he's wanted to. I think this kind of life keeps you the same. It's almost as if you've been mummified."

"I don't think of Christopher as mummified," Marianne interjected.

"Think about it. When you said he was unchanged, you were right. Close your eyes and listen to him: you could be hearing the Christopher Fermoyle of fifty years ago. The expressions are the same. The lilt in his voice is the same. His opinions are the same. He's like a Chinese mandarin during the Ming dynasty. And I think this comes from never having to deal with the ups-and-downs of life that most people experience."

"You're probably right. At any rate you make a pretty good case as to why he's unchanged."

"I don't mean this analysis in any critical way. I think it helps to explain his unique characteristics," Frank said.

"Then there's me," Marianne continued. "I'm half mummified."

"Oh, no," Frank interjected. "You're Marianne the Magnificent. You were the liveliest gal during my school years. How can you be mummified? Half or whole?"

Marianne looked both elated and saddened by Frank's comment. Her oval face seemed opaque, as if the Marianne of her late-teens and twenties lay just beneath the face of the still beautiful but older Marianne of her sixties. There was something wrong with the lustrous eyes, though, Frank thought. The sparkle was still there...but not as much. Those eyes were still beautiful, still luminous, but they seemed dead, as if something had died in Marianne...something that she wished to hide.

"Oh, Frank, you're wonderful, but you're wrong. I was brought up, as you know, as a privileged only child of a well-off family. I married and then divorced a wealthy man. I have never worked in my life. I didn't have children. I haven't even had very many close relationships. Don't you think that this has been—and is—at least a half-mummified life?"

Before Frank had a chance to respond, Marianne continued. "I love the fact that I've been able to study Sophocles and Virgil and Dante and Aquinas and Kirkegaard and to discuss them...often with you and Christopher. I've had great rambles and fun times. I loved acting in the plays at St. Ignatius...and I really loved the cast parties afterwards. But none of this made me a whole person. Mine has been a wasted life."

Marianne looked as if she were on the verge of tears. Frank was stricken by the vehemence of her self-castigations.

"Come on, Marianne, how can you say that?" Frank leaned toward her, and took her hands in his. "You have led a superb life. You were like a Madonna to us when we were in school. You were attractive, you were bright, and you were fun. Conversing with you was sheer delight. And how many of us have gotten divorced? Others haven't had children. What are the characteristics of a fulfilled life? Damn it; don't say that yours is a wasted life."

Marianne patted one of his hands. "Frank, you're a sweet man, but, however you configure a fulfilled life, mine wouldn't be considered one by any definition. It's been too selfish. What I studied...what I loved to converse about...the parties I went to...my marriage...even my divorce—don't you see all these things were about me? The fact that I never had children was sign of my barrenness; it was a symbol that I never in my life lived in any way for others. That's a wasted life."

Frank was startled and confused by his friend's deprecations of herself. He couldn't get rid of his images of the glamorous, sophisticated Marianne—the Marianne sitting with him and his friends, discussing the meaning of life and variations on this theme, holding forth on the ideas of Gabriel Marcel, Marianne at the opera, Marianne at the symphony, Marianne playing Joan of Arc in The Lark. How could her life be a wasted one, Frank asked himself, and, if it were, what about his? True, he had children, but, then, so did other people—many of whom he considered truly to have led wasted lives. And, true, he had worked, but then, he had had to. Would he have worked if he had been the recipient of a large trust fund?

"Frank, let's go out into the garden," Marianne interrupted his musings. "It's one of those few days in San Francisco when it's possible to do so."

"Sure, sounds great."

The two arose, both pleased to have a respite from their conversation. Marianne's self-doubting was troubling Frank. For her to feel that her life had been wasted shook Frank's sense of what constituted a good life, a fulfilled life. Her thoughts unnerved him, threw him into a morass of doubt.

They walked through the French doors into a manicured garden, splayed with the unusual warmth of a San Francisco afternoon, and sat down on a stone bench facing a small fountain. The sound of the gurgling water and the garden's sunny tranquility tempered Frank's internal anxiety. They sat in silence.

"Do you remember when Tony Ghilardi forgot to come out on stage as the messenger, and Tom Riley had to summarize his lines as if he had received a vision?" Marianne asked with a soft laugh.

"How could I forget?" Frank answered, chortling. "It was my first play at St. Ignatius and I thought I was going to die of embarrassment. But, you know, not one person that I asked later noticed the gaffe. I was amazed."

The two friends traded anecdotes about their college years for an hour. Giggling and laughing about their reminiscences, they reached back into the recesses of their memories for those events they thought the most amusing. Some Frank remembered, but Marianne did not; others Marianne related, but Frank did not recall. As they told their stories and laughed once again at them, both felt that the nearly half-century that had elapsed since had disappeared; in reliving them it was as if they were once again living in the 1950s. The intervening years—years of graduate school, of marriage and divorce, of raising children, of work, of relationships made and ended, of financial travail—all seemed to disappear. Frank and Marianne lived once again in an era when life spread before them as if it would never end and that happiness and fulfillment in their lives were a birthright.

"We'd better stop this," Frank said after chuckling over yet another anecdote that Marianne had just told. He was pleased to see her become enlivened by their musings and storytelling about the past. "We're going to 'split a gut,' as my mother would have said. Thank God Paula's not here. She hates it when I go on with stories about a time and place where she wasn't present and about people she didn't know."

Marianne became serious again. "How is Paula, Frank, and how is your relationship?"

Frank was surprised at the question. "Oh, she's fine…busy as ever. And our relationship is fine. We get along very well together."

"I'm happy to hear that. I think she's very good for you, and I think you make a great couple. But, I must say that I was surprised when the two of you got married."

"No kidding? Why was that?" Frank was intrigued.

"Oh, I don't know…I didn't think…at that time…you know, when it appeared to be a serious relationship…that the two of you…um…well, had that much in common."

Frank could see that Marianne was embarrassed by her comment and by having to answer his query. But he wanted to hear her reasons why his choice of a wife seemed so improbable.

"What were the dissimilarities?" Frank pursued.

"Oh, you know, you were such an intellectual, and I didn't think Paula had the interests you did in history, literature, philosophy, and so forth. Your idea of exercise is picking up a glass, and she's an avid skier and runner. I don't know…it seemed that your temperaments were so different. She was precise, and organized, and pretty contained. And you were the opposite: vague, disorganized, and a volatile Italian."

Frank laughed. "Well, you know what they say: opposites attract."

"That was true for you the first time, and somehow the attraction didn't last," Marianne replied acerbically.

Frank winced. He didn't expect Marianne to start an argument about his choices of wives.

"Claudia was a youthful mistake. I didn't know myself and I had no idea of the nature of a marital relationship. I don't think the fact that she and I were so different entered the equation, even though I know a lot of people felt that it did.

"With Paula it was different. I had been single after my divorce for more than 15 years. I'd had a lot of experience with women. I had certainly contemplated the nature of relationships—marital and otherwise. And I had a lot of thoughts about how to make a marriage work—ideas that, fortunately, have proved to be helpful."

"Oh, Frank, I didn't mean to disparage your choice of Paula as a wife. I just didn't think she would stimulate you enough; that's all I meant. And, obviously, I was wrong."

"You're not alone in thinking that. A lot of people have told me or implied to me that they didn't think Paula would be intellectually stimulating to me. But the truth is that intellectually stimulating women have never been prime candidates for a wife as far as I'm concerned."

Marianne looked crestfallen. "Why is that?" she asked.

"Oh, I don't know. I have found most intellectual women I have known not to be overly concerned about domestic arrangements—something that is very important to me. Then there's the matter that competition raises its ugly head. I have found that I can get intellectual stimulation from friends or others. I don't feel that I have to marry it."

Marianne's expression had stiffened, "What do you and Paula talk about?" she inquired.

"The usual things, I guess. The truth is that we don't have all that much time together. We both work, so we don't connect, except maybe for a brief phone call each day, until we get home at night. We'll chat before dinner and during dinner about our day or about business matters...by that I mean things having to do with the nuts-and-bolts of our lives...about mutual friends...that kind of stuff. Then, after dinner, we'll read or maybe watch some television. When we're in Healdsburg, we're both busy during the day. During the evening we have the same kinds of conversations we have in the city. And, keep in mind, that in San Francisco many evenings we're busy with social engagements and meetings."

"Hmm. Then you really don't discuss ideas."

"Well, I wouldn't say that. We do discuss ideas. But I can't say that we sit down and discuss Plato's ideas or Thomas Aquinas' definition of 'the good.' Our conversations are not just idle chit-chat, if that's what you're asking."

A shadow of annoyance had crept into both of their responses. Frank was puzzled by Marianne's pursuit of the topic. There were many people who had questioned his intellectual compatibility with both of his wives. But, while he thoroughly enjoyed conversations with intellectual women (and loved to screw them), he had never contemplated marrying one. Both Claudia and Paula were bright, intelligent women; it wasn't as if he'd married the town airheads.

"I wasn't saying that you and Paula only engaged in idle chit-chat," Marianne countered. "I was just curious about the content of your conversations, that's all."

Frank thought later that he should have changed the topic. But that was not his way. Instead, he continued it as a dog gnaws on a bone.

"I guess I always get defensive when people imply that I, the big intellectual, married some dumb-shit, that…"

"I never said you married some dumb-shit. I merely…"

"But you implied it by asking the questions you did."

Marianne suddenly stood up. "No, I didn't. I was only asking a friend a question about his life. I wasn't implying anything."

Frank could see that she was angry. What had happened? he asked himself. What had caused their pleasant nostalgic conversation to become contentious?

"Okay, okay," Frank stoically responded, "Let's let it drop. I don't know how we got embroiled in such a silly subject. If Paula's happy and I'm happy, what difference does any of it make?"

Marianne did not answer. Frank looked up at her and saw that there were tears glistening in her eyes. Her head sunk down, and she began to sob.

Frank stood up and gently put his hand on her arm. "Marianne, what's the matter?" he asked with concern.

She shook her head, as if trying to stop crying, but the sobs continued to convulse her body. Eventually, they began to subside.

Marianne looked at Frank and said, "I'm sorry, Frank, but at one time I thought that we might be together…that we might be closely connected… that…"

So that was it. They together had caused the boil to be lanced. Frank was stunned. He had never suspected that Marianne had been in love with him and thought they might marry.

He was momentarily nonplussed, but then put his arm around her waist and murmured, "Marianne, I'm sorry. I never knew."

She angled away from his arm, took out a handkerchief to daub her eyes, and, in a harsh voice, said to him, "Of course you never knew. You were too busy fucking all those other women."

"Now, Marianne, this is unfair. We were both divorced, we got together for dinner, had a little too much to drink, and tumbled into bed. We repeated the sexual experience several times more, and then we didn't. I've always thought of you as a cherished friend, a sister, not a lover."

"Yeah, well I didn't think of you as a brother. Even during those chaste days when you were at St. Ignatius, I wondered why you never asked me out on a date. Oh, I know, we palled around together—you, Christopher, and I...and sometimes others—but you never asked me out on a date, even though we always had a good time together."

"I was a mess in those days. I was shy around women. I had low self-esteem about my looks. Even to kiss a girl I dated was beyond me. And you were like a goddess...tall, good-looking, smart, sophisticated...and you dated older men. Sure, we hung out together, but Christopher and I were like part of your court. I no more dreamed of dating you than I did of dating Marilyn Monroe."

Marianne had seated herself once again on the stone bench in her garden. "How about after your divorce, when you had become a man of the world?" she asked. "You weren't so in awe of me then."

"I've always been in awe of you, Marianne. I have never gotten over my image of you as the 'golden girl,' the desirable, but unreachable goddess, even during the brief period of time when we were sleeping together."

Marianne sighed and was silent. She looked somewhat embarrassed by her tears and outburst. Both of them seemed unsure of what to do or say next.

Marianne broke the silence. "I'm sorry, Frank, it was unfair. I've always liked you, maybe even loved you. When we were in school, I knew you were pretty gauche with women, uncomfortable with them in romantic settings, but I could never figure out why you never asked me for a date. Now I guess I know why.

"When we 'tumbled into bed,' as you put it, I thought that finally might have been the connection. We were both available. You had gotten over your sexual constraints. We went out, had a wonderful time every time, as we had always had, and were sleeping together...having sex. This was it, I told myself. But, then, you didn't call to go out anymore. You moved on to some other woman or women. I was very hurt and disappointed. It was my fault for expecting so much."

Frank felt abashed. What he thought had been a fling with an old friend hadn't been so for Marianne. He had adored her as a friend, but he had not found her as exciting as a lover, and never considered her as a potential wife. Funny thing, he thought, you finally bed someone who for years had dazzled you and you're...well, if not disappointed, then not carried away enough to make you propose. The thought of Peggy Lee's song, "Is That All There Is?" crossed his mind.

"I'm flattered, Marianne, and surprised. I don't know what more to say. Even if I had known your feelings, I don't know if anything would have worked out differently. I could never get over my sense of awe of you... and awe of another is not a great component in a committed relationship."

"Okay, okay, Frank. Enough. What's past is past. I certainly couldn't have changed your feelings."

"But, Marianne, I want you to realize that my love for you, my deep friendship with you, wasn't...isn't...a romantic love. I love you, but not in that way."

"I understand, Frank. Let's let it be. If whatever ails me hadn't made me so depressed and feeling lonely, I never would have cried and blurted all this out. But, thanks for your love and friendship."

"You've had that since I've known you."

They settled once more into an uncomfortable silence. Their recent exchange had made any light conversation impossible. Each sat wrapped in a cocoon of embarrassment. What could they say next? Frank decided that they had to part, sorry that their next encounter would be shadowed by Marianne's revelations and his guilt and sorrow that he couldn't have fulfilled her desires. They could not control how they felt. He felt dispirited that this splendid woman was aging and ailing, alone and depressed, and he felt helpless to do anything about it.

Frank broke the silence. "Well, I think it's time that I best be getting home. I've got a number of things I need to do for work. Is there anything I can do for you? Anything I can get you?"

"No, I'm fine. Anna has done the shopping and has prepared meals for me...not that I'm very hungry. I'll be fine."

Frank began to head for the French doors that led from the garden into Marianne's house. Marianne followed him. When they reached the front door to the house, Frank turned to look at Marianne. Her head hung down, afraid to meet his gaze.

"Marianne, it's been great seeing you. I had a lovely visit. I had no idea about the feelings you expressed...really, I'm so sorry. I..."

"Don't worry about it, Frank. We feel what we feel. I'll be okay. It was great of you to come over. The next time I see you I'll be more chipper."

Frank leaned over, put his hands on her shoulders and softly kissed her cheek. Her head continued to hang.

"Goodbye, Marianne," he said.

"Goodbye, Frank. I'll see you soon, I hope."

He opened the door and walked down the stairs of her house. On the sidewalk he turned and waved. She looked wan and sad. He could see tears in her eyes. She smiled, waved, and then the door closed.

Morose and at odds with himself, Frank slowly walked up the steps into the house. Paula had a fire in the fireplace and was sitting reading in the living room. She looked up and smiled.

"Hi, Sweetheart," she welcomed him. "How was your visit? How is Marianne feeling?"

Frank slumped into a leather chair. He wasn't in the mood for a cheery conversation, but he also felt that he couldn't let his glumness pervade the room.

"It's always great seeing Marianne," he responded to his wife, trying to manage to smile. "We go back a long way. But I'm concerned about her health. The doctors don't seem to know what's wrong with her. It's depressing her."

"That's really too bad. It's bad enough to be sick, but it's terrible not to know what's wrong with you."

"No kidding. But, anyway, we shared a lot of memories."

Frank couldn't decide whether to tell Paula about Marianne's revelations of her feelings for him, but quickly decided not to. What would that accomplish? he asked himself. It would probably only create ill feelings on Paula's part toward Marianne.

"You're filled with memories. You must be getting old," Paula joked.

"So old that I think I'm going to take a short nap before we go out. Will you wake me up in forty-five minutes?"

"Sure. I'm going to sit here and read until then."

Frank walked upstairs to his bedroom, removed his shoes, pants, and shirt, and lay down on his bed. He felt exhausted. This has been some week, he thought. There was the intense time when he thought his wife was having an affair, only to discover that his ex-wife had become a lesbian. And then, today, Marianne's revelations. He felt overloaded, wrung out.

He was softly snoring when Paula came in, kissed him on the lips, and gently nudged him. "It's been an hour, dear. Time to go."

CHAPTER 15

Frank was tying his somber blue tie in front of the mirror. Thales of Miletus had said "All is water," and Frank felt that Thales, considered to be the first Greek philosopher, may have been right. The rain poured in windy gusts outside, beating a loud tattoo on the windows.

As he finished tying his Windsor knot, Frank looked at his disgruntled face in the mirror. He did not remember a time in recent years when he had felt so morose. He was in no mood to go out in the teeming rain to the event that he must attend: Marianne's funeral at St. Ignatius Church.

Two weeks after Frank and Marianne had seen each other, when Marianne had made her confession of love, Christopher called him to say that Marianne had been readmitted to the hospital. It had been Frank's intention, after Christopher's call, to buy her a large bouquet of flowers and visit her. But several days had elapsed, and Frank still hadn't gone to visit Marianne. Then Christopher had called to say that Marianne had died. Frank was stunned…and filled with bitter regrets.

Today he was to be one of the pallbearers at Marianne's funeral mass. A chapter in his life had closed, he thought. The Magnificent Marianne, as Frank and a few of his friends had called her when they knew her as students, was no more.

Paula was to meet him at the church, so Frank guided the Jaguar by himself through the beating rain to St. Ignatius Church. Water poured down the gutters, even down the streets themselves, as Frank drove to the church. At almost every corner there was one of those ponds created when the sewer intake got plugged.

There had been no viewing of the body at the funeral home. Marianne's instructions for her funeral were quite specific: a funeral mass at St. Ignatius Church and then burial at Holy Cross Cemetery. No vigil at the funeral parlor, no reception afterward.

Frank parked in a lot reserved for the St. Ignatius faculty. He wasn't in the mood to drive around, looking for a legal parking place. He would take his chances.

There was a lull in the intensity of the rain, but Frank still needed an umbrella. He walked rapidly towards the church that loomed above him.

St. Ignatius Church stood before him—a superb example of Italian baroque, dominated by two spires, a campanile, and a dome. Built after the earthquake and fire of 1906 had destroyed the existing church and college, the church, which continued to be the largest church in San Francisco, was the first structure constructed for the reconstituted college; and virtually all the Jesuit community money had gone into building the magnificent church. The fathers stinted on everything else. Classes were held in nearby ramshackle buildings. There was virtually no library. The science laboratories were primitive. The Jesuits had made the decision to honor God with a magnificent temple—this was their first priority—and the rest would somehow follow. It was an ultimate act of belief in God's Providence...and, in most eyes, an act of folly.

Frank entered a side door into the church and walked up the narrow staircase to the sacristy. He knew the way well, as he had traversed it many times when he was a student at St. Ignatius College, frequently serving mass as an altar boy.

The sacristy was just as big as he remembered it—one of two cavernous spaces flanking the church's sanctuary, where dozens of priests would vest each morning before going out to say mass at the main altar or one of the many side altars. How times have changed, Frank thought: today, perhaps two priests vest in the sacristy, and the side altars were being dismantled.

Christopher Fermoyle had already arrived and was standing silently contemplating the vestiges of a departed religious sensibility.

"I feel as if I'm standing in the midst of an abandoned Sumerian temple," Christopher said when he saw Frank, "or a Druid grove, after Druidism had been proscribed, and only one Druid priest continued to secretly tend the sacred fires."

Frank smiled as he reached out his hand to shake Christopher's. His friend tended to make dramatic and colorful comparisons.

"I know," Frank said, "I feel as if I'm seeing ghosts at the vesting tables."

"We'd be standing here now, in cassock and surplice, waiting to accompany Father So-and-So down to one of the side altars, listen to him murmur the mass, and then return here before going off to classes. Lovely."

"It's amazing how, as we get older, we look back on so many changes. I thought then that all these things would stay the same. Now, the priests have dwindled to a handful, the side altars are being taken out, the mass is said in English, the liturgy has changed, and the church seems like an empty tomb."

"Is it only our generation that feels as if it has experienced such changes," Christopher mused, "or is it endemic to all generations?"

"Hard to say. I think people coming to our age in any generation believe that they have experienced great changes. But, maybe our generation has experienced more...hard to tell."

"Can you imagine anyone building this church today?" Christopher pondered.

"Hardly. There isn't the will for it. Everyone would condemn the idea and say that the money should be given to the poor."

The two men chuckled over the thought of anyone suggesting the construction of such a church. Instead, churches were being closed and pulled down.

Another set of footsteps was heard coming into the sacristy. Christopher and Frank recognized a friend from college days, Tom Lambert, one of Marianne's pallbearers. The new arrival shook hands and mumbled some words about Marianne's untimely death, and the three of them stood silently.

Tom Lambert had been a close friend of both Christopher's and Frank's during their college days, but he had never been an intimate. Tom's family had been wealthy, and Tom had grown up in a mansion. Tom had not lived in the St. Ignatius dormitory, where truly intimate friendships were nurtured.

There had been little contact after they had graduated—enough to maintain the friendship, but not enough to grow it. Tom became an international financier, and had lived in New York, Europe, and Hong Kong. The three friends saw one another only during one of Tom's occasional visits to San Francisco.

Tom had married twice but by now had been divorced for many years. He had retained the good looks of his youth, and his still-handsome face was set off by perfectly coiffed hair with touches of gray along the temples.

Tom broke the silence. "This seems to be our connection these days: to meet at funerals. I preferred it when we got together and pulled an all-nighter, studying at Mel's, or acting in one of the school's plays."

"We all prefer those days," Christopher said, "but I think they've gone, never to return."

"Interesting," Tom continued, "that we thought that our college lives, somewhat transformed, would continue for all of our lives. But they certainly haven't."

"You're beginning to sound like Francis, here...hankering after the past," Christopher said.

"Well, they were great years...years filled with excitement and hope."

Frank had decided to stay out of any conversation on the past at St. Ignatius. Being once again in the church, and on the occasion of Marianne's funeral, was having a powerful impact on him. He knew it would be better if he stood silently with his thoughts and emotions.

"Welcome back to St. Ignatius, Gentlemen." No one had heard Dick Mahoney walk into the sacristy.

"Dick, how the hell are you doing?" Tom greeted him.

"Fine, and you? Are you finally settled down here after your rambles?"

"Yep, I've finally come to reclaim the heart I left in San Francisco."

"Welcome home," Dick responded to his school chum.

Dick silently shook hands with Frank and Christopher. Tom had had only perfunctory contact with his friends from St. Ignatius since graduation, but the other three had kept in contact. Marianne's death was like a thunderbolt: none of them wished to say much about it, each knowing the others were deeply grieving.

Tom, the only one among them who dated Marianne in college, began to speak of her. "I couldn't believe it when I heard that Marianne had died. Of course, I didn't even know that she was sick. A shame. She was probably the most alive woman I have ever known."

No acknowledgments came from the others, but Tom went on.

"She could talk your ear off about Descartes, Spinoza, Kant...and, of course, Aquinas...and then be dancing on a table at a cast party. Some gal."

A vague feeling that Tom's comments were somehow desecrating Marianne's memory bubbled up within Frank, and he intuited that Dick and Christopher were feeling the same. He was sure that they were remembering their distaste when they were in college and Tom would talk about "making out" with Marianne after their dates. All three had felt that such conversation about Marianne was indecent.

Christopher cleared his throat in disapproval at Tom's reference to

Marianne's exuberance at parties and said, "Let's all lunch at Malloy's after the interment."

"I haven't been to Malloy's since…the last funeral in which I was a pallbearer," Dick laughingly responded.

"Why would anyone go to Malloy's unless you had been to a funeral?" Frank joined in, smiling.

"Sorry, guys, but I've got an appointment right after the committal. But, hoist one for me at Malloy's."

Once again, Frank thought, Tom has removed himself from any intimacy with his friends. Malloy's would be fun after the shock and sadness of seeing Marianne committed to the ground at Holy Cross Cemetery. How many times had he been to the funky Irish bar in Colma to anesthetize the sorrow of some burial or, perhaps, if he were not sorrowful, to celebrate the deceased's life with a group of friends? Malloy's had all the earmarks of the perfect watering hole after funerals. The memento-filled walls somehow radiated the Irish moods about death: weeping into one's beer one moment, laughing and drinking it the next. It would be comforting.

Two distant cousins of Marianne's came into the sacristy. This would complete the complement of pallbearers. Frank had never met them before. They introduced themselves and then stood somewhat awkwardly in the somber group.

A door slammed and into the sacristy came a priest, dressed in black pants, a black shirt with short sleeves, and the white Roman collar, about as clerically dressed as priests got these days. Frank had never seen him before.

"Hi, I'm Tim Bailey," the priest introduced himself to the six pallbearers.

Frank detested such casualness. Priests were supposed to be called "Father," not by their first names. Today everyone wanted to be cool.

All six of them shook hands and murmured their names. The priest then went to put on his vestments to celebrate Marianne's funeral mass. Frank watched as Father Bailey slipped what looked like a white sheet over his head, and remembered when he had been an altar boy, both in his parish church and at St. Ignatius, when the priest had solemnly put on his vestments before mass, kissing each and saying a prayer as he put each one on. He couldn't remember all their names…what were they?…maniple, chasuble…Ah, drat it. He hated not having instant recall of all those things he once knew so well. And, most of all, he hated that the reverence in vesting and the several components that constituted the priests' vestments had been swept away. Almost every part of life was being reduced to the lowest common denominator, a kind of homogenized blandness.

"I think we're ready," Father Bailey announced.

Book in hand, he led the men out of the sacristy into the church, walking past the long line of side chapels to the entrance of the church. One of the chapels had been taken out and the space converted into a meditation room; and Frank had heard rumors that the priests at St. Ignatius were thinking of ripping out confessionals. When would it all end? Frank asked himself.

Marianne's casket stood at the entrance to the church, guarded by two somber employees of the funeral parlor that had had custody of her body. They directed the pallbearers to line up along the casket, and then waited for the priest to begin the service.

Father Bailey read the prayers that are said at the reception of a body into the church for a funeral, and then reached over for the container of holy water and sprinkled the casket with its contents. The priest then turned around and led the pallbearers, the representatives from the funeral home, and, of course, Marianne's remains, to the sanctuary of the church.

Very few people were in the church for Marianne's funeral. The two cousins who were pallbearers were the only family that remained. She had lived a somewhat reclusive life during the past several years, and the friends she had had from school and from when she was married had all, more or less, drifted away.

Frank spied Paula among the handful of mourners in the front pews. She knew about the role that Marianne had played in his life, and, out of loyalty to him, had volunteered to come to the funeral mass.

The procession stopped just short of the church's sanctuary, and Frank and his fellow pallbearers took their seats in the front pew. Father Bailey continued into the sanctuary, where he said a few words of introduction, made the sign of the cross, and then began the prayers inaugurating the mass of Christian burial.

Christopher and Frank had been deputed to do the readings, after which Father Bailey read the Gospel and gave the sermon.

Father Bailey had met Marianne a few times, but had not known her well. His sermon was a stock set piece about death and being with Jesus. It could have been given for the funerals of any number of deceased individuals.

Following the sermon, the mass progressed to its conclusion. Father

Bailey then proceeded to say the final prayers at Marianne's casket. Once again he sprinkled it with holy water and incensed it. At a signal from one of the funeral directors, the pallbearers once more lined up along the casket and accompanied it out of the church.

Frank felt a tinge of depression as he walked down the aisle. He remembered the funerals for which he had been an altar boy since he was eight years old, the funerals he had attended until the late-1960s. They had been solemn affairs: the liturgy employed to explore the mystery of death, especially the requiem high mass with its black vestments; the chilling words of the "*Dies irae*"; and the serious understanding that death was both the end of one's physical presence on earth and the time of one's judgment by God. Think of all those composers—Verdi and Mozart among them—who had poured their talents into writing requiem masses.

Now the liturgy was called "the mass of the resurrection." It was an upbeat affair, with the priest wearing white vestments. In Frank's mind, it totally lacked the beauty and solemnity of the discarded liturgy.

Frank and his fellow pallbearers waited while Marianne's casket was placed in the hearse for its slow ride to Holy Cross Cemetery in Colma, "the city of the dead."

Paula went up to Frank to say goodbye, explaining that she had to get to work. A few of those whom had been at the funeral mass came up to Frank to say hello and to express surprise at Marianne's death.

One person at the funeral was Vince Piccirillo, who had been a friend at St. Ignatius. He and Frank had drifted apart after college, victims of the tides and choices that swirl around one after graduation. They saw each other only in accidental encounters every five or six years. Vince remained as thin and wiry as he had been in college...and still had the same engaging smile and warm personality.

"Frank, we meet again." He shook Frank's hand and flashed a broad smile.

"Vince, good to see you. We've got to stop meeting like this. The last time was a funeral too...Jim Sullivan's about six or seven years ago."

"One by one, off we go. Too bad about poor Marianne. I guess it was all that high living when we knew her in college...all that smoking and drinking."

"Who knows what people die from? She stopped being a heavy smoker and drinker in her late 20s, when she got married. The doctors couldn't figure out what was wrong with her. Maybe she was tired of life."

"It's hard to imagine Marianne being tired of life. She was always so full of it."

"People change. The hard realities set in. Your dreams and aspirations aren't realized...you know, a certain weariness sets in."

"That may all be true," Vince responded, "but of all the women I knew while we were at St. Ignatius, she was the 'golden goddess.'"

"Yes, yes, she was. Venus and Minerva wrapped into one. Everyone thought she would have a dazzling future. But it didn't work out that way."

"What do you think went wrong?" Vince inquired. He had not known Marianne as well as Frank, Christopher, and Tom when they were in college, and he hadn't had any contact with her after they graduated.

"Oh, I don't know," Frank mused. "She was so fabulous in her late teens and early twenties that everything after that seemed anti-climactic. Her audience disappeared after graduation. She didn't have to go to work. The man she wound up marrying was flawed, and the marriage didn't last. She didn't have any children. She never had had any really close girlfriends. And she never developed any hobbies or interests...didn't volunteer...I don't know what went wrong...maybe too much too soon."

"Could be," Vince mused.

Christopher walked up to the two of them and shook hands with Vince.

"We were just talking about Marianne's life," Vince addressed Christopher.

"Ah, what about it?"

"I was wondering what had gone wrong."

Christopher winced. His instinct to defend and protect Marianne came immediately to the fore. "Who said anything was wrong with her life?" He shot a glance at Frank to determine whether he agreed with Vince.

"Well, it just seemed as if her potential was never realized. And then she dies relatively early."

Christopher drew himself up to his full height. "Marianne's life was in and of itself a work of art. Sure, she didn't work; but, one, very few women of her class worked in those days; and two, she didn't have to work. She married unsuccessfully, alas, and had no children; but I never thought that Marianne should ever have married. It was a mistake to commit to one man. She belonged to the world. I envisaged her as a nun—a Teresa of Avila, a Mother Theresa."

One of the funeral directors came to summon Frank and Christopher to the limousine, which would follow the hearse to Colma. They said goodbye to Vince, who stood wide-eyed as Christopher was soaring in his assessment of Marianne.

"I thought Vince would come unglued when you were talking about Marianne," Frank whispered to Christopher as they entered the limousine.

"Well, after all, he's a certified public accountant. You have to dramatize things for him to understand."

"You did a good job of summarizing Marianne's life, Christopher."

"Thank you. I shall go to my grave with glowing memories of her...as I am sure you shall."

"No doubt about it."

The car with the six pallbearers followed the hearse south toward Colma. The cortège, with only two additional cars, slowly made its way to the town of Colma. Frank looked out at the gloomy, rain-slicked streets. Dark clouds had gathered against the hills.

There was little conversation in the limousine. The presence of Marianne's two cousins, who lived in the Midwest and had not known her well, inhibited the four college friends from talking. Some polite conversation developed between Dick and the cousins. He tried to extract information from them about what they did in Indiana, how well they had known Marianne, and how they liked San Francisco. Their laconic replies did not encourage a lively, general conversation.

The tract houses of the second quarter of the twentieth century in San Francisco's Sunset District rolled by and soon the funeral caravan was on Highway 280, which would take them to Colma, "the city of cemeteries." The houses were visible from the elevation of the highway, where the hearse, leading the small number of vehicles, turned off onto a ramp that brought the mourners to Holy Cross Cemetery.

The quartet of hearse, limousine, and two cars stopped briefly at the cemetery office before proceeding to the site of Marianne's burial. The grave had already been dug, and the coffin was placed by the pallbearers onto some wooden beams that had been placed atop the grave.

As soon as the coffin had been placed, a white Saturn drove up to the gravesite. Father Bailey got out, his surplice draped over his arm and a book gripped in his left hand. He appeared to be in a hurry to get back to San Francisco, flashing a smile to the small group of assembled mourners. He put on his surplice and immediately began to read prayers from the book he held. The prayer, *In Paradisum*, one that Frank had always enjoyed (particularly when it was sung), ended the service, and Father Bailey issued a general goodbye and scooted to his nearby car.

The two funeral directors and the drivers of the hearse and limousine also seemed anxious to leave the cemetery. There would be no lingering around the gravesite. Frank and his fellow pallbearers threw carnations into the grave. Frank gently touched the coffin and bade his friend farewell. Then he joined the others in the limousine.

Christopher had left his car at Malloy's, so he instructed the limousine driver to deliver them to the famous watering hole, where they said their brief farewells to Marianne's cousins.

"Certainly no family resemblance to Marianne there," said Dick after closing the door to the limousine. "They're a couple of stiffs."

"Whoever said that family members were all alike?" Dick responded. "Mine certainly aren't. And Marianne may not have been so lively if her parents had stayed in Indiana."

"I can't imagine Marianne as anything but lively, even if she had been raised in the Gobi Desert," proclaimed the ever-loyal Christopher.

The three friends entered Malloy's. The familiar funkiness cheered them. The bartender looked up at them and nodded when they walked in, recognizing them as part of a decades-long procession of mourners that came to Malloy's to mourn or celebrate a death—perhaps both simultaneously.

Frank, Christopher, and Dick selected a table far from the few customers at Malloy's. The place was dark, even for a bar. They silently arranged themselves around the table.

"What will it be, gentlemen?" asked the bartender.

Christopher looked at his companions and responded, "I think we'll have martinis all around...Bombay Sapphire gin."

The bartender nodded and walked away to the bar. "I think martinis in honor of Marianne are called for, wouldn't you?" Christopher inquired of his companions. Both nodded their heads in agreement.

No one spoke until the drinks had been placed in front of them. It was once again Christopher who broke the silence. He raised the old-fashioned martini glass and said, "Here's to Marianne the Magnificent. May her soul rest in peace."

"To Marianne," Frank intoned, raising his glass.

"To Marianne," Dick echoed his friends. "I never dreamed that the three of us would be sitting here, mourning Marianne," he continued. His still-handsome face was hunched over his martini; to Frank, he resembled a good-looking gargoyle.

"Death seemed very far away when we were at St. Ignatius...and for years afterward," Frank chorused.

Christopher ignored the musings on how the reality of death had sneaked up on them and changed the subject.

"It amazes me how someone as popular as Marianne when she was in school wound up with so few mourners. Look at the three of us...we adored her...even Tom was a fan of hers. But I doubt there were even ten others in the church today."

"I guess we could give the usual answers," Dick replied. "She had no family. She was divorced. And she had become pretty reclusive during the past ten or so years."

"I think there's more to it," Frank added. "Many of those who enjoyed Marianne's company years ago have moved away...or they're ill...or they can't get off their asses to go to her funeral. It gives me a sense of how quickly we fade away."

Christopher sat back in his chair. His right arm was slung over the back of his chair. His left hand held his martini glass.

"Last year I went to St. Ignatius for the funeral of Patrick Moylan...you know, the shipping mogul. The guy was a prick, but you know what? The church was packed. I kept wondering why there were so many people. I realized that you began with a large family. Then you add those who work at the shipping company and those who are with companies somehow associated with it. Then you add family friends, who think it important that they be seen at the funeral. And, finally, let's not forget, the people from various non-profits to whom Moylan may have given some money and who came expecting that they'd be given more. What it all adds up to is a packed church."

"But why do we want a packed church at our funeral?" Dick asked. "Whether we are mourned by one or one thousand, we are still dead. Those who continued to love Marianne were there today, and that's all that matters."

"I guess I'm trying to chip away at something that's more mysterious to me," Christopher tenaciously continued. "I can intellectually understand the reasons why there were so few people there today, and I agree with you, Dick, that none of us needs a big send-off when we die, but I guess that I'm more fascinated with the contrast: Marianne in the late-1950s, golden girl, extremely popular, beloved not only by the three of us, but by scores of others; Marianne, forty-some years later, remembered by a few, mourned by fewer. How does someone so remarkable fade out so completely?"

Only silence met his query. Both Frank and Dick had offered solutions, but both agreed with Christopher that it was a mystery how this vivacious, intelligent, and popular young woman could have been forgotten by the many whose lives had somehow intersected with hers.

All three simultaneously sipped their martinis, as if each had thought that some answer could be found in the gin.

Dick spoke next. "We don't have enough experience with life when we're in college to realize what might happen to us as we grow older. We thought that because Marianne was so popular there that her magnetic aura would be part of her later years...that hundreds of people she had known would be at her funeral. There isn't any correlation, as we can tell by Marianne's life."

"Then the question is, 'How did Marianne go from being the belle of the ball to being a recluse?'" Frank asked. "I can't say that she actively excluded people from her life, but there was certainly a disconnect from when we knew her in college to her life afterward."

"Something happened during the time of what I call the diaspora— when everyone scatters after they graduate." Christopher continued the analysis. "She entered a tight community when she came from St. Agnes to St. Ignatius. We'd see her at morning mass. We'd see her at rehearsals and during the performances of the plays we all did together...and at the cast parties. We'd go to the movies together. Hang out together and talk in Golden Gate Park.

"That all disappeared after graduation. People scattered to the four winds. That life was totally over. I never thought that Marianne could make the transition. She was lost without the tight community that adored her and had plenty of time to be with her. She thrashed around...then got married, pretty late in life for those days, and when that didn't work out she basically cut herself off from life."

Frank stared into his martini glass. As usual, Christopher's intuitive grasp of situations made sense. He remembered that he had been at odds when he graduated; no longer part of that community that had so nurtured him...teachers and his fellow students. He was out of the rules of his family's household and not yet responsible for a job and family. That sudden change left him disoriented, lonely.

"I think you're on the mark, Christopher," Dick began, "but I don't understand why she couldn't make the transition. We all adapted. We scattered—some to work, others to grad school; we married and had children; we worked at jobs; and, in those new lives, we held onto some of the friends we had in college. That's the normal course of life. What happened to Marianne?"

"Everyone is different," Christopher responded. "Look at the three of us here. Each of us responded very differently to life after college. But none of us was quite the star Marianne was in college. She could never quite adapt to not having a *coterie* of adoring friends around her after she graduated."

"Yeah, I can remember when we'd see her at morning mass." Frank smiled at the memory. "The fact that she was pious as well as beautiful only increased our lust."

Dick laughed. "I was always surprised that we didn't start fighting about who would carry her prayer book to mass."

"Do you see what I mean?" Christopher pressed his point. "It's very hard to go from that experience to being out in the world without a group of adoring fans around you."

"What I can't understand," Dick mused, "is why none of us ever dated her. Only Tom had the nerve to ask her out."

"Well, that's not entirely true," Christopher said, with a toss of his head. "Mr. Molinari, here, many years after we graduated, not only asked her out, but had carnal knowledge of her."

Dick knew this, but laughed. "No, I was talking about when we were in college."

"Speaking for myself, dating was never something that moved me," Christopher asserted. "I was perfectly content to be in her presence, whether it was a cast party after a play, walking in Golden Gate Park, or having coffee after mass."

"For me it was, I guess, a low sense of self-esteem around girls, as we used to call them," said Frank. "I loved her company, and I think she liked mine—in fact I know she did—but I could never imagine asking her out on a date. And this was not only my own shyness or reticence; most of us felt that Marianne was so much above us that we would have sooner thought of asking the Blessed Virgin Mary or Marilyn Monroe for a date."

They all laughed at Frank's extravagance, but knew it to be true. Only Tom, of those they knew, had been able to overcome shyness, a sense of inadequacy, and an awe of Marianne's beauty and personality. And his courage was most likely because he had been "born with a silver spoon in his mouth."

Christopher raised his martini glass. "Here's to you, Marianne. You were great. We loved you. Enjoy the peace that you never seemed to find in your life."

"To Marianne," Frank and Dick joined him in his toast.

The trio sank into a gloomy silence. Each felt that something very important had passed from his life. Marianne was a vibrant human being in their college years, but she had been something more—a symbol of what they considered to be the golden years of their lives. A tangible portion of their youth was buried with Marianne in the ground of Holy Cross Cemetery.

Christopher attempted to alleviate the melancholy. "The three of us have good health. We're reasonably happy with our lives. And we're engaged in life. I think we'll carry on for some decades in similar fashion. Here's to us." And, once more he raised his martini glass.

"To us," the three men toasted.

"And to a long and healthy life," Frank added.

The air of melancholy was not dispersed by Christopher's optimistic toast. Each of the three friends sitting on that day in Malloy's was beset by his own dread. Friends and contemporaries had been dying or were ill. The emotional glow that life would somehow stretch into eternity had dissipated. At this point in their lives the three friends had a sense that, while it may be a few years or many, the years of their lives were numbered. And recent experience had shown them that whatever years remained would evaporate in a flash. The languorous sense of time they had felt in their youth was no longer so slow moving.

"Frank, how's your place in Healdsburg?" Dick joined Christopher in trying to change the mood by changing the subject.

"Paula and I love it. I didn't ever realize how relaxed I can be as when I'm up there. But it's a sump for money. There's always some expense or other coming up."

"I suspect that's the nature of places in the country." Dick was valiantly trying to lighten their moods.

"The two of you will have to come up again for a weekend. You know the rule: entertain yourselves except for mealtimes and after dinner."

"Invite us after the planting season," Christopher joked, with a mock grimace on his face. "The last time I was at your place you handed me boots, a ragged pair of pants, a sweatshirt...and a shovel. I had to help plow up the garden you were planting."

"Planting?" Frank laughed. "You went out to the garden in a white Oxford shirt, ascot, wool slacks, and Bally loafers. You gingerly put one of your shoes on the shovel, and then said you couldn't bear to disturb the microorganisms in the ground."

Dick and Christopher joined in Frank's laughter. It appeared that the melancholy had begun to dissipate. The three friends began to revert to their good-natured raillery and cheerful conversation.

"I'm sorry Tom wasn't able to join us," Dick said.

"Tom continues to lead a very, very busy life," Christopher answered him, with a touch of irony.

"Yes, Tom has tried to straddle many worlds since we were at St. Ignatius." said Frank.

"As I've gotten older I think a lot about the nature of friendship...why some people are your friends, and others not," mused Christopher. "How you have friends at one time of your life, but don't have them at another time. All three of us were close to Tom when we were in college, but all I think any of us could say today is that he is an acquaintance."

Dick signaled the bartender for another round of martinis and responded to Christopher's inquiry.

"What fascinates me in addition is the changing nature of friendship. The three of us have known each other since we were fourteen. For four years we saw each other for a good chunk of every day, including weekends. How much do we see each other these days? Maybe once a month...and sometimes those meetings are only for a short time. And yet we consider each other among a handful of our closest friends."

"I find it all very hard to explain," said Frank. "I have no friends from grammar school, three or four from high school, and the two of you and maybe a couple more from college...and then it stops. No one since we graduated has entered what I call 'the sacred circle' of intimate friends that I made in high school and college.

"Sure, there have always been a half dozen or so people that I've considered good friends at any given time...we get together for dinner or maybe for some events, but I don't have anywhere near the relationships that I have with the two of you."

"They say that the first growth of roses is always the best," Christopher commented. "Perhaps the same thing is true of friendships. High school and college are very special times in one's life for bonding, making for more intense and intimate friendships...and keep in mind that for all of us we had no distractions of the fair sex for those eight years."

"Well, I won't go that far," Dick laughed. "But you're right. When you're in an all-boys high school or an all-men's college, your relationships are going to be with other boys and other men."

"But that still doesn't explain why we never achieved the same level of intimacy with those we met after college," Frank wondered.

"Well, think back to our college days," Christopher mused. "The sap of youth is running in our veins. We're addicted to exploring life. We're into ideas, experiences...and we want to share them with others. We live in dormitories, where we have constant access to those to whom we've gravitated as friends. It's a magical time for coming together as friends."

Christopher had captured the essence of how their friendship had come to be, but both Frank and Dick were laughing.

"My goodness, how eloquent," said Dick.

"You're a true philosopher," Frank joined in.

"Well, it's true, isn't it?" asked Christopher with a mock look of defending himself.

"You're absolutely right," Dick exclaimed. "You're absolutely right. My God, how much I miss those days."

"Yeah," Frank added. "Not a day goes by when I don't think back on the excitement of those days at St. Ignatius. I love my life these days...my wife, my children, what I do for a living, my collecting, my friends...but it's...well, it's different. It's..."

"Getting older," Christopher interrupted. "It's a stable, mature love of life. It's not the unfettered, exuberant love of life that we had in our teens and twenties."

"We'll never have that experience of life again," Frank said.

His statement caused the three friends to lapse into another melancholy silence.

Christopher broke the silence. "I think these martinis are causing us to lapse into depression. "The Irish in us—I don't know what your excuse is, Frank, but it's casting a pall on our celebration of Marianne's life. But, at the risk of my getting a DUI, let's have one more round."

He called over to the bartender for three more martinis. He quietly chuckled, looked at his two companions, and said, "We've been lamenting the changes in our lives since we left St. Ignatius, and here we are, experiencing it as we did back then. The three of us are together talking about the meaning of life, as we did then, whether we were gulping cups of coffee at Mel's or swilling drinks at the Cozy Cove. There's something to be said for that."

Frank and Dick joined in Christopher's quiet merriment. The martinis seemed to bring forth both a melancholy at the disappeared youth and elation at leading fulfilled lives. Imbibing a third martini following Marianne's commitment to the earth at Holy Cross Cemetery was causing them to feel a warm glow, increasing their sadness and their happiness, relishing their companionship on this occasion of saying farewell to a cherished friend who was a symbol of their happy youthful days.

Dick lifted his glass. "Here's to the three of us. May we be together until we join Marianne."

Three glasses clinked together. The bartender looked up from his task of drying glasses at the sound, and then looked away. He had often witnessed the conviviality of mourners at Malloy's.

"And here's to Marianne the Marvelous, Marianne the Magnificent," Christopher toasted.

Once more the trio clinked their glasses together.

"To Marianne," Dick said.

"To Marianne," Frank repeated.

"You know, it's just occurred to me that there were no flowers at Marianne's grave," Dick noticed. "Why don't we stop at one of the florists on the road and bring her a bouquet of flowers before we head home?"

"Great idea," Christopher agreed.

"My mother used to say, 'Bring me flowers while I'm alive, not when I'm dead,'" Frank said.

"Don't be such a Grinch," Christopher countered. "We'll bring her flowers for ourselves, not for her."

"What flowers would best represent Marianne?" Dick asked.

"I think roses," Frank answered.

"And I'd like to see violets. I've always thought of Marianne as a violet—but not a shrinking one," Christopher said.

"How about orchids?" Dick countered. "Robust, beautiful, delicate."

"It's too late for Daphne, which she had in her garden, and gardenias are too funereal. How about roses, violets, and orchids?" Frank's martini-induced expansiveness collated all responses to Dick's question.

"Agreed," said Christopher.

"Let's do it," Dick chimed in.

The three quickly finished their third round of martinis and arose from the table.

"I'm treating," Christopher proclaimed. "And we can all chip in for the flowers."

"Thank you, sir," Frank acknowledged.

"*Urbanus et intellectus,*" said Dick.

Christopher paid the tab and the three men walked out of Malloy's' murky atmosphere and got into Christopher's car. They drove a short distance along the main road, lined with various necropolises, monument makers, and other businesses catering to laying the dead to rest, and parked in front of the first florist shop they came to.

The friends walked into the shop and asked the florist for a bouquet of the flowers they had selected. The florist gave them a quizzical look, no doubt thinking their request an odd assortment but quickly fulfilled their request.

They drove once more to Marianne's gravesite, got out of the car, and placed the bouquet on top of the coffin, which still lay on the wooden beams, awaiting the workers to place it into its final resting place.

The three friends stood back a few paces, their heads bowed in silence.

"Goodbye, Marianne." Again, Christopher broke the silence. "We love you."

"Rest in peace, Marianne," said Dick.

"May your life in heaven complete all your desires," whispered Frank, thinking back to their last conversation.

After a moment or two of silence, they turned away from the gravesite and walked to Christopher's car. Frank tried valiantly to restrain the tears that were coming unbidden into his eyes. He surreptitiously glanced at his companions and saw that they, too, had eyes glistening with tears.

None of them spoke, and each avoided looking at the others.

CHAPTER 16

Frank sat in the steamer chair in front of his modest home in Healdsburg, looking out at the undulating hills surrounding him. The book he had been reading lay at his side, and he now contemplated the oak trees that stood on the twenty-acre parcel that he had purchased a quarter-century before.

It had become a refuge from his busy life in San Francisco, and, despite the area having become in recent years an increasingly popular place for second homes for San Francisco socialites, Frank had been able to steer clear of any replication of his city social life. His Healdsburg retreat had become a place to take walks, to read, and to garden.

Paula and he would occasionally invite guests, as they had done this weekend. When there were guests, they would be feted to simple but imaginative meals and good wines, taken to explore the area, and guided to some of the adjacent wineries; but part of the weekend they were expected to entertain themselves, to take walks or read, while Paula and he would withdraw into the quiet realm they so cherished. When the guests left, usually sometime on Sunday, they would look at each other and repeat the mantra, "It was great having them here, but it's best when it's just the two of us."

Frank gazed toward the garden, where Paula was deadheading the rose bushes, and experienced a serenity he never felt in San Francisco. Each of them had invited a friend for the weekend: Frank had invited the newly-divorced Greg O'Connell, a friend since high school, and Paula had asked Ann Morris, who had been a neighbor of hers when Paula was single. Ann had never married, but the fact that she and Greg were single was not the reason for their being invited to the Healdsburg retreat. Neither Paula nor Frank thought of either of them as having any romantic interest in the other.

It was now the late afternoon on Saturday. Greg had retreated earlier to his bedroom to take a nap, and Ann had gone on a hike. The respite had allowed Paula to do some gardening and Frank to laze in the sun and read.

Across the meadow directly in his view, Frank spied Ann walking down a hill headed directly toward him, her hand clutching a walking stick. His contemplative couple hours had come to an end. Oh, well, Frank thought, it's almost the cocktail hour anyway.

Ann strode to where Frank was sitting. She was slightly flushed from the exertion of her vigorous hike, and seemed suffused with the sense of physical well being that accompanies physical exercise.

"How was your walk?" Frank inquired.

"It was terrific," Ann responded. "I really got going up the hill, and my reward was that splendid view from the top. My God, what a wonderful place you have here."

"Thanks. We love it."

"Are you going to retire here?"

"I'm not sure what is meant by 'retire,' but, yes, when I decide to hang up my calculator at Blakesley and Montgomery, I'd like to spend the bulk of my time here. We'll also keep our place in the city."

"Is Paula excited about spending that much time here?" Ann asked the question as if she already knew the answer.

"Well, as you know, Paula is considerably younger than I, and lusts more for the urban fleshpots than I. I suspect that the way we'll arrange our lives is that I will occasionally spend a few consecutive days in San Francisco and then return here. Paula will spend long weekends here and then return to San Francisco. I think the arrangement will work out very well for both of us."

Ann looked dubious but did not pursue the subject. Frank had always liked Ann Morris. She was a woman of strong opinions, had an acerbic sense of humor, and was a brisk and interesting conversationalist. He enjoyed her company, and was pleased when Paula invited her to dinner in San Francisco or for a weekend in Healdsburg.

Frank looked at Ann, who was now sitting across from him. She was in her mid-50s, her face, more handsome than beautiful, had a strong, confident cast. She had been married once, long ago. After her divorce Ann had not shown much interest in dating, and Frank had only known her as a confirmed single person.

"So, Ann, how's the practice of law these days?" Frank inquired, hoping to get his guest on some favorite topic with the heat and gusto of which she was capable.

"Oh, you know, after thirty years of practice there's not much new. You go over the same problems, just different clients."

Ann's law practice was largely corporate and estate planning. However, every once in a while she would take a criminal defense case pro bono, if she felt there was an issue of justice at stake and that a specific and worthy case needed competent legal counsel. And, when such a situation came to her attention, Ann pulled out all the stops. She would become a one-person O. J. Simpson legal defense team.

"Any interesting criminal cases currently?" Frank pursued.

"Interesting that you should ask," Ann responded earnestly. "I've just taken the case of a man who's been in prison for twenty years, accused of rape. There was some evidence that he may not have committed the crime, but last week we got the clincher: the DNA didn't match."

"So, if there's no match, he didn't commit the crime?"

"That's right. And he'll be out free after twenty years of incarceration."

"Wow, talk about injustice."

"I can't entirely blame the system...and let me stress entirely. There was no DNA technology twenty years ago, so that wasn't available to his defense. There was some pretty compelling circumstantial evidence... and, let us not forget, the defendant was an African-American. So, he was convicted and has been in jail for a couple decades."

"What happens if the DNA evidence clears him?"

"He'll be released and he'll get some minimal compensation, and then he's out in the world after having spent half his life in jail for a crime he didn't commit."

"If he didn't commit the rape and he's released, I can imagine how bitter he'll be."

"Amazingly enough, I don't think so. He's become quite religious while in prison...seems to think that whatever has happened to him is God's will. So I don't think he'll go on any rampages if he gets out. What I'm concerned about is that if he does get out, how will he manage in society? He was a wild-ass guy before he was incarcerated and the prison system didn't really give him any skills. So, the question is, how is he going to make a living?"

"Knowing you, Ann, I'll bet you have a plan."

Ann chuckled. "Well, it just so happens that I do. I'd like to see him get out of the Bay Area, where the cost of living is so high. There are people I know who have contacts in Oregon, where it costs so much less to live, who I think can get him a decent-paying job that doesn't need a huge amount of skill. From there he's going to have to do his best to fashion a life for himself."

"You sound pretty detached, Ann. After all, if he is found innocent, this is a pretty big thing that happened to the poor man."

"I guess I am somewhat detached. When I take a case like this, I'm pretty sure that an injustice has been committed. I try my best to rectify the injustice, and in the matter of Clarence Possner—he's the guy I've been talking about—that means if he's released from prison, trying to get established in the world...But I can't take it upon myself to make this a perfect world. I just do the best I can in a few situations and hope that others will do likewise."

"You're right. If we look back on the horrors that have occurred just in the last century one could get pretty depressed."

"And that outlook can lead you to the trap that there is nothing you can do to alleviate suffering in the world. A person then becomes wrapped in a cocoon of selfishness."

Paula, who had finished her gardening tasks, joined Frank and Ann.

"Well, what have the two of you been discussing?" Paula inquired.

"Ann was just saying how she was dedicating her life to making this a perfect world," Frank joked.

Ann laughed. "And Frank was telling me how he was going to move to Nepal and become a Buddhist monk."

"Sounds as if the two of you were having an interesting conversation," Paula remarked.

"Frank and I always have interesting conversations. He's one of the only people I know with whom you can discuss ideas."

"That's very flattering," Frank said. "And you're one of the only individuals I know who has ideas that I can discuss."

"Okay, you two, stop the mutual admiration society. You're becoming nauseating."

"Seriously, Ann, I enjoy our conversations. Thanks so much."

Frank was sincere. Ann Morris didn't hesitate to bring up sharply defined ideas and dialogue about those ideas. Frank didn't always agree with her views, but he always cherished their talks.

"Don't mention it," Ann responded to his compliment. "The pleasure is mine."

"I think it's time for cocktails," Frank announced. "The sun is somewhere near the yardarm...at least somewhere in the world. And I presume that Greg will be getting up soon. What's your pleasure?"

Frank went into the house to pour a vodka and tonic for Ann, a chardonnay for Paula, and a rum and Coke for himself. He heard stirring in the bedroom where Greg was taking his nap.

"Greg, time for cocktails," he called out to his friend. "What'll you have?"

The bedroom door opened, and a tousled Greg O'Connell walked out yawning.

"That felt great," he proclaimed, stretching his body. "Why don't I ever take naps when I'm home?"

"Because you don't allow yourself to take them," Frank answered. "You're always on the move."

"Yeah, well, I love to take them here. What are you serving?"

"Tell me what you'd like and I'll tell you if we have it."

"How about a Campari and soda?"

"You're on."

"I can always count on you dagos to have Campari."

Frank rolled his eyes and laughed. Greg and he had been friends for more than fifty years...they had roomed together in college. From the moment they met, Frank had noticed Greg's gravelly, loud voice and outrageous statements. Frank accepted his friend's quirky behavior with amusement; others were not so amused. Greg tended to set many individuals' teeth on edge with his sometimes-boorish comments.

"And you can always count on my having a pint of Guinness for you micks," Frank responded.

"Not Guinness. Whiskey for the Irish. It takes too long to get sloshing drunk with beer."

"Whatever. Here's your Campari and soda. Open the door for me while I bring the ladies their drinks."

Greg opened the door, and Frank, juggling three glasses, stepped onto the patio and over to the chairs where Paula and Ann were chatting. Greg followed, clutching his Campari and soda.

"*Salute*, as the wops say." Greg lifted his glass. Paula chuckled, but Ann looked at him with arched eyebrows. Frank knew that she was not a fan of Greg O'Connell's.

Still looking grim, Ann asked, "What are you doing these days, Greg?" The emphasis on "what" was such that Frank thought that Ann expected Greg to say that he was a pimp or was operating a pornographic shop.

"Same old, same old," Greg responded. "I'm still into 'juice' work: you know, easing the path through the political thickets."

"That's a job?" Ann archly inquired.

Frank and Paula relaxed and sat back to listen to the unfriendly repartee between their two friends. Frank could have told Ann, who was trying to verbally crush Greg, not to bother; Greg was uncrushable. He had the hide of a rhinoceros.

"Are you kidding? It's the best kind of job. I make a lot of money and it's easy work. I introduce people to each other. I have lunch and dinner with politicians. And I occasionally appear before commissions and agencies. Not bad for a poor kid from the Mission."

The outline of Greg's explanation about his job was roughly correct, but it wasn't the essential truth. It was true that Greg had been born in San Francisco's Mission district, then an Irish working-class area, but his father had been a stockbroker who had moved his family to the Sunset when Greg was a baby. While his father had chosen a modest lifestyle for himself and his family, he had accumulated a fortune, which had been divided among his wife and two children after his death. It was the return on these inherited assets that accounted for the bulk of Greg's income.

After half-hearted attempts at law school and a doctorate in education, Greg had turned his gregarious personality to lobbying. His engaging smile, companionable manner, and backslapping bonhomie were valuable traits in persuading bureaucrats and politicians to approve some measure desired by his clients.

"Why don't real estate developers and companies just present their desires to whoever has jurisdiction over such matters and let the laws and regulations govern the decision?" Ann persisted. Her mentioning of real estate developers and corporations showed that she both knew what Greg did and the composition of his clientele.

Greg smiled and threw back his head and roared with laughter. "My God, you're naïve. In what world do you think such a thing happens? At what time in history do you ever think there was no attempt to influence public officials?

"You may disapprove of the process, but I can assure you that it has always existed and will always exist. The only thing you might find redeeming is that in this country the system is reasonably free of corruption. Sure, some member of the board of supervisors may vote your way because he or she may want a contribution from you at the next election. And a bureaucrat may perform a favor because they may be looking for patrons to advance them up the civil service or appointive ladder. But, compared to the rest of the world, this is the Garden of Eden."

Greg had sensed that Ann was needling him because of her dislike of him, and his response was a "shot across her bow." Yes, he was easy-going and jovial, slow to take offence, but he was going to retaliate if someone pushed him too far.

"I still think influence-peddling is wrong." Ann began to retreat. "It's a perversion of the process by which the deliberations and decisions of a public forum should rise above money and who you know."

"Yeah, well, often it does. I tried to get Wal-Mart permits to put a store in San Francisco. I know all the players to get a decision in its favor, and it had plenty of money to 'grease the skids' for the politicians. It came to nothing. The neighbors rose up, and the bureaucrats and politicians backed off. But, here's my question: were the interests of San Francisco best served by their decision?"

"I'd say they were," Ann replied to Greg's question. As the conversation continued, she was sounding increasingly prissy.

"Oh, is that right? Well, here's the picture. Wal-Mart buys some crumbling buildings that generate virtually no property taxes, and builds a huge store that they're willing to make more aesthetically pleasing than their usual 'big boxes.' They hire hundreds of people—mostly seniors seeking to supplement their income or young kids working their way through school. They pay gobs in property taxes, they offer a choice to consumers who can buy more cheaply there than at other stores. So, what's the problem?"

Ann stiffened. "For one thing, Wal-Mart's pay and benefits are so low that their employees are forced to use welfare services. Your taxes and mine go into supplementing their compensation. And, second, they make competing businesses fold and…"

"That's all a lot of bull crap." Greg was pressing his verbal advantage over Ann. "I said earlier that most of Wal-Mart's employees were seniors or students. Only losers would go to work for Wal-Mart and expect to raise a family on their pay and benefits. And, as for competing businesses folding, that's the capitalist way. That's the same thing that was said fifty, sixty years ago when supermarkets began to become popular. And what do you have today? Lots of supermarkets and lots of independent grocery stores."

Frank and Paula looked at each other. Neither of them ever objected to vigorous arguments and discussions, but the confrontation between Ann and Greg was becoming more personal than either of them thought beneficial for a late Saturday afternoon in the country. Their nods confirmed that both of them felt the need to step in and defuse the conversation.

"I know I personally don't like to shop at Wal-Mart," Paula began, "but I don't think they should be stopped from building a store."

"You sound like some pro-choice hypocrite," snapped Greg. "I'm against abortion personally, but I think everyone should have a choice.'"

"Okay, ladies and gentlemen, time out," Frank called out. "Everyone to their neutral corners and take a deep breath."

Frank had rarely seen Greg so argumentative. Was it post-nap crankiness? Or had Ann's thwacks gotten to him? Whatever it was, his harsh response to Paula's attempt to bring down the temperature of the conversation threatened a nasty exchange. It was time to intervene. He began anew.

"I think tomorrow we'll hit a few wineries...maybe a couple old standards and a couple new ones that have opened up since you were last here. What do you think?"

"Sounds great," said Greg, sounding as if he were calming down.

"I think that sounds wonderful," Ann agreed.

"Okay, it's settled. Tomorrow...some wine-tasting."

"I think it's time to put on the coals for the barbeque," Paula remarked. "Ann, would you like to join me?"

"Sure, let's do it."

"We'll be back as soon as the coals are set," Paula said to Frank.

Frank nodded and thought that he would like to overhear Paula's conversation with Ann. Both of them thought that Greg was ordinarily too loud, boisterous, and overbearing, but this last conversation would really have set their teeth on edge.

"Do you think I was a little too harsh?" Greg inquired, after Paula and Ann had left.

"Oh, no, Greg, I thought you were sweeter than Rebecca of Sunnybrook Farm."

"My big mouth again, huh?"

"You were even more vociferous than usual."

"Well, that bitch got me going. She thinks her shit doesn't stink because she occasionally does some high-profile defense case that gives her a lot of publicity, and she thinks that gives her a license to high-hat me."

"Where is your chivalrous spirit?" Frank inquired good-humoredly.

"Chivalry, my ass. I gave her what was coming to her."

"Well, you didn't have to fire your cannon at Paula, as well."

"I'll apologize to her. I'm sorry. It's just that she got caught when my guns were blazing."

"Is everything Okay? You seem a little testy today."

"What, I'm not my usual cheerful self after I get blitzed by a self-righteous bitch?"

"Greg, please stop calling Ann a bitch. It's going to poison the weekend, and I don't want to return to San Francisco tomorrow night exhausted because of your cantankerousness."

"Okay, okay."

"So, what's wrong? You're usually loud, but you're not usually this... feisty."

"They just found some cancer in my prostate," Greg blurted out. "They say it's in the early stages, so there's nothing to worry about. Sure. If you believe that, then you can believe in the tooth fairy. What's worse is that I've got to make a decision about treatment: whether to have surgery or chemotherapy. Neither is particularly attractive."

"Jesus, Greg, I'm so sorry." Frank leaned forward, filled with concern for his friend. "But if they caught it in the early stages that means that it's not life-threatening."

"So they say."

"When do you have to decide what kind of treatment you'll have?"

"By the end of the next week. They want to do surgery or start the chemo the week after next."

"Which treatment are you leaning toward?"

"I don't know. With the surgery you can't use your pecker again...not that I've been using it much the last few years. And with the chemo people say that your internal organs get all screwed up."

"Well, at least you'd be alive."

"Yeah, alive with a permanently limp dick or burned-out insides."

In all the years that he had known him, Frank had never seen Greg so disconsolate. So that was the reason for his earlier rude behavior. It was certainly understandable.

"You're going to come out of this just fine," Frank said, with exuberant assurance. "The feisty Irishman will triumph over adversity."

"You're full of shit. Even under the best of circumstances, it's not going to be great. Getting older sucks."

"Now Greg, I've never known you to be gloomy in the face of adversity."

"That's because I've never had to face adversity...except maybe when Deborah and I split up."

"So you start now," Frank told his friend, eager to stamp out the moroseness he saw in Greg. "They say that negative attitudes impede the healing process."

"My God, you sound like one of those whacko New Age dames."

"There's nothing New Age about my wanting you to keep a positive attitude as you start the process of getting rid of prostate cancer. Despite your cynicism, I believe that healing is helped by not being negative."

Greg seemed resigned to not countering Frank's views. He continued to look both gloomy and angry, as if he were saying, "Why me?" But he had stopped lashing out. The two men sat silently watching Paula and Ann as they fiddled with starting the fire in the Weber.

Frank felt inadequate about his attempts to console and buck up his friend. Women seemed to do these things better. They cried, chattered incessantly, and expressed sympathy in a thousand different ways...it all seemed adequate to get them through whatever crisis threatened them. Men had a more difficult time. Rational approaches didn't seem to fit the bill, and, while Frank didn't consider himself a cold person, hugging Greg and crying together didn't seem a viable alternative. And so they sat in silence, each wrapped in his own thoughts and feelings.

Paula and Ann wandered back to the patio. They noticed the changed atmosphere but didn't inquire as to its reason.

"How about another round of drinks?" Paula asked. Each person nodded. Something must be wrong, Paula observed to herself, and went into the house to bring out another round of drinks.

Frank felt it was his job to lift the pall that had descended on them, but he struggled to find the right pitch to stimulate pleasant, even inconsequential, conversation.

"Have you to been to any good concerts lately?" he asked Ann. Ann was a music lover.

"Aside from my regular symphony performances—and it's been a good season—I've been to a couple Early Music Society concerts at St. Gregory's, and they've been great."

Frank could feel how stilted the conversation had begun, but soldiered on. "What other types of music do you hear during the year?"

"Well, you know, Paula and I get tickets for three ballets each year. I usually see about four operas, and...well, that's about it. Occasionally, I'll go hear Chanticleer or the Philharmonic Baroque. I'd go to more concerts, but I'm frequently working late at night."

"The curse of maintaining a successful career these days," said Frank. "Greg and I grew up in a more leisured society. When we were starting our careers, attorneys, even those at the big, prestigious firms, worked nine to five—maybe six some days—and almost never worked on weekends."

"Those days have certainly changed," Ann interrupted.

"People who worked for corporations had similar hours. Stockbrokers started at work earlier here in the West, but they left earlier. But now people work till midnight and beyond...Saturdays...Sundays...and most of them don't eat lunch. It's barbaric."

"Two workaholic careers are the norm today, especially in the Bay Area," Ann declared. "Everyone is driven to duplicate the lives of their parents and grandparents, and they can't accomplish this if they don't pull out all the stops. It's tough."

"I used to think that people could do with less, and I guess in some cases they can," Paula joined in, "but in most cases I think their expenses are about the same."

"However you analyze the situation, the standard of life for the middle class is declining," Greg stated, breaking his silence. "After World War II—for about a quarter century after—you had the golden age of a huge middle class. Now you have overworked serfs killing themselves for the things that their parents took for granted."

"Where will it all end?" Paula wondered. "Prices for everything, especially housing, continue to go up. People can't work any more hours; they'll just have to do without some things."

"That's what is called a lower standard of living," Greg said.

"I guess we'll all get through okay," Frank said, pleased that the rancor that had marked their earlier conversation had disappeared. "And I think our children will be okay. But I think that if all this continues, unless they have very high-paying jobs, our grandchildren will have a heck of a time."

"We'll be gone by that time," said Ann. "*Après moi le deluge* and all that."

"Or they can migrate to China or India," Greg said smiling.

It pleased Frank to see his friend come out of his earlier gloom. The wit and humor, so characteristic of Greg, had begun to re-emerge. Frank hoped it would last.

The sun had disappeared behind the hill. The still twilight, with only the occasional chirp of a bird punctuating the silence, came over them like a blanket. The day was ending.

"I think it's time to get dinner going," Paula announced as she stood up.

"I'll help you," Ann added and joined Paula in an exodus to the kitchen.

"And I'll have another drink." Greg handed his glass to Frank.

"Me, too. I'll be right back," Frank responded.

Paula and Ann were quietly speaking to each other as Frank entered the kitchen.

"Don't make it too strong, Frank, or he'll start getting more obstreperous," Paula admonished.

"Okay, dear."

"Your friend has quite a mouth," Ann added. One could easily see what the two women had been talking about.

"Now, Ann, don't depart from the harmony that has been re-established," Frank said in a mockingly patronizing way. "Think good thoughts about everyone."

"That's tough to do sometimes," Ann continued.

"Let it be a challenge, then, for someone as smart and focused as you are."

Frank went back out to the patio with the two replenished glasses and set them down on the table.

"I'll bet they were talking about me," said Greg, as Frank once again sat down.

"What makes you say that?"

"Oh, I know women...I think. And I can tell that as far as Paula and Ann go I've overstepped the boundaries of proper behavior."

"Well, if they were, I didn't hear anything," Frank lied. "They were fussing about preparing dinner."

"I guess I don't always behave like I should."

"Don't let this epiphany stand in the way of your self-expression," Frank said, chuckling.

"I often vow to change my boisterous personality," Greg continued, ignoring Frank's humorous sally, "but I can never seem to accomplish it."

"To know you is to love you."

"My God, you're filled with bromides today."

"It's a beautiful evening. The birds are darting around, giving their final chirps of the day. The temperature is just right. A little bromide seems just right."

"So, you don't want me to expose my tortured soul to you?"

"How many years have we been exposing our tortured souls to each other? Has much changed? At this point in our lives I think we need to make peace with our personalities, whatever they are, and let them be what they are."

"You've become a philosopher," Greg chuckled.

"I've always been a philosopher."

"As the years go by you're going to need your philosophy more and more."

"I can see that already. Getting older seems to bring out the need for it."

"And if you get something like I've got, God forbid, you'll really need to be a philosopher. But, of course, you've also got religion."

Greg made his last statement in a mocking tone. He and Frank frequently joked about their religious differences. Greg, from an intensely pious and religious home, a former seminarian, had become what had once been called a "fallen-away Catholic," a vocal non-believer. Frank had continued to be a practicing Catholic. For years, the two had bantered about their respective belief and non-belief.

"You're going to have it, too, at the end. Don't forget, if you go before me I'm arranging a full requiem mass for you," Frank joked.

Greg held up his hands in mock horror. "I'm leaving instructions in my will that you're not to come anywhere near my body. My requiem is going to be a big party."

"Oh, come on, Greg, how can you stand to go out of this world without a rousing rendition of the *Dies irae* or the *In paradisum*?" Frank teased.

"Well, maybe you could have a memorial concert, where you could have a component of sacred music…but mostly I want Mozart. But no mass."

"You'll change your mind when I'm bringing over a priest to your deathbed to give you extreme unction…or whatever they call it today."

Greg chortled. "I'll warn my heirs against your wily ways."

"Dinner is ready," Paula called out from the porch.

"That was fast," Frank answered.

"The chicken is still on the coals, but the pasta is ready to serve. Better come in right now. You know how quickly it cools off. And bring in your glasses."

Frank and Greg took up their empty glasses and walked toward the house. Frank had enjoyed the banter with Greg, and was relieved that his depression about his prostate cancer had at least momentarily disappeared. Hopefully, Frank thought, this pleasant mood would last for the rest of the evening.

Frank noticed that Paula and Ann eyed Greg warily as they entered the house. They had not experienced his change of mood outside.

"Greg and I have just been planning his obsequies," Frank announced.

Ann, always a little starchy, peered at Frank, while Paula, used to her husband's joking about death, laughed.

"No one can do a better job for the final arrangements than Frank," she said.

"I don't want him anywhere near my 'final arrangements,'" Greg proclaimed with simulated anger. "I don't want him to bring his Catholic voodoo into my final days or to my memorial. He's got to be stopped."

"Most people praise the cook when they're sitting down to dinner," Ann said, "or talk about their forthcoming vacations, or the weather, sports, whatever. But I've never before heard funeral arrangements discussed during dinner."

"Discussions of funeral arrangements are much more interesting than sports or vacations," Frank responded. "The next thing you'll want me to discuss is my grandchildren."

Frank always insisted on saying grace before meals. Paula joined him in making the sign of the cross, while Greg rolled his eyes and Ann stood stiffly at attention.

"Okay, let's hit the tortellini," Frank said, as he concluded the brief thanksgiving.

Four forks simultaneously stabbed at the small succulent pasta "doughnuts" on their plates. Paula had purchased them at her favorite delicatessen, Molinari's, in North Beach, and they were covered with the gravy Frank continued to make from his mother's recipe.

Greg issued a satisfied smack of his lips after tasting his first forkful of tortellini. "This is great. You wops certainly know how to eat."

Frank chuckled. Ann again raised her eyebrows. Paula smiled.

"It's too bad we were never able to teach the Irish how to cook a decent meal," Frank continued the ethnic banter.

"That's because we were always too drunk to learn," Greg responded.

"Ah, well, Greg, you know you have an open invitation to dine with us whenever you want a good meal," said Frank.

"Thanks. I've taken you up on your offer many times, and will continue to do so in the future."

Paula got up to clear their dishes from the table. "Sit," she enjoined Ann, who was getting up to help her. "It'll just take a minute. I'll call you when I need some help."

She rinsed the dishes and put them in the dishwasher. Frank admired his wife's domestic competence and organization, and was grateful that he was its beneficiary. He knew that if he were left to his own devices, he would be living in chaos.

Paula brought the platter of barbequed chicken into the house. The aroma of barbeque, the tang of the charring that Paula did so expertly, immediately filled the air.

"That smells great," Ann announced as she arose to help Paula serve the asparagus and zucchini. The platter of chicken was placed on the table, where Greg and Frank greedily eyed it. Ann set down two platters that contained the vegetables. And Paula followed up with a basket of French sourdough bread.

"I think that should do it," said Paula, visibly proud of her gastronomic accomplishment.

The platters were passed, creating intermingled, pungent food odors that in turn created an eagerness among the quartet of diners to begin consuming the food.

There was silence as they ate, with only the sounds of clicking and scraping utensils, chewing, and an occasional "um" from one of them. Frank enjoyed participating in such a meal. He had eaten well at his family's table ever since he could remember. His father's extensive garden had provided fresh vegetables, and friends of his parents had provided fresh fruits from their orchards near San Jose. And his mother's culinary skills, honed from the time she was eight or nine years old, turned each meal into a delightful experience.

Simple peasant fare was served at his mother's table. Often there would be dishes that were, in modern days, looked upon with disgust—tripe, for example, or tongue. The members of his family would comment on the food: "The pasta is too al dente," one would say. "The roast is cooked to perfection," another would proclaim. "You've overcooked the peas," yet another would remark.

Frank's mother, often joined by his aunt, had spent many days each year canning. The huge wooden cabinets his father had built in their basement contained hundreds of jars of vegetables, fruit, jams, and a concoction of vegetables and tuna, known in his family as antipasto.

Food was central to his family's life. In a way it was still central to Frank's life, but without the prissy self-consciousness that had come to surround food during the past couple of decades. Portions in restaurants were not sufficient to feed a gerbil. "Presentation"—food arranged according to a color palette—had become the hallmark of a good meal. One food critic's comment on a restaurant in which it was almost impossible to obtain a reservation was, "Here you must not judge by the quality of the food; the experience is one of performance art."

The chattering of many of his friends about this restaurant or that repelled Frank. Most of them had grown up on nothing but macaroni and cheese or peanut-butter-and-jelly sandwiches, and were now setting themselves up as experts on the yak piss dressing on the arugula salad or the aardvark turds so artistically presented on the plate.

It was a disgusting display of shallowness, he thought. In Frank's opinion, people thronged to the latest trendy restaurant like lemmings following one another to check out a new chef. Food had become a religious experience for people who neither knew nor cared about food, but didn't want to be left behind in the latest fashion.

Frank stood up to clear the plates, while Paula put a vinaigrette dressing on a platter of sliced tomatoes, basil, and red and green bell pepper—Frank's favorite salad. Ann and Greg sat together in silence.

"Salad at the end. How European." Greg spoke teasingly.

"Not the end, you clod. Dessert is at the end," Frank teased back.

When all were again seated Ann said, "It's a full moon tonight. It should be beautiful here, away from all the lights of the city."

"I think we should all go out and dance naked under the moon," Greg declared.

Paula and Frank laughed. Ann rolled her eyes. There is certainly no chemistry between those two, Frank thought.

"We can appoint a master or mistress of the revels," Frank suggested. "But I don't think there were orgies involved in the worship of a moon goddess. I believe that the moon goddess was always pure."

"What a shame," Greg said, "maybe we can do a Baal worship ceremony instead."

"Okay, you two, we know you studied classics in high school and college." Paula knew that both men could go on ad nauseum in a display of such esoteric knowledge.

"Well, what's the point of having studied it if you can't trot it out at times like this?" Frank countered.

"Because it becomes boring after a while," Paula answered. "Not everyone likes to discuss minute points of long-dead pagan religions."

"That's because this is a debased society," Greg said. "What do people discuss these days? The gym where they work out. Their health. The latest trendy restaurant."

"You and Frank's other friends are so harsh on the world around you and so critical," Paula said. "There isn't anything wrong with a little light conversation."

"Do most people ever discuss anything but light topics?" Frank now entered the fray. "What Greg enumerated is a pretty good list of what people talk about constantly...oh, he forgot golf, pets, and grandchildren."

"I think the two of you should be more tolerant of other people's conversations," Paula declared.

"Tolerant?" Frank said. "You have also expressed how boring it is when people go on about how well or badly they play golf, incessantly about their grandchildren, or some ailment."

"Yes, but I don't keep criticizing those people as they're talking," Paula answered.

"That's because you're too polite," Greg said. "Frank and I were trained in the cut-and-slash techniques of debate...take no prisoners."

"I think that this discussion is getting boring," Ann said. "Why do any of us care about what other people talk about?"

"Because it's a pollution of the atmosphere," Greg shot out. "It's like rap music, universal bad grammar, people wearing $400 blue jeans that come faded and with holes. Pollution. It has to be stopped."

Frank relished Greg's outburst. "You're on a roll, Greg. Flay the Philistines."

Greg appeared abashed at Frank's rousing encouragement, as if he had been awakened from a dream.

"All that crap really fries me," he mumbled.

"I couldn't agree with you more," said Ann, becoming cheerful at the opportunity to find an area of agreement with Greg. "The music is abysmal. The people who sing it are classless tramps. The society is rotten with materialism, and it's become dumbed-down to an extent that I find unbelievable."

"Go, girl," Frank called out. "I didn't know you were so disaffected with contemporary society."

It was Ann's turn to be embarrassed by her outburst. She looked as if she regretted her spontaneous diatribe.

"I don't know what all of you are getting so excited about," Paula joined in. "All young generations express their rebellion against the older generation through different music, linguistic peculiarities, and adopting different attitudes, clothing, and so forth."

"That's not historically accurate," Frank countered. "I grew up listening to the same music my parents listened to...Frank Sinatra, opera...my clothes were pretty much duplicates of my father's. There was not as much dissonance between the generations as there is now."

"I don't know if all that's true," said Paula, desiring to defend the particularities of the younger generation. "To begin with, you were an old stick-in-the-mud from the time you were born, so you're no judge. Second, I'll bet there was more rebellion in your generation than you recognize."

"I think you're wrong," Frank persisted. "There was certainly some rebellion. Some guys wore 'DAs.' Occasionally we'd use slang that wasn't known to our parents, and every once in a while we'd put on weird articles of clothing, like glow socks in the early 1950s. But the young generation, those growing up, was relatively stable. They didn't idolize the trash-heads that dominate the young today and listen to music which not only gives one a headache, but which is nihilistic."

Greg's and Paula's comments had struck a nerve in Frank. He loathed and despised the culture of the young in contemporary society. He saw it devoid of intellectual curiosity, and watched in dismay as those in their 20s, even their 30s, forsook reading for innumerable hikes, ski trips, gyrating in dance clubs, or a variety of activities such as river rafting, hang gliding, and surfing. Their conversations were devoid of any interest to him, and conducted with a narrow vocabulary and with little grammatical precision. They had no depth of knowledge: you mention Winston Churchill and to them he might have been a pharaoh from the Middle Kingdom.

For Frank, it was as if the world he had grown up in and known was ending. Elegance in dress and manners was gone. He had seen young men at the opera in T-shirts and torn, faded jeans. One looked in vain for a necktie along Montgomery Street. Frank felt as if he were living in a developing Dark Age.

"You're all sounding like old farts," Paula said. "While you're blasting the modern generation, let me get dessert."

She placed a lemon tart pan on the table and began to cut slices for each of them.

"This is fabulous," Ann exclaimed. "Why can't I make creations like this?"

"Because you never try," Paula laughed. "When was the last time you cooked anything?"

"Oh, I guess a couple Thanksgivings ago...for my family. It was a disaster, and I vowed I'd never try again."

"Oh, a woman of great domestic achievements, I can see," said Greg.

"Ann's achievements are in areas other than cooking," Frank quickly commented, anxious to prevent any recurrence of the bickering between Ann and Greg.

"Yes, and besides she helps keep the restaurants in San Francisco in business," said Paula.

"You may laugh all you want," Ann replied, not minding the humor at her expense, "but I figure I am making money by not cooking."

"How is that?" Greg demanded.

"I work the time that I would be cooking, and what it costs me to eat out or for take-out is less than the billable hours I charge."

They all laughed at Ann's whimsy, even Greg. Frank felt that Ann may actually have believed what she had said, as a way of defending her not ever cooking.

"I love cooking," said Paula. "Not only do I like to see—and eat—the results, but I find it a meditative experience."

"I do a little cooking, when I'm in the mood," said Greg, "but it's no fun to go through all the preparation just to fix a meal for yourself."

"Invite people over," Frank proposed.

"Then not only do I spend the time cooking, but then I have to spend the rest of the evening entertaining people...or someone. It's easier to eat out, by yourself or with others, so that after dinner you can simply go home."

Greg had become somewhat bitter about domestic arrangements after he and Deborah divorced. It was a story typical of their early adulthood. Greg and Deborah began to quarrel and their marriage began to fray. It was the time of the Sexual Revolution, which had become prevalent in cities such as San Francisco, New York, and Los Angeles. Greg began to fool around; then Deborah had a full-fledged affair. When Greg found out about Deb's affair, the marriage went kaput.

Greg had loved to cook, and prided himself on his ability to cook delicate sauces and prepare to perfection cuts of meat. His divorce had soured him on the domestic arts on which he had once prided himself.

"It's such a beautiful evening," Paula said. "Let's go out to the patio. It's a full moon tonight."

Frank helped his wife clear the dishes from the table, rinse them, and place them in the dishwasher. Ann and Greg continued to sit at the table, making stabs at conversation.

Frank carried out a tray containing a bottle of port and four glasses. They sat in the same chairs they had sat in before dinner. This time it was dark, and the sky was studded with stars. In the east, the pale, cold light of the newly risen moon glistened through a screen of oak trees. The music of Frank Sinatra gingerly came forth onto the patio. Frank poured four glasses of port.

"You can never see the stars in San Francisco," Ann said dreamily, her head tilted back.

"God, I love this place," Frank announced, after handing a glass of port to Paula. The light of the moon, the myriad stars, and the just-so temperature combined to overload his senses with pleasure.

"I can see why," Greg said. "It's the perfect retreat. Both during the day and during the night it's beautiful...it induces peace and tranquility."

"You're getting so poetic, Greg," Paula commented.

"I may be poetic, but my comments are true. I am never as relaxed as when I'm here."

"That's very sweet of you to say," Paula responded, "and we love to have you here...and relaxed."

"It's like going to a spa," Ann added. "You two cook. We swim in the creek. And the setting is just too beautiful for words. Thank you. Thank you."

"Just wait until you check out and get the bill," Frank joked.

"Whatever it might be, it's worth it," Ann laughed.

The quartet lapsed into silence, broken only by the rhythmic sound of crickets punctuating the pervasive silence. Each seemed wrapped in personal thought, unwilling to have private musings interrupted.

Frank broke the silence. "Yeah, no buses going by. No car alarms going off. No police or ambulance sirens. No sense of the urban dynamo."

"Frank, you know you love the city. This place does have different amenities, but the excitement of city living is wonderful." Paula's defense of living in San Francisco was her standard response to Frank's love of their country place. She lived in fear that he would retire and move them to Healdsburg.

"I felt its excitement much more when I was younger." Frank countered. "The sap was running then. I was running all over town with big plans and dreams. I was caught up in the buzz of city life. On Friday nights I used to love to go to North Beach and wander around...browse at City Lights, walk along Broadway, watching the freak show there, eat at the La Pantera or La Felce, go to the Savoy Tivoli. Now on Friday nights I want to come up here or sit in front of a fire at home with a glass of wine in my hand."

Paula returned to the fray. "You'd miss the city if you didn't live there. Where would you go for the opera or the concerts we go to? What would you do for a library? Who would you talk to?"

"You get to a point in life where these things don't matter as much," Frank answered. "I could listen to CDs for music. As it is, I go to one or two operas a year. I've heard the great singers of the world. Do I want to hear a second-rate Bulgarian soprano sing *Tosca*? As for books, I could make one trip a month to the city to get a batch of books from the library. And, as for talking to people, the people I want to talk to I can invite up here. Besides, I am talked out. It's a time for listening to myself."

"You know you'd miss the city." Paula concluded the discussion.

"Maybe," Frank concluded dreamily. "Maybe."

Paula knew that it was futile to continue the conversation. If and when the time came that Frank retired and proposed moving to Healdsburg, she would deal with it then.

"Well, while the two of you discuss where you would like to live in the future, I'm going to get ready for bed," Ann stated, getting up from the comfortable Adirondack chair. "This clean, country air has made me sleepy. Thanks for everything, I'll see you in the morning."

"I think I'll tuck in too," Paula said, also standing up. "And don't the two of you stay up all night, talking, drinking, and smoking your cigars."

"We'll be in shortly," Frank answered. He realized that the days of his and Greg's staying up until dawn, drinking, smoking, and engaging in wide-ranging conversations were long past. Neither of them had the stamina any longer for such sessions.

Frank kissed Paula goodnight and planted a chaste kiss on Ann's cheek.

"It has been a pleasure chatting with you both," Greg said. "And,

Ann, don't take my sometimes harsh comments personally. Not even the Molinaris have been able to totally civilize me."

Ann laughed. "I'll get over your barbed and hostile comments," she said.

The two women walked into the house while Greg and Frank re-lit their cigars.

"She's not as much of a bitch as I had thought," Greg said. "I probably should have been more diplomatic."

"If that had been the case, I would have wondered who I had invited. It wouldn't have been you."

"Am I really that bad?"

"I can't say that you're 'bad,' but I wouldn't nominate you for a position in the foreign service."

"No, I guess not. I've never been able to contain my abrasiveness. It hasn't served me well."

Frank glanced at his friend, his face illuminated in the darkness by the glowing end of his cigar. There was a look of deep contemplation—and sorrow—on his face.

"You've done very well in life. We all come into this life with our own personalities. It wouldn't do to try to change them too much."

"Ah, there you go. Do you know that as you've gotten older you've become almost saccharine sweet? You've become too mellow. In the old days you would have responded to my revelation that, yes, I have a shitty personality, that I treated Ann badly, and that I should change my personality, using behavior modification techniques, because my lousy personality turned off people and made more enemies. And, now, you've joined the 'I'm O.K., you're O.K.' crowd."

"When I said that years ago, I meant it, and it was applicable. It no longer is. You're too old to change. You might as well live with your shitty personality."

Greg quietly chuckled, but didn't respond to his friend's assessment. He seemed to be pondering the implications of Frank's statement. After a moment he said:

"You know, Frank, you may be right. The damage has been done. What is the difference if I occasionally insult or shock the Anns of this world? How can their disapproval affect me in any way?"

"I wouldn't take this revelation too far. If you and Ann—or anybody else—were to slug it out by yourselves, that's one thing. But, when there are others around, those people can become uncomfortable...as Paula and I were tonight. You don't want to create too much of a wasteland around you."

"I'm sorry for tonight."

"You don't have to apologize to me. I've known you for fifty years. We've roomed together. We've been intimate friends. I have come to take you as you are. And, despite your quirks, Paula loves you. But she is going to feel uncomfortable and hurt when she sees you bulldozing her friend."

"Please tell Paula I'm sorry."

"Nonsense. If you're sorry, you tell Paula you're sorry."

"So, how is it that you're becoming so squishy in your opinions and mellow in your assessments of individuals? You used to be much tougher."

"Age, I guess. I don't feel as vehement about things as I used to, and I don't feel the need to declaim against people whose ideas or lifestyles I don't like as much as I did in the past."

"It's funny seeing the new you. I preferred the old you—the raging prophet. You were never constrained in holding forth unpopular opinions, whether at dinner parties or at other polite social gatherings. I can still remember you thundering against abortion at a dinner party...I forget where. And then there was the time at a cocktail party when you were holding forth on your theory that golfers were inherently shallow. That was your Golden Age. You were magnificent."

Both men quickly laughed at Greg's reminiscences. Frank was flooded with memories of similar harsh critiques of ideas and individuals. More than one person had accused him of being "judgmental"—a pejorative term among the "I'm O.K., you're O.K." crowd.

"I guess I can still get into arguments about ideas," said Frank meditatively, "but I don't slash at others as I used to. I guess I'm into discussing more than arguing. The other day I got drawn into a discussion on affirmative action. I stated my opinion as softly and mildly as I could, and then listened to the opposite position from the person I was having lunch with...and there the discussion ended."

"In the old days you would have called that person's ideas 'absurd,' 'totally lacking in internal logic,' and, let's see, probably 'moronic,' and you would have attributed such opinions to a lout or to an unthinking person."

"Yes, I would have done that."

"And do you really blame getting older for your increasing mellowness?"

"You know, I haven't given it all that much thought, but I think it is. I still feel as strongly that abortion is murder, that affirmative action creates more problems than it solves, that most welfare programs provide welfare for the bureaucrats who administer them, but I don't feel compelled anymore to be so vociferous and insulting as I used to be. I realize that I'm not going to change anyone's opinion, so I just state my position and let it go. The fire has gone out."

As Frank finished his description of how he had changed from the flamboyant debater and upholder of unpopular opinions to his current mild expositions, the telephone rang.

Frank's brow was furrowed as he looked at his watch.

"It's 11:30," he said. "Who could that be?"

He loped into the house from the patio and hastily grabbed at the insistently ringing telephone.

"Hello," he answered.

A woman's voice was at the other end. Frank listened intently, his face now a mask of concern and worry.

After a short, staccato conversation, Frank said, "Okay, I'll leave tomorrow and see you tomorrow night."

CHAPTER 17

Frank walked quickly down the antiseptic white corridor of St. Vincent's Hospital on Twelfth Street in New York City, eager to see his Uncle Vic.

Vic Bonfiglio, Frank's mother's brother, was a favorite relative. Twelve years younger than Frank's mother, Vic had escaped the proscriptions against going to college and the family demands that he be a grocer or farmer. Instead, he had worked while attending college, moved to New York, and found employment in an advertising agency, where he became a successful account executive.

Frank became close to his uncle. When he was growing up, he looked forward to Vic's annual visit to San Francisco. As an adult, Frank cherished visiting his uncle in New York. Although looked upon by the rest of the family as odd, Uncle Vic maintained warm relations with his family, and would go out of his way to encourage the intellectual, social, and economic ambitions of his nieces and nephews. Frank had found his warmth, generosity, and humor nurturing qualities while growing up and even as an adult.

Frank's cousin Joy had called him while he was chatting with Greg under the stars in Healdsburg. Vic had suffered a stroke. Frank packed a suitcase early the next morning and Greg had driven him to the San Francisco airport. It was midnight when he arrived at Kennedy—too late to go to the hospital—so he checked into the Windham Hotel on 58th Street. Because it was still early by his West Coast clock, he decided to spend an hour or so wandering around the vicinity of his hotel.

Frank walked across the street to the Oak Room in the Plaza Hotel. It was a Monday night, and the bar was not crowded. He ordered a Pimm's Cup, which he ordered only when he was in the Oak Room, and sipped it at a table while his eyes once again happily ran over the wooden walls of the elegant bar.

He had first experienced the Oak Room in his mid-twenties, during his first trip to New York as an adult. Frank remembered the excitement of viewing the great hotel and its famous bar during that visit. Not only was he impressed by the cavernous elegance of the Oak Room; his imagination soared as he wondered about the notables who might have visited the bar in the past.

Tonight the Oak Room was subdued. It was near closing time, and tomorrow was a workday. Frank sensed a feeling of winding down in "the city that never sleeps," and he was enjoying the lull in the manic energy of New York.

He paid for his drink and walked out of the Plaza, deciding to stroll down Fifth Avenue toward downtown. It was nearly 2 a.m., and yet there was action on the street. Cabs and autos swooshed down Fifth Avenue; a fair number of individuals were on the street; the occasional wail of a siren punctuated the mild night air.

Frank noticed the familiar stores: Bergdorff's, Van Cleef & Arpels, Tiffany's, Cartier's. Within a few hours their doors would be open for customers eager to purchase their wares. Who had the money to buy such expensive goods? Frank asked himself. It came to him how much money had been made in the past four decades—through real estate, oil, leveraged buyouts, technology—and how eager these newly-minted multi-millionaires and billionaires were to spend it.

Frank decided to walk a couple blocks on 57th Street. He loved to look into the windows of the art galleries—another venue for the newly moneyed to spend. If he had that kind of money, Frank thought, these would be the shops he'd haunt.

A bell somewhere sounded two o'clock. Frank still wasn't tired, but he decided to retrace his steps to his hotel. He wanted to get to the hospital early.

Within ten minutes Frank walked back into the lobby of the Windham Hotel. It was, as usual, dowdy. One person sat behind the desk, nodding to him as he walked to the creaky elevators.

The Windham was a hotel without amenities—no room service, almost surly desk attendants—but the location was superb, the rooms large and clean (Frank always asked for one in the rear of the hotel to be free of the noise of the garbage trucks), and the price for the rooms quite reasonable.

The elevator reached his floor, and Frank walked the short distance to his room. He opened the door and snapped on the light. He brushed his teeth, slipped into his sleep coat, and took a book from his briefcase. Frank read for about fifteen minutes before his eyes began to close. He turned off his bed light and slipped into sleep, wondering what his visit to Uncle Vic would be like.

There it was: room 438. Frank took a deep breath and walked in. His uncle had no roommate, and the television was silent. The curtain was drawn, and the light in the room was muted. Frank saw a shrunken old man in a hospital gown, dozing beneath the coverlet of his bed.

When had he last seen his uncle? About ten months before, Frank recalled, when Vic had been on his annual visit to San Francisco. The man dozing in the bed appeared to be a different person. The stroke had taken its toll, had squeezed and compressed his physicality. Frank could tell that Vic's facial muscles had been affected. A strange asymmetrical look had taken over his uncle's features.

Frank sat down on a leather chair next to his uncle's bed, ready to wait until his uncle awakened. The squeak of the chair when Frank sat down caused the sleeping man to open his eyes. A smile spread over his face when he saw his nephew. He tried to raise his right arm, but the limb would not respond.

"C—c—c—caro, h—h—how are..." His uncle stuttered.

Frank got up from the chair and embraced his uncle. "Zio, how are you?" He had always called his aunts and uncles by the Italian words for aunt and uncle.

His uncle's response was in the form of indistinguishable sounds. Frank saw the look of frustration and fear on his uncle's face.

"Don't bother trying to talk, Zio. You'll be back to your old self soon. Joy called me late Sunday night to tell me you'd had a stroke. I flew out yesterday, but got in too late last night to come by. I haven't had a chance to talk with Joy yet, but I guess she'll be by soon."

Frank looked at his uncle and saw his attempts at a welcoming smile. He also saw a man who loved him. Frank's earliest memories were of his uncle's affection for him—an affection that he had always returned. Uncle Vic was different from Frank's father, who was a martinet and who could never understand why Frank had no interest in athletics or in hunting and fishing.

Instead, his uncle was demonstrative in his love and always encouraged Frank's pursuit of knowledge and his interest in the arts. When Vic came to San Francisco, he would give Frank several books as presents and take him to the opera. Surrounded by family members who were grocers, farmers, and laborers, Frank looked at Uncle Vic as if he were a knight from one of the medieval tales he loved to read.

Despite Uncle Vic's college education and work in the advertising business, he still had some of the rough-hewn edges of the Italian peasant. He had an earthy sense of humor and a ferocious fund of commonsense. Frank delighted—as an adult—in his uncle's use of certain expressions that were common in his boyhood. A sofa was a "chesterfield." One "wiped," not dried, the dishes. And one "closed," not turned off, the lights.

His uncle's continued use of such expressions always brought Frank back to his years of growing up. It was as if he were watching a family sit-com on television: "Frank, close the lights. I haven't got stock in PG&E." "Frank, it's your turn to wipe the dishes." "Frank, don't sit on the chesterfield. It's brand new."

"Let me give you a rundown on the family, Zio." Frank wondered how he would continue a one-sided conversation with this man who had so much relished the give-and-take of talk. "Paula is well and sends her love. The children and the grandchildren are well. My life is pretty much the same…still working."

How quickly one could summarize his or her life. Frank didn't feel like elaborating on the details and nuances of his life, as he would have done if he and his uncle were sharing a meal at a restaurant or at one of their homes. He felt that his uncle was preoccupied with his own health and not really interested in the commonplace news of other lives.

 Frank became quiet. He reached for his uncle's hand and clutched it. Vic was the last of his parents' siblings—and the one he had loved the most. His uncle made no more attempts to speak or to move. His face showed his affection for Frank and also displayed his resignation to his paralyzed state. Frank prayed that his uncle would either die soon or have all his facilities restored.

To languish as a paralytic was not what his uncle would want. Here was a man who was a voracious reader, a superb conversationalist; a man who, after he had retired, volunteered to build houses for Habitat for Humanity. No, a life as a bedridden, helpless individual is not what Vic Bonfiglio would want.

"Oh, Frank, how wonderful of you to come!"

Frank looked up and saw his cousin Joy, Vic's only child. Joy was twenty years younger than Frank. They had never been close, but Frank dutifully contacted her whenever he came to New York. Often she and her husband Ted would have dinner with him. Frank had found it curious that his uncle had never suggested that Joy and Ted join them when the two of them got together.

"Hi, Joy. I got on the first plane I could."

The two of them hugged. Joy then bent over her father and kissed him on the cheek. Then she straightened up and took Frank's arm, gently steering him into the hallway.

"This was completely unexpected," Joy began. "Dad had his annual physical about two months ago and got a clean bill of health. He worked out every day and he always ate well...and he has never smoked. And, poof, he has a stroke. I can't figure it out."

"What have the doctors said?"

"What do doctors always say? They can't account for the stroke. They don't know when or if he'll recover. He needs to stabilize, they say, and then it's onto a rehab center. God only knows what's going to happen."

Frank was uncomfortable with Joy's directness about her father's condition. They entered Vic's room again. Frank could see his uncle's wide-open eyes fixed on Joy. Resoluteness mixed with sadness was evident on his face.

"Most people recover from strokes," Frank cheerfully stated. "Your father's health and habits have been good, and there's nobody I know who's tougher. He'll come out of this just fine."

"I hope you're right, Frank. I pray that you're right. How long are you going to be staying?"

Frank hadn't given any thought to how long he would stay in New York. When Joy had called, his first instinct had been his desire to see his uncle. It was obvious that his uncle would be in this paralytic state for some time to come. There was nothing that Frank could do for him. Joy would obviously deal with doctors and with all the details of his care during the time of recovery.

"I hadn't given it any thought. I just wanted to get here to see Zio Vic. I don't know...I'll probably stay around for at least a couple days."

"That would be great. Why don't Ted, you, and I get together for dinner tomorrow night?"

"Yeah...sure. We can work out the details tomorrow. You'll be here, of course."

"Where else?"

"I think I'll go now and come back this afternoon. I'll see you then." Frank turned to his uncle. "Goodbye, Zio. I'll be back this afternoon."

Zio Vic was staring at him, his eyes vacant. Had something happened to change his expression to one of mute unawareness? Frank leaned over to kiss him and squeeze his hand, but Vic made no movement in response.

There was no point, Frank thought, in staying by his uncle's bedside. Joy probably would want to speak to the doctors, and he felt it was not his place to be present at such a conference. He would run over to the Met or the MOMA and spend some time there before returning to the hospital.

Frank decided on the Met, and, as was his custom when in New York, he would go first to the current exhibition, if it was something he wished to see, and then select one or two galleries to visit. It was all that his eyes could take, he reasoned; and, over a number of years, he would be able to savor most of the treasures of this world-class museum.

None of the temporary exhibits held any interest for him, so he decided to visit the Met's collection of primitive art. But, before doing so, he would begin, as he always did, by walking through the medieval collection.

Frank had been fascinated with the Middle Ages since he had been a little boy. He could still remember his excitement at age eight reading *Medieval Days and Ways* and his ongoing interest in this field. During college he had even contemplated getting his Ph.D. in medieval history.

The fascination had not gone away, and Frank took every opportunity when in a museum to look at its medieval art and artifacts, and, when in Europe, to track down every piece of medieval architecture he could locate. He felt that he knew every piece of medieval art shown at the Met; he no longer lingered devoutly at each piece, but strolled through the galleries, his eyes quickly but lovingly resting on each piece of art.

Having accomplished this pilgrimage, Frank walked the corridors and stairs to the Met's collection of what he still called primitive art. He had always enjoyed looking at these artistic products of Africa, Oceania, and parts of Asia; he lamented that he had not become a collector many years before, when pieces were still modestly priced.

Frank began to look carefully at an array of masks from New Guinea, but he couldn't concentrate. Instead, in each mask he saw the face of his uncle. Masks, he remembered reading, gave a new or second identity to the wearer, and Frank wondered whether his uncle had worn a mask. To have escaped from a family that had limited social, intellectual, and economic goals, to have provided for himself an excellent education, and to have gone on to a successful career in advertising in New York meant not only that his uncle had to have had a laser-like focus and an iron determination, but also that he could exhibit multiple facets when he had to explain to his family why he was working two jobs so that he could afford to go to college, his pleadings to college administrators for scholarship funds, to his classmates so that he wasn't labeled an outsider.

Had all this taken its toll on his uncle? Frank didn't know, and now he might never know. As much as he had loved his uncle and all their conversations, Frank could not remember any time that his uncle opened up about difficulties in his life, problems he had, or the sharp edges in his relations with his family. Nor had his mother or other members of his mother's family ever revealed their thoughts or feelings about Uncle Vic. If there were secrets, they had gone to the grave. Vic would be described as "smart," a "hard worker," "adventurous." He was held in awe, but Frank could intuit that he was also seen to be an outsider.

Frank tried again to focus on the collection, most of it coming from Nelson Rockefeller, and soon began to put his uncle out of his mind. He could see how the African masks could have influenced the art of painters on the early part of the twentieth century. There was a stylized freshness in their elegant forms. Frank liked the fact that they gave a different identity to the wearer in a ritual. How very nice to become someone else for a time.

The thought brought him back to his uncle, and Frank's thoughts about his uncle led him on to his own life. What were his masks? What had he used them for? Did he use them to display a deeper truth about himself? Or did he use them to conceal himself?

Frank realized he couldn't concentrate on the exhibits. I might as well leave the museum, he thought and was at odds with himself as he walked down the steps of the Met. He wasn't ready to go back to the hospital, and he wasn't in the mood to go to another museum. Central Park seemed to invite him, and Frank decided to find a secluded spot far from the traffic of Fifth Avenue or Central Park West to sit and daydream.

This park's too skinny, he thought. You can lose yourself in Golden Gate Park, but it's tough to do here. After walking for ten minutes, Frank flopped down on a bench at the edge of a lawn. Two teenage girls, deep in conversation, passed him, but he saw no one else on the meandering lane.

I think Uncle Vic's stroke has got me spooked, Frank said to himself. He's only fifteen years older than I—time that can go by in the wink of an eye—and in fifteen years, or ten, or five, I can be lying paralyzed in a hospital bed.

His sense that time had become like a racing car at the Indy 500 had caused this preoccupation with death. If you sat close to where the race took place, you could barely see the cars as they zoomed by. That's what time had become for him. Someone would say about his granddaughter, for example, that she just turned fifteen; and his response would be, "Why it seems just like yesterday that she was born." And, indeed, the sense of time since the birth of his granddaughter did seem compressed. Then he would project fifteen years in the future and think that in a similar short space of time he could be incapacitated or gone.

Frank decided to leave the park—it was allowing him to sink into a depressed state of mind—and to visit his uncle at the hospital. He wandered out of the park and walked to Madison Avenue, where he entered the subway station.

Frank's trips to New York in recent years had impressed him with how clean and efficient the subway had become. Along with the restoration of the subway system, Frank had noticed how few homeless people inhabited the streets of the city. What a contrast to San Francisco, where the proliferation of panhandlers seemed to increase daily, becoming in the process more and more aggressive. Whatever Giuliani did when he was mayor of New York should be patented, Frank thought.

Frank emerged from the subway station and walked the short distance to St. Vincent's. He dreaded walking into the hospital and dreaded even more seeing his uncle in his current state.

As he walked down the corridor Frank saw Joy leaving his uncle's room.

"The doctor just told me that there isn't much hope for Dad's recovery," Joy said by way of greeting.

"What do doctors know? Did they predict that he would have a stroke?"

"No, but now that he's had one, I'll bet that their prognosis is pretty accurate. I'm going to have to figure out what to do when his time in the hospital is over...probably a long-term nursing facility."

Frank had never particularly cared for Joy, and now he despised her. She had inherited little or none of her father's warmth, charm, or generosity. A fading beauty, she was interested only in her status in society and in the material possessions she kept acquiring.

It seemed to Frank that she had no empathy for her father's plight and that she was ready to dump him in a nursing facility as an expedient way of not having to have to spend time and energy to make his life comfortable.

"Couldn't you hire people to take care of him at your place? He certainly has enough money for that," Frank inquired, fully knowing what Joy's answer would be.

"Are you kidding, Frank? Can you imagine our co-op smelling like a hospital...with all the entertaining for charities that I do?"

Frank looked grave, but didn't respond. He did not trust what might come out of his mouth.

"By the way, how about dinner tonight? We're both free, amazingly."

Frank nodded in acquiescence. Not really wanting to do so, but without a ready way to decline.

"Great," Joy responded to his mute agreement. "Let's say 8 o'clock at Babo's. Do you know it? It's on Washington Place. Great food and a lovely ambience."

"I'll see you and Ted there."

Joy flashed a smile. "I'm sure my father will be pleased to see you. See you tonight."

Frank entered the hospital room, and, even though his uncle looked grayer than he had looked earlier in the day, it was a pleasure to get away from Joy.

"Hello, Zio, how are you doing?"

Uncle Vic tried to speak, but only what sounded like stunted groans came from his mouth. His attempts to return Frank's embrace and kiss came to nothing. However, despite his futile efforts to return his nephew's hug, Uncle Vic's face flashed a happy radiance at seeing Frank.

Frank drew up a chair close to his uncle's bed, angling it so that he could look directly at him.

"Are you comfortable, Zio? Don't worry about talking. You've just had this stroke, and it takes a while to recover. You'll be in rehab for a few days, and that will be time enough for you to work on recovering your speech and your movement.

"I'll do the talking for both of us now. Not the first time, huh?"

Frank laughed and thought he saw some corresponding humor in his uncle's eyes.

"This gives me an opportunity to tell you how much I have cherished our relationship and how much I have loved you," Frank began, astonished at the outpouring of his deep feelings for his uncle. "I'm sorry that it takes an event like this for me to say what I've always known, but I think you've always known how I've felt about you. You've been like a father to me. And this is a good time to thank you for all you've done for me all my life...for your presents...remember, you gave me the first book I ever owned...for your good advice...for your encouragement. You're responsible for much of what is good in me today."

Uncle Vic was staring directly at Frank, his face impassive. But Frank could see tears collecting in his eyes.

Frank continued. "I know that in a few months, a year, two years, when we're chatting and enjoying a glass of wine and a cigar we'll both be embarrassed by this effusion of mine. But, because I know you can't interrupt me, I thought I'd say it now. There, I've said it...and I'm glad I did. I love you, Zio."

Frank squeezed his uncle's hand. Tears were flowing from Uncle Vic's eyes, and after a moment of quiet, he tried again to speak. Only a variety of unintelligible sounds came forth; and, after several attempts, Uncle Vic gave up and became content only to look at his nephew.

"Zio, I'm going to go back to the hotel now. I'm having dinner with Joy and Ted tonight. I'll be in to see you tomorrow morning, and then I'll be heading back to San Francisco. But I'll be back in New York to visit you again soon. See you tomorrow."

Frank got up and leaned over to once more hug and kiss his uncle. As Frank straightened up he looked down at a sad, frightened, and suddenly old man.

Babo's was crowded. An unctuous maître d' ushered Frank to the table where Joy and Ted were already seated.

Frank leaned over to give his cousin a kiss and then shook hands with Ted.

"Hi, Frank, good to see you again. Welcome to New York."

"It's great to be here, but I wish it were under better circumstances."

"Yeah, too bad about the old man. You just never know in life."

Ted Henderson was just about fifty years of age. Tall, good-looking, from an upper-middle-class family in Boston, educated in tony schools, he had inherited all the bonhomie and shallowness of his class and upbringing. He and Joy had constructed a life that was in constant motion: an endless series of social gatherings, vacations where their social peers were going, and just enough athletics—tennis for both, golf for Ted—to allow them to converse with their friends about their games.

Ted had had the foresight to get his M.B.A. after college. Then he'd used his good looks and social connections to obtain a position with an old-line investment banking company. He brought neither brilliance nor hard work to his firm, but his connections had been useful in delivering business—and the financial exuberance of the 1980s and 1990s had helped mask Ted's deficiencies.

His income was substantial, which, combined with the income from several buildings that Uncle Vic had given to Joy, provided them with the extravagant lifestyle they both so enjoyed.

Frank prepared himself for the condescending recommendations of dishes and wines from both Joy and Ted. He wasn't disappointed. They both recommended a variety of exotic-sounding, trendy dishes: absurd combinations of foods that emulated from creative chefs who had to cater to fickle, jaded diners who had forgotten that meals were about eating, not about innovation.

After listening to Joy's and Ted's suggestions, Frank selected what sounded the most edible and the least exotic of the recommendations.

"You won't be insulted if we drink a French wine?" Ted inquired. "I know you Californians think your wines are superior; but, regional chauvinism aside, you and I know better." Ted looked at Frank over the wine list, which he had been perusing with his square, half glasses.

Frank was in a mellow mood and had resolved not to be provoked by his cousin and her husband. "I'm sure you'll choose something with your usual good taste," Frank said graciously.

Ted went back to the wine list with no comment. He signaled their waiter and ordered a bottle of Chateau Y'Quem. Frank estimated that the bottle probably sold at the restaurant for about $300.

"So, how did you find my father this afternoon?" Joy asked.

"He seemed tired and not in as good shape as when I saw him this morning," Frank responded.

"The doctor says that if a stroke victim doesn't show substantial recovery within three or four days of the stroke, it is likely that he or she won't recover."

Frank tried not to show that he was irritated with Joy over her clinical analysis of her father's chances for recovery. While her reports may have been accurate, there was no sign of compassion for the frightened old man—her father.

"Whatever the prognosis is, Uncle Vic is going to need a lot of love to get him through this. He's been independent all of his life. He's always been very active, even after he retired. And, now, to be incapacitated like this, even if he does partially recover his speech and the use of his body, it's going to be tough on him."

"Yes, yes, no doubt," Joy responded dryly. "I've been looking into nursing homes for him...places that have good physical therapy facilities, and aren't...you know, too dreary."

"Joy, nursing homes aren't spas for the middle-aged and restless. They're places for old, sick people," Frank couldn't help letting out a bit of his exasperation.

"I know that. But I saw a couple places today that were terrible. The smell was horrible. A number of the patients there were constantly yelling. It was like being in an insane asylum."

"Well, Joy, as I said, people who go into nursing homes are either physically or mentally ill...or both. They're at the end of their lives, and both their bodies and their minds are breaking down. What you're going to see and hear...and smell...are people who are dying."

Both Joy and Ted grimaced at Frank's words. Frank didn't want to add that if Joy was so offended by nursing homes then she should keep her father in her home or in his, with around-the-clock help.

"I'll just keep looking until I find a well-managed care facility that isn't as...well, gross...as the ones I've seen so far," Joy said, swallowing her distaste for Frank's comments.

"I'm sure something will turn up," Frank mumbled, looking down at his plate.

Ted cleared his throat. "Well, Frank, old man, when are you going to take up golf? A man in your position should be out on the course a couple times a week, driver or iron in hand...good for the waistline you know...and for business."

Frank had been dreading this moment. Ted made the same inquiry every time they saw each other. How had his family acquired such dolts as Joy and her husband?

"I'm a little old for golf, Ted. I do some aerobic walking for exercise and I'm not actively pursuing business. I'm very pleased with my life and don't have much time for new activities, especially golf, which consumes the bulk of one day."

"Ah, you've been missing one of the great pleasures of life."

"I'm sure. How are things at the firm? I see that you've been getting some big underwriting deals." Frank was eager to change the subject.

"Oh, same-old, same-old," Ted replied. "We're one of the biggest—and the best, I might add—and we're always aiming to get more than our share." Ted gave a hearty laugh.

"I see that you've been eliminating the competition," Frank continued. "You've bought a couple of West Coast boutique investment banking firms."

"Oh, yeah. Well those firms do okay in the beginning, but they have no staying power. They can't compete with the big boys."

"Why don't 'the big boys' just wait for them to fold?" Frank asked, genuinely interested.

"That would complicate things. It's much easier to buy the existing clientele of the firm through an acquisition. Most of the clients stay with you, and you're not out there scrambling and competing for the clients of a defunct firm."

"That makes sense. Do the acquisitions impact your bonus? There are a lot more mouths to feed."

"No, not at all." Ted looked somewhat annoyed at the question.

"It's a shame you won't be here next week, Frank," Joy interrupted. "I'm co-chair of the annual museum gala. It would be fun to have you there with us." She had clearly been bored with the earlier conversation and wanted to interpose with topics more congenial to her interests.

"Unfortunately, I'm still employed…and I should get back to Paula."

"Ah, yes, how is Paula?" Joy asked.

"She's terrific, and sends her regards to the two of you."

This was a lie. Paula hadn't said to him on his departure to say hello to Joy and Ted, both of whom she detested. Both his cousin and her husband had looked on Paula as a cute diversion of his, not someone to be taken seriously. Their condescension to her each time they met was palpable.

"Oh, that's lovely. Please send her our love and hugs and kisses," Joy intoned.

Their appetizer consumed, they were now working on their entrée. Joy had eaten about a quarter of the appetizer and was now picking at whatever it was that she had ordered. Frank hadn't heard her order and couldn't recognize what was on her plate. Ted nodded to the server to refill their wine glasses; the server acted as if he were pouring liquid gold, which Frank thought, it is.

"Joy, you must have had a big lunch today. You're not eating very much," Frank coyly needled.

"Oh, no, I barely ate at lunch. But, you know, a girl's got to watch her figure." Joy trilled a dry laughter.

Frank had witnessed such gastronomic habits in San Francisco, as well. Society women talked incessantly about the trendy restaurants and trendy chefs, about the food and the ambience. They spent fortunes to dine at these places, but never ate.

"My gosh, you're as thin as a rail. I can't imagine your having to watch your figure."

Joy looked pleased by Frank's comment. "Staying thin is the result of not overeating, you know," she replied.

Frank wondered why women like Joy didn't just stay home and nibble on some lettuce a few times a day, instead of spending fortunes each year eating out at restaurants twice a day. The results would have been the same and they would be saving tens of thousands of dollars.

"Whatever your regimen is, you look terrific, Joy...you, too, Ted," Frank said.

"Nothing that a couple golf games a week and a daily workout at the gym can't do," Ted noted.

"Why, Frank, that's very nice of you to say," Joy interjected. "As you know, you've got to work at keeping fit. I don't eat too much. I work out... and play a lot of tennis. And, then, of course, I go to the spa four times a year."

Frank wondered what the purpose was for all this effort. He thought, Joy is almost fifty years old. Does she want to perpetually look thirty? Does she expect to live forever? Is there some sort of competition in her social circle as to how young one can look or how thin one can be? A woman starves herself to look thin and spends hours each week working out, or spends a fortune to go to a spa and be tortured for a week—and what is the result? You still start to look old at a certain point or you get breast cancer or ovarian cancer...or you get dementia.

Joy and Ted both turned down dessert, and Frank did also. The waiter brought decaffeinated coffee and a cognac for Ted. The conversation was petering out, with Joy and Ted muttering about how good the food had been at the restaurant and how they should come more often.

The waiter brought Ted the bill, and, when Frank took out his wallet to retrieve his credit card to either pay the bill or pay his share of it, Ted dramatically put up his hand to signify that Frank should put his wallet away.

"Now, Frank, you're our guest tonight. I'll pick up the tab. You host us when we're in San Francisco. Both Joy and I are grateful that you've come out to see Vic."

Frank knew that the next morning Ted would give the bill to his secretary for his expense account, but he was nevertheless grateful to be spared the tab of several hundred dollars for the dinner.

The threesome rose to leave the restaurant, and both the waiter and the maître d' fawned over them as they threaded their way among the tables to the entrance of the restaurant.

The air was warm but not moist. There was a soft breeze. The cacophony of New York was evident after the soft murmurings of the bistro.

"I think I'm going to walk to my hotel," Frank announced as the three of them stood in front of the restaurant. "It's a gorgeous evening. I'm going to see your father tomorrow morning and then take an afternoon flight to San Francisco. Will I see you at the hospital?"

"No...no, not tomorrow. I have a hair appointment in the morning and a committee meeting in the afternoon. And I'm going to have to find some time to look at some more nursing homes."

"I'll call you in a couple days to see how your father is doing. Ted, thanks so much for dinner. It was great seeing the two of you. Take care of Uncle Vic."

Frank shook hands with Ted and gave his cousin a hug.

"Have a safe trip home," Joy called out as Ted hailed a cab.

Frank walked along 72nd Street until he came to Central Park West. He loved walking in New York—day or night. Frank Sinatra was right, Frank mused: it's a city that never sleeps. Vehicles zipped along the street. Electric lights flashed everywhere he looked. And even in the residential area in which he was walking at eleven o'clock, Frank could feel the pulsating dynamo of activity and energy that was New York.

He had enjoyed coming to New York ever since his first trip there as an adult in the mid-1960s. He had had numerous pleasant adventures in the city and had encountered a number of fascinating personalities—from romantic liaisons to business connections. A great city to visit, Frank thought, but I wouldn't want to live here.

Smiling at the truism that had come up in his mind, Frank felt sadness overcome him as he anticipated his visit with his paralyzed uncle the next morning. He tried to expunge the sadness and instead concentrated on his trip home and how happy Paula would be to see him.

CHAPTER 18

Back in San Francisco, Frank decided one morning to walk to his office. The earlier overcast had cleared, and it was a mildly warm, sunny day. San Francisco's downtown area sparkled in the sunlight. He didn't reminisce about businesses that were no longer at the locations he was walking by as he headed toward his office. Instead, he attempted to fix his mind on the conversation he had had the previous day with Marcia Cantor, his therapist.

He would have to set out the questions she had asked him and allow his mind to play with them. Frank had found that solutions to problems could frequently be found by intensely contemplating the situation. He had experienced that the more he thought about some problem or some situation, the more multi-faceted it became, giving him more choices of action or more solutions.

From his thoughts there came forward one resolve: he would no longer share his thoughts on death with friends and family. They were beginning to think he was crazy or obsessed. Also, he needed to wrestle with his thoughts and feelings deep inside himself; it didn't help to have conversations with others about them.

Frank arrived at the Russ Building, strode briskly through the lobby, and stepped into an elevator that lifted him hundreds of feet into the air. Jessica greeted him with her usual broad smile as he walked up to her desk. "Welcome back, Mr. M. Did you work through all your problems?"

"Absolutely. We decided that if I was your age again, and as good-looking, I wouldn't have any problems."

"Good luck," she said, with her customary giggle. "You've got a ton of messages. I put them on your desk. Oh, and Mr. Hopkins came by and asked if you could stop by to see him when you have a moment...whenever."

Frank was somewhat surprised by this request. He almost never saw the managing partner except at office meetings. They had a good relationship, but had never been socially close. What business they needed to transact together was almost always done in the context of a partners' meeting or one of the firm's committee meetings.

"Okay, I'll go see him after I've looked at my messages. Thanks, Jessica."

Frank was feeling overwhelmed by the amount of work that had piled up on his desk ever since he had made two trips to New York after his uncle's stroke. He thumbed through the sheaf of messages that Jessica had put on his desk. Three or four friends had called. He'd call them later. Several clients had called, but none of the messages seemed urgent. Most client calls, Frank had long ago decided, were meaningless. Something might come up in one of their minds, and, if they had some time, he or she would call. There would be nothing substantial in what they wished to talk about: they just wanted to call. Then there were those who had been told something by a friend—something that usually had to do with the fact that their portfolio wasn't doing as well as their friend's. Ego suddenly would begin to rear its ugly head.

Of course, Frank always returned each call. But, as he had gotten older, he had done so less cheerfully, and he noticed that hints of sarcasm had crept into his conversations. He needed to watch that, he noted.

Well, might as well go see Calvin Hopkins, Frank thought. He was not in the mood to answer these calls.

Frank walked down the corridor to the managing partner's office. "Hi, Greta. Is Mr. Hopkins available? He told Jessica that he wanted to see me."

"Let me check, Frank." She picked up the intercom phone and stated, "Frank Molinari's here to see you, Mr. Hopkins." There was a short pause and she looked up at Frank, "Okay, go right in."

"Hi, Frank. Good to see you. It's nothing urgent…just wanted to chat about some things. It could have waited."

"I got your message when I came in. I figure there's no time like the present."

"I was sorry to hear about your uncle's death. I gather the two of you were pretty close."

"Yes, we were very close. He was my mother's younger brother, so we were not that far apart in age."

"Well, again, sorry to hear about it."

The managing partner of Blakesley & Montgomery was movie-star handsome. In his mid-50s with touches of gray at his temples, Calvin Hopkins was tanned from frequently playing golf and tennis. He lived across the bay in Piedmont, where he was part of an affluent country-club set. Frank had admired his skills as the firm's managing partner. He was fair and did an excellent job obtaining consensus among the partners for decisions that had to be made. And his affable personality, his exquisite manners, and patrician good looks combined to make him an effective marketer for the firm.

Hopkins got up from his desk and pulled a chair from another part of his office over to where Frank was standing.

"Frank, something has been flickering through my mind, and I thought I would bring it up to you in a preliminary way. We can continue to discuss it over the months to come.

"What came into my mind was my need to inquire what, if any, plans you have to retire or cut back in any way your involvement with the firm. You may not have thought about any of this...at least, you haven't shared any thoughts with me. That's why I said that we can explore this issue in the months to come. The reason I am bringing this up to you is that in my capacity of managing partner of Blakesley & Montgomery, I've got to think about the long-term management of the firm. That means from time to time bringing in young associates as partners. But, to do that, we need meaningful partnership interests to offer them. You know how it goes.

"As you know, we don't have a 'sixty-five' rule here, as, let's say, most law firms do, which automatically sets an age for mandatory retirement from the firm, and I don't think we want one. And, obviously, I am not saying that you're not a continuing valuable asset to this firm. You most certainly are. It's just that I would like to have some indication of your individual plans so that I can do some long-term planning."

Frank couldn't speak. He sat, stunned.

"I know this can't be easy to hear, Frank, and I'm sorry to be the one to say it," Hopkins said, looking directly at Frank. "Please, please, keep in mind that I am in no way trying to push you out the door. My only purpose in asking you the question I did is to help me make some decisions about the before long-term planning for the firm."

Hopkins' additional attempt to sooth him helped Frank catch his breath and try to recover from his shock. His first inclination was to start shouting, stomp out of the room, and write out his resignation. Instead, he took a few deep breaths and attempted to slow down his racing heart and thoughts. He needed to get out of the managing partner's office.

"Of course you need to plan for the firm," Frank began. "It's just that you caught me by surprise. But, sure, let me think about it and we'll discuss it."

Frank stood up, followed by his partner, who held out his hand to shake Frank's. Frank's trembling hand took it limply.

"Let me say once again, Frank, that I consider you, and everyone here considers you, an invaluable asset at Blakesley & Montgomery. I can't tell you often enough that my query is merely to ascertain your own wishes, so that I can incorporate them in my planning."

"I understand," said Frank. "I'll spend some time thinking about it and then we'll talk."

Frank closed the door to Hopkins' office behind him and stopped for a moment. He felt that his face was flushed and he knew that his mind was racing. Why hadn't he anticipated this meeting, this revelation, he asked himself? Was he really going to be put out to pasture? Were they going to kick him out of the firm? He needed to sit down...and calm down.

Thank God Jessica is not at her desk, Frank thought, not wishing to encounter his secretary. He went into his office and closed the door. Instead of sitting at his desk, Frank sat on the settee where his clients generally sat when they visited.

I've got to be calm, Frank thought. I need to think this through. Hopkins is as smooth as silk, I know. What is he really trying to tell me? Does he want me out of here? Do the other partners want me out? Well, I'm not going.

Anger began to supplant the surprise that had overwhelmed him in Hopkins' office; and Frank began to tell himself that he would defy any order to leave. He knew the partnership agreement: there was nothing in it about no longer being a partner after a certain age. He had been a major contributor to building up the firm, by God, and he was still more than pulling his weight.

On the other hand, he thought, he had been playing around with semi-retirement in his mind for the last couple years. He hadn't come to any decision, but he'd thought about it. That would have meant altering his partnership situation. And he certainly understood Hopkins' need for long-term planning for the firm. It wouldn't be able to keep the youngsters, the kids who were out there hustling as he had hustled in his twenties and thirties, if he couldn't offer them partnership interests in the firm. No, that made sense. And it made sense that Hopkins would ask him what his plans were. The anger began to recede.

But what about me? Frank asked himself. Am I ready to retire? Am I even ready to cut back? Look at my friends. A couple of them who had retired subsequently went to seed. Most of the others had cut back to the point of effective retirement, but wouldn't admit it. If you used the "R" word about them, they went ballistic.

Frank could see that Jessica had returned to her desk. He knew that her delicate antennae would be able to surmise that he was agitated. Perhaps he should leave the office...take a walk.

Jessica walked over to another desk to speak to one of the other secretaries, and Frank bolted out of his office door, saying to her without stopping, "I'll be back in an hour."

Montgomery Street was quiet even though that it was almost the lunch hour. One no longer saw the "movers and shakers" of the financial district on the street anymore, as you would for the first decade or so when Frank had worked there. The financial district was now spread over many blocks; and one had never heard of most of the new "movers and shakers."

Frank felt better in the late morning sunshine. A mild breeze wafted down the street, unlike the wind tunnel that Montgomery Street so often was. He didn't even perform his daily ritual of muttering about how badly dressed those walking down the street were. His mind was fixed on the conversation he had just had with the managing partner.

Why am I so resistant to retiring or to cutting back? he asked himself. Was it because the suggestion constitutes a conclusion to my work life—yet another symbol (or, omen, perhaps) of my getting near to the end of life? The walk was clearing his head, but he realized that this was not the time for him to be making decisions or getting down to the nitty-gritty of his death phobia. He needed to be sitting down with a paper and pencil for that.

"Frank Molinari, you look as if you've got the weight of the world on your shoulders." A hand clapped him on the shoulder.

Frank turned around to see the smiling face of Chris Martini.

"Christ, Chris, you scared me to death. How have you been? I haven't seen you in ages."

"I've been great. I feel fine. No complaints."

"And if you did you wouldn't utter them."

"What's the use? But what's with the long face? I saw you from down the block and it looked like you were going to jump off the Golden Gate Bridge. What gives?"

Frank didn't feel like discussing his concerns, but he realized that it would not do to blow off his old friend. "Something I didn't expect," Frank began. "The managing partner called me in this morning to ask me if I had any plans to retire or to cut back. He said my input would be helpful to him for his long-term planning for the firm. It took me by surprise."

"Hell, I've been telling you for two years that you should retire or cut back," Chris retorted. "You've got enough money to live well and you've got lots of interests. I can't figure out why you're still banging away."

"Well, you're not exactly my role model. If I say you're retired, you explode, telling me you're not retired. And then you tell someone else that you're playing golf two or three times a week."

Chris chuckled. "Well, I guess you're right. I'm not fully retired, but I have cut back. And I don't want the word to get out that I'm retired, because then people whose work I don't like wouldn't come to me."

"'O, what tangled webs we weave...' Why don't you just chuck it all as you've advised me to do?"

"Well, you can't play golf in the winter. So what are you going to do?"

"I'm going to take a month or so to think about it and then make a decision. There's no age limit at the firm, so they're not going to throw me out. Their big thing is giving partnership interests to the younger people, and that makes sense."

"Take my advice and get out. There's nothing worse than being in a place where they want to give your partnership to a younger person. It's like being in a family where the children are waiting for you to die so that they can inherit your money."

"Are either of these scenarios from personal experience?"

"No. That's because I sold out my interest in my firm a few years ago. And now I pay my share of office expenses and take on whatever work I want. So no one's breathing down my neck waiting for me to retire."

"All that went on because you wanted to retire...maybe not fully, but you decided you didn't want any more administrative responsibilities and you didn't want to work as much as you once did. But that's not my situation. I may have thought a little about the possibility of retiring or cutting back, but it wasn't that I was planning to do so anytime soon."

"It sounds as if you've been given a wake-up call to start seriously thinking about it."

"There's no way that they can force me to retire or cut back, and I am still carrying my weight at the firm."

"They might not be able to force you out, but I'll bet they can sure make it uncomfortable for you. And why in hell are you resisting this so much? You're beyond the age when most people retire. And you've got enough money to retire comfortably. Why hold on?"

"I don't know. I guess I haven't thought that much about it." Frank was now feeling uncomfortable with Chris' probing. He didn't want to tell him what was probably the true reason for his not wanting to retire: that continuing to work full time helped him to lessen his aggravation with getting older and with his recent obsession with death.

"I'll take your advice and give it some thought," Frank concluded.

"Good. I think you'll see that what I've said makes sense. Go out at the top of your form, whether you're a boxer, a baseball player...or an investment advisor."

"Thanks, coach, that was a great pep talk. I really feel fired up."

Chris smiled. "Don't get goofy, now. Just give it some thought, and I'm sure you will make the right decision.

"I've got to go, but one more thing. Are you going to the reunion? Monica and I will pick up you and Paula and we can drive there together."

"Ugh. I'm sorry I haven't said something sooner, but I'm pretty sure I'm not going to go. I just don't feel like it."

"You're going to go if I have to hog-tie you. Are you kidding...not going to go?"

"The one we went to twenty-five years ago was depressing, and this one will be even more depressing. I'm not into masochism."

"Oh, get off it. Just go because you're curious about what the people we graduated from high school with a half-century ago look like now. You've got to go. You are one of the stellar graduates of our class!"

"Did you see the last copy of the alumni magazine? Art Grogas, who lives in Canada, wrote an article for it and provided some photographs for the article in which he tells about driving out West and getting together with three of our classmates. Somewhere in the Southwest, I think. There they were, fifty years after getting out of high school and all looking old. It was depressing. And can you imagine their conversations? Chatter on 'the good old days' and sentences that began 'And do you remember when...' No thank you."

"Don't be so cynical. We only get together every quarter century, and I don't think there will be a big gathering for the next one. Come on...it should be fun."

"What should be fun about it? Why should I want to see those whom I didn't particularly want to see during four years of high school? And those I did want to see then, I see today."

"You're going just because I want to discuss the evening with you after it's over. And if you persist in telling me that you don't want to go, I'm going to call Paula and tell her to cut you off."

"Okay, okay, I'll give it some more thought. I'll let you know."

"Tomorrow. Tomorrow you'll let me know."

"Yes, yes, yes…tomorrow. Now get going and let me finish my ambling while I think of all the things you've told me to think about."

"Come to the right decisions about both matters. I'll talk with you tomorrow. So long."

"It's been a real pleasure running into you," Frank called out to the retreating figure of his friend, his voice dropping with irony.

"Yeah…yeah…me too," Chris shot back, as he disappeared among the crowds that now had begun to fill Montgomery Street.

Frank continued his walk and his musings. Of all the people to run into, Frank thought. Chris had been one of his closest friends since they had entered high school together fifty-four years ago. Their temperaments were quite different, but their friendship was an intimate one. Chris never felt constrained about giving Frank advice, based upon his own sensible and conservative approach to life. His advice on the retirement issue certainly made sense. He would have to plug Chris's thoughts into his own thinking about what he should do about retirement.

And what would he do about Chris's pressure to attend his fifty-year high school graduation reunion? High school had been a difficult time for him. For a number of reasons he had not done well academically. He had felt that the priests who taught him had not understood him. And he hadn't known what to do with the sexuality that was burgeoning within him.

He'd certainly had some enjoyable times—appearing in some school plays and winning some oratorical contests came to mind—and he'd certainly made a handful of close friends; but did that warrant spending an evening trying to remember the names of people you hadn't seen in at least twenty-five years, trying to find topics of conversation and trying to incorporate Paula and other spouses in the interaction? Augh.

On the other hand, as Chris had pointed out, he *was* curious about how his classmates looked fifty years after graduation, what they had done, and what they were doing. He knew that he would probably have the youngest and the best-looking wife at the gathering. He'd certainly had a successful career, perhaps not the most successful in position and financial recompense, but certainly successful enough.

Frank realized that he had never been fond of his high school. He was not one of those for whom high school was truly alma mater. His four years in high school had been filled with anguished loneliness, of yearning for female affection and companionship, of giving in to the eccentricities that resulted a dismal academic record. During that time there had been some pleasant moments, some triumphs, and comradeship with a handful of friends. He had stayed in touch with these friends.

Still, the question remained in his mind: did he want to spend several hours with a miscellaneous assortment of classmates that he didn't particularly care for a half century before and who were nothing to him but pictures in his yearbook?

Frank was now strolling along Broadway. How do these sleaze places stay in business? he asked himself. Signs advertising "Naked Love Acts," "Strippers Galore," "Get Off On Our Gals" littered the block. Do people still come to these places? It was too early for the barkers, whose funny patter always enlivened a walk along the block of Broadway that contained the remnant of the 1960s sex shows. The bright sun gave the buildings a tired, depressed look.

He had driven down Broadway one night when he and Paula were returning late from a party in the East Bay. It was about 1:45 a.m., just as the places were about to close, and substantial numbers of people were leaving the various sex-show venues. It was a Friday night, and the crowd looked like guys in their late-teens and twenties from places like Hayward or Pleasant Hill for a night in the strip clubs. A night in the big city.

Frank's "monkey mind" now began to go into overdrive. His memory flitted to Broadway in the 1950s, when he and friends would go to the Hungry i, Enrico Banducci's now legendary night-club; the Purple Onion; and another venue for young, undiscovered talent, the Bocce Ball, where a small orchestra onstage would play for young men and women singing opera arias and duets.

But his favorite place was probably the Matador, a small, elegant bar that featured such young jazz artists as Dave Brubeck, Cal Tjader, George Shearing, and Vince Guaraldi. Frank had smoked Marlboro cigarettes then. He would sit at the bar or one of the small tables, have a drink, and smoke a few cigarettes, listening to the mellow jazz of men who would become legends. It had been one of his great pleasures.

Where have all those intimate, quiet places gone? Frank asked himself. The Yerba Buena, down the hill from the Fairmont Hotel, with its piano bar. The Fairmont itself with the Cirque Room. Sitting around the piano bar at the Rendezvous, listening to Inez Jones sing her bawdy songs.

Oh, boy, I better get back to the office, Frank thought, before I go over the bend with this nostalgia. But, where did all those places go? he once again asked himself. Can it be that no one wants to sit down with a drink in a quiet place and listen to a jazz trio or the mellow music of a good pianist?

Frank looked up Montgomery Street. Should he climb the few blocks to the top of Telegraph Hill and look out over the bay? No, he thought, I feel better and I need to get back to work. I can think about retirement and the high school reunion tonight.

CHAPTER 19

Exactly 100 teenagers—either 17 or 18 years old—had graduated from St. Aloysius High School in 1955. They had spent four years in one of three classes—A, B, or C—determined when those applying for admission had taken an entrance examination.

One of Frank's first interests when Paula and he entered the Olympic Club's golf club, called Lakeside, where the fiftieth reunion of his graduation from high school was being held, was to determine how many of his classmates had shown up. There were probably a hundred people in the spacious room in the clubhouse, where drinks and hors d'oeuvres were being served. If you subtracted a handful of individuals associated with the school and the spouses of the alumni attending, about forty of his classmates were in attendance, Frank computed. He seemed to remember that a handful of his classmates had died...so, let's see, about half are here...not bad.

Frank was nervous...far more nervous than when he was introduced to some large group of strangers to whom he had to give a talk. Fortunately, Paula and he received large-print nametags just as they entered. Frank attached his to his suit coat lapel and hoped that he could quickly read those of his classmates. Frank also wondered how many of his classmates he would recognize. Fifty years, after all, represented a significant amount of time. Hair turned grey and fell out. People limped from arthritis or knee replacements that didn't work out.

He decided to get into the evening slowly. First, he decided to get a drink and then try to single out those whom he had liked to talk to in high school. The bar looked empty, and he guided Paula to it by a circuitous route.

"A glass of chardonnay and a gin and tonic," Frank ordered from the bartender.

Frank instantly recognized the voice behind him. Paula turned toward him with a slight, expectant smile, wondering which of her husband's classmates would be the first she would meet.

"Well, Timmy Sullivan, nice to see you," Frank began. "This is my wife, Paula. Paula, Tim Sullivan."

Frank had despised Sullivan in high school. The only child born to parents well in their forties, he had grown up in economic affluence—the arrogant, pampered son of elderly parents. Sullivan's perpetual, condescending smirk had annoyed Frank in high school, had annoyed him twenty-five years ago at the last reunion he had attended, and annoyed him now.

Tim Sullivan had become the vice chairman of one of the largest of the Fortune 500 companies—quite a corporate success, but one that mystified Frank, as he had never seen any imagination or creativity in Sullivan. Frank thought him bright enough, but certainly not brilliant. Perhaps it was true that large corporations chose snots with a good golf game as their top executives.

"Are you still working or have you retired?" Sullivan asked, after nodding to Paula and giving the bartender his drink orders.

"I'm still working, I'm happy to say. How about you?"

"I retired about six months ago," Sullivan laconically replied. Frank had seen the announcement of his retirement in the newspapers, but hadn't wanted to acknowledge that he had in any way followed Sullivan's career.

"Are you working because you want to or have to?" Sullivan asked as he grabbed the two drinks he had ordered and began to walk away.

"I believe in sticking with things I like doing," Frank answered, suppressing his inclination to start choking his old nemesis.

"Well, this is a great beginning," Paula said. "Hell of a guy. Were you close?"

"Your irony is not without cause. A bad omen…to encounter as the first person at one's reunion someone who was the biggest jerk in the school."

"It's got to get better from here."

"It certainly can't get any worse. Let's plunge into the maelstrom."

Frank and Paula moved away from the bar and headed toward a small knot of people laughing and talking. Frank took Paula's elbow and veered her away from the cluster of chattering couples.

"What's the matter?" Paula inquired.

"Oh, it's a group of people whom I barely knew in high school. If we were to join their group, they would think that aliens had landed from space. Let's see who else is out there."

"I can see that this is going to be a most unusual evening," Paula said with upraised eyes. "Why didn't we just have a cocktail or dinner party for those people you do want to see?"

"That would have been too simple." Frank responded, his eyes scanning the room. "Ah, there are Chris and Monica talking with Len Maestri and I guess his wife. That should be great."

"At last, an acceptable person."

Paula had known Chris Martini and his wife Monica for as many years as she had known Frank. She went up to them and gave each of them a hug and a kiss. Frank greeted Len, whom he had not seen since their last reunion, a quarter century before, and who introduced him to his wife, Emily. Frank then introduced Paula to this couple she did not know, and, with greetings and introductions completed, the sextet began to describe what they had been doing for the past twenty-five years.

Len Maestri had been a close friend of Frank's during their high school years. They had lived near each other and shared similar intellectual interests. They had gone to different colleges in the West, and as a result, their friendship had diminished. It had evaporated after Maestri had gone east for law school. For perhaps a couple of decades after they had graduated from high school they had seen each other every two or three years, either in New York, where Maestri was practicing law, or in San Francisco. That desultory connection came to an end, and they hadn't seen each other since the last reunion. There had been no quarrel, but time and distance, and different lifestyles, had effectively put an end to their relationship.

That was O.K., Frank thought. Life brings organic changes. Those who had been old friends are winnowed into being acquaintances; and you meet people along the way who become new friends. Friendships change as one progresses through life.

"Are you still living in Manhattan?" Frank asked Maestri.

"Still there. I love living in the city. My two oldest daughters are now in their early 40s and the youngest is her mid-20s. We're empty nesters and can enjoy all the city has to offer."

"And, I guess...at least I've heard...that you're retired. What have you been doing since then?" Frank asked.

"I've signed up for the Ph.D. program at Columbia," Maestri laughed. "Don't ask me what I'm going to do with the degree. Nothing, I suspect.

Even though I was a philosophy major at Stanford, I've always been interested in history, and decided to go for a Ph.D. in history."

"Now that's what I call an ambitious post-retirement plan," Chris said, chuckling.

The three women in the group all smiled politely, knowing that this conversation was only the first of the evening's spousal retrospectives.

"I figured that I could complete the program in five or six years. I'll be in my early 70s. Maybe I'll feel like doing a little teaching after that...or maybe not. We'll see. In the meantime I'm having a good time being back in school."

"You make me feel like a sluggard," Chris said.

"I'm sure that you're doing what you want to do now that you're retired," Maestri responded.

"Well...I'm not fully retired. I'm no longer a partner in the firm, but I go into the office two or three times a week and work with a few clients I really like," Chris said in an almost apologetic way.

"And, Frank, have you retired?" Maestri asked.

"You've hit a sore subject," Chris laughed. "I can't get Frank to pull the plug."

"I don't see you pulling the plug entirely," Frank shot back at Chris. "But, to answer your question, thanks to our friend here I'm turning the question over in my mind. I'm not sure I'm ready to fully retire yet. I still like the business...but I'll probably start pulling back soon."

Paula looked at Frank with some surprise. He had not yet discussed with her his conversation with the firm's managing partner or his conversation with Chris.

"I'm sure you'll make what decisions are best at whatever time is best for you," Maestri said with bland suavity. "And, Paula, how about you, are you still working?"

"I'm an interior designer on my own, and I work at whatever pace I choose. I take off whatever time I want to go to our place in the country or to go on vacation, and, when I get tired or bored with what I'm doing, I just won't do it anymore. It's no big deal."

"A perfect situation," Maestri declared. "And, Monica, how about you?"

"I haven't worked outside the home since I was married. I am doing now, and I guess will continue to do until I die, exactly what I've been doing for over fifty years. The only difference is that instead of raising two children, I'm helping to take care of four grandchildren."

In order to cover all bases, Frank took the opportunity to ask Emily Maestri about what she was now doing.

"I practiced law until about ten years ago and then quit," she responded. "Now I serve on some boards of charitable organizations and try to have as much fun as I can."

"Sounds pretty good to me," Frank said.

There was a pause in the conversation. It struck Frank that each alumnus and his wife had given a brief synopsis of their recent lives. Retirement and what one was doing after retirement were major topics at any fifty-year reunion. This seemed to be the end of that conversation, and there appeared that there was very little else that anyone wished to say. The six of them were certainly not going to discuss the intimate details of their lives during the past half century: divorces, fears and tragedies, disappointments and failures, the extinguishing of many hopes, thoughts about impending old age and death. No, maybe it was time to re-group and recycle the same conversations again. He had his part down...so did Paula. It was time to listen to different scenarios.

This was accomplished by the arrival of two new couples. Foster Huntley had been bright enough but was remembered as being a star on the school's football team. Frank had seen him every school day for four years, but they had never been friends. Every so often they exchanged a bit of banter, but for neither had there ever been the slightest desire to enhance the fact that they shared the same classroom.

His wife—the second, Frank seemed to remember—looked like an aging floozy. She was well into her fifties, with bleached blond hair, dressed in clothes that would have embarrassed a pop tart. Her makeup had been put on with a trowel, giving her in addition the look of a harlequin.

With Huntley was Doug Jackson, whom Frank had never known very well. He had been famous in high school as a lothario; but the good looks that Frank had remembered a half century before had faded. He was bald and paunchy. His face was creased and wrinkled.

Doug Jackson's wife, his girlfriend during their senior year of high school, also looked old. Frank seemed to remember that she had been a year behind them in school, pretty in a conventional way, with an engaging smile and a voluptuous figure. The prettiness was gone, and the figure had become thickset and dumpy. Her hair was gray without any of the handsomeness of white.

"So, there are the intellectuals," Foster Huntley proclaimed with forced heartiness. "How you doing, guys?" He dramatically stuck out his hand for handshakes all round.

Once more the introductions of spouses were made. And once more the queries about what each had been doing for the last number of years began.

The fact that there were now ten people in the group allowed Frank a chance to escape. Why hadn't the school just solicited from each alumnus an essay about what he had been doing for the past quarter century, and sent them out with a current photo of all alumni? Frank wondered. That could have been the reunion.

Frank nudged Paula, and the two of them eased themselves out of the group. He looked back to see the resulting octet engaged in animated conversation, smiles and guffaws punctuating whatever they were saying.

As Frank was trying to ascertain whom he could espy who would be somewhat interesting to talk to, a woman who retained the remnants of good looks approached him. She looked familiar, but Frank couldn't remember how—or if—he knew her.

"Hi, Frank," she said, coming up to Paula and him. "Don't say you remember me, because I'm sure you don't. Margie Callahan, now Margie Schumpater."

"My God, of course," Frank exclaimed, stunned by seeing one of the beauties from a nearby Catholic girls high school. "I mean...why are you here? Oh, of course, you must have married Mike."

"You got it. A third for us both. And, hopefully, this one is the charm."

"Margie, this is my wife, Paula. Paula, this is Margie Callahan Schumpater, an old acquaintance from high school and even college days."

The two women exchanged greetings, each looking slowly and avidly at the other. Frank could tell that Paula's antennae had caught the bat squeaks of interest on his part as Margie had come up to them and in his almost stuttering excitement as he had greeted her and introduced them.

"Mike's over with some guys babbling about 'the good old days' and reliving the great days of high school," Margie said with a smile that reminded Frank of the Margie Callahan of the years that had flanked his high school graduation. "I saw you out of the corner of my eye and thought I'd come over to say hello."

Margaret Ann Callahan had been one of the great loves of his life—a girl and a young woman who had captivated him with a specific kind of beauty and adroitness of mind. In his youth Frank had gazed upon her as an unapproachable goddess.

Her father had been one of the top vice presidents at Wells Fargo Bank, and the family had lived in the kind of post-World War II upper-middle class opulence that was in stark contrast to the working class, immigrant environment in which Frank had grown up.

Margie herself had been tall and willowy, with elegant good looks, not the conventional prettiness of so many of the high school girls he had known. Her exquisite facial bone structure was set off by a hint of dark complexion—perhaps a "black Irish" heritage Frank had thought. And she had dressed in a style that Frank still thought was the best look ever devised for girls and young ladies: a kilt skirt to the middle of her knees, knee socks and penny loafers, and a Brooks Brothers Oxford shirt. My God, she was a vision, Frank remembered.

"Your husband was a tough nut to crack, Paula, and I never succeeded in doing so," Margie said with arched eyebrows.

"How do you mean?" Paula asked.

"When we were in high school, I was somewhat sweet on him. I had heard him converse at various gatherings that we attended together, and I loved his ideas and the way he presented them. He was certainly what we would today call a 'geek' or a 'nerd,' but he had a wonderful mind, a splendid mind.

"I put some opportunities out here for some possible dating, but he never responded."

"I think he's changed somewhat since then," Paula responded ambiguously, but with a smile.

Frank felt himself blush. He was suddenly, unpredictably light-headed. He remembered so well a couple of these overtures, but he had not realized at the time that they were overtures. Margie had been an excellent student and interested in history and literature, as he was. Once, when they were seniors, she had called him. He had been so surprised to hear her voice that he had almost dropped the telephone. She said to him that she was having some trouble understanding some issues in her U.S. history course and asked him if he would mind coming over to her house and explaining them.

Frank remembered that he could barely stutter out a "yes" and that he was trembling with excitement when he hung up the telephone.

The next evening he went to the mansion where she lived, was admitted by the family's maid, and shown into the library. Margie entered within a few moments and thanked him profusely for coming over to help her with the essay she was writing. Frank could only stare at her; she reminded him of the portraits of women painted by the Renaissance artists he had only recently begun to discover.

Margie had a sheet of paper in her hand with five questions dealing with issues on some aspect of U.S. history on which she was writing a term paper. She invited Frank to sit beside her on the sofa in front of a coffee table on which there was a tablet and a pen to write down the thoughts he was conveying to her. Frank felt like putting his arms around her and passionately kissing her; he could still remember her scent as he sat close to her.

Instead of following his impulses, Frank dutifully began his disquisition on the issues of U.S. history that were contained on the sheet of paper Margie had handed him. She jotted down notes in her tablet of the analysis he was expounding.

When Frank had finished, Margie once again thanked him and offered him a soda. He accepted, and watched her as she walked to the door of the library with the walk and posture of a thoroughbred horse. Just before she opened the door there was a knock, and then the door opened. It was Margie's mother, who gave a perfunctory greeting to Frank and then said to her daughter:

"Margie, you have a telephone call."

Her mother left, and Margie turned to Frank. "Frank, I'll be right back."

The door closed, and Frank was left with his thoughts. A telephone call, he thought...probably from one of her boyfriends. He knew that she dated young men from college; he had seen some of them at various events—very good-looking, self-assured, with the easy social graces of college students from wealthy families. And why not, Frank thought: with her sensuous beauty, social position, intelligence, and sparkling conversation, Margie would not be interested in high school boys.

The minutes ticked by, measured by the grandfather clock in the library, until Frank wondered if she had forgotten about him sitting in the library. He gauged that it had been about twenty minutes since she had left. Should he let himself out of the house? At that moment she returned with two cans of Coke. She looked flushed.

"Frank, I'm so sorry to have left you waiting," she had said to him. "The call took longer than I thought it would, and then I had trouble finding the Coke. My mother says it's bad for your teeth and doesn't stock much. Here, let me get some glasses."

Margie went to a cabinet and pulled out two glasses into which she poured the Coke. She seemed distracted as she handed one to Frank and started sipping the other.

"Have a seat," she said to him.

She sat where she had sat prior to her departure from the room, and expected Frank to take his same place. Frank remembered seeing a look of surprise on her face as he, shy and embarrassed, sat down on a leather chair facing her.

"What are you reading these days?" she inquired.

"Umm...Sir Walter Scott's *Heart of Midlothian*," he was able to force out, mesmerized by her beauty and grace and tantalized by sexual desire.

"We're in the same period, roughly. I'm reading *Jane Eyre*."

"I read it last summer. I loved it."

Margie smiled. "I'm only halfway through, but I'm very much enjoying it. I love the English novel."

"What are you going to read next?" Frank asked.

"*Wuthering Heights*, I think."

"You're going to love it."

"Have you read all the English novels?"

"No, not really...but a lot of them. I love the novel, and I especially love the English novel."

"We'll have to compare notes some time," Margie suggested.

"That would be great."

There was a lull in the conversation. Frank wondered whether he should ask her to go to a movie with him...or go out for a cup of coffee. Would she laugh at him, or, more politely, offer an excuse as to why she couldn't? Why would she go out with him? She had these good-looking college men hanging around her. He decided against asking her out for a date.

"Frank, I've really enjoyed our time together," Margie said, "and I can't thank you enough for giving me your insights into those points regarding the Civil War. Do you mind if I call you again if I need some help?"

"No, not at all. I'd be...be...pleased to do anything I could." Frank felt like a puppy dog when that last statement came out of his mouth.

"Well, I guess I need to get upstairs and get started on my term paper. Thanks again for coming over."

She stood up, and Frank stood up as well. They walked in silence out of the library into the entry hall. Margie opened the front door and looked up at Frank, smiling.

"I had a great evening, Margie," Frank said, annoyed with himself that he hadn't asked her for a date—and felt he couldn't ask her now— and that he couldn't fulfill his impulse to throw his arms around her and kiss her. "I always enjoy your company."

Margie Callahan smiled warmly at him. "You're always great to talk with, Frank. Goodnight."

Frank had walked out into the darkness, pining with love and frustrated by his inability to connect with the object of his desire in a romantic way.

A second overture Frank remembered was the summer after their senior year. He had encountered Margie in Guerneville on the Russian River, when he had been invited for the 4th of July weekend by Russ Borti, whose family had a cabin there. Margie had been invited to spend the weekend by a classmate whose family had a substantial vacation home overlooking the river.

Margie and her friend were leaving the local grocery store with some provisions as Russ and he were strolling down the road. Frank and Russ both knew Margie and her friend, Clarissa. Margie seemed pleased to see Frank, and the four of them chatted amiably in the hot Sonoma sun. They were recent high school graduates anticipating their transition to college.

"Clarissa's having a barbeque tomorrow afternoon," Margie addressed Frank and Russ. "Three or four people we've encountered here from our schools are going. Why don't you join us? Is that okay, Clarissa?"

"Sure."

Frank and Russ looked at each other and simultaneously said, "We'd love to."

Frank felt his heart race and strange sensations play through his body.

"And we're going canoeing tomorrow morning at about nine," Margie continued. "Why don't you meet us at Burke's Canoes and then we'll paddle down to Guerneville? We'll be picked up there, and you can then go home, change, and be at Clarissa's at five."

"Sounds great," Russ immediately said. Frank nodded in silent agreement.

"See you tomorrow morning, then," Margie said, as the two girls walked toward Clarissa's car.

Frank and Russ continued their walk along the road paralleling the Russian River, which was filled with vacationers and tourists enjoying the mid-summer holiday. Frank looked back to see Margie and Clarissa deep in conversation as they approached Clarissa's car. "Clarissa is probably asking Margie why she invited the two of us to spend the day with them," Frank said. "The two of us are not exactly in their social set."

Frank and Russ exchanged some banal comments about how nice it was to be invited to spend the following day with some contemporaries and wondered who else would be there. As they walked to Russ's family cabin, both seemed wrapped in their own thoughts. Frank tingled with excitement at the unexpected pleasure of spending the day with the girl he so much loved.

When they gathered the next morning at Burke's, there were eight in Clarissa's party. Two were Margie's and Clarissa's classmates, whom Frank knew slightly, and two were graduates of another Catholic high school in the area, a much tonier school than St. Aloysius. Those students came from the affluent upper-middle-class Catholic professional and business class.

Introductions were made. The gleeful chatter of recent high school graduates, animated by the commingling of the sexes and further fueled by the festive holiday spirit bubbled up among the canoers.

The plan was to rent two canoes and put four of them in each. Frank prayed that he would be placed in the canoe with Margie, and, when the decision was being made as to who would go in which canoe, she announced, "Put me in the canoe with Frank. I want to discuss some books we've both been reading."

Frank's heart leapt with excitement. He stepped into the last place in one of the canoes. Margie took the place in front of him, and Clarissa and one of the young men from the tony high school filled out the canoe. Shortly thereafter, the two canoes began their voyage along the Russian River.

The morning fog had begun to dissipate, and the warm sun shone on their bodies. Margie had on a two-piece bathing suit. The vaguest line of blondish-brown hair went along her spinal column to where they disappeared into her swimsuit bottom. Frank looked at this line with fascination. His penis hardened, and his body fluttered with erotic desire. He felt an impulse to put down his paddle, throw his arms around her, and nuzzle his face in the nape of her neck.

He didn't, of course, and the canoe trip was spent in banter and an occasional flurry of conversation with Margie about the English novels he had been reading. If he said something that Margie thought was funny, she would turn around and flash him one of her extraordinary smiles. Frank would then resume his contemplation of the fine line of golden hairs that cascaded down her back.

The canoe trip ended, and the canoers returned to their venues to shower and change for the barbeque at Clarissa's. Frank, dazzled and desirous, contemplated asking Margie for a date while they were at the barbeque. After all, she had asked that both be on the same canoe.

The bright, late-afternoon sun shone over the deck of Clarissa's parents' vacation home overlooking the Russian River. Clarissa's folks were a progressive sort, and allowed beers to be served in the early part of the evening to the twelve, under-age high school graduates whom Clarissa had assembled.

Clarissa's father barbequed steaks and Clarissa's mother brought forth vegetables and potato salad. The beverages now became soft drinks, but the exuberant teenagers still felt some alcoholic glow from the beers they had earlier consumed.

Margie had changed into a short skirt and a tank top. Her hair was pulled back into a ponytail. And, while she was certainly friendly to Frank, there was no sign as the evening went on of her singling Frank out for special attention.

The ebullient spirits and interplay among the guests offered Frank no opportunity to sequester Margie and ask her out on a date. His inherent shyness around girls and his awe of her beauty and her social position combined to derail his question to her.

The barbeque ended at midnight, and the guests went back to their lodgings. Sad, disappointed, and disgruntled—but still filled with longing and desire—Frank tumbled into bed in a small room of Russ's parents' vacation cabin.

The summer passed. There were no calls from Margie; there were no more casual encounters. In the fall, he knew that she would be entering Stanford; he would start his college years at St. Ignatius College.

The years passed. When he was in his late-twenties, about a decade after he had been with her at Clarissa's barbeque, Frank saw Margie at a cocktail party. Frank was still married to Claudia; and Margie was then married to her first husband, a "golden boy" type she had met at Stanford and who was practicing law at one of San Francisco's large, prestigious law firms. They lived in Atherton, one of the upscale towns sprinkled south of San Francisco.

Once more, Frank began to feel the desire and erotic excitement that he had felt for her ten years before. But their conversation was short and insignificant. They introduced their spouses, made a few banal comments, and then each couple disappeared into the maw of the cocktail party.

He had not seen her again until this evening at his high school reunion.

Frank's reverie came to an end when he heard Margie say to Paula, "Well, if he had changed fifty years ago, he and I might have been attending this reunion together."

"I'm glad he didn't," Paula responded with a smile.

"The last time we saw each other was about forty years ago," Frank said, eager to change the conversation. "You were married to a tall, good-looking attorney."

"Eric. Yes, he was tall and good-looking...and, yes, he was an attorney. He also worked twenty hours a day, including weekends. He began to cheat on me after we had our second child. Goodbye, Eric. I was single for a few years, and then I married Lance Hopkins.

"The name should have been the tip-off. Lance, like Eric, was good-looking. He was the CEO of a chain of hospitals, was funny, and was a great step-dad to my kids. But he was totally disinterested in sex. I thought he might have been gay...and he may be. We went to therapy. I did everything I could to entice him, but nothing worked. Finally, I came to the conclusion that a marriage without a component that I considered very, very important was not a marriage. Marriage number two ended.

"And then there was Mike...and here he is."

A cheerful, smiling Mike Schumpater, holding a half-empty martini glass, shook hands with Frank and quickly introduced himself to Paula.

"Frank, me boy, it's been a long time...twenty-five years, I think, since the last gathering."

"And you don't look a day older," Frank responded.

"Aah, that's a bit of blarney."

Michael Joseph Schumpater, as Frank remembered from Mike's yearbook listing, always spoke as if he were from the Old Sod, even though his ancestry was German and English. Mike had been the consummate "all-round guy." He had been an excellent athlete, got good grades, was good-looking with wavy blonde hair and was a jovial, "hail-fellow-well-met" type. He and Frank had not known each other well in school.

Frank seemed to remember that Mike had become one of the top executives for some local utility company. Presumably, he was now retired—and married to Margie. Hard to imagine Margie discussing

English novels with him, but perhaps he provided more of what her second marriage lacked.

"I didn't realize until tonight that you and Margie knew each other in high school," Mike said to Frank.

"Yes, yes, we did...not well, but we knew each other. We had some people we knew in common and would occasionally see each other at parties or other events."

Frank decided to spare the group his memories of Margie Callahan or the fact that he had once considered her the love of his life. Even so, he saw Mike, Paula, and Margie looking at him intently as he spoke.

"I barely knew who she was in those days," Mike continued. "Never had much contact with those Convent of the Sacred Heart girls. "I'm surprised that the two of you never dated. I remember you reading all those fat, obscure books in high school. You know, Margie loves to read the same kinds of books now."

"It takes more than a common interest in English literature for two people to date," Frank responded, feeling somewhat uncomfortable with Mike's probing.

"Yeah, I guess so. Who knows why it is that people get together."

"How did the two of you meet?" Frank asked, hoping to change the conversation.

"Nothing sensational. Friends of both of us invited us separately to a cocktail party, and we met there. Margie was a couple years out of her second marriage, and I had been divorced a couple years. We liked each other, went out, and the rest is history."

"Never count on Mike to give the entire story," Margie countered. "In reality, he had seen me at a golf tournament charity event to which I had been invited by a cousin of mine, found out who I was, did some research, and had mutual friends invite us to the cocktail party at which we met."

"Kismet," Paula said, softly.

"How about the two of you...how'd you meet?" Margie asked Paula.

"I had done interior decorating for Frank and his first wife—not much, I should say, because Frank despised interior decorators. We'd run into each other from time to time, and then I married and moved away, and he subsequently got a divorce. Then I got a divorce and moved back to San Francisco, and one day we bumped into each other on the street. He asked me out, and we started dating. Here we are. Kismet."

A fine, sanitized version of the entire chain of events, Frank thought.

"Isn't it amazing how many of us, brought up Catholic in the 1950s, educated in Catholic schools, have gotten divorced," Margie said, looking at Frank.

"Oh, I guess there are a lot of reasons," Frank responded. "Not only did the immigrant ghettoes dissolve, so did the Catholic ghetto. The permissiveness of the 1960s contributed to it—the 'I'm O.K., you're O.K.' attitude that followed. Social pressures against the divorced lessened. All of these things combined to make the divorce rate among Catholics about the same as among non-Catholics."

"Frank, you can still analyze as well as when you were in high school," Margie said to him.

Paula looked at Frank with arched eyebrows, but said nothing. She's going to have a million questions when we go home, Frank mused.

"Thanks," Frank said. "But now I've got a bit more experience under my belt to help my analysis."

"Experience is always a good thing," Margie said, looking somewhat wistful. "I seem to remember that you were somewhat naïve and idealistic in high school. That wasn't a terrible thing...but you seemed unsure of yourself then."

"I was very unsure of myself in my teens and early twenties," Frank said, "and in a lot of ways. It took me a long time to find out who I was and how to get along in this world."

Mike was looking bored with the conversation. He probably prefers sports talk or some banal thoughts about politics, Frank thought. Paula was uncomfortable with Margie's statements and questions. He wondered if she was serious when she told Paula that he had been a "tough nut to crack" and that she had made "overtures" to him. Had she wanted to date him fifty years ago? Was she sorry now that their acquaintance had not ripened into a romance? Why didn't he put his arms around her and kiss her during those two opportunities so long ago?

The conversation went no further. Bob Barnes, a classmate who had played football with Mike, approached the foursome.

"Hey, hey, how's the old make-out bandit?" Bob fairly yelled out as he approached. "Some shindig, eh?"

Mike and he slapped each other on the back. Spouses were introduced, and Frank and Bob shook hands and exchanged cordial greetings.

"Where's your wife?" Mike inquired.

"Wife? Have no wife. Been divorced for five years...and happy, happy.

I've been seeing someone, but we broke up last week. Too late to find someone for tonight. That's O.K. Maybe I'll find a new love here."

Bob's audience all smiled, but Frank could see Paula's slight pout of disapproval and Margie slightly rolling her eyes.

Bob Barnes had been one of the class comics. He had retained his slight physique—Frank had always wondered how he'd made the football team—but his former black hair had turned white. Fifty years after he graduated from high school, Bob still thought of life as a good joke.

"I'm going to get another drink before dinner," Frank announced, unwilling to spend any more time with Bob. "Mike, Margie, Bob, see you in a bit."

Frank steered Paula away from the group and toward the bar. He awaited Paula's questions and impressions, but they were aborted by Jim Ahern, president of the class of 1955, announcing on the microphone that dinner was being served. Frank and Paula changed direction and headed for the club's elegant dining room, passing a dozen or so couples to whom he nodded in recognition or commented, "Hey, how are you? Good to see you. Catch you later."

There were about fifteen tables with eight settings at each. Frank looked for Table Seven, where he would be sitting with three friends from high school and their spouses. He had done everything he could to avoid sitting with classmates he had barely known, or worse, had disliked, and he had been successful. Frank was ambiguous about having gone to this reunion: he didn't want to spend the evening in agonizing boredom, and so had selected his three closest friends from high school to be his dinner companions.

The four couples were arriving at their table at just about the same time. They sort of mingled about the table until an announcement was made that Father Dingel would say grace, which served as a call for them to establish their seats around the table. Frank sat down in the chair in front of him, and Paula sat to his right. Next to her sat Chris and Monica. There was then some confusion about making it "boy-girl, boy-girl," but, as grace began, Len Maestri and his wife, Emily, had arranged to establish the acceptable seating pattern.

Grace was concluded, and a few welcoming speeches ensued. The torrent of words from the podium dampened the usual flow of banter that would have come from the friends at Table Seven, but the speeches did not stop the waiters in their white jackets from placing salads at each place.

Thus the class of 1955 began to eat dinner and to drink the wine and water that was before them.

As the dinner progressed, Frank realized that he was not his usual ebullient self. He didn't engage in banter with his friends. His laconic replies to queries were uncharacteristic, and his unwillingness to proffer his ideas and comments most unusual.

Paula, he thought, also noticed it, without assigning any reason for his taciturnity; she seemed determined to make up for his quiet by engaging in animated conversation with Chris and Monica.

Frank knew why his spirits were tamped down or, more accurately, why he was so reflective in the midst of the reunion party and dining with close friends of more than a half century: it was seeing Margie Callahan and it was the conversation she had had with Paula and himself.

Frank noticed his physiology when Margie had walked over to them: his heart began to beat rapidly, his face felt flushed, and he felt chills throughout his body. He felt light-headed. This was the physical reaction he had to a woman with whom he had seen only once in fifty years, since they were both seventeen.

The physical reaction was paralleled by his emotional turmoil: the flood of memories of their encounters, his teenage love for her, and the frustration of his never having had any romantic interaction with her. Margie indicated that she would have liked to have dated him; but, even if that were true, what would it have meant: a few movies, coffees together, walks during that summer of 1955...perhaps some kisses. But, in that September she would have gone to Stanford and he to St. Ignatius College; the romance would have ended.

Even so, Frank thought, what a blissful few months that would have been. He couldn't figure out why he had been so bashful with girls in high school. To ask someone to dance or to go to a school dance was torture for him. To think of asking someone out on a date left him tongue-tied.

Frank couldn't experience then—at his fiftieth reunion dinner—the feeling of love, of yearning, of desire that he had felt for Margaret Ann Callahan fifty years before. He tried, he tried hard, to do so, but he couldn't; but he could remember what those feelings had been. It was as if a piece of opaque glass stood between the Frank Molinari in his late-60s and the one who had existed a half century ago. He knew that certain sights or smells could trigger the memory of those emotions—seeing a pretty girl in a ponytail, for example, could summon the sweet nostalgia of seeing Margie during the summer of 1955—but these triggers could not reproduce the emotions themselves. It was trying to look at a faded photograph and see the voluptuous beauty of long ago.

Why would he want to? Frank thought. Why do I want to recreate the angst of my teenage years or of those of my early 20s? Elation followed by agony. Because you thought you were really alive then, he answered. Because to the tips of your fingers to the ends of your toes to the top of your head you were pulsating with excitement. You miss those electrifying emotions, even when they brought you sadness and loneliness. You miss the exhilaration of erotic desire, of a young, healthy body bicycling long distances, of the most delicious hopes and dreams for the future.

By now they had finished their entrees, and it was time for the evening's speeches. Frank hated the blather of such events: talks taking twenty minutes when they could have been compressed into five. The self-congratulatory nature of such events, the surreptitious attempts to extort money from the alumni, the rah-rah, "good old days" nature of the oratory all combined to trigger Frank's cynicism—and to bore him.

The evening's rhetorical fare began with the school's current president, Father Dingel. He welcomed the graduates and gave a rousing account of how the school has become better and better year-by-year and assured the alumni that it would continue to grow in every way. Father Dingle was followed by the development and alumni directors, who bubbled with enthusiasm for the school and urged all those present to participate in helping make their school even greater. The third speaker was Jim Ahern, who had been the senior class president, and who now began to give a series of anecdotes about their years at St. Aloysius.

Jim Ahern had been, in Frank's eyes, the quintessential Irish-American bullshitter while at school. Friendly, gregarious, and an All-American type, Ahern had managed to be both a good athlete, playing basketball all his four years in school, and an excellent student. His social skills and self-assurance had been amazing to Frank. And his Celtic charm and good looks would have made him a Don Juan on the dating trail. Jim had begun to date a classmate in the eighth grade, dated her throughout high school and college, and married her immediately after he had graduated from college.

Diane Marcy was her name, and her appearance and personality had mirrored Jim's. Apparently, they had had a splendid marriage and produced six children; but last year Diane had succumbed to breast cancer.

Even though Frank and Jim had never been close friends, Frank had written a letter of condolence to Jim after he read of Diane's death. It was curious, Frank thought, that they hadn't become friends. Jim was likeable. He lacked the arrogance that had marked a number of their classmates. And he was bright. But, somehow Frank had always found him too conventional to form a basis for friendship, somewhat like a "Goody Two Shoes," the types who become corporate executives or Roman Catholic bishops. Everyone was always wonderful in Jim's eyes; everything was always delightful. This was the person, after all, who had dated someone exclusively for nine years before he married her, and then had by all accounts a wonderful marriage for forty-five years.

Frank had always thought that it was preordained that Jim Ahern would become a certified public accountant.

And now, Jim Ahern was at the podium retelling stories about their lives fifty years ago and more: the undefeated football team of their senior year; the collapse of a large, flower-covered lattice-work at their junior prom; the eccentricities of Father Pettingill, who had taught them English; and Don Cardelli's getting drunk one night and roaring obscenities outside of the priests' residence. Frank closed his eyes and remembered his charming, friendly classmate addressing the class fifty years ago with ebullience and enthusiasm; he sounded exactly the same tonight. There was no trace of the disappointments and frustrations he may have encountered during the past half century; there was no sign of the sorrow that must have seared him the previous year when his wife had died. Frank admired Jim's imperturbability, but he would not have traded their lives.

Jim finished his comments to a rousing ovation. He accomplished his task well, Frank thought...for the task that was assigned. But, couldn't he have talked about whether four years at St. Aloysius gave the hundred graduates on June 11, 1955, aside from an education to get them into college, the moral vision to make them better human beings? Could he not once have touched on the emotions that so frequently rocked the lives of the class of 1955 during their four years at St. Aloysius? And how did the class of 1955 respond in the past fifty years to the *sturm und drang* of the previous four?

The evening was to end with dancing, but Frank decided he had had enough of the bonhomie of this reunion evening. He felt over-stimulated and had no appetite for more backslapping from his aging classmates, or for seeing the tired faces and gray hair of their dumpy wives—and certainly not for the banal comments and pathetic reminiscences.

He turned to Paula and said, "I've done my duty by my friends. Shall we go?"

"Oh, why don't we stay for a while and dance?"

"Dance? I'm not a big fan of dancing under any circumstances, and I need to escape from my classmates."

"How about two dances and then we'll go?"

"O.K., but you've got to pretend that we're filled with teenage lust and that we're dancing slowly at a prom fifty years ago."

"You should be writing Harlequin romances or teen-age fantasies. You are too much. O.K., two dances and I'll pretend I've got an up-sweep hairdo, a strapless, backless, white prom gown, and whatever the 'fuck-me' shoes of the period were."

"Now, that isn't very nice language. The girls and young ladies of that era didn't use words like fuck."

"But it was the naughty girls that you guys would lust after."

"Au contraire, my dear," said a smiling Frank, as he pulled back Paula's chair from the table. "It was the sweetest, the purest, the most pious—if they were at all pretty—that the Catholic boys of my time lusted after. The trash tongues, those girls who 'put out,' those who had sleazy reputations. You might French kiss, or dry hump them. You might finger fuck them after a party, but you would never have contemplated them as serious girlfriends, nor ever, God forbid, thought of marrying them."

"I just love your 1950s language and concepts," Paula laughed. "You should be put in a museum, along with green Jell-O molds and pink bathroom tiles."

"That's what you get when you marry an older man," said Frank as he led Paula onto the dance floor and began to fox trot with her to "My Blue Heaven."

Frank had never been a good dancer, and, as he had gotten older, he danced less and less. Paula, on the other hand, loved to dance and would prevail on him to dance at least a couple dances.

After a moment Frank began to imitate the slow dancers of his high school years. He draped his arms around Paula, with his hands on her rear end, lay his head on her shoulder, and began to sway softly to the music.

"Oh, my God, you're incorrigible," said Paula, shaking loose from him. "Either dance properly or let's go. I'm not going to participate in one of your bizarre fantasies." She sounded somewhat annoyed.

Frank laughed. "O.K., O.K., let's be conventional and dance like grownups."

"What's with you tonight?" Paula asked. "You've been all over the place. At one point you're blushing and nervous, the next you're cackling and making jokes. What's happening with you?"

"Oh, you know, reunions are always hard on people. They bring up a lot of emotions...especially when it's your fiftieth."

The band had now swung into "Tutti Frutti," and Frank eased Paula off the dance floor. A conventional song you could fox trot to was one thing, but one that took more skills was another. It was a cue to end the evening.

They walked to their table to say goodbye. Their six companions were sitting there, engaged in earnest conversation. Why does one come to a reunion to have conversation with people you see all the time? Frank wondered. But, on the other hand, it's safe, meaningful palaver, not forced and boring talk with people you have nothing in common with.

"Are you going already?" Chris inquired. "What cowards. Aren't you going to drink this event right down to the dregs?"

"I've already gotten to the dregs," Frank said. "I'm feeling both over stimulated and tired."

"I wonder how many will attend our seventy-fifth," Len asked, smiling.

"I promise I'll attend if you do," Frank said.

"It's a deal," Len said, rising to shake Frank's hand and give Paula a kiss on the cheek.

Frank's classmates and friends had all arisen to bid them farewell. Having made their goodbyes, Frank and Paula walked to the main entrance. Frank fervently hoped that none of his classmates would waylay him as he was leaving.

None did, and within minutes Frank and Paula were in the Jaguar heading out of the Olympic Club's parking lot.

The couple was silent for several minutes, each preoccupied. Each wondered what the other was thinking.

Paula broke the silence. "So, what's the story on Margie Schumpater? You have never mentioned her before."

"There is no story," Frank answered. "She was someone I knew in high school, but never dated."

"I think there's more to the story. You looked and sounded like an emotional train wreck when the two of you were speaking."

"I don't know what else to tell you. I was certainly attracted to her in high school, but she was a beauty and I wasn't handsome; her family was rich and socially prominent, and mine wasn't; she dated college guys. I guess it just wasn't in me to make the effort to date her."

"She said she had wanted to date you."

"Yeah, well that was said fifty years later, when we all sort of look the same and we've been dinged by life. A romantic haze colors our memories."

"You looked very nonplussed during your conversation, as if you had regrets for not dating her. Why didn't you connect while you were single and during one of the times she was single?"

"That's a good question, and I'm afraid I don't have a good answer. I certainly thought about it, and by accident, I did connect with a couple women I had known or dated in high school, but I never thought about contacting Margie to see if she were single."

"I'm surprised. You certainly seemed to have a case on her when you were in high school. And tonight it certainly sounded as if she would have been responsive."

Frank was intrigued by Paula's fascination with his old love for Margie Callahan. "I didn't go looking for adolescent loves when I was single. As I said, a couple popped into my life by accident. But I didn't compile a list and call them to see if I could see them decades later."

"Why not? You fucked virtually everyone with a skirt when you were single."

"That was a transitioning time. And a lot of my screwing was based on trying to accomplish what I didn't do in my adolescence. But then…but then I realized that one can never get enough as an adult of that which you felt, that you did not get enough of as a young person."

Both were quiet, as Frank piloted the Jaguar through the dark, quiet streets of Pacific Heights. It had been for Frank an emotionally draining evening. For Paula it had provided some insights into her husband's past.

There was a parking place in front of their house. Frank decided not to park in their garage. As he and Paula walked up the front steps into the house, Frank felt the twinges of sexual desire. It must be the result of the evening's memories of his desires fifty years ago, he thought.

Paula checked her phone messages while Frank began to pull off his clothes. He went into the bathroom to take the few pills he needed to take for his high blood pressure and decided to slip a Viagra into his mouth.

Frank had just gotten into bed when Paula walked into their bedroom. "How about a more intimate fifty-year reunion?" Frank asked her.

Paula laughed her soft laugh. "I'm probably the recipient of the most unusual seduction lines of any woman on the planet. Sure."

She brushed her teeth and then languorously removed her clothes. She paused for a moment in thought and then opened a drawer looking for an appropriate piece of lingerie, pulling out a red teddy that she knew Frank liked.

Frank looked at her tall, willowy body, lean, yet sensual. From the bed he examined the luxurious patch of auburn pubic hair. How pleased he was to be married to someone of her youthful attractiveness. He thought about his classmates that evening, most of them with dumpy, wrinkled spouses with gray hair. That's pretty shallow of me, Frank thought. After all, we do get older and old looking, and marriage is about "for better or worse." But he still relished his young-looking, trim, and attractive wife.

Paula climbed into the bed and turned to Frank. "I'm sorry, sweetheart, if you had a hard time tonight."

"No, I didn't have a hard time. But I can say it was an unusual time. We take an evening to go to a fiftieth reunion, and the only people we spend any time talking to are the friends we see frequently. The rest I pretty much couldn't care less about."

"But you enjoyed seeing Margie."

"Yes...yes, I did. It's always interesting seeing someone fifty years after you've had teen-age lust for her."

Frank held his wife in his arms, facing her on his left side. His right arm was free, and he used this hand to softly feel her body beneath the silk teddy. As his fingers played over her silk-covered breasts, he felt her nipples harden. Frank kissed the nape of her neck and let his tongue and lips play with her left ear. Paula let out a moan of pleasure. Frank sought out her lips and passionately kissed her, his tongue thrusting deeply into her mouth.

"Nothing like a little necking on the occasion of one's fiftieth high school reunion," Frank murmured.

Paula giggled. "You can have more than necking and petting, if you want."

"Sure, why not. Let's work on it."

Frank's fingertips slowly traveled down Paula's hard stomach, playing for several seconds with her navel, and descended to between her thighs, where they probed through her pubic hair and sought her clitoris.

Another moan of pleasure escaped from Paula's lips. She planted kisses on his face and shoulders with increasing fierceness, as his fingers played with the now-hard kernel of pleasure beneath the hair and lips of her vagina.

Paula reached for his penis and began to massage the shaft. Aware of the increasing difficulty he had had recently to achieve a stiff enough penis for penetration, Frank concentrated on whether his penis was hardening. It felt hard, he thought, but was it hard enough?

Ripples of pleasure cascaded through his body and through Paula's. She gently nudged him onto his back and straddled him. With her hands she tried—unsuccessfully—to bring his penis into a sufficiently hard state for her to be able to shove it into her vagina.

To compensate for the long, hard thrusts into her body, Paula used Frank's penis to stimulate her clitoris. Frank tried to thrust completely into her, but he quickly realized that this was not going to happen. But he was receiving great pleasure from Paula's manipulation of his shaft and her use of the tip of his penis to pleasure herself.

Paula bent over him so that they could kiss, slithering her thighs around his penis and thus continuing the pleasurable stimulation he had been receiving from her hands. Frank cooperated with her massaging thighs, feeling increasing pleasure in his genital area.

Frank flipped the two of them over so that he was now straddling Paula, and continuing the genital stimulation that, though outside of her vagina, was exciting and brought them both pleasurable sensations.

They both increased their rhythms and the intensity by which they ground their genitals together. Their pleasure was heightened...and suddenly Frank felt a subtle spasm of conclusive pleasure pass through him. He felt the semi-hardness of his penis become flaccid. His and Paula's grinding together slowly stopped, and the two of them slowly suspended their sexual activity and lay quietly in each other's arms.

Frank tried to suppress the image that had formed in his mind that it had been Margie Callahan and he who had been making love fifty years ago rather than Paula and he a few minutes ago.

He fell asleep with that image implanted in his consciousness.

CHAPTER 20

There was some fog in the west as Frank sipped a vodka and tonic in the Bank of America Building's Carnelian Room, but the remainder of San Francisco was bathed in sunshine.

Frank loved any view of San Francisco, and the view from the Carnelian Room gave him a panoramic vista not just of San Francisco, but also of Marin County and the East Bay. San Bruno Mountain blocked his view to the south. But Frank had to admit that he preferred more intimate sights of the city to the more distant vistas provided from the eyrie of the Carnelian Room.

He remembered as a child going with his parents to the Top of the Mark—the place for San Francisco views then. Now the Mark Hopkins Hotel looked like a toy building far below his perspective. Probably the favorite distinction of his young life had been Coit Tower. Frank could remember clambering around Telegraph Hill in the 1950s—his parents often visited friends of theirs who lived on the hill—and he would often escape their hot, stuffy flat and the boring conversation and be allowed to explore the area by himself or with his brother.

The view from Coit Tower allowed Frank to both see and hear the cauldron of excitement from San Francisco's docks. Bags of coffee beans from Latin America would be delivered just a few blocks away to the coffee roasters: Hills Brothers, M.J.B., and Folgers. Bananas and other tropical fruits would be lifted off the ships and sent just a few blocks away to the Produce Market. The creaky sound of cranes, the thump when goods hit the docks, the orders barked by the foreman, were all part of a symphony—a symphony of work—that delighted Frank.

From Coit Tower he could see North Beach, the East Bay, the cluster of office buildings along Montgomery Street and at the foot of Market, the hotels on Nob Hill, the chic residential area of Russian Hill, and to the southeast to where San Francisco was expanding its airport. From this delightful, fluted, art deco tower Frank felt that he could reach out and touch the buildings and the people in his immediate vicinity.

He felt similar sensations when he would bounce down the stairs of Filbert Street, just beyond Montgomery Street, only a block east of Coit Tower. That particular block on Filbert Street was so steep that the street was composed of wooden steps that cascaded along the inhabited part of the street and then plunged to Sansome Street along the sheer cliff on the quarried part of Telegraph Hill. Three small streets ended in that block of Filbert, one of which was covered with wooden planks.

Filbert Street was a splendid oasis in an urban landscape. Frank's earliest memory of the street was that the considerable area flanking the wooden steps was a jumble of weeds and junk, deposited there, presumably, by nearby residents. But, when he was in college, he noticed that someone had begun to remove the old tires and abandoned bedsprings and replace the weeds with flowers, shrubbery, and trees. He had been told that this was being accomplished by a recent transplant from Los Angeles, who was doing it as therapy for her arthritis.

Frank snapped out of his reverie and looked at his watch. It was 5:20. Vanessa was late. He was somewhat surprised by her telephone call. True, they had spoken about getting together a couple months ago when they had met by accident on the street and then had cocktails at the Compass Rose; but many people say things, mean them at the time, and never follow through.

Out of the blue, Vanessa had called him, talked about getting together, and suggested a specific time and place. Had she wanted merely to exchange pleasantries—or was there something specific that she wanted?

Frank looked up as he took another sip of his cocktail and saw that Vanessa was bearing down on the table he had selected by the window. He rose to greet her; and, when she got to the table, spread out his arms and gave her a warm embrace and kiss.

"What a nice surprise to hear from you," Frank said as he pulled out a chair for her to sit on and signaled the waiter to take her order. "I've been meaning to call you, too, but the last few months have been hectic."

"Isn't it amazing how life gets away from us?" Vanessa responded. "A day goes by...then another...and pretty soon it's years."

"It was such a delight bumping into you a couple months ago and then having drinks. I'm glad we're doing it again."

"If we don't do it now, one day we'll pick up the newspaper and see that one or the other of us has died."

"You're sounding like me now," Frank replied. "People say that I'm sounding morbid."

"But it's true. We can let weeks…months…and then years go by, not contacting old friends…and then you're too embarrassed to contact the person."

Frank smiled in recognition. How many times had he done exactly that: not contact friends for years? There came a point when he became too shame-faced to reinstitute the connection.

"I'm pleased that we're not doing that." Frank said sincerely.

"We had what I consider some of the best years of my life together… yours too, I hope. It would be a shame never to be in touch again…just because we've gone on to other partners."

"I like your thinking," Frank laughed. "And I'm so delighted to see you." He was trying to keep the conversation bland until he could determine if Vanessa had called him with a specific purpose in mind.

It was as if she had read his mind. "I know you, Frank. You're thinking, 'What is it that she wants? Why is it, really, that she called me?' And I'm going to give you the real reason. I'm going to turn 65 in a couple weeks—and don't tell me how good I look for 65, I know I do—and I was feeling nostalgic for my 30s, when you and I were together."

"Don't get me wrong. David and I have a wonderful relationship. It's been a wonderful relationship for over twenty-five years. But it was that explosion right after I turned thirty that still stays with me."

"Explosion?"

"Yes, explosion. Meeting you, falling in love, moving to San Francisco and establishing a new life here for myself and the girls…the several years in which we were inseparable…that was an explosion."

"It was pretty amazing, wasn't it?" Frank recalled, dreamily. The impact of meeting Vanessa and having such an intense relationship could never leave his mind.

"It was more than amazing. I have never been more alive. Part of it was getting out of a dreary marriage. Part of it was the passionate romance of our relationship. And part of it was discovering myself in ways I had never dreamed of."

"How well I remember those Frank mused. "How could I ever forget them? We were drawn together by an overpowering magnetic force. What wonderful days—and nights—we had. It was a magical time in my life."

"I guess I have to be truthful. It's the sex that I remember most," Vanessa said, with almost a lascivious smile. "I was a virgin when I was married, and Aaron's idea of love-making was putting out the lights when we were in bed, slipping off my nightie, and, after little or no foreplay, entering me. He came and then he said goodnight.

"You unleashed me. We would make love night and day, in positions I don't think the Kama Sutra has, in places that I still laugh about. Do you remember one night we had smoked some grass and had drunk a lot and we climbed under the table at the Caffe Sport and made love?"

Frank laughed and looked around to make certain that no one was sitting close enough to hear them. "How could I ever forget," Frank said. "You were the willing and enthusiastic partner for every sexual fantasy I have ever had. It was unbelievable."

"But it just wasn't the sex," Vanessa continued. "It was the excitement of being on my own, three thousand miles away from my family, engaging in a career I really loved, exploring the city and the West with you. I loved every minute of it."

The waiter came over to their table to ask if they wanted another round. Frank ordered another vodka and tonic for himself and another Campari and soda for Vanessa.

Frank enjoyed the reminiscences, and the discussion of their explosive sexual life brought on a tingle of desire. He remembered so well—and with a twinge of sadness as he recalled his current diminution of sexual desire and the abatement of sexual performance—the countless times he and Vanessa had made love: in virtually every room of the house and his apartment, on beaches, in the woods, in restaurants, and other public places where the possibility of discovery *flagrante delicto* made the experience doubly delectable, on couches and tables, as well as beds. Two people with a fierce sexual hunger had found each other.

But it was more than just the sex. It was, as Vanessa had pointed out, the explorations of life, the lively and penetrating conversations, it was the laughter, the anticipation of new adventures; and it was seeing Vanessa grow as a new human being, away from the tutelage and often, the suffocation of her parents and her husband.

Frank was staring into his glass, happily suffused with memories, when he felt a presence hovering nearby. He saw that Vanessa was looking up, and he followed her look right into the face of Christopher Fermoyle.

"Good afternoon, Francis. You're looking well," Christopher intoned, as he looked down at Frank and Vanessa.

"My goodness, Christopher, you gave me a start. Sit down and join us. You probably don't remember, but you met my old friend Vanessa Walker a few times years ago. Vanessa, this is Christopher Fermoyle."

"Ah, yes I remember...Frank's concubine many years ago. How very nice to see you again."

Vanessa looked somewhat startled, while Frank chortled. It was impossible to take any of Christopher's outrageous comments as insulting. They were just too funny to take seriously.

"What brings you to the Carnelian Room?" Frank inquired of his friend.

"A couple of old acquaintances of mine are in San Francisco for a few days, and they invited me to have drinks with them here. They wanted to experience the views. I haven't been here in years. And, finally, when I do come, who do I see but my old and dear friend, Francis Molinari."

"You never know where I'll turn up."

"And you, my dear," Christopher turned to Vanessa, "what have you been doing in these years après Frank?"

"Getting on with my life," Vanessa responded somewhat tartly. "I'm working. I travel. I see people. I've had a live-in relationship with someone for almost a quarter century. I live."

"How very nice," Christopher responded to Vanessa's litany with more than a hint of sarcasm. "How very nice. I'm so pleased that you haven't pined away from lovesickness and withered and died. That shows fortitude."

Before Vanessa could say anything, Christopher proclaimed, "Well, I must be going. I've got an early English-Speaking Union board meeting. Can you imagine me in the English-Speaking Union? It's too amusing. I'll leave you two former lovebirds to your reminiscences. Goodbye."

With that, Christopher wheeled around and strode to the bank of elevators.

"I see you still have the same whacko friends," Vanessa remarked.

"Yes, I guess some of my friends are eccentric. But, still, they're friends," Frank retorted.

"It's very nice to have friends from that long ago. I'm sorry that I don't."

"Well, you know, you've spent half your life in New York and half in San Francisco. It's tough to keep up with old friends clear across the continent."

"Yeah, I guess so." Vanessa turned her head to look at the view. The fog had made no more progress, but the overcast had turned the waters of the bay into a silvery gray. There was silence, as Frank took a swallow of his drink and also turned to take in the view.

Vanessa turned back from looking out the window and looked at Frank straight on. "Frank," she said, "there is something that has always puzzled me."

"And that is?" he inquired.

"I have never been able to figure out why we didn't stay together."

Frank could feel his eyebrows go up in surprise at Vanessa's statement. He had to give her a considered and truthful answer, and he had to think about the components of that answer. He pursed his lips and began to look around the Carnelian Room. Mostly tourists, Frank thought. There were two Indian men chatting a few tables away. A couple, badly dressed, were oohing and aahing about the view. Midwesterners. Four Japanese men were speaking softly at another table—possibly businessmen visiting San Francisco or possible expatriate Japanese involved in one of the many Japanese businesses in San Francisco. At another table a couple that appeared to be in their mid-twenties sat holding both hands and looking dreamily into each other's eyes. Probably honeymooners.

"Why didn't we stay together?" Frank mused, half to himself and half to Vanessa. "Boy, that's a good question, and I don't know if I have a complete answer.

"The subtext of your questions is, I think, that with such passionate love that marked our relationship and the magnificent time we had together, why didn't we stay together, either married or living together? Let me enumerate some of the barriers that..."

"Frank, you're sounding like a lawyer. Just tell me what's on your mind."

"I am telling you what's on my mind, and to do so I have to marshal what I see as the reasons in a logical manner."

"Okay, okay, sorry for the interruption."

"Let's begin with the external pressures. Your parents didn't like me, and that generated problems for us both. Your ex-husband made gobs of problems for a few years. And your daughters, to say the least, were ambivalent about me. It's not easy to defy one's family, and I think that your family's attitudes placed a major obstacle in our staying together.

"Then there were the internal problems. I dreamed that if I married again I would want more children. You certainly didn't want any more.

There was also the religious difference. That may sound strange for those days, but for me it was a real issue. I wanted the person I was going to be married to or live with to go to church with me."

"But you didn't have children when you did re-marry, and you seemed to not mind going off to church by yourself when we were together."

"Actually, we tried to have children, but none came. And, while you may not have known, I found going to church by myself, even though I've done it many times, to be a lonely experience."

"I'm sorry. I didn't know that."

"There's nothing to be sorry about. It's just one of those things."

"There is one more thing," Frank went on. "For whatever reason, at that point in my life I wasn't ready to settle down with one woman. Perhaps it was because of the problems between us I've already enumerated, or maybe it was because at that time and place I hadn't exorcised my demons about having sex with multiple women—not simultaneously—and that kept me from committing to a relationship...I don't know."

Vanessa looked pensive, and once more turned her head to look out the window. Frank felt a sense of relief, an unburdening; at the same time he felt as if a chill had descended upon them. Both Vanessa and he retreated into a thoughtful silence. Each wondered what the other was thinking.

Vanessa sighed and turned her head from the window. She didn't look at Frank, but rather into her Campari and soda. "Thanks for the honesty, Frank. I appreciate your analysis, even if it did sound like a legal brief."

Both gave a sad smile. Frank thought he knew why Vanessa had asked the question. Their relationship had been such an explosion of passion, such an intimate exploration of each other, and such an exciting adventure that neither of them thought it could ever end.

Neither of them had been young when they met: Frank was in his mid-thirties and Vanessa three years younger. But, as the steady flow of water erodes the hardest stone and as frustration, anger, and unfulfilled dreams create a sour atmosphere in a relationship, their love story had ended in hostility and recrimination until time had soothed the wounds, and they were able to come to an accommodation as friends.

Vanessa had gone on to a romantic liaison with David Young, a successful surgeon. A short while after they had begun to date, they moved in together and lived like husband and wife—for whatever reason they had decided not to marry—for more than twenty years. Frank had had a major relationship with Regina Tresam for several years before he met Paula, and had continued that relationship during the early phases of his relationship with her. Five years after he met Paula they had married.

Many years had elapsed since Frank and Vanessa's relationship had come to an end. There was stiffness between them in the first few years after their break-up, but, eventually, a friendship had been established. She and David had come to his and Paula's wedding, and every once in a while one couple would invite the other to dinner.

This low-key friendship had gone on for many years; and Frank wondered why Vanessa was now so patently reminiscing about their previous relationship and probing for the reasons for its failure. Could it be that she wanted to resume the relationship? Frank put the thought from his mind. Both were in happy, fulfilling relationships; neither wished to disrupt those. What could be the reason, then, for her excavation of their romantic relationship, Frank asked himself.

Vanessa once more broke the silence. "I can't imagine why I'm getting so nostalgic about the years we were together. For some reason our relationship has been very much on my mind as of late. In fact, I can't get it out of my mind. I feel as if it's my connection with my younger days...I don't know...it's weird."

"I'm not a psychologist," said Frank, tugging on his chin, "but I think this is a normal process. As we get older and age takes its toll, we tend to take pleasure in remembering those days when the sap was flowing. Perhaps we even obsess on them, as if they can substitute for the slow diminishing of our physical, mental, and emotional capacities." Frank felt a bit pedantic after saying this.

Vanessa smiled. "Frank, you're always so god-damn rational. Do you have an analysis and an answer for everything?"

"Only for those things that can be analyzed and for which there are answers," he responded. "Many things, I've found, can't be analyzed and have no apparent answers."

Vanessa looked straight at him. "I wonder how it would be if we were to resume our sexual relationship."

Frank looked at her intently and gulped. Was this a suggestion? A proposition?

An abstract wondering? Frank had been turned on by their conversation earlier; and the reminiscences of their relationship had stimulated his sexual appetite. If Vanessa were serious about a sexual encounter and he replied in the affirmative, the Omni Hotel was across the street and would supply a suitable venue for their tryst. His desire to reach back to those passionate years was certainly there.

Almost instantaneously Frank pulled back from the surge of lust, from the desire to see if they could recreate the orgasmic delights of their years together more than a quarter of a century before. Idealistic and practical considerations flooded his mind. His marriage vows came to mind, as well as Vanessa's commitment to David, although not cemented by marriage. The disloyalty to Paula that such a momentary sexual encounter would represent would always skulk around in his being. And, if she found out, which, from Frank's experience, was the more probable scenario, there was a strong probability of separation and divorce. She had warned him of such several times during the course of their marriage, knowing of his past infidelities, and Frank had absolutely no desire to end his marriage. It was this consideration that caused him to beat back any temptation.

"I've wondered the same thing many times," Frank began, with an audible sigh. "And I wonder about it now. But wondering and acting are two very different processes. What could be a momentary diversion, a moment of great pleasure, even a successful capturing of the past, could also wind up with tragic consequences. I have never believed in 'Nobody will ever know' as something to count on in life. If we were to resume our sexual relationship, I would bet that Paula and David would find out, and our lives would inevitably end in shambles. And, even if our relationships would survive, we would be marked as disloyal and any sense of trust would have evaporated. There are times when we have to keep our experiences buried in the past. What did Thomas Wolfe say...you can't go home again."?

Frank felt somewhat of a prig after he had finished his speech. It had helped to dissipate his sexual desire. But he still felt like a patronizing old moralizer.

Vanessa's intense gaze had vanished, and she was once more looking out the window at the swirling fog. "Frank, you've come a long way," she said. "Of course, you're right, and you've put it very well. What's in the past should stay in the past."

Frank felt as if the fog had filtered into the Carnelian Room. There was a sense of dejection that had settled on Vanessa and him. Neither of them wanted to admit it, but neither of them could contain it. Each of them avoided looking at the other. Vanessa gazed out of the window and Frank stared into his almost empty glass.

What was it, Frank asked himself, that had triggered the depression that settled over the two of them? Was it backing off from a momentary fling or a longer sexual liaison, if that had actually been on the table? Or was it a more profound recognition that no matter how pleasant life was for each of them presently, they knew down deep that they would never again experience the volcanic sexuality, the longings of love, and the appetite for adventure that had so passionately consumed them many years before?

"You know," Frank said, attempting to lessen their gloom, "I'm not sure we would want to return to those earlier days. My God, what a roller coaster ride it was…missing each other so much when we were apart, the anguish when we were quarreling, the sheer quivering…"

"You're right, Frank, but whatever kind of gloss you want to put on it, I miss the emotion, that soaring sense of being alive in every particle of my being. I miss that."

"I miss it, too. And that's one of the things that weighs on me presently: the knowledge that I'll never soar like that again, that my entire being won't ever pulsate like that again. But for my own self-preservation, I've got to counter those feelings with the wisdom that for everything there is a season. Otherwise, I'd be in a perpetual funk."

"So, you don't believe that anything will ever come along that will duplicate—possibly in a different way—those feelings, that sense of aliveness?'

"No. Unfortunately, I don't. I can't tell you how many times I've thought about it. I expect nothing. What I do expect, if I can bring myself to accept it, is greater tranquility in my life, a certain detachment, a mellow enjoyment of life."

"That's not a great substitute for what we were talking about." said Vanessa with a wan smile.

"Listen, I'm speaking theory here. I'm saying things that my mind says are true, but my emotions can't fully accept. You're looking at someone who would dearly love to f…make love like a satyr again, go on that emotional roller-coaster ride of love, experience all that tingling excitement of working at a job I loved, the constant anticipation of some new adventure. But, you're also looking at someone who doesn't want to drive himself crazy with disappointment, frustration, and lack of fulfillment in the remaining years before he leaves this earth."

"It seems a shame." Vanessa spoke softly and wistfully. "We spend maybe two decades of our life—maybe somewhat more—with the possibility and,

I guess, often the actuality of, a pulsating exciting life. And then for the rest of our lives we lament the end of that time and desperately try to recreate it."

Frank listened to Vanessa's complaint. Yes, she was right. The kind of excitement she was describing began in puberty and began to fade at about the half-century mark, and steadily declined after that. Then one would spend two, three, four decades unsuccessfully trying to recapture the past.

But Frank's recognition of Vanessa's justifiable lament also triggered other thoughts deep within his being. A line from Scripture—he had forgotten where specifically from—"Your young men shall dream dreams, your old men shall see visions." Wasn't that the wisdom of old age? One had to detach from those ideas dreamed up in adolescence and youth and make one's peace with the mellow tranquility of old age. Such detachment should not be merely the passive acceptance of the difference between youth and old age, but the embrace of what life gives us in old age. One could still retain pleasant memories of youth and middle age, but one shouldn't let them dominate later life.

And, bottom line, this meant confronting the reality of mortality.

Frank decided against sharing his insights with Vanessa. He had waxed too philosophical already. On some level each of them grasped the realities, and each also knew that following these prescriptions for happiness in old age was more difficult than recognizing them.

"Would you like another drink?" Frank asked.

"No, I don't think so. Liquor, they say is a depressant and I don't need to get any more depressed. Plus, these days if you sniff a drink you're legally intoxicated. Get a DUI, and you can kiss your life goodbye."

"Once the tide turns get out of the way," Frank declared. "It does make the roads safer, but you can't even drink modestly if you go out to a party. I guess it's good for the cabbies."

"Frank, I can't tell you how wonderful this has been, and how grateful I am for your time. I don't know what I came looking for, and I don't know if I've found it. But I do know that I feel better now than when I called you and before we had our tete à tete."

"Don't be silly. I don't know what you were looking for...I don't even know what I'm looking for...but it helps to talk things out. That's what friends are for. And, if you feel better now than before you sat down there, I'm thrilled."

"You've been kind and very helpful...and very noble," Vanessa said with a warm and endearing smile.

"I can say the same to you."

Frank signaled the waiter for the check.

"Can I give you a ride home?" Vanessa asked.

For some reason he couldn't fathom, Frank didn't want Vanessa to drive him home, even though after they departed he would have to take the bus across town.

"No, thanks, I need to go back to the office to clean up some things," he lied.

The waiter brought Frank's credit card and the slip for him to sign. Then he and Vanessa stood up from the comfortably upholstered chairs in which they had been sitting. They walked slowly to the bank of elevators, silently entered them, and were quickly whisked in an ear-popping descent to the main floor.

Vanessa and Frank walked out into the foggy early evening. Darkness had fallen on the city, and Frank was reminded of some Sherlock Holmes films he had seen, especially those starring Basil Rathbone. All that was missing was the deep-throated rumble of foghorns that he remembered from when he was a boy.

They strolled the half block to Kearny and California Streets, where they stopped. They looked at each other. Vanessa broke the silence.

"I parked a couple of blocks away."

"And I'm going to walk down to Montgomery Street," said Frank.

"Thanks for everything, Frank. Being with you just now has meant more than I can tell you."

"Thank you, Vanessa. I always love it when we get together. Meditate on my thoughts."

Vanessa didn't respond. Instead she put her arms around him and kissed him on the cheek. Frank reciprocated with a hug and a chaste kiss on Vanessa's cheek.

"Goodbye, Frank," Vanessa said, disengaging from the embrace.

"Goodbye, Vanessa. Stay well."

Vanessa walked down Kearny Street to the garage where her car was parked. Frank stood rooted on the corner and watched as she disappeared into the swirling fog.

CHAPTER 21

Frank looked at himself in the mirror as he shaved. Not bad, he thought, for someone in his mid-sixties. He was not a health or exercise fanatic, but he looked good for his age. At 5'11" and 170 pounds he looked trim enough. Not for him, he thought, all the boring work that it takes to have a body that would make one look as if he were in his twenties or thirties.

Yes, around his eyes one could observe the ravages of age; and the two ropes of flabby skin along the upper part of his neck definitely delineated his time spent on this planet. But, all in all, his skin was clear, his eyes were lustrous, and he didn't have a paunch: he looked O.K.

Paula called to him that breakfast was ready, and he put on his robe and padded down the stairs to the kitchen, where she had cut a melon and placed it at his place on the small table where they ate when they were alone.

Frank refilled his coffee mug and sat down, while Paula scooped out some oatmeal for them to complete the menu for this first meal of the day.

"What's on schedule for you today, Sweetheart?" Frank inquired of his wife.

"Nothing unusual. Off to see some things in the wholesale area. Meeting with a couple of clients. Going out to see how the installations are going at the Merrimans' house. Oh, but I am going out to dinner tonight with Betsy and Ellie. I shouldn't be home too late—stop, no, no that's tomorrow night."

Frank wrinkled his nose, but said nothing. Any comment of his would only cause unpleasantness between them. He didn't like either Betsy or Ellie. Frank thought these friends of Paula's were obtrusive in his relationship with Paula, frequently counseling her about some aspect of their marriage.

He thought them two busybodies whose values were totally different from his and Paula's. Their interference in his and his wife's marriage was exceedingly annoying, but Frank had been unable to break the bonds of her friendship with them.

"How about you? What are your plans for the day?" his wife asked, as she sat down at the table.

"I'm going to work half a day today, and then go do some errands... maybe even haunt some galleries and bookstores. Anyway, it will only be half a day of work today. Tonight I've got to pack to go on retreat tomorrow."

"I almost forgot you're going on retreat this weekend," Paula said. "How nice. You'll have to pray for me."

"And for myself as well."

"That goes without saying. So what is it that you're going to be working on?"

"I haven't been down to El Retiro for a few years, so I thought I'd go and think about and pray over a few issues in my life right now."

"For example."

"Oh, you know...this work thing has got me stymied. Should I retire? Should I cut back? And, then, I'm really going to try to get my head straight on my obsession about getting older."

"Thank God," Paula exclaimed. "It's about time."

"Yeah, yeah, yeah..."

"Don't 'yeah, yeah, yeah' me. You are driving your family, including me, and your friends nuts with your obsession on getting older and on dying. Do you think you're the first person who's gotten older or who will die?"

"O.K., let's drop it. I told you I'm going to work on it this weekend. So, don't bug me about it now. I've got to run."

Frank put his dishes in the dishwasher, poured himself another cup of coffee, and walked upstairs to his bedroom to dress. He quickly put on his attire for the day, brushed his teeth, and grabbed his briefcase. Today, he decided, he would take the bus downtown.

He found Paula puttering in the kitchen and gave her his usual hug and kiss. "Bye, honey. See you tonight. Love ya."

"Love you, too."

Frank walked the few blocks to catch the 3 Jackson bus. He generally alternated between driving to work, certainly when he had to make calls on clients or potential clients, and taking the bus, which allowed him to read during the journey and avoid the high parking fees downtown.

He boarded the bus, which held only a handful of riders, most of whom were chattering away on their cell phones. What is this world coming to? Frank asked himself. Do people have to be blabbing to each other constantly? He felt cranky, he realized, but he felt that the technology capable of allowing people to talk with one another constantly and from any location would lead to even greater shallowness in society. Oh, what the hell, why should I care, he thought. I don't have to deal with any of them.

Frank opened the *Chronicle*. What a lousy newspaper, he said to himself, as he scanned the front page. There is truly nothing in it. Here is another part of an interminable series on some woman diagnosed with cancer. A sad story. But should it be reported in countless pages in the newspaper? Another long series on the Burning Man phenomenon in Nevada. Another example of the San Francisco Bay Area's restlessness and shallowness. If it weren't for the obituaries and the occasional bit of news that was important to him, Frank thought, he would cancel his subscription.

He rifled through the paper, set it down on the seat next to him, and pulled a book out of his briefcase. But then Frank noticed that he had just about reached his destination and tucked the book back into the briefcase.

Joining some riders getting off at his stop, Frank walked the familiar short route to the office building that housed Blakesley and Montgomery. He stood mute with others on the elevator ride and watched as they piled off onto various floors. The process reminded Frank of a colony of ants.

"Good morning, Mr. M." Jessica's cheery voice was always an antidote to his morning grumpiness.

"Good morning, Jessica. Hope you had a pleasant evening."

"I'll have to tell you about my date last night when you've got a minute."

"I'm all ears. I've got a few things to go over with you. Why don't you come in in about five or ten minutes, and I'll hear about your date."

"Will do. Would you like some coffee?"

"You're a dear, and the answer is yes."

It was tantamount to a felony to ask a secretary to fetch you a cup of coffee these days, and Frank was grateful to Jessica for offering to do so.

Frank hung up his suit jacket and sat at his desk to look at the day's calendar. No firm meetings. No client meetings. Terrific. This would give him the opportunity to review his accounts. He would make it his objective to look at A through F today. And he had about ten to fifteen memos and letters to dictate. It was rare that he had an entire day—in this case a half day—to catch up on reviewing portfolios and handling correspondence.

Jessica came into his office carrying two cups of coffee. She placed them both on his desk and sat down opposite him.

"Well, where shall we start...the date or your assignments?" she asked.

Frank chuckled. "Oh, let's ease into the day. Why don't we start with the date?"

"You're going to love this. I pass this guy almost every day coming in to work. He's cute and seems cool. After a few weeks we smile at each other as we pass. Then, last week he's in the lobby of this building with a bouquet of flowers, which he hands me. 'I just like you without having met you,' he says, 'and if you're willing, I'd like to take you to dinner. Here's my card so you know I'm not an unemployed weirdo. If you'd like to accept my invitation, call me and we'll set up the time and place.' And with that he was gone."

"Now that's an unusual introduction," Frank laughed.

"I was really touched by it. And he seemed a little shy, which was cute. I looked at the card and saw that he works for a big law firm downtown. What the heck, I said. So I called him.

"We arranged for the date and when he would call for me. And I could tell that he was really pleased that I called him."

"I love to hear stores like this," Frank chortled. "It restores my faith in humanity."

"Me, too. Well, he arrives right on time and brings me another bouquet of flowers. A real gentleman, I think. He takes me for drinks to the Redwood Room at the Clift Hotel and then to dinner at Masa's. It was very romantic. I was a little bit uncomfortable, because I didn't think I was appropriately dressed for the restaurant. But he was so charming that I forgot about it."

"And, so, apart from going to nice places to drink and eat, how was the date?"

"I think I could marry this guy."

"What?"

"I know it sounds crazy, and who knows what the future will bring, but, yeah, I have a gut feeling that this date could turn into a relationship."

"My goodness," was all that Frank could say. He had gone through several such "gut feelings" of Jessica's that had ended disastrously; and Frank had grieved at her resulting pain.

"He told me that he would bore me giving me an account of his life and his values, and then asked me to do the same. By the end of the evening I had a pretty good sense of who he is and what he has done in his life, and he had a pretty good idea about me. Then when he took me home, he asked if he could call me again. I said yes, and then he kissed my hand and left. My heart went pitter-patter."

"Oh, boy. You've got to keep me up to date on this one."

"Oh, I will. I will."

Frank could see the joyous expectation on Jessica's face. There was no doubt that she wanted to get married and have children. And, while she was very attractive, bright, and personable, her Prince Charming had eluded her. This, after all, was San Francisco. He uttered a silent prayer that this time the relationship would end up in a happy marriage.

"Okay, you've taken my breath away with your story of romance," Frank said. "Now, let's do some work."

Frank gave Jessica about a dozen tasks to accomplish. He looked at his calendar to see if he needed to anticipate anything for the remainder of the week, but found nothing.

"Let's see," Frank mumbled. "I'm going to start off my day dictating a flock of memos and letters. Why don't you get going on the items I've given you, and, when I'm finished dictating, you can start typing what I've done."

"Sounds like a plan, Mr. M.," said Jessica, with the joy of a woman in the early stages of love. She left Frank's office, clutching her notebook.

Frank proceeded to dictate into the old IBM machine that he had used for more than thirty years. He leaned back in his chair with a sheaf of notes in his lap and talked into the handheld contrivance that had for many years patiently listened to his letters, memoranda, and instructions to a succession of secretaries.

It took him about two hours to complete seventeen letters and memoranda. It was now late morning, too late to begin the portfolio reviews he had planned. He'd look at how the stock market was doing for a bit and then go to lunch, Frank thought. After lunch he would begin the portfolio reviews, forgetting that he had planned to work only half a day.

He pushed the buzzer on his telephone, summoning his secretary. She appeared immediately.

"Jessica, I'm finished with my dictation. Why don't you take the tapes now? I'm going to get caught up with the market for about fifteen minutes or so and then go to lunch."

"O.K., I should have everything done by the end of the day."

A quiet day, Frank thought, as he switched on the television monitor to watch the day's stock market action. No messages. No telephone calls. What a relief. His pleasure in not having to respond to a raft of telephone calls triggered in him an uncomfortable sensation that he hadn't as yet come to any decision about his future in the firm: whether to retire or to cut back. Ever since his talk with Cal Hopkins he'd felt ill at ease whenever he saw him and whenever he encountered one of the younger associates.

If he was so pleased not to handle telephone calls, wasn't that a sign that he should be retiring or cutting back? Well, he would pay attention to this dilemma this weekend when he went on retreat.

The Dow and the NASDAQ were both up by a substantial number of points, he noticed. He checked the prices of several stocks in which he had an interest...all up nicely. Great, Frank thought, it's always better when the market is up. Less nervousness among his clients. It's just the lunatic fringe that will complain that their investments are not up as much as those of their friends.

Frank tried to ascertain what the market trends were, what industries were particularly strong, but it appeared that what was occurring was a broad, general market rise. That made it easier when evaluating the portfolios of his clients.

The clock on his desk chimed twelve times. Noon already. He would have a quick lunch and come back and review the batch of portfolios.

"I'm off to lunch, Jessica. Won't be long. I'm dining alone today."

"I'm sure you'll have a fine conversation," Jessica quipped. "Enjoy."

Frank decided on Sam's for lunch. Ordinarily, when he had no luncheon engagement, he would eat a sandwich at his desk or sit at a counter of some diner; but today Frank felt like a proper lunch. He would order either the sand dabs or the Frank's salad—a concoction named for one of the waiters at Sam's. This signature salad contained romaine lettuce, avocado, hard-boiled eggs, avocado, and generous portions of shrimp and crab.

The maître d' nodded his head as he entered. "How many today?" he inquired.

"Just me."

"Follow me." The maître d' had seen him countless times in Sam's, but his stoical demeanor never changed. No joke. No smile. No chitchat.

He led Frank to a small table in the back of the restaurant. Almost immediately one of the waiters came up and asked him what he'd like to drink. Frank ordered a glass of chardonnay and the Frank's salad.

The restaurant was beginning to fill up, and as he waited for his lunch to be served, Frank looked at the diners. Sam's was a traditional San Francisco restaurant, one of the few left in the city. Most of them had closed; others, like Tadich's, had become more upscale—and noisy. Sam's wooden panels that bisected the dining area and separated the kitchen at one end and the bar at the other hadn't been stained in decades. The walls were dingy. But the food was plentiful and prepared well.

Frank remembered first lunching at Sam's more than forty years before. A large, round table in one of the corners in the front of the restaurant had for years been the luncheon venue for the major producers from a nearby Merrill Lynch office. The movers and shakers of what was once a compact financial district along Montgomery Street frequented Sam's. He remembered a jovial Tommy Adams, descendent of presidents, telling jokes at the bar, loud guffaws emitting from his jowly, jocund face. Come to think of it, he never saw him eat, only drink, Frank remembered. The always-friendly stockbroker, now dead, was a type no longer tolerated in the more relentless business world.

It had been mostly the financial types that had lunched at Sam's: stockbrokers, bankers, savings and loan executives. This clientele had largely disappeared as the financial district had expanded to the south of its traditional venue and as long lunches had become a thing of the past. To Frank it felt as if the barbarians had overrun civilization. Today's younger financial types either ate at their desks or went out for inedible health food and swigs of carrot juice or water. Those more concerned with how their bodies looked spent their lunch hours working out at fitness centers.

His waiter, dressed in the traditional black suit of old-time San Francisco waiters, brought Frank his order. As his fork began to cut away at one of the tomatoes, he felt a hand on his shoulder.

"Frank Molinari, how the hell are you?"

Frank looked up to see the grinning face of Al Bruning, a friend of many years, from the days when they had both worked at Wells Fargo Bank. He was pleased to see him. For whatever reason the two of them had not seen much of each other for the past couple of years. There had been no falling out…just, well, maybe just laziness on his part, Frank thought.

Frank stood up and shook his friend's hand. "Al, good to see you," he said sincerely. "Why don't you sit down and join me?"

"I can only sit for a few minutes. I'm over there with a few people." Al pointed to the corner table that had once been the preserve of the big producers from Merrill Lynch.

"It's been ages since we've gotten together," Frank began, as they sat down. "I miss you."

"Both of us need to remember how to dial a telephone," Al laughed.

Frank had forgotten how positive Al always was. Instead of being miffed because Frank hadn't been very assiduous in their getting together, Al remarked that both of them had been remiss.

"Here we are again," Frank commented, "in this place of memories."

"Well, don't forget we couldn't afford this place when we were at Wells at $275 a month."

"That's right. It was Tadich's every two weeks for an abalone steak and Goldberg Bowen's most days for a sandwich and a Coke."

"But once we got into the big money—$1000 a month—we ate here often."

"Hard to imagine those days. How are you? How's business?"

"I've been fine. Health is good, thank God. And business has been great. But, let me give you a head's up. I'm going to retire in a few months."

Frank was speechless. He looked at Al with an uncomprehending look. "Retire?"

"Yes," Al said, "people do retire, you know."

Frank recovered somewhat. "Yes, I do know, but I don't think I've ever known a stockbroker who has retired."

"I'm not the first, nor will I be the last."

"I've got to say that I'm stunned. I don't know why. We're the same age, and we're of retirement age. But, I don't know, I never thought about you retiring."

Al had been a stockbroker ever since they had both left Wells Fargo in the early 1960s. They had both worked for Sutro & Company for a few years, after which Frank moved on to Blakesley and Montgomery and Al went to another brokerage firm.

"I'm happy to say that I've made a fair bit of money, saved a decent percentage of it, and invested it pretty well. That allows me to retire with a more than comfortable income. Liz and I love to travel, which we'll be doing.

"Plus, I've gotten tired of holding hands during bad markets and going through all the constant chatter that goes along with being a broker. It's time for me to go quietly into the night."

"I know. I know. I'm finally thinking about either retiring or cutting back myself. I don't know…retirement sounds so final."

"It's not like you don't know what to do in retirement."

"No, I wouldn't be bored, believe me. But there's something about the word retirement that I don't like. It has a sense that life's almost over."

Al laughed. "I'll have to sort that out. I've got to go. Call me for lunch."

"I promise, honest Injun. I'll call you tomorrow and we'll set it up for next week."

"Sounds great." And with a smile and a wave Al walked the length of the restaurant to the group waiting for him.

There he had done it again, Frank thought, despite his resolves, moaning about his life coming to an end if he retires. People will start thinking he had lost his mind. This coming weekend he would have to come to grips with this retirement issue, he resolved.

Frank proceeded to devour his salad. Whoever the waiter "Frank" was, he had concocted a splendid assortment. And he didn't ruin it by giving it a gooey, creamy dressing; the vinaigrette was perfect. It should have received some gastronomic award, Frank mused as he ate.

As he finished his lunch, Frank let his eyes wander over the restaurant and allowed his ears to overhear snatches of conversation at the nearby tables.

Aside from Al, he knew nobody in the restaurant. A goodly number were probably tourists, he speculated, many from outlying communities. People from Redwood City, Danville, and Mill Valley—all the suburbs— loved to come to San Francisco for entertainment, shopping and eating. There was a time when on any given day he would know more than half the people having lunch at Sam's. Where had they gone? Retired or dead, he said to himself.

"I just can't find a dress," a middle-age woman was saying to her companion at the next table. The woman across from her was nodding with appropriate sympathy.

At the table across the aisle a young couple was making every effort at speaking sotto voce. Both were frowning and speaking intently. Domestic quarrel, Frank thought. How many had he witnessed over the years? What is it about sharing a meal at a restaurant that prompted arguments among couples? And how many couples had he seen in restaurants that ate in silence, never speaking to each other, their heads bobbing in synchronism as they placed each morsel of food in their mouths.

The waiter brought Frank coffee, and Frank slowly sipped it as he continued to observe his fellow diners. What a pleasure it was to sip a hot cup in a leisurely fashion after lunch.

Frank saw two men deep in serious conversation a couple tables away. One of the two was stretched out over the table, attempting to make a point to his companion. A business lunch, he thought. The fellow doing the talking, his neck craning across the table, was obviously trying to sell something.

Over the years the faces have changed, Frank thought, but the functions stay the same. The selling goes on, friends continue to socialize, and visitors wishing to experience an old-line San Francisco restaurant still frequent the same places.

Frank motioned to his waiter to bring the bill, and when he delivered it, Frank handed him his credit card. Frank continued to peruse the restaurant. The woman of the couple that had been quarreling was crying now, and trying her best to hide her tears. The two women at the next level sounded as if they were gossiping about a mutual friend. No, Frank thought, people don't change.

He added a tip to his bill and signed it. It was time to get back to the office. Al was deep in conversation with his companions. Frank decided not to go to his table and say goodbye. He walked out into the pallid sunshine of an early San Francisco afternoon and headed slowly toward his office. Al's announcement that he was going to retire had shaken him. Frank knew that it would be a catalyst for his making a decision about his own work situation.

Jessica was not at her desk when he arrived at his office...probably out to lunch. But on his desk were drafts of some memos for him to approve and letters for him to sign. Also on his desk were the folders of the accounts he wanted to review. Frank loved to have Jessica working for him. Not only was she pleasant to have around, but she was also efficient.

Frank took off his coat, placed the folders on the couch in his office, and sat down next to them. He peeled off the first one and began to examine its contents. The department responsible for assembling the information had done its usual excellent job of presenting all the figures necessary for him to determine whether the portfolios were well positioned and whether they were performing adequately.

It took him only a few minutes to come to a conclusion about a portfolio's health. By late afternoon he had reviewed thirty portfolios: only two had been put aside for further consideration. There was a batch still beside him, but Frank was not in the mood to continue his review.

Let's see, 4:30, he said to himself as he looked at the clock on his desk. He suddenly recalled that he had planned to work only half a day. Ah, well, he thought, it doesn't matter. He probably would have wound up spending money if he had. I think I'll call Paula. He went to his desk and dialed his wife.

"Hello."

"Hi, Sweetheart, what's for dinner?"

"You must be bored if you're calling at 4:30 to ask me what we're having for dinner."

"Not bored, just eager to get home and see you."

"Ah, that's so nice. And I can hardly wait to see you."

There was a certain amount of fun in such conversations they had, but both appreciated the sentiments expressed.

"So, we're having a nice, quiet night at home tonight?" Frank inquired.

"That's the plan. Unusual, no?"

"I love it. Unfortunately, it is too unusual."

"Back to what we're having for dinner. We have string beans and halibut. How does that sound? And I'll make a salad."

"Sounds terrific. Let's see…it's not quite 5 yet. But I'm not too enthusiastic about reviewing any more portfolios, and it's too late to start any more projects. I think I'll leave now. I should be home by a quarter to six. We'll have a nice, long evening."

"I knew you were bored. That's great that you'll be home early. See you in about forty-five minutes."

"Love you."

"Love you, too."

Frank put down the receiver. He was a fortunate man. Despite his recent concerns and obsessions, he had a good life. He didn't have as much money as he would have liked, but he had enough to lead a comfortable life. His needs were taken care of, and he had a sufficient surplus for such luxuries as travel, collecting books and art, and for contributions to his favorite charities.

Feeling thus pleased with his life, Frank threw some papers in his briefcase and left his office.

"I'm off, Jessica," he told his secretary. "Here are the signed letters and the corrected memos. Tomorrow is time enough to get them out. Why don't you take off, too?"

"Thanks, Mr. M. I'll see you tomorrow."

Frank walked the short distance to Sutter Street, where he waited for the 3 Jackson. The usual clutch of bus riders at the end of the workday awaited one of the three busses that would take them home. Rather than pull out a book to read while he waited for the bus, Frank spent the time observing his fellow travelers.

There were probably twenty people there, a few couples but mostly individuals. One couple, probably two women friends in their mid-twenties, chattered away; another couple, no doubt in a romantic liaison, joked and touched each other in the playful way that young lovers manifest their enjoyment of each other's company.

Half the group was on cell phones, which always set Frank's teeth on edge. This need for incessant chatter, Frank thought, drove him crazy. A woman in her thirties, with pendulous breasts and a sour face, stared vacantly into space. I wonder what her story is, Frank asked himself.

The bus arrived as he was about to create life scripts for the people grouped around him. Several got on the 3 Jackson, and then the bus lunged forward to its next stop a block away.

Frank settled into one of the seats near the front of the bus, reserved for seniors and disabled people. What would happen if all the seats were full, and he asked some young or middle-aged person to give up his or her seat to him? It had never happened. Would he be bold enough to ask?

He reached into his briefcase for a book he was readying—Thackeray's *Vanity Fair*. Some years previously he had determined to read the spectrum of English novels, books that he had first read in his high school and college years. He had started with the nineteenth century, plowing through the enormous output of Dickens, Eliot, Trollope, and now Thackeray. And while he believed he was enjoying what would probably be his last reading of these splendid books, he couldn't help but remember the excitement that had gripped him when he had read them in his teens and twenties. He had turned the pages with such an expectant eagerness, tingling with a palpable excitement as he read about Becky Sharpe, Oliver Twist, Archdeacon Theophilus Grantly, and the entire pantheon of the unforgettable characters that peopled the hundreds of novels written by the prolific nineteenth-century authors. He often ended the novel he was reading in those years as he looked out a window and saw the dawn. A depression would settle on him as he finished a book...but then it was on to the next one. And so it went for years.

And, now, as he reread them, he could remember those pleasurable hours of excitement...but they didn't return. Yes, he still enjoyed reading novels, but he enjoyed them in a tranquil, autumnal way, not with the quivering pulsation that he once had.

Frank closed *Vanity Fair* and closed his eyes, trying to recapture those feelings of long ago. He hovered over them, remembered them—but couldn't recapture them. What was it, he asked himself, that had gone out of life as he got older? Why couldn't that excitement that permeated life when he was in his teens and twenties continue? What had sucked out his life the tremulous chiaroscuro that he had once experienced?

Frank opened his eyes just in time to see that his stop was only a half-block away. He pulled the overhead cord to signal the driver to stop, and when the bus pulled into the designated stop, he exited through the rear door.

Frank walked the few blocks to his home, entered, and put his briefcase down in the entry hall. Paula had heard him come in, and walked down from the second floor to greet him. They embraced and kissed. He felt the smooth skin of her cheek and rubbed his hands along her lithe body. She was wearing dark slacks and one of his Brooks Brothers Oxford shirts.

"I've got an idea, Sweetheart. How about a 'roll in the hay' before cocktails?"

Paula threw back her head in laughter. "Oh, you smooth-talking romantic. Sure, why not?"

They walked up the stairs arm in arm. A great day, Frank thought.

CHAPTER 22

Frank walked toward the chapel along the well-tended path to his assigned room for his annual retreat at the El Retiro Retreat House in Los Altos. He knew the grounds and the routine well. The room he had been given was in the oldest building on the property, the home of the original owner of the estate. It was large and had its own bathroom.

Frank had been coming to El Retiro since he was in high school. His father had gone for years, and, after Frank's inaugural high school retreat, he went with his father and the group his father went with.

He cherished his annual retreat: the quiet, the ability to wander the extensive grounds thinking about—what?—So many things. He had inherited the piety of his parents, and the opportunity to pray and the exhortations of whatever Jesuit was the retreat master that week were balm to his soul.

Frank unpacked his suitcase and put his toiletries put away in the medicine cabinet above the sink in the bathroom. There was nothing scheduled until dinner at 6 p.m., so he had a couple hours to himself until then. First he looked out the window at the front entrance of the building where his room was. It looked west, over Highway 280 and over the campus of Foothill College, farther still over the hills that barred the view of the Pacific Ocean.

Leaving the vicinity of his living quarters, he walked toward the central area of the retreat house: the chapel, the dining room, the Jesuit residences, other residences for retreat guests, and the conference center. The view here was to the east: the bay, the range of mountains beyond the bay, the southern end of the peninsula, and the broad Santa Clara Valley.

Frank gazed at the panorama in front of him, amazed at the changes that had taken place in that terrain over the half century that he had been coming to El Retiro. In the mid-1950s the towns and cities that lay below him were hamlets at best. San Jose, now larger than San Francisco, was then still a provincial market town. One could still see the massive palette of pink and white blossoms of the fruit and nut trees that blanketed Saratoga, Campbell, Mountain View, and the other agricultural towns that dotted the valley. Since then, the area had become a major population center of the San Francisco Bay Area. The explosion of technology had turned it into the greatest producer of wealth in the world. Now, instead of Santa Clara Valley, it was known as Silicon Valley.

Here he stood in an oasis of spirituality, where men and women attempted to save their souls, looking down on multi-million dollar houses and on companies worth billions of dollars.

Frank thought back on the years he had gazed on this view—as a student, when he had been single, and during both of his marriages, sometimes stupefied with loneliness and perplexed about his life. There were times when he felt elated, sure of success, and other times when he felt singed with failure. And, now, he felt...well, okay...not great...okay.

He pivoted from the spot where he had stood to view the tableau before him and walked up the stairs to the chapel. It, like all Catholic churches, had changed. A spare table stood in the middle of this sanctuary. The traditional altar, where for many years the Latin mass had been celebrated, stood bare, denuded of the altar linens and the cloth that covered the tabernacle, the color of which indicated the liturgical season—white, green, purple, red. The remainder of the chapel was very much as he remembered it fifty years before.

Dipping his right hand in the holy water font, Frank slowly made the sign of the cross and walked to a pew in the middle of the chapel, genuflected, and knelt in the pew. He asked God to help him with his problems, to give him guidance on the issue of his work situation, and to cure him of his obsession with getting old and dying. He finished his petition with a silent recitation of the Our Father, a Hail Mary, and a Glory Be to the Father and walked out of the chapel into the late afternoon sunlight.

Cars were coming into the parking lot, and men and women were filing into the registration office and then going to find their rooms. A man probably in his early forties walked past him. He was wearing a white shirt and khaki pants. Noticing Frank he wheeled around and, smiling broadly, stuck out his hand.

"Hi, I'm Father Mike. I'll be co-directing your retreat."

"Hello, Frank Molinari. Nice to meet you, Father." Frank shook his hand.

"Where are you from?"

"San Francisco. Been there all my life."

"Great city to be from. I'm from Los Angeles, but I hope you don't hold that against me. Enjoy your retreat. And I'm always available if you'd like to talk."

"That would be great. I'll look you up tomorrow or Saturday."

"Do that. I've got to go to see if any of your fellow retreatants need any help finding their rooms. See you later."

The priest quickly walked to the registration office.

Father Mike, Frank thought...and in khakis...another of the changes of the last forty years. During the early days of his coming to El Retiro, the priests had worn long, black cassocks and birettas on their heads. They were addressed by their last names and had become legendary among the pious Catholic men—women had their own retreat houses—who went there year after year...a group of Catholic doctors from Marin County one weekend, members of the Knights of Columbus from San Mateo another weekend, groups that would frequently number 100, enjoying the sociability of friends as well as feeling that they were somehow feeding their souls.

Men and women were now passing Frank as he stood at the bottom of the chapel steps. The retreat had a specific theme—"spirituality for older men and women"—and, as a result, those attending were in late-middle age or beyond. Frank had chosen this specific weekend because of his dilemma about his work situation. It would be, he hoped, "on point."

Most of his fellow retreatants nodded and smiled as they saw Frank, and he returned their greetings. They were wandering about before dinner was served, as people do who are in unfamiliar circumstances, unsure about what they should be doing and unwilling to sit back and read a book or wander about meditating...or just looking at the view.

A woman who was probably in her late forties or early fifties caught his eye and smiled. Frank nodded and smiled, thinking that she, like the others, would pass on in aimless wandering. Instead, she stopped in front of him.

"Well," she asked, "what brings you here?"

Frank was startled by her question, and thought that it might be someone he had known but didn't recognize. He played for time. "I'm here to see if

I can get a grip on becoming old and eventually dying. How about you?"

The woman laughed. "You put it so forthrightly," she said. "Most people wouldn't be so honest. I'm Mary Lamb."

"Hello, I'm Frank Molinari. Well, there's no point in covering up what we're here for. Otherwise, what's the point?"

"You're absolutely right. But I still feel that if all the people here were asked, very few would be so up front."

"How about you, why did you come to this particular retreat?" Frank asked.

"I could answer the same as you have...in a general sense. My specific circumstances are that I've just turned fifty, just retired from my job as a partner in a big headhunting firm, and have been divorced for five years. Given that my health is good and that I've got longevity in my genes, I thought I'd take this opportunity to think out my future."

"I wish I had done that when I was fifty."

Mary Lamb was tall and slender. She wore what seemed like an expensive blouse and a pair of Ishimisaki pants that highlighted her height and her lissome figure. (He knew the name of the designer because Paula had a pair.) Mary had an elegant attractiveness and an air of having come from money...or, certainly, having made a goodly amount of money.

"Oh, I'm sure that you've never lacked for timely introspection. What do you do now?"

"I'm still working, and that's something I'm trying to work out this weekend, whether to retire or cut back or keep slogging away."

"What is it that you do?"

"I'm an investment advisor for a good-size regional firm."

"Ah...," was Mary Lamb's reaction.

"And you? Do you think you'll develop a new career—you're certainly young enough—or just spend the rest of your life taking cruises?"

"Well, I'm certainly not going to spend my life taking cruises, but I don't know what I want to do from here on in. Like you, I'm hoping to get some enlightenment this week."

"Where are you from, Mary?"

"Boston, originally. But I lived mostly in Manhattan after college. I've been in California for about fifteen years."

"Do you live in the Bay Area?"

"Yes, in Piedmont."

Frank liked the exchange he was having, and decided to continue. Mary didn't seem to want to rush off anywhere. "So what do you do beside work...at least until you retired...and keep house?"

"How does one describe what one does with one's life? I see friends frequently. I travel some. I do a great deal of reading. There is always a fair amount of business stuff and household work one has to do. You know... the days go by."

"I know. I realize all the time what a complex life I have. Each day evaporates. Then, suddenly, one year is gone, then another...then a decade."

"I was thinking that the other day. It seems as if it were yesterday that I was married and having children, and now they're grown and out of the house."

"Where do they live?"

"Both of them work and live in the East. One's in Greenwich, Connecticut, the other in Manhattan. We see each other two or three times a year."

"Unfortunately, children don't tend to stay near their parents anymore."

"I'm not sure that's so unfortunate, but, no they don't."

Frank felt as if he were on a date...what do you do? What do you do when you're not working? What are your likes and dislikes? And this in front of the El Retiro chapel. Next he'll be asking what her sign is. And, he reminded himself, he was a married man.

Frank plunged ahead. "Does your ex-husband live in the area?"

"No, he moved back to New York shortly after we divorced. He's an investment banker...came out here to run the San Francisco office of his firm fifteen years ago, and then went back to New York after we divorced."

"Tell me...I'm curious...what made you decide to retire so young from what sounds like a pretty good job?"

"For one thing, I've been at it for twenty-five years. I'm happy to say that it was a successful career. My retirement benefits were quite substantial. The company also offered a 'golden handshake.' All that, plus a good-sized inheritance from my parents and a substantial divorce settlement gave me the wherewithal to retire comfortably.

"But what really motivated me was my desire to do something totally different—whether it's starting my own company or something in the non-profit world—while I'm still young enough."

"Sounds like you've got some big decisions in front of you."

"There are, but it's a good sort of decision making. I'm not against the wall financially. I can take some time to really think about what I'd like to do, and then see if it's possible.'

"Still, when you're making those kinds of life decisions, it's a big deal."

"Yes, but a nice big deal."

Frank enjoyed talking to Mary Lamb. He thought he might ask her if she'd like to sit with him at dinner and at subsequent meals, but decided against doing so. But he still didn't want to break off their conversation.

"You said you're a voracious reader," Frank opened up a new subject. "What do you like to read?"

"Literate fiction and well-written nonfiction…history, biography…that sort of thing."

"No kidding!" Frank exclaimed, his interest in his companion heightened. "Those are my interests, as well."

"Reading is one of the great pleasures of my life. And I read all kinds of things—international intrigue and espionage, good mysteries, solid novels, the classics. I think the last number of years have seen brilliantly researched and written biographies and histories."

"You're absolutely right," Frank replied, quite excited about finding someone to discuss his love of reading with. "I think this began in the 1960s; and I think it began with Holroyd's biography of Lytton Strachey."

"Do you? I read that biography about ten years after it was published. I loved it. I thought the presentation of this massive amount of details on Strachey's life made the biography most interesting. So, you think that this biography began it all?"

"Well, you know, it's hard to pinpoint something like that, but at least it's a symbolic beginning from my own experience After that you get an enormous number of detailed, well-written biographies. And, in history you get Barbara Tuchman and others who revolutionized the writing of history."

Mary had a broad smile. "I can't tell you how pleased I am to find someone with whom I can discuss the books I read. Even those of my friends who are readers will read only light fiction and the occasional how-to nonfiction book."

"I'm a little encouraged about more literate fiction," Frank rejoined. "About a year ago I discovered an excellent writer who writes espionage intrigue books—Alan Furst—and I've been amazed at how many people I've encountered who've read him."

"I love Alan Furst," Mary almost shouted.

Frank was smitten. A way to a man's heart may be through his stomach, but the way to his head was through an intelligent conversation about books. "Oh, my God, I'm in love," he said, laughing.

Mary's smile expanded to a gurgling laughter. "This is great," she said.

The chapel bell began to ring. It was the call for the *Angelus*, but also the call to dinner. Mary and Frank walked slowly toward the dining room, along with other men and women who began to converge from the several paths that wound around El Retiro's buildings. They continued their conversation about books as they entered the monastic-like dining room, with its expanse of glass that allowed the diners to enjoy the magnificent panorama of the valley below.

Frank chose an empty table. There was no doubt that Mary and he would be companions at meals. He pulled out a chair for her, and the two of them sat down. Within seconds two others—both men—had seated themselves at the table…and then the remaining four chairs were occupied by three women and another man. Frank would have preferred eating solo with Mary and continuing their delicious conversation, but that would have been too eccentric. Maybe at Esalen, but not at El Retiro.

Instead, Frank introduced himself to the five strangers who were at his table. As was his wont, he began the process of asking questions to prime the pump for conversation: what do you do? Where do you live? Why are you here?

It worked. Soon the four men and four women were chatting amiably about their lives and what had brought them to El Retiro. With the exception of Mary, they were in their sixties. All but two at the table—Frank and one of the other men—were retired. They felt young, and they wanted meaningful occupation for as long as their health was good.

"I don't want to spend the rest of my life just playing golf and puttering around the house," Sam announced, summarizing what the others were saying.

It occurred to Frank that the people he had met at El Retiro were looking for some sort of career counseling…perhaps not about what kind of job or career they would like, but about what might be appropriate to do after retirement. There didn't seem to be much interest in the more abstract area of spirituality for older people.

"How about you, Frank?" one of those sitting at the table asked him. "What are you looking to get out of this retreat?"

"One of the main things is what everyone at this table has just said: what to do with the rest of my life. I plan to come to some decision while I'm here about whether to retire, to stay full-time at my job, or to cut back. But I also want to go deeper, to see if I can formulate spirituality appropriate to my getting older."

Frank looked around the table. Everyone had stopped eating as he spoke. With the exception of Mary and Sam—they looked at him with puzzlement. His thought on spirituality appropriate to getting older obviously seemed somewhat odd to them.

"That's a lot to figure out," was the response of the man who had asked the question.

"There's always a lot to figure out in life," Frank concluded.

Heads went back to bobbing up and down in silence as they continued to eat their dinner. Meals at El Retiro were always in silence, except for the first and the last. Tonight's momentary silence was a pause in the tendency for strangers to tell about themselves, and incidentally, to hear about others. Frank counted the seconds before someone began the autobiographical odyssey. It was less than a minute.

Sally began. "I've just got to figure out who I am and what I want to do after a divorce and now that my kids have left the house. I was a stay-at-home mom and wife for many years until my bast...I mean my husband... left me for a younger woman. And I taught grade school. But teaching is for younger people. Teaching kids these days is a killer."

"What do you think you'd like to do?" Frank asked. "Would you want to get married again? And do you want to work after you give up teaching?"

Sally looked at Frank as if he had interrupted her desire to give more details about her life. "Get married again? Oh, I don't know...I guess, if I met the right man. I don't know about work. I really should retire. But what would I do? No husband and no children to take care of."

"Oh," Frank continued, "that's the bane of getting older. Spouses die and couples get divorced. Children grow up and move away. We get bored with our jobs and we either want new ones or we want to retire. And nothing prepares us for all this."

Sally's face scrunched. She didn't want philosophical exegesis. She wanted to tell her story. She should have been in an encounter session at Esalen, Frank thought, not at a Catholic retreat house. But the rest of the table nodded, seemingly in agreement...all except Mary, who had a serious, contemplative cast to her face.

Jim, the man who had asked Frank why he was there, plunged into the conversation. "You know, Frank, you're absolutely right. We go to school. We get jobs. We get married. We have children. We struggle to support our families. And, then, just at the time you feel you can relax and enjoy the results of your hard work, your life falls apart. My wife left me last year after forty years of marriage because she said she was bored. My three children avoid me like the plague. They don't want to hear about my life. I've just retired. I was bored with my job…I'd been with the same company for more than forty years…but I can't seem to figure out what to do with my days. And on top of all this, I've started to have health problems. What the hell is all this about?"

Frank had begun to stroke his chin as Jim was uttering his *cris de coeur*. Maybe I should have been a psychologist, Frank thought. "That's probably why you're here, Jim, to figure out what the hell it's all about."

"Yeah, I guess maybe so."

And now it was Barbara's turn, as dessert was being served and the early evening twilight made its way across the valley. "I'm hoping that we get just a few answers to these questions this weekend. I realize that in two and a half days we're not going to entirely change our lives, but I hope to change a little bit of it."

More nodding…and more silence.

"This is a process," said Mary. Frank looked up from his chocolate pudding and gave her his full attention. "We're all looking for specific answers to our questions, questions about our individual lives. Those answers lie within us. I think we need to use this weekend as a catalyst to bring those answers out."

Astute, Frank thought. And perceptive. She's smart as well as good looking.

There was a clinking on a glass. Father Mike had just walked into the dining room and had some announcements to make. In a relaxed, jovial manner he explained the schedule for the weekend, enjoined the retreatants to keep silent over the course of the weekend, and said that he and Father Pat would be happy to talk with any of the retreatants, if they so wished. He finished his talk with some housekeeping details. Where to get toothpaste if you forgot to bring some, where the library was, and so forth.

The retreatants began to file out of the dining room. Some sequestered themselves to smoke; most of the others gathered in little groups, chatting until it was time for the first conference at 7:30 in the chapel. After a fifteen-minute interval, the chapel bell began to ring, signaling that it was time for the conference. The retreatants walked up the steps and sat in the pews of the chapel.

Father Mike began with a short prayer and then sat down at a small table. His talk lasted about forty-five minutes, and was essentially a prologue for the retreat. He pointed out that there was an appropriate spirituality for different times in a person's life: for example, spirituality in one's teens is different from that of a person of sixty or more. We need to be conscious, said Father Mike, of developing a spirituality that is appropriate to our circumstances: whether married or single, working or not, sick or well. One of the components of the retreat, he said, is for us to look at the inevitability of death—a subject that occupies the minds of most people increasingly after they turn fifty.

That component, Frank thought, was something he could relate to.

We think that life's decisions are made when we're younger, Father Mike continued, but numerous decisions need to be made when we're older—decisions having to do with work or volunteering, family relationships, where we're going to live, and so forth. "We're going to try," said Father Mike, "to help you make these decisions by a prayerful reliance on God."

This should be a good retreat, Frank thought.

Father Mike ended his colloquy, knelt to say a short prayer, reminded the retreatants to keep silent, and walked out of the chapel. The retreatants followed, quietly filing out into the clear Los Altos night. Stars twinkled overhead, and a half moon was rising over the bay. It was a mild evening. Frank looked at his watch. It was only 8:30. He didn't feel like going back to his room. He tried to seek out Mary Lamb, but she was nowhere to be seen.

He would take a walk around the property, Frank thought, and then go to his room and read. As he had now done for many years, Frank began his silent hegira around the grounds of El Retiro. His favorite view was toward the east and to the south. Even before the population exploded in more recent years, the twinkling lights in the distance represented for Frank a stark contrast to the darkness and silence of El Retiro. Especially on Friday and Saturday nights, during those long weekend retreats, Frank underwent a sad melancholy. He envisaged young men and women out on dates, having dinner, perhaps, or at the movies, or parked in cars, necking and petting. It all seemed like a comforting thing to do.

Here he was again. This time the frustrated lusts of his youth had been, more or less, laid to rest. He had had a successful career, he was happily married, his children seemed to be leading happy lives, and he was fulfilled in his various interests. But, still, as Frank looked out over the multiplicity of tiny lights in the distance, he felt twinges of that same sad melancholy he had experienced in his younger years. The Peggy Lee song that had haunted him for so many years, "Is That All There Is?" filtered through his head.

Frank forcibly turned from such thoughts as he walked around the hilltop near the retreat house. The darkened buildings with an occasional light were silhouetted by the light of the moon. He tramped by the water tank. His view was now north and west, large, ranch-type houses on large lots, affluent neighborhoods, and the college across Highway 280. He tried to focus on making a decision on his work situation.

Frank made the sign of the cross and said a prayer, asking God for help in making the right decision, and then began to mentally construct a balance sheet of his options.

What were the reasons for staying? he asked himself. A major reason was that he would be earning a high salary and putting more money away. Another reason was that working full time helped to ward off his consciousness that he was growing older. Anything else? he wondered. Nothing came to mind.

What were the reasons for retiring or cutting back? For one thing, he was getting tired of working. He could tell that psychologically he was not as patient as he had been before and less interested in the details of the business. But what irritated him most was having to listen to the irrational whining of some of his clients.

What affected him the worst was that his "seat," so to speak, was wanted for some of the younger associates, those eager, enthusiastic, and energetic young men and women who had done well at the tasks given them and now thought that they had put in sufficient time for them to become partners. The problem was that you could only cut the pie in so many pieces. Frank realized that he stood in the way of one or more of the firm's promising associates. He further realized that this was harming the firm's future. If energetic, creative young men and women at the firm didn't get ahead, they would leave.

There must be some way that he could resolve his dilemma, Frank thought. Much of what kept him from retiring was nonsense. He had his mother's fear of penury: there was never enough money. However, he realized that he could retire comfortably, that he would have no financial constraints in retirement.

Working to ward off his fears about growing older was also absurd, he realized. The reality was there. No amount of working out or work was going to change that. He needed to confront getting older and dying without the barriers of doing things that would blunt his consciousness.

What should he do? Frank didn't feel like making any decisions tonight. It was after 9 o'clock. He had the pros and cons in his mind. He also knew the direction in which he must go. Tomorrow…tomorrow he would deal with it and make his decision. Now he would amble toward his dormitory, go to bed, and read until he was ready for sleep.

He gazed at the cars traveling Highway 280, their lights speeding along, emitting "thump-thump" at various intervals. He slowly turned to walk the slight hill to his room.

Frank noticed that a few of his fellow retreatants were sitting and reading in the expansive living room of the house where his room was. They looked up as he walked in, and Frank smiled and gave a nod to those who caught his eye.

His room was different from most of those at El Retiro. Each room at the newer residence buildings was spare but comfortable, with a private bathroom, a single bed, a small desk, a chair, and a clothes closet. Frank's room was in what had been a large estate's substantial house and was large, carpeted, with a double bed, a large desk, a large chair, and a settee. The bathroom was as large as most of the newer rooms. It even had a balcony that looked toward the southeast.

Frank sprawled on the settee and reached for the book he had been reading. He usually tried to read books with spiritual themes when he was on retreat, and he had two or three in his briefcase, but the book he reached for was an espionage thriller that he had read half of—Alan Furst's *Dark Voyage*—and he was eager to finish it.

Furst's books had been a delight during the past few years, but he only read them when he wasn't faced with pressing duties, as he found it hard to put down the novels.

After about an hour Frank began to doze. Time to go to bed, he thought, as he woke up with a start.

The next day began with mass at 7:30. The chapel bells rang the wake-up call at 6:45. By 7:20 the retreatants began to appear from different locations, walking toward the chapel. Since not all the retreatants were Catholic, not all went to mass, although some non-Catholics did.

Father Mike and Father Pat concelebrated. Out of the corner of his eye Frank saw Mary Lamb and noticed that she was looking in his direction. He turned his eyes toward the altar.

There was no homily, and the mass was over by 8:10. Once more retreatants left the chapel and congregated in silence in the patio in front of the dining hall, where they awaited the bell for breakfast. Frank loved the bell-driven schedule at El Retiro. It lessened the need for decision making, giving him time and energy for more substantive decision making than when to eat.

The same people sat at the same refectory tables in the dining hall, and each stood at his place at table, waiting for Father Mike to say grace. He said the standard, "Bless us oh Lord…" and then added, "We ask your blessing on these retreatants who seek your love for the rest of their days."

With the conclusion of the blessing, all sat down. Father Mike announced that breakfast was buffet and indicated the order for the retreatants to get up and file along the two tables that contained scrambled eggs, bacon, sausages, rolls, coffee, water for tea, and various condiments. No one went hungry here.

Breakfast, and all the meals until lunch on Sunday, was eaten in silence. No chatter as there had been at dinner the evening before. That suited Frank well. He disliked a constant menu of inconsequential conversation. Occasionally he looked over at Mary Lamb and their eyes met. I wonder what she is thinking about? Frank asked himself. Both would smile when their eyes met, and then they would look down at their plates.

Retreats at El Retiro were composed of three conferences each day: one after each meal. In the late morning there was an examination of conscience, during which one of the retreat masters read from a list of possible faults, followed by instruction on how to eradicate these faults if one was prone to them. In the late afternoon, there was reading and discussion of selected Biblical texts.

In the past decade or so, retreats at El Retiro had had specific themes; the one Frank was attending, for example, explored spirituality for older people. There were retreats for the divorced, for those with addictions, for young singles. The conferences were oriented toward specific themes, and there was an attempt to fit the examination of conscience and the discussion of Biblical texts into the themes, as well.

On Friday morning, at the conference following breakfast, Father Pat lectured for about an hour on developing a spirituality that was suitable for those over fifty years of age. He pointed out the immense changes that took place during the years following fifty: retirement, a decline in sexual desire and potency, children out of the family home, an increase in illnesses, the loss of friends and family members, and an increased sense of the eminence of death.

One's relationship with God, Father Pat proclaimed, had to incorporate these changes. One's prayer life needed to encompass these massive changes; and one's attitudes, frequently buffeted by disappointment and a sense of loss, needed to be guided by our prayerful responses.

Father Pat, a man in his early sixties, put forth a well-reasoned and logical presentation. It was, Frank thought, an excellent introduction. What came next, he presumed, would elaborate on this initial presentation.

The conference was over at about 10:15, and Frank decided that he would continue his walks on the El Retiro grounds, contemplating his work dilemma. He whispered a prayer before he left the chapel, asking God for guidance, and then stepped out into the bright morning sunshine to begin his wanderings.

Frank preferred staying on the top of the hill looking east out over the Santa Clara Valley. The slightly mysterious sense that he had experienced the night before while viewing the landscape had given way to a sense of bustling expectation, as the area experienced the last day of the work week.

Kneading his mind into a contemplation of the pros and cons that he had thought about the night before, Frank began to realize that fairness compelled him to consider others in making his decision. This realization led him to postulate that some or total diminishing of his position at Blakesley & Montgomery was imperative.

"I've got it," Frank said out loud as he looked down, vaguely seeing it, on the town of Los Altos. "I'm gong to ease out beginning now."

His mind quickly calculated what his plan would be. He would tell the firm that he would eliminate his partnership interest over the next five years, cutting back at a rate of twenty percent per year, becoming fully retired at the end of five years. And, should he find after a year or so, that he wanted to accelerate the process, he could do so.

Frank was pleased with himself. In less than a day from his arrival he had come up with a workable solution to his work dilemma. This was the catalyst to begin the process. Once the process was in place, he thought, his fears would dissolve and he would probably make the decision to retire.

His pleasure was such that he gave a couple skips when he continued his walk up the path. Frank looked up and saw Mary Lamb smiling at him.

"I hate to break silence, but I couldn't help notice you speaking to yourself and then skipping up the lane," she said.

"Oh, that. Well, you know how Italians are...a little crazy. I was just celebrating my decision about working. I'm going to cash out my partnership and ease out of my working life over a five-year period, sooner if I want to. I'm thrilled that I have this off my mind."

"I'm so pleased for you. Congratulations. I'm sorry to say that I haven't received any revelations yet."

"You will. You've only just begun."

"This morning's conference didn't reach me, for some reason. It was a good statement, but it didn't trigger any responses within me."

"These things don't happen overnight. Last night I kind of framed the problem, and just now the solution came to me...at least the solution I'm comfortable with at this point. You'll start clicking on yours. I find that when I have the time to start concentrating on what I want to achieve and am in a place such as this without distractions, I'm on my way."

"You're encouraging. Thanks."

"No problem. Just focus and start jotting down what comes to mind."

"You should have been a psychologist."

"I've thought that myself many times," said Frank, smiling.

"We'd better get on our way before the silence police arrest us."

"See you at lunch."

The two continued their walk in opposite directions: Mary Lamb still seeking her path, Frank pleased that he had made a major decision. He looked at his watch to make certain that he wasn't too far from the chapel when the bells rang for the examination of conscience. His thoughts turned to Mary Lamb as he continued to amble. He regretted the demand for silence, as he would have liked to have continued their conversations. Maybe he would invite her to lunch when they returned home. And, then again, he thought, maybe not.

The remainder of the day sped by for Frank. He had now turned his mind to issues other than the one he had solved, notably his obsession with getting older and dying. This had been much on his mind since the morning, when he had resolved his work situation. As he usually did, he let his mind play over the problem, but this time it was not a problem capable of a practical solution. This was something deep in his psyche that troubled him, something that wouldn't go away, something that defied his attempts to bring it under control. Perhaps he should speak to one of the two priests about it. Maybe they would have a thought or two that would help.

Not that he lacked any philosophical knowledge on this matter. As far back as he could remember, he had known that people get older and die. Disease, he knew, was part of life. No one could escape death. He had known all of this; he had read the classics on death and dying. He could have been another Buddha, except that his knowledge was not sufficient to rid him of the increasing fears he had of the debility of old age and then of death itself.

For all of his life Catholicism had told him that death would be welcome, that he would then be in paradise with God. And for many years that was a comforting, if abstract, thought. But, as getting older and the imminence of death became a present reality, the comforting thought of an eternal life in Heaven's happiness became less of a help. He was stymied as to what to do about these fears.

The evening conference had been over for about an hour, and Frank found himself sitting on a bench, once more gazing at the twinkling lights in the landscape beneath him. The sense he gathered from tonight, Friday, differed from what he mused upon last night. Tonight's scene reeked of release, the end of the workweek, a night for letting off steam, a night of relaxation.

Frank heard footsteps on the gravel of the path that came to the bench on which he was sitting. He looked up to see Mary Lamb.

"Do you mind if I talk with you?" she inquired.

"Of course not. What's up?"

"Oh, I don't know. I've been up above you, looking at this same view, and I've been feeling a bit blue."

"Yeah, I know what you mean," Frank responded, somewhat wistfully. "I've been coming here almost every year for the past half century, and I always feel blue, too, on Friday and Saturday nights as I look at this view. I don't know what causes it. Maybe it's because we feel that everyone out there is having a good time, while we're up here engrossed in morose thoughts."

"Are you having morose thoughts?"

"Well, not exactly morose, but I am concentrating on getting rid of some of the devils that have entered me."

"Performing an exorcism, huh?"

"Yeah, I guess in a way I am. I hope it's successful."

"I'm sure it will be. You're very focused."

"So, what's making you blue?"

"Oh, I don't know. I feel at odds with myself, all at sea. I've got lots of things to be thankful for, but I find something's missing at the core of my being."

"Have you been getting anything out of the retreat?"

"I think so, but nothing yet that's transformed me. Maybe I'm just impatient."

"Sometimes—probably most of the time—these processes take time. You work them over slowly in your mind, and then you try to establish a solution. I was lucky in my work dilemma…my other matters aren't so easy."

"I guess I'm asking for a miracle. I really do want to do something meaningful for the next quarter century of my life, whether it's a work career or something in the non-profit field. And, then…I guess I want a partner in my life."

"Those two things shouldn't be so hard to accomplish. Just find the right job and the right guy."

Mary's black eyes shone as she smiled. "Yeah, that's all."

"You know, in a way, Mary, I'm not kidding. The career situation is probably the easiest. You've got some great experience and talents. A good career counselor could help you to use those talents, and, once you've figured that out, a good headhunter can place you with a company or a non-profit where your experience and talent can best be utilized. And, keep in mind; it need not be a lifetime commitment. If one thing doesn't work out to your satisfaction, you can go on to another. As for a partner, I'm afraid I can't help you there."

"Thanks for the advice on the former. I'll take it to heart. As for the second, I know you can't offer any advice. And I'm embarrassed that I even brought it up.

"You know, I have a lot in my life. I've got sufficient income so that I don't have to work. I've got lots of interests and a lot of friends. I don't think I'm unattractive. But, with all of that, I am fundamentally lonely, I want some 'special fella' to share my outings, my interests…my life."

Frank could see tears gathering in the corner of her eyes. "I can't believe that there aren't a ton of guys out there who wouldn't be thrilled to death to share your life."

Mary smiled, as one or two tears rolled down her cheeks. "You're a sweetheart to say that, but the truth is there hasn't been one."

"I can't believe that. Are you picky?"

"Well, of course, I'm picky…but not picky as you might think. The person doesn't have to be handsome or have a buff body, but I don't want a stupid person, or a selfish one. I want someone with some sensitivities… by that I mean someone who will occasionally ask how my day was. And I want someone who will share the bulk of my interests…music, theatre, reading, travel. It doesn't sound like much, does it?"

"Finding someone to share your life is always a difficult thing…"

"And I don't necessarily mean marriage or even living together," Mary interrupted. "I just mean someone committed to a relationship who will share my life."

Frank could hear the exasperation in her voice. "Well, as I was saying, this is a difficult thing, because it's not predicated on something logical, but on an unpredictable chemistry between two people."

"Even when I've shared a chemistry with someone, the connection came to an end for one reason or another. The guy wanted a mother. He wanted sex but not commitment. He was totally into himself."

"It's hard to imagine how you could have had chemistry with men like that."

"You know…you're attracted to someone initially, but the more you know that person the more his negative qualities come out."

Frank nodded, but kept silent for a moment. "Where do you meet men?" he asked.

"All over. I meet them through friends. I meet them at events I attend. Some I even meet in coffee shops…you know, someone says something to you, you reply, then there's a conversation, then he's got my card."

"And then what?"

"Some never call, and that's okay. Some call and ask you out, and immediately after dinner or a movie, they want to jump in the sack. Others bore you to death almost immediately. Then there are those who show great promise. They are flattering and interested in you. They seem to have their lives together. They're not pushing right away on the sex thing. And, then, after a few weeks they unravel. And then there are those who you never hear from after you've had sex with them."

"Ah, an oft-told female tale in the San Francisco Bay Area."

"Now, where are those hundreds of eligible suitors, just waiting to be with me?"

Frank smiled. "Okay, not hundreds."

"I feel humiliated that I'm even telling you this. I feel as if I'm weak and needy."

"Wanting someone special to share your life doesn't make you weak and needy. I suspect that most people in this world are looking for the same thing. Some are successful; some are not. I will pray that you are one of the successful ones."

"Thanks, Frank. Thanks so much," she said sincerely.

"I also believe that such things are part of fate or luck. You know, you go through all the jerks, and then, one day, out of the blue, there's someone you mesh with right away. And you keep meshing. Then your quest is finished. You have to kiss a lot of frogs before you find Prince Charming."

Mary chuckled, and Frank was pleased that she had found humor in his last statement. "That will keep me going," she said.

Their eyes met. Neither of them turned away from the other's gaze. Both of them seemed expectant of something…neither of them knew what. Suddenly, Mary thrust her head forward and began kissing Frank, murmuring, "Oh, Frank, if I could meet someone like you." Simultaneously, she clasped him in her arms.

Frank felt a surge of desire. He returned her kisses and flung his arms around her. They sat passionately kissing on the bench. An immediate thought that entered his mind was the paradox that here he was in his 60s, embracing and kissing an attractive woman at El Retiro, when he had spent his teens and much of his twenties and thirties yearning to have a special relationship with a woman, looking down on the twinkling lights of the peninsula and feeling lonely and alienated. Should he sneak her back into his room? he asked himself.

As if a cold breeze had blown its chilling blast over him, Frank suddenly felt fear. What if someone would walk along the path? What if someone were watching from above? What about his marriage vows, which in his marriage to Paula he had never violated? What if this momentary desire should turn into a full-fledged affair that would in time destroy his marriage?

His fears and questions became buried in the convoluted embraces and kisses. Frank wasn't in a hurry to resolve his dilemma.

Mary suddenly broke away from him, and stood up. She covered her face with her hands and began to cry. "Oh, Frank, I am so sorry," she exclaimed. "I was feeling so confused and so lonely. I just wanted to hold someone and to be held. I am so sorry."

Frank stood up and put his hand on her shoulder. "Mary, Mary, I know. I know. I wasn't exactly an unwilling participant…"

"Frank, I'm so ashamed."

"There's nothing to be ashamed of, Mary. Our beings have been stretched here, and it's natural to want some physical affirmations. Neither of us has done anything we should be ashamed of.

"But, now, I think it's time for both of us to go to our rooms and have a good night's sleep. Tomorrow is going to be another long day."

"Yes, that's a very good idea," Mary responded, wiping her eyes with a handkerchief. "Frank, thanks so much for being so understanding and for such good advice."

"Maybe I should get a job on the staff here," Frank laughed. "Mary, you're terrific. It's all going to come out just fine. Sleep well."

"Goodnight, Frank."

The two separated, taking separate paths to their rooms. Frank felt greatly relieved. He felt that he had stood at the edge of the abyss—the chasm of desire betraying his marriage vows, opening the door to something he did not want to happen: the erosion or ending of his marriage.

Whew, thought Frank, that was close. Thank God that she pulled away, or who knows what might have happened. It will be very nice to pull the covers over my head.

It was lunch on Sunday, and the rule against speaking was suspended. Saturday's schedule had gone by quickly, as had that of this morning. Frank had listened avidly to the conferences and participated in the religious services. He had even scheduled some time with Father Mike to discuss his increasing obsession with getting older and death.

Father Mike had been eager to help, but didn't help much. He had rehearsed all the ideas that Frank had known all along, but which hadn't helped him much as he wrestled with his demons. But Frank had been grateful for Father Mike's solicitude and help. And, as a result, he felt less obsessed.

And, now, it was time to go. After lunch he would put his baggage in his car and head back to San Francisco, back to his normal life. In the meantime, he chatted amiably with his table companions, who spoke glowingly of their experience.

There had been little contact with Mary Lamb the day before or this morning. They had exchanged cheerful greetings when they encountered each other, but there had been no conversation about their physical coming together on Friday night.

And, now, at lunch both of them participated in the exuberant conversations of a handful of people who had just removed themselves from the normal rhythms of everyday life and placed themselves for few days in a quasi-monastic environment for a spiritual purpose. Everyone was convinced that his or her life had been transformed by the experience. Frank knew better: a change for the better, possibly, but a complete transformation? No.

The restraint with which Frank and Mary were conversing was palpable. Each felt somewhat embarrassed by their physical encounter, but neither of them wished to allude to it. They did exchange addresses and telephone numbers, and Frank went as far as to tell Mary that he would call her and invite her to his home for a drink and to meet Paula.

Frank shook hands with Mary, and the two of them lingered to tell each other how pleased they had been to have met the other. And then they parted.

As he put his luggage into the trunk of the Jaguar, Frank felt pleased about his retirement decision. He would announce it tomorrow at the firm. He felt lighter and less harassed about his obsession with getting older and dying. He realized that he would have to continue his struggle in that area.

CHAPTER 23

Frank arrived home in the late afternoon. He felt refreshed and tranquil. Paula was pleased to see him, and they spent their cocktail hour and dinner discussing his insights while on retreat. She seemed pleased with his decision to begin the process of cutting back at the firm.

"I think this will be great for you," she announced. "It will give you a lot more time for your interests, and you won't be so grumpy when you're annoyed with things at work."

"Yeah, I'll be terminally cheerful."

"Well, I wouldn't get carried away. When will you tell the firm about your decision?"

"Tomorrow morning. It will be interesting to experience their reaction."

"I'd say, from what you've said to me, that they'll be pleased to replace the burned-out giant with fresh, young energy."

"Thanks a lot."

"You know that's true, as well as I do. I know you keep up with the investment world, and I know you're out there hustling new business…but nowhere near what you did thirty or forty years ago."

"You're right. And I fully realize that we need to be replaced with people who are still hungry to succeed."

It was a pleasant, mellow evening. Frank did not talk about Mary Lamb, except to say that she was one of the few "interesting" people he had met at El Retiro. Frank had watched closely to see if Paula's antennae would pick up on this small fact, but it appeared that they did not.

After dinner they watched a couple episodes of *Sex and the City*. Frank had mild sexual desire, but not enough to inaugurate sexual activity. Instead, he read for half an hour and went to sleep.

The next morning he set off for work in a good mood. He was eager to lay out his plan, and his first task was to arrange an appointment with Calvin Hopkins. After he returned from arranging his appointment with Hopkins, Frank asked Jessica to come into his office. He closed the door and asked her to sit down. The perennial smile faded from her face as Frank outlined his five-year plan, keeping from her that he felt he wouldn't last past three. She pursed her lips and wore an unaccustomed serious look on her face.

"Gee, Mr. M, this comes as a surprise. You've never talked about retirement before," she stated in a halting voice. "What do you think they'll do with me?"

"Are you kidding? They're all going to fight over who's going to get you. You're a terrific executive assistant."

"Thanks, Mr. M, I appreciate the compliment, but it'll be strange working for anyone else. You're the only person I've ever worked for. I came here right after school."

"I wish I were twenty years younger so that we could have that many more years together, but I was born too soon or you were born too late. Besides, within a couple years you'll be hitched to 'Mr. Right' and you'll be staying home raising babies."

Jessica giggled. "From your mouth to God's ear," she said, borrowing one of Frank's favorite expressions. "But, who knows. I can't imagine staying home, however...not with what it costs to live these days. And nobody's going to be as good of a boss as you have been, that's for sure. I'll probably get some stuck-up jerk."

"Thanks, Jessica, that's very nice of you to say. But I'm not gone yet. Within the year I'll probably have to share you with someone else. But I'll try to make sure it'll be with someone you will like."

Frank understood Jessica's concern about whom she would assist. He realized that he was one of the few in the firm who treated the secretarial executive assistants as colleagues instead of "go-fers" and menial clerks. The senior executives were haughty and patronizing—both men and women—and kept the assistants at arms' length. Frank realized that Jessica cherished their work relationship because he was appreciative of her hard work and dedication, but also because he realized that a great deal of his effectiveness could be attributed to her. And...she had also become a friend.

"Okay, Mr. M, I'll try not to sweat it. Please try to protect me from the bad guys."

Frank had no luncheon plans and decided to work at his desk until his appointment with Hopkins at 2:00 p.m. He looked over the piles of papers and files on the credenza in his office and took a handful and put them on his desk. He would not miss the abundance of paperwork and the myriad details his job demanded. Within a few moments Frank was methodically reducing the tasks that he had placed on his desk, and the habits of decades as an investment advisor began to stop the mental reservations of his occasional reluctance to tackle paperwork.

At one point Frank happened to glance at the clock on his desk. It read 1:55 p.m. Better get over to see Hopkins, Frank thought. He's a stickler for punctuality.

He put down the folder he was reviewing and walked out of his office, and down the corridor toward Hopkins' office.

"Go right in," reeled off his secretary. "He's expecting you."

Frank walked into the managing partner's office. Calvin Hopkins had just picked up a telephone call, but motioned for Frank to sit down and indicated that the call would not take long. Frank looked around the office and noticed its austere, bland look. Just like its occupant, Frank thought. Whereas Frank's own office was filled with photographs of his family, works of art, and mementos, Hopkins' office had no marks of his taste or indications of his life. There were a few pieces of art that were owned by the firm that had been used for the wall space in the corridors, but nothing else. But, Frank thought, despite this desiccated personal presence, Calvin Hopkins was an excellent managing partner. He orchestrated the members of the firm in a fair and equitable way, without emotion and without fear or jealousy. His sole concern was two-fold: what's best for the clients and what's best for the firm.

"Good to see you, Frank," said Hopkins, putting down the telephone. "What's up?"

No small talk. No bonhomie. Hopkins' approach was to get down to business immediately.

"I promised you a decision on my duration with the firm," Frank began with a smile, "and I'm here to give you my decision."

"Great," Hopkins responded.

"I've decided to eliminate my ownership over the next five years, reducing it twenty percent each year, and decreasing my responsibilities proportionately. And, if I decide to accelerate the process, I'm at liberty to do so."

Hopkins was silent and impassive for a few seconds, and then said,

"Okay, that's it, then. I'll have our lawyers prepare a memorandum for our signatures. Your payout will begin at the end of our current fiscal year and will be proportionate. If you wish to accelerate the process, give us thirty days' notice, and we'll establish the value of your payout."

There it was—the agreement with his proposal—and without emotion or superfluous comment. Frank even felt that he had noticed the slightest spasm of disappointment on the managing partner's face—annoyance that Frank was taking five years to fully retire. But, he admitted, that might have been paranoia on his part.

"And, Frank, I don't need to tell you what a vitally important person you've been over the years to the success of this firm. I am only one of many of your fans here at Blakesley and Montgomery, and I'll be sad when you do finally end your association."

It was a gracious peroration, Frank thought. Conventional, but gracious. And, whenever the time came when he left, Frank knew, Hopkins would pull out the stops to honor him.

Both Frank and Hopkins stood up. Frank put out his hand, and, as the two shook hands, Frank felt a sadness descend upon him. "It's been a very happy place for me to work," he told the managing partner.

"It's been a happy circumstance for us to have you here, Frank," Hopkins replied with a smile.

Frank walked down the corridor to his office in a haze. After all these years, he had committed to retirement. What had defined him, captivated him, interested him all these years would soon be gone. He'd have plenty of money to live quite well; but for the first time since he was a teenager, he would no longer be working.

There was something else that gnawed at Frank: the idea that Hopkins was somehow unhappy that he had not totally resigned, but that he would be being bought out of his partnership over the next five years. He had no evidence that this was the case. In fact, Hopkins' blandness would successfully disguise the deep disappointment he felt.

Frank knew his feelings were irrational, but somehow he couldn't excise them from his psyche. He realized that this disappointment was part of the retirement cataclysm that had begun.

Jessica was away from her desk when Frank went into his office. He felt deflated, and certainly didn't feel like resuming his work. It was almost 3 o'clock, he saw on his clock. He would take off the rest of the day, he decided.

Frank put some papers in his briefcase and left a note for Jessica that he was gone for the rest of the afternoon.

He had driven to work that morning, and he went into the garage to retrieve his car. At first Frank had thought about going home...maybe taking a nap...but when he seated himself in the Jaguar's luxuriant leather seat, Frank decided that he would drive out to the shore of the Pacific Ocean and contemplate the view there. He maneuvered himself onto Geary Street and drove west to the ocean.

Frank parked the car at the entrance to Sutro Park, the former estate of one of San Francisco's most colorful historical figures—collector, businessman, and mayor—Adolph Sutro. Frank walked onto the wide, graveled path that led into the park. Very few of Sutro's classical statues still graced the space; and the trees, shrubs, and flowers, although presentable, were not the elaborate horticultural spectacle that they had been when Sutro lived there. The house and the observatory no longer existed—only a white gazebo reminded visitors of the structures that had once been there.

Frank walked up the steps to the platform where Sutro's observatory had been. There was a chill in the air, but there was no overcast to cover the opaque blue skies. The view from the platform, over the Cliff House and the ruins of Sutro's entertainment complex, was balm to Frank's troubled soul. The panorama was extraordinary, Frank thought: south along the western edge of Golden Gate Park all the way to the zoo, north to Land's End and the Marin Headlands.

Other than few hearty souls surfing along Ocean Beach, Frank was alone. He half-sat on the stone wall that surrounded the platform and gazed out at the splendid scene before him. He had visited this area from his earliest years. His parents had taken him as a child to the zoo, to swim in the chilly waters of Fleishhacker Pool, to Golden Gate Park, to the Sutro Baths and Museum. He had enjoyed these excursions as a small boy, as he now relished the quiet contemplation the beauty that this area offered him.

Frank looked down at Ocean Beach. How frequently after his divorce would he walk, both during the day and in the evening, along its sands, thinking about his life, about the wife and children he was leaving, drenched in sadness and fear for the future. He had received strength from those walks; they had given him the ability to reshape his life.

And now he was facing a new juncture in his life: retirement. Most people he knew looked forward to this moment. At least, they said they did. And, thought Frank, I'd have been happier than I am if retirement hadn't come along when physical and mental deterioration had become a matter of concern to him, prompting him to become obsessed with death. Would he ever live a fully tranquil life? Frank wondered.

Frank closed his eyes and listened to the gentle sound of the waves crashing onto the beach below him. What would he do with the increasing amount of leisure time that he would have?

It wasn't as if he didn't have any interests. He was a voracious reader. He had always done some writing. He loved to watch old movies and to listen to music. The lessening involvement with the firm would also allow him more time to travel. Frank knew that he wouldn't be bored. What, then, was bothering him?

Frank decided not to dwell on whatever it was that was making him uneasy. He had made and announced his decision. It was time to move on. I need to change the script in my head, he thought.

The barren Seal Rocks no longer had the long-familiar sea lions on them. Isn't nature strange, Frank thought: after centuries of cavorting and mating on these rocks, they decide to move to one of San Francisco's principal tourist attractions, Pier 39. Go figure.

The sun had begun to dip in the west. The air was still, and, except for the light splash of waves on the sandy beach, it was quiet. It was the time of melancholy—late afternoon, just before darkness. A few darting birds and some soaring seagulls provided the only movement. Downtown, thousands were anticipating liberation from their jobs for the day and would soon be scurrying out of tall office buildings into buses and cars, eager to get home or to carry on whatever leisure activities they had planned, eager to lay aside the tasks of that day.

Frank was grateful that he had never been eager to end his workday. He had always enjoyed what he had done. Sure, there were troublesome days, even boring days, but the days had passed very quickly. Even if he was anticipating some particularly delectable activity in the evening, Frank had always relished his workdays.

He realized that his thoughts were leading him back to his concerns about retirement, which, given his natural susceptibility to the melancholy of late afternoon and early evening, would begin to depress him. He needed to turn his mind to more pleasing or comforting paths.

Frank reached into his pocket and pulled out his Blackberry. He might as well check on his schedule for the evening and tomorrow. Ah, great, he thought, a quiet evening at home tonight. Tomorrow, an appointment with his dentist at 8:30 and five business appointments scattered throughout the day—a fairly busy day.

Noticing his dental appointment brought about free association. He had gone to the same dental office since he had been in high school. Only two dentists had worked on his teeth since he was sixteen years old.

Frank began to chuckle. He remembered an escapade shortly after his divorce. A dental hygienist by the name of Pandy was in her mid-twenties, cheerleader cute, and always wore tight-fitting cashmere sweaters that accentuated her ample bosom. As she bent over him cleaning his teeth, Frank could feel the firmness of her breasts swathed in the softness of the cashmere. Simultaneously, he could feel his penis stiffen; he hoped she wouldn't notice.

Shortly after he and Claudia had separated, he was having his teeth cleaned and telling Pandy about his separation. She listened sympathetically and asked, "Are you lonely?"

"I guess I am," he had responded. "It's tough going from a big house with a wife and four children to being by yourself in a one-bedroom apartment."

"You need to start seeing someone."

"In time, I guess."

"Seeing someone will help with the loneliness."

"I suppose so, but it's kind of hard to do that when you've been married for a number of years."

"You'll get over it."

Frank had felt a hand on his groin. Startled, he looked up at Pandy. She was now fumbling with his zipper.

"Let's start now with some post-marital experience," she said.

The dental chair in which he had been sitting went back when Pandy released a lever, and Frank found himself prone on his back. She had undone his zipper, belt, and the button of his pants, and with a deft move, pulled his shorts and his trousers down to his knees. Pulling down her panties and lifting her skirt, she straddled him. Her left hand clutched his immediately stiffened penis and quickly inserted it into her moist vagina.

"This won't go on your bill," she said with a smile, as she began to lift herself up and down.

Frank's initial surprise quickly gave way to intense desire. He reached up to pull up the cashmere sweater and to edge upward the brassiere beneath it. Her breasts were as firm as they had appeared during his twice-annual dental visits. His fingers played with them and his index finger brushed against her hard nipples as Pandy's up-and-down movements accelerated. He arched his hips to heighten the connection between his penis and her vagina, which brought forth a moan from her.

With difficulty Frank pulled himself up so that they were now face to face. They began to kiss, their tongues flickering in and out of their mouths. Frank's fingers greedily massaged her breasts, while Pandy quickly and rhythmically exercised herself on him, her breath becoming quicker, punctuated by moans of pleasure.

And then it was over. Frank exploded within her. Pandy whimpered as her body went limp. He lay back, spent from the unexpected sexual act, and Pandy lay on top of him.

It was only a moment before she gave him a peck on the cheek, and hopped off the dental chair. "Well, I think it's time to get back to work," she said, re-arranging her clothes to their more conventional attire.

Frank did the same. "Maybe I should come in every week to get my teeth cleaned."

"It's always a pleasure to see you...and to clean your teeth, or whatever."

Frank smiled when he had remembered opening the door and booking his next appointment.

Two weeks later he had called Pandy for a date, but had been told that she had left his dentist's employ and was now working in San Jose. He hadn't pursued it. San Jose was a long way away.

Long shadows were being cast by the sun's decline into the Pacific Ocean. It was time to go home, Frank decided. He felt refreshed, even buoyant. His recollection of his adventure with Pandy had lightened his heart. His had been an interesting life, he thought, even though today it would be doubtful whether he would be able to slide so easily into Pandy— or anyone else for that matter.

Frank walked to the Jaguar and drove eastward. The buildings along Geary Boulevard slipped quickly by. Some were painted in garish colors, but this part of San Francisco had changed hardly at all, unlike much of the city. Even though the houses and businesses along the thoroughfare were not superb architecture, Frank felt reassured by their familiarity.

He felt most reassured when he pushed his garage door opener and entered his garage. Frank loved his home and felt secure there. Paula met him in the hallway as he entered from the garage.

"I thought you'd be home earlier," she said, after they had kissed and greeted each other. "I called the office and Jessica said you had left early."

"I did, but I drove out to the ocean for some contemplation. I gave Cal Hopkins my retirement plans today, and, afterwards, I just wanted to get away and think."

"What did he say?"

"Just what I had expected. He made no comment on the five-year buyout, and said that I had been a great asset to the firm. I felt that he may have been disappointed that I didn't say I'd be totally out in a month or two; but I have nothing to base that on."

"I'm glad it's done. You might decide that you want to accelerate the time, but at least you've put a terminal date out there."

The two of them walked into the living room. Paula went into the kitchen to pour them each a glass of wine. Frank took off his coat and tie and sat down on the sofa. He enjoyed this time of day: having a glass of wine and conversing with his wife as darkness fell. He felt enveloped in comfort.

Paula brought Frank his glass of wine and said, "Here's to your retirement. And to a long life together."

Frank smiled and raised his glass. "To enjoying lots of leisure time together."

They clinked their glasses together. Paula sat next to him.

"I know this has been hard for you to do," she began, "but I think you made a very wise decision. You need to make way for the younger associates in your firm and you need to enjoy the time you've worked so long to appreciate without the concern of work. Believe me; you're going to wonder why you took so long to make this decision."

"Whatever. I'm happy I made the decision. Now...what's for dinner?"

"How about some grilled salmon and green beans?"

"Sounds great. Let me check my telephone messages and then we can eat." Frank listened to his messages, but heard nothing of importance. After listening to a dreary litany of telemarketing advertisements, he thought, what a plague on this earth. Then he walked into the kitchen and poured himself another glass of wine.

"How nice to have a quiet night at home," he said.

"It's always nice to be here with just the two of us," Paula responded, smiling.

"We should do it more often. And I think we will, now that I'm retiring. No more hustling for business."

"See? You're already seeing the benefits of your decision."

Frank smiled and began to thumb through the mail that had arrived that day. "Nothing but crap in the mail or on my answering machine," he said grumpily. "These are the times we live in: lots of stuff, but nothing important. Just think of all the resources that go into a constant stream of advertising."

"Dinner is almost ready. Will you set the table?"

Paula and he worked well together, Frank thought, as he set the table. It was a different relationship from his parents', with his mother doing all the domestic chores. But, then, his mother did not work outside the home, as Paula frequently reminded him when he would complain about the chores she assigned him. But the relationship worked well. He was not overburdened by what he had to do, and Paula seemed pleased by his help.

"What are your plans for tonight?" Paula asked him when they sat down to their meal.

"I think I'll do some reading and then go to sleep on the early side. I'm tired. How about you?"

"I'm going to pay some bills and get out some invoices. I think I'll tuck in early, too."

They finished dinner and separated to perform the tasks they had set for themselves. Frank once more settled in the living room and decided to finish his Alan Furst novel. He remembered that once he had canceled a business lunch so that he could finish a Helen MacInnes novel; another time he called at the last minute to excuse himself from attending a dinner party so he could continue to read a Michael Thomas novel.

At about 11 o'clock he began to feel sleepy. Paula came by to say that she was almost finished with her tasks, and he was in a place where he could put the novel down. It was time for bed.

Frank brushed his teeth and took a couple of pills, peeled off his clothes, put on his pajamas, and climbed into bed. He flipped through a magazine that was on his nightstand until Paula came into the bedroom.

"Good night, sweetheart, I'm going to put out the light."

She came over to the bed, hugged him, and gave him a kiss. Frank remembered that not too long ago he would have pulled her down upon him and they would have had sex. Not tonight...not most nights. Sexual desire seemed to have drained away.

"Good night, dear," she said, as she straightened up. "Sleep well. I'm going to climb in in a few minutes."

Frank turned off the reading lamp and turned over on his right side.

Soon he was asleep.

Frank dreamed that he was walking along a grassy meadow. The sun was shining and the birds were chirping. Suddenly the sky began to fill with dark clouds. The wind picked up and swiftly grew into a howl, and heavy rain began to fall. Frank started to run, trying to reach the shelter of a nearby oak tree. He had almost reached the tree when he stumbled and started to fall into a hole in the field.

Frank desperately tried to find some footing or something to hold onto, but there was nothing he could use to stop his plummeting descent. He felt weightless and helpless. Faces began to appear around him in the hole: his parents, his brothers, relatives, friends, enemies—all looking intently at him as he plummeted. Fear consumed him as he continued his fall, waiting to hit a surface where his body would explode on contact. And around his fall continued the faces of those whom he had known in life, some of whom he recognized, others whom he did not.

He let out a scream and found himself being shaken. He awoke frightened and disoriented. Paula was shaking him.

"What's the matter?" she asked, visibly shaken, "You've been screaming out."

Frank realized that he had awakened from a nightmare—one that was vividly imprinted on his mind. His skin was clammy and his heart was pumping. He still felt the sensation of falling through space.

"I guess...I guess I had a nightmare," Frank responded, his breath short.

Paula threw her arms around him. "My God, you scared me to death. Your arms and legs were thrashing and you were screaming out. What was your nightmare?"

Frank sat up in bed. He described falling down the hole with the faces of all the people he had ever known surrounding him, projected on the sides of the hole, as he fell.

"What do you think it means?" Paula asked him.

"How the hell should I know?" he replied in an irritated voice. "I've just been scared to death, and you're asking me what my dream 'meant.' It was a nightmare! How do you interpret a nightmare that has you falling down an interminable hole being watched by people you've known? Everyone was there: my parents, people I've met once."

"Okay, okay. You don't have to be so testy. I was concerned. And dreams do have meanings, you know."

"Yeah, yeah, yeah. Let's try to get to sleep again...and, hopefully, this time I can sleep peacefully."

"Goodnight, Sweetheart. Sweet dreams." Paula gave him a kiss.

"Goodnight, Darling."

This time Frank rolled over onto his left side and put his arms around his wife. He closed his eyes, hoping that there would be no repetition of his nightmare. But he felt wide awake. He couldn't get the frightening dream out of his mind. What did it mean? he asked himself.

CHAPTER 24

Father O'Sullivan's funeral mass had gone as Roman Catholic funeral masses go: propelled by a traditional ritual. But it was a different ritual than Frank had grown up with. No longer the stately, solemn cadences of the requiem high mass, with its black vestments and the doleful lines of the *Dies Irae*, the commitment of the soul to God's mercy. Now it was white vestments and the half-hearted optimism that had renamed the funeral mass "the mass of the resurrection." Frank did not approve. He longed for the rich symbolism and formal cadences of the old funeral mass.

St. Ignatius Church was about half full. Not nearly so many as those whose lives had been touched or even changed by Father Michael O'Sullivan, S.J., in his decades of ministry at St. Ignatius College, Frank thought. The passage of time had dulled what Frank felt should have been the gratitude of many who had graduated from St. Ignatius College.

Father John Smythe, a Jesuit at St. Ignatius whom Frank knew slightly, ascended the elaborate pulpit to deliver the eulogy. He first read the gospel, and, when he had finished, adjusted his white vestments and began his comments on his deceased confrere. He touched on most of Frank's mentor's salient features: his reaching out to young men and helping to transform their lives; his seeking contacts in the worlds of fine arts, music, books, and other areas that introduced high culture to the sons of working-class parents; and his involving parents in cultural presentations on the campus. Father Smythe also described Father O'Sullivan's warmth, good advice, and encouragement for those whom he served as a confessor.

But, Frank thought, while Smythe's catalogue was accurate, the eulogy failed to capture the excitement that O'Sullivan's "boys" felt in their association with him and with one another. But, then, how could he? He hadn't experienced in his late-teens and early-twenties the extraordinary magnetism of O'Sullivan. Smythe had known him only as a fellow Jesuit many years later.

The eulogy was concluded and the funeral mass continued. Frank looked around the huge, baroque church and saw a number of his classmates and friends. It was Father O'Sullivan who had brought most of them together and helped to forge their friendships—friendships that had lasted half a century. These individuals had been the core of his relationships since they had encountered one another, and Frank's mind wandered over the many years of warm, interesting conversations, mutual help, and encouragement during rough times. The memories created a warm glow in him.

When the time for communion came, Frank stepped into the aisle and slowly progressed toward the sanctuary of the church. He was deep in thought and didn't notice the man kneeling in a pew near the front of the church. Christopher Fermoyle elbowed him. Frank looked at his old friend and clapped him on the shoulder. There were tears glistening in Christopher's eyes. Sadness was splayed across his face.

Frank moved up a few feet. Father Smythe handed him a wafer. "Body of Christ."

"Amen." Frank answered and put it in his mouth.

He passed up the woman holding the chalice with wine in it and walked back to the pew where he had been sitting. He knelt but could not keep his mind on the sacrament he had just received. Frank's interior dialogue and impressions could only fix on his days at St. Ignatius College under the guidance of Father O'Sullivan, of the thrill of learning new things apart from the academics, of his delight in meeting fellow students engaged in the same path of discovery...and of the wonderful relationships, such as the one with Christopher Fermoyle, which had existed for several decades as a result of Father O'Sullivan's tutelage.

Then the end of the funeral mass began. The three concelebrating priests came to the edge of the sanctuary for the final obsequies. They incensed the coffin, read prayers, and removed the white pall from the simple, wooden coffin. The coffin was now surrounded by about twenty-five of O'Sullivan Jesuit confreres who had come in the tradition of bidding their "brother" farewell, and it progressed slowly down the principal aisle of the church's nave, from whence it would be placed in a hearse that would take it to the Jesuit cemetery at the University of Santa Clara.

Very few of those at O'Sullivan's funeral would be making the almost-fifty-mile trip to Santa Clara. Frank and his friends would be going to the large dining room on campus to attend a luncheon for those attending the funeral.

One by one Frank's friends gathered around him: Chris Martini, Terry Donohue, Christopher Fermoyle, Dick Mahoney, and Dick Lambert. Their usual volubility was muted; each seemed preoccupied with his own thoughts. It was a gray, overcast day, reminiscent of the so many foggy, gray days when they were undergraduates.

"I guess we're all here," Christopher Fermoyle proclaimed. "Let's have lunch."

The six friends walked slowly the short distance to what once had been the dining commons when they were students. It had been transformed into a multi-purpose room used for lectures with large audiences, entertainments, and, occasionally, such as today, a special lunch or dinner.

The large room was now called the Bellarmine Room, and as the friends entered it the room resembled a restaurant. Numerous tables were set, awaiting the mourners; about forty students lined one of the walls, ready to serve the meal. Several others were walking around with glasses of white wine and glasses of water.

"Let's get a table so that we can all sit together," said Dick Mahoney. "We'll put our coats on the chairs and then get some wine."

The tables were set for eight; there were six old friends. Other people might attempt to sit at their table, but it would be an unwelcome intrusion.

Dick Lambert signaled one of the student waiters, and all of them except Lambert took a glass of wine. "Watching my waistline," he explained.

They huddled together, not wanting anyone to disturb their reflections or the distinctive ways in which they wished to express their feelings regarding this momentous occasion. Their silence continued as they took the initial sips of their wine.

"I don't know why I'm so bummed about Father O'Sullivan's death," Christopher Fermoyle began, "after all he was in his eighties and in bad health. It's just that…"

Fermoyle drifted off into silence. The others did not break it. Their looks continued to be sad and serious.

Dick Mahoney attempted to get the conversation started again. "You know this is an awesome occasion when the six of us have a tough time talking," he laughed.

"That's never happened in my memory," Chris Martini added.

"Let's face it, we're not just mourning Father O'Sullivan," Frank noted.

"We're also mourning the passage of time in our lives."

There was no derision or playful raillery when they heard Frank once again lament getting older. They all felt that sense of mortality catching up.

Frank continued. "When we met O'Sullivan he was a young priest with a passion for civilizing clueless kids from Catholic working-class families... most of us anyway. And we were eager teenagers who had read a great deal and were full of ambition and piss and vinegar. He collected us and helped civilize us."

"Well, I don't know if I would go that far," Dick Lambert interjected.

"I will give you that you and Fermoyle are somewhat exceptions," Frank shot back. "You were both from the Catholic ascendancy, the upper-middle class. You didn't need as much civilizing as the rest of us did."

"There were a lot of factors involved," Terry Donohue added. "One was that the six of us happened to find each other, like each other, and saw our friendships blossom while under O'Sullivan's tutelage. Another was the sheer thrill of the intellectual and emotional stimulation we were getting.

"Christ, we'd go to operas, symphonies, and chamber music concerts together. We were able to sit and chat with Gabriel Marcel, Martin D'Arcy, and Frank Sheed. I still look back on it as if it were a dream."

"It was a dream," Christopher said. "We all thought we'd be young forever and that all of our dreams would come true. And what's happened? Fifty years have gone by. We're beginning to feel the travail of getting older...and we've realized that most of those dreams aren't going to come true."

"But it was just during our lives at St. Ignatius that we dreamed those big dreams," Chris Martini offered. "And I guess that at that time we did believe we'd accomplish them."

"There's even a line from the Bible that describes this situation," Fermoyle interjected. "Let's see...ah, yes, 'Your young men shall see visions, your old men shall dream dreams.'"

"I'll have to figure out what dreams I'm dreaming," Dick Lambert said, laughing.

"No one I've ever encountered would make us dream like O'Sullivan," Frank said. "He was like a wizard with a wand. It takes a sort of genius to be able to take guys in their late teens and early twenties and launch them into intellectual and cultured lives."

Frank's friends nodded in agreement. Each of them had been touched by the enthusiasm, commitment, and passion of Father Michael O'Sullivan, S.J. Not only were their interests awakened, but the sharing of those interests among a band of classmates created bonds of friendship that had lasted a lifetime. And their interests had remained, with the memories of their first introductions to chamber music concerts, rare book dealers, and fine printers.

"Gentlemen, I see the clan has gathered for reminiscing." Frank and his friends turned to see Jim Stella.

"How could you ever guess?" Dick Lambert answered.

"I know you guys," Stella said. "You never get together without raking up the past. You've become the elders, the keepers of the flame, and the upholders of the traditions."

"I'm going to grow a beard," said Chris Martini. "It will make me look like an elder."

"You'll have to let your hair become its natural gray, however," cracked Christopher.

Chris Martini shot his namesake a cross look. He was sensitive about people bringing up the fact that he had his hair colored.

Someone on a microphone began to call for quiet.

"I'd like to welcome everyone here to a luncheon to celebrate the life of Father Michael O'Sullivan." Frank recognized Father Albert Rivera, the president of St. Ignatius College. "Mike was a splendid Jesuit and a great credit to the college. And I know that virtually everyone here has been significantly touched by him. He was everything that a member of the Society of Jesus and on the faculty or staff of a Catholic college should be: a person committed to others. And, now, let me say grace and continue to celebrate Father Mike's life."

Rivera said the standard grace before meals and the assembled 200 mourners sat down to lunch. "Mike?" Frank thought. How modern. How with it. And, then, Frank mused, if "Father Mike" was so great, why had no one taken his place at St. Ignatius College? Frank answered his own question when he realized that an institution can't just replace someone like Father O'Sullivan the way you can replace a U.S. history or chemistry professor. Individuals like Father O'Sullivan came along rarely, impelled by a special charisma, driven by a distinctive passion. Still, Frank did not find that Rivera's bland introduction captured the essence of Father Michael O'Sullivan.

Jim Stella joined the group, and the seven friends began to fork the salads in front of them. Frank was seated between Jim and Christopher Fermoyle. It was strange for Frank to experience the silence of these friends, usually so voluble; but he realized that the death of this priest had deeply affected each of them.

Christopher Fermoyle broke the silence. "I wonder how many of our generation had similar experiences to those we had in college?" he asked, to no one in particular. "I know that you will have athletes on a winning or championship team that will bond for life...perhaps the coach of that team served as a mentor. Or maybe a military unit that faced and survived great danger might have great ties to one another. And I know that there have been professors at colleges who have greatly influenced their students—Chauncey Tinker at Yale, for example. But I really wonder how many students in the 1950s and early 1960s fell under the influence of one man, were both educated and civilized, and in the process formed a coterie of friends with similar aspirations."

The entire table had stopped eating while listening to Christopher's soliloquy.

Dick Lambert was the first to respond. "I think you're making a bit much of this," he remarked. "A great guy held out all sorts of goodies to us. We were predisposed to be interested, and most of those who became involved liked each other and became friends. I mean...well, this isn't the Vienna Circle or the Bloomsbury Group."

"Dick, why is it that you're always downplaying the influence of Father O'Sullivan in our lives, both personally and collectively?" Christopher countered. "Is it that you don't want to give credit to someone else for your sophisticated interests?"

Frank felt uncomfortable with the direction of the conversation. Storm clouds were brewing between Dick and Christopher, and Frank wanted to direct the conversation away from quarrelsome, contentious topics.

Dick was stung by Christopher's remarks. His face showed the hauteur that many believed had always been beneath Dick's urbane, hail-fellow-well-met exterior.

"You can't judge the state of the interests of individuals from your own background, Christopher. My parents went to operas, symphonies, museums, and a whole host of cultural venues from their earliest days. Those interests were passed on to me. I enjoyed them here at St. Ignatius, and I particularly enjoyed them here because I was able to share them with people I liked."

Frank nudged Christopher's knee with his hand, just in time to forestall a retort.

Dick Mahoney slid into the conversation. "Whatever our backgrounds and whatever we assign to Father O'Sullivan's influence on us, let me raise my glass to a great groups of friends and to the late Father Michael O'Sullivan."

Each person hoisted his glass. "To each of us and to Father O'Sullivan," said Terry Donohue, and the rest of the table chorused, "Hear, hear."

The crisis had passed. Frank noticed—or felt—that a sense of joviality had replaced the tension caused by Christopher's and Dick's exchange. He was relieved.

"You know we should have a Father O'Sullivan commemorative event once a year," Frank offered. "We could sponsor a lecture or a concert at St. Ignatius, and then all of us could get together for dinner."

"You were born a century too late, Frank," Chris Martini responded. "You would have been great—not that you aren't great now—but you would have been perfect in the nineteenth and early twentieth century, with formal gatherings, testimonial dinners..."

"Does that mean you don't like my idea?"

"No, no. I'm just saying that you are one of the only people I know—if not the only one—who..."

"...would make such a suggestion," Christopher interposed. "And that's why we all love Frank. He holds out to us the 'city on the hill,' a world where few people wish to go these days. I think it's an admirable idea. It will recapture the days of old, when we'd help Father O'Sullivan put on an event at St. Iggy's and then adjourn to La Pantera for dinner. Remember? $1.25 for a five-course dinner."

Everyone smiled. Christopher's approbation of Frank's enthusiastic suggestion jogged their memories of the excitement they felt when they would work together to set up, advertise, and manage the operations of a lecture, a concert, or some other event that Father O'Sullivan had inaugurated, after which they would take a bus to North Beach, where they would eat a large Italian meal and drink a carafe of raw red wine. It had been a time of warm humor, exuberance, and delight in one another's company. It was a time that each of them looked back upon with fondness... and with regret that those days could not be recaptured.

"I miss those days," Dick Mahoney said. "Miss them more than I can say. And I'm sure everyone at this table does. Sometimes, when I'm in bed, trying to get to sleep, or maybe on a hike or just letting my mind go fallow, I try to recapture those times, try to re-live or re-experience my days here at St. Ignatius...the emotions, the thoughts, the smells...you know, all those things that excited us."

Each person was quiet and looked at Dick. Dick Mahoney was universally liked and respected by his friends, and he was known for his commonsense assessments. What he had just uttered was not what his friends expected him to say.

"I think that everyone here agrees with you." Terry Donohue broke the surprised silence at the table. "I tend to try to look back and try to recapture my feelings from those days as I've gotten older. I can remember them...but I can't make them come back."

"There are a couple movies on this topic," offered Dick Lambert. "One is *Somewhere in Time*...you know, Christopher Reeves and Jane Seymour. I forget the details, but the movie is about someone having a sense of a great love in a previous life, I think, and his going back in time to recreate it.

"The other one is a Japanese film I saw about a year ago, *Odd Obsession*, in which the principal character wants to experience things by creating what he wants to experience. The thing I remember is that he wanted to experience jealousy of his wife, and he had to create and summon up the concept of jealousy."

Jim Stella throatily laughed. "This conversation sounds like the ones we used to have in high school and college. After we'd seen a Bergman film or whatever passed as intellectually heavy in those days, we'd go out for a pizza, a hamburger...or a drink...and have these interminable discussions about the meaning of the film. I'll tell you one feeling I have no trouble recapturing from those days, and that's the intense feeling of boredom when I saw *L'Aventura, Hiroshima Mon Amour*, and *Last Year at Marienbad*."

The group laughed. How well each of them remembered the compulsion to see and to react to the European movies that began to flood the art houses in the 1950s. Frank and his friends thought of themselves as intellectuals, and, as intellectuals, they often went to the Clay or Vogue Theatre. They had to see these movies, praise them, and discuss their significance. One censored oneself; one could not admit that he thought the film pretentious or numbingly boring. Only later in life would each of them admit that they had carried these feelings as a running subtext in their minds.

"I've tried to re-experience the past, too," Frank admitted. "But Dick Mahoney is right: you can remember fragments of the past, and smelling a madeleine may open your memory to some part of your past, but you cannot recreate the emotions and feelings that surged through us."

"What I want to know," said Chris Martini, "is why we're so anxious to re-live the past. Why do we want to recreate or re-experience the feelings and emotions of the past? What's wrong with the present?"

Christopher Fermoyle looked at Chris and started to speak again in a soft, almost conspiratorial tone. "This is old men's talk...the talk of old men who lived rich, interesting lives as young men. Those of us who had wonderful relationships in high school and college, who thrilled to reading, ideas, the arts, who struggled through intensely hormonal sexuality—as least those who did—and who kept asking ourselves, 'What's it all about, Alfie'—to continue our conversation about movies—no longer have those experiences, no longer can achieve the intensity of those emotions, of those feelings.

"They say that one begins to die in the extremities," Christopher continued. "Have you ever had your leg fall asleep and you go hopping around to restore feeling in it? This is what we're doing now...trying to restore feeling throughout our beings.

"But the feeling in your leg will come back. What we're looking for is something that can't be brought back. Being 16 or 18 or 20 again can't be done. We experience life in very different ways now, because our experience of it fifty years ago has been dying. We didn't notice this for a long time, but in the last decade we have. And we're thrashing around because we now realize that we're dying and that in a countable number of years we'll be dead...poof.

"But Chris is right when he asks, 'What's wrong with the present?' All of us have to come to terms with the present...and with death. Otherwise, we'll be going out in a miserable fashion, looking back with longing at a time that we'll never see again and can only bring up fitfully in our memories."

Nobody spoke when Christopher had finished his comments. Frank scanned the faces of his friends. Most looked serious, as if they were trying to digest what Christopher had said; one or two looked as if they were trying to stifle laughter.

Dick Lambert broke the silence. "Wow, the philosopher king has spoken," he said.

Everyone smiled or laughed, breaking the tension caused by Fermoyle's remarks. But the smiles and laughter did not mean that his comments had been dismissed; each man had entered deeply into his own consciousness.

"It's a cruel joke that each of us comes suddenly and early to this supposed 'golden age' in our lives, and, before we know it, it's gone and we're looking backward with longing." This was uttered by Terry Donohue.

"Years ago I asked my father-in-law why people like Henry Ford and Nelson Rockefeller had affairs, divorced, and remarried," Frank said. "That was a big deal in the early 1960s. It's become commonplace now. He told me that both men were in their fifties, that this was a time when men lose their sexual potency, their careers have peaked, and their children are grown. They begin to panic about getting old, and they try to rejuvenate themselves by having affairs. He said that the excitement of being with someone new and younger and the illicit nature of the action gave them the illusion that they had become younger. But, he said, it didn't work, at least not for long."

"Does that mean we shouldn't start having affairs?" Jim Stella sardonically asked.

"No. It just means that you shouldn't expect to become young again if you do," Frank retorted.

"One can have fun while looking for the Fountain of Youth," Chris Martini added.

"Ah, gentlemen, denial is not just a river in Egypt," Christopher interposed. "You may make light of my insights, but on some level you will have to grapple with them."

"Lighten up, Christopher," Dick Lambert said. "It's bad enough to be getting older without having to think about it."

"I'd like everyone who has never thought about the implications of getting older or about their own death to raise their hands," Dick Mahoney asked.

No hands went up, but each tried to avert his face.

"And let me ask each person who has never tried to re-connect on some level with the time when he was in his teens or twenties to raise his hand," Dick continued.

Only Chris Martini's hand went up.

"Ah, Dick, you need to enter the real world," Christopher said to him. "You're the most practical person here, but this practicality has cut you off from reality."

Dick was about to utter a sharp retort, but Frank cut him off. "Dick has established that, for the most of us, getting older and facing death has been on our minds. Why, I wonder, do we want so desperately to connect with our youth?"

"I think it's because that time of our teens and twenties was truly a utopian time, a golden age," Dick Mahoney explained. "We didn't have the aches and pains and various diseases we have today; it was a life of little or no responsibility—no job for most of the time, no marriage or family; and it was a time when we were pulsating with excitement and all of our emotions were engaged...all the time."

"Yeah, but I could have done without a lot of the *sturm und drang* of that time," Terry Donohue added. "It was pretty wrenching to go through all those emotions."

"No kidding," said Chris Martini, "I far prefer the calm of this age."

Frank began to detect a sense of fatigue about the subject they had been discussing and a reluctance to delve deeper. He decided to change the subject.

"I'd love to have Father O'Sullivan here right now, to hear him discuss what we've been talking about, to see what his take would be on various contemporary topics, and to hear him talk about our lives today."

"That's going to be pretty hard to do," Christopher dryly said. "And what's more, during the past few years he never wanted to get involved in here-and-now things. He was fixated on the next world—both for himself and for all those he knew."

"Yeah, I know," said Dick Mahoney. "Every time I spoke to him during the past two or three years he was only interested in whether I was prepared for death and extolling the world to come."

"That fits right in with our conversation today...a memorial conversation for Father O'Sullivan," said Chris Martini.

"Okay, wise guys, go ahead and mock the ultimate ideas, the lost things," proclaimed Christopher. "But I know the day is coming when you'll all be too eager to discuss what we've been talking about today."

"Until then, let's lighten up," Chris Martini proclaimed.

After a short silence, Frank asked, "Who has read any interesting books?"

"I've just discovered an excellent fiction writer," Jim Stella responded. "Every once in a while I read in what I call "international intrigue," and I've started to read Alan Furst, who writes about Europe just before World War II and during the war. He's excellent."

"And I've just finished Jeffrey Myers' biography of Edmund Wilson," said Terry Donohue. "A great critic and writer, but a jerk of a human being."

"I've got to get going before you literary types put me to shame," said Dick Lambert, getting up from the table. "As always, it's been a pleasure being with you."

"Yeah, I've got to get going, too," said Chris Martini. "I've got to get back to the office."

The friends stood up from their seats at the table. The gathering to commemorate death and celebrate the life of Father Michael O'Sullivan, S.J., was coming to a close. Not just the table where Frank and his friends were sitting, but all the people at the gathering were making their farewells and leaving.

Frank shook hands with his friends and exchanged some quips with them. They saw one another with some frequency, so there were no long goodbyes.

Christopher came up to him, as he was walking out. "May I join you?" he asked.

"Do you have to ask?"

"That was a most interesting exchange today. It's interesting to observe those who choose not to deal with the topic of getting older and the prospect of dying."

"I thought you were very eloquent on those subjects."

"Yes, I'm beginning to share your obsession with them. I'm even beginning to troll through my past and attempting to relive the sights, sounds, smells, and emotions of my high school and college."

"And have you had any success?"

"About what you'd expect. I can remember things, but I can't duplicate the emotions. It's as if I'm looking at a pentimento or a palimpsest."

"Pentimento or palimpsest. Sounds like a vaudeville team."

"I'll see you Saturday night."

CHAPTER 25

Frank enjoyed parties, especially those he and Paula hosted. Normally, he and Paula would invite eight to twelve people to dinner, where there could be conversational interplay and where humor and wit could be displayed. And, normally, he did not enjoy large cocktail parties, nor did he host them.

But this Saturday was different. About three months ago Paula and he were talking about how many people had invited them for cocktails or dinner to whom they had not reciprocated. These were mostly marginal friends and acquaintances—nice, pleasant, somewhat interesting, but not scintillating, dynamic, or fun. Rather than invite them to a series of dinner parties, Paula and Frank decided to host a large, catered cocktail party that would incorporate both their close friends and the acquaintances to whom they "owed" entertainment. Both agreed to this method of repaying social obligations, even though neither of them relished such gatherings.

They had sent out 200 invitations for staggered hours, so that there wouldn't be a great crush of people all at once. They hired Fernanda de Maistre and her husband Rene to cater the event. Fernanda and Rene would provide a large amount of very good hors d'oeuvres, serve drinks, take coats, and generally manage the evening ...all for a reasonable price. Frank would buy the alcohol and the ingredients for the hors d'oeuvres, according to the de Maistres' requirements.

So here it was Saturday evening at five o'clock, and Frank and Paula had just finished dressing: Fernanda, Rene, and their two daughters had just arrived to set up.

"I hope everybody leaves by nine," Frank announced to Paula.

"Why are we having this affair if you're already looking forward to everyone leaving?"

"It's an accommodation. I find cocktail parties superficial and shallow. We're only doing it because we want to have a number of people over whom we don't particularly want to have at a dinner party."

"I hope you develop a better attitude as the evening goes by," Paula continued. "We have a lot of good friends coming. And the other people who are coming, even if we don't find them terribly exciting, we certainly enjoy their company."

"Tanya Devereaux?"

"You know as well as I do that if we didn't invite her, she'd bad-mouth us all over town. Inviting her was just insurance."

The conversation reaffirmed Frank's realization that Paula wanted peace and tranquility whenever possible and that she disliked what she considered his harsh and negative attitude. She is a much kinder person than I, Frank thought.

"Let's go down to see if Fernanda and Rene need anything," Paula said.

The couple walked down to the first floor. The rooms were ready, awaiting the people who would shortly cram into them. Rene, Fernanda, and their two daughters who were helping out were busy and focused in the kitchen, making the final arrangements for serving the hors d'oeuvres.

The white wine was being chilled. Bottles of both red and white wine had already been opened. Bottles of liquor and mixes were ready for consumption. Frank relished the quiet competence of these caterers. There were no hissy fits, no demands, no officiousness; they knew what to do, and they did it.

Fernanda politely responded to Frank's inquiry of whether they needed anything by asserting that everything was under control. And so Paula and he decided to sit in the living room and await their guests. There they sat impatiently waiting for the evening to begin, chatting about inconsequential matters, both feeling nervous about whether the evening would be a success.

The doorbell rang. Their first guest had arrived. The clock in the living room said it was 6:02. Fernanda was at the front door immediately. She opened it, greeting the guest, and offered to take her coat. As soon as this inaugural guest had peeled off her overcoat, Frank and Paula were there to greet her.

It was Doris Metcalf, a woman in her late-seventies whom they had met several years before on a group trip to South America. Doris was sweet and pleasant, and they had invited her to dinner shortly after they returned from the trip. Doris responded by inviting them several times to dinner. They had become embarrassed by their failure to reciprocate; this was their attempt to make up for their not having invited her to their home for dinner.

"Thanks so much for having me," Doris said to Frank and Paula. Frank could detect in her voice an annoyance that there had been no dinner invitation, only an invitation to a large cocktail party. Frank also decided he would not allow himself to feel any guilt.

"We're thrilled you could come," Paula said enthusiastically, flashing one of her engaging smiles. "Why don't you get a drink and help yourself to the hors d'oeuvres?"

Paula's invitation reminded Frank of why he hated cocktail parties. You invite people to your home, greet them when they arrived, and then pass them on to the caterers, hoping that they'll meet someone with whom they can have a conversation.

Doris smiled wanly and headed for the bar. One out of two hundred. A hundred and ninety-nine to go, thought Frank.

The doorbell rang again. It was Terry and Melinda Donohue.

"Hi, Doc. Hi, Melinda," Frank warmly greeted them. "Welcome."

"We came early because we've got theatre tickets." Terry was almost apologetic.

"But we can stay for about an hour." Melinda added.

Paula had begun to chat with Terry, while Frank sought to make small talk with Melinda, whom he had known since his undergraduate days. She was three years younger than Terry. They had met when they were in high school—Melinda a pert, cute freshman and Terry a serious, bespectacled senior—and started dating the following year, when Terry was a freshman at St. Ignatius College. They married when Terry was in medical school and Melinda had finished college.

Melinda was no longer cute. As her looks had faded to blandness, her weight had increased. She now looked positively dumpy. She had never been interesting or exciting. Now she seemed like a bored and tired housewife. Frank felt sorry for his old friend.

The doorbell rang again, and Frank suggested that Terry and Melinda join Doris in the dining room and sample the refreshments. This time several people walked into the house. Frank and Paula greeted them, while Fernanda deftly and quickly took their coats. The ballet had begun of greeting guests, making them feel comfortable with a few snippets of conversation, and then shuffling them off toward drinks and hors d'oeuvres, where the hosts hoped fervently that they would connect with others and have a good time. Frank and Paula pumped hands, kissed and were kissed on the cheeks, and tried to come up with a sufficient number of witticisms, bon mots, and one-liners to make up for the lack of real conversation.

At about 6:45 Frank and Paula were still at the front door greeting their guests. Frank could hear a buzz in the adjoining rooms—a buzz indicating that the party had achieved a sufficient density, that the alcohol had loosened a sufficient number of tongues, and that the gathering had been kick-started into a party.

Those who knew one another—and many of them did—were clustered into small groups and picking up on conversations they had had the last time they were together at a cocktail party. The groups would become like amoebas, constantly breaking apart and reforming.

Those who knew no one or who had already exhausted conversation with the one or few people they did know would be wandering around expectantly, looking around eagerly for someone to talk to. Frank hoped that these "loners" would find others and generate exciting conversations.

Frank had not progressed beyond the entry hall, as guests were still streaming in. He had just greeted the Foleys, the Simons, and Alden Capellini and his date. Alden was recently divorced and had just begun to date. The long-legged blonde he had brought to the party was tan and sleek. Frank was convinced that her internal gyroscope began to vibrate when she learned that Alden was a venture capitalist and when she saw that he was shy and somewhat naïve.

Christina Winckle was her name, and her smile tried to denote both sincerity and sexiness. Frank had seen this type of woman often; they hung out in fancy resorts around the world, gravitated to upscale events in cities, and could be counted on to be prominent at yacht clubs and country clubs...in short, wherever wealthy men gather.

Alden seemed somewhat uncomfortable. Frank remembered how it was several months after his separation; he was extremely nervous about going to a gathering where his friends would be and going with someone who wasn't his wife. It had been strange, vaguely unsettling, and embarrassing. He knew that Alden felt a similar disquiet tonight. I'll be sure to check in on him later, Frank thought.

As Alden and Christina proceeded in to where the party had begun to reach its critical mass of hilarity and chatter, she flashed Frank a wide smile, as if to encourage him to advance her cause with Alden. Frank quickly and silently uttered a prayer that her blonde hair, lascivious looks, and sensuous body would not influence Alden's decision on the nature of their relationship. She was definitely not a good long-term investment.

"Frank, you asshole, why don't I get a dinner invitation sometimes?" Even though his back was toward the front door, Frank immediately knew that Tanya Devereaux had arrived.

Frank turned slowly toward her. "Because I want to share you with as many people as I can," he replied.

Tanya gave Frank what he would describe as an "air-kiss on both cheeks," but, before she could say anything, Frank said to her, "My God, Tanya, you look like Ottoline Morrell."

"Who in the hell is Ottoline Morrell?"

"It's hard to explain, but she was a great character and patron of the arts in England...let's see, late nineteenth, first third of the twentieth century. Quite avant garde."

And, indeed, tonight Tanya looked like an exotic bird with its plumage in full display. Her clothes could have been purchased from a group of Bedouins camped in an oasis, Frank thought: floppy, bright colors, generally outré. She seemed to have exhausted her store of bangles, dangling earrings, and exotic jewelry. Her head was wrapped in a turban, and her make-up highlighted her fleshy features.

"Ah, yes, well..." Tanya didn't know whether Frank was complimenting or insulting her. Her lack of knowledge about whom she supposedly looked like deterred her from responding.

"Where is your wife?" Tanya demanded. "I've got great news about my new career as an artist."

"I presume she's gotten swept away into the dining room." There was noticeable acerbity in Frank's voice.

Without another word, Tanya Devereaux swept out of entry hall and down the corridor, leaving Frank with a heightened aversion to her. Her mentioning "my new career as an artist" is what set off Frank into new heights of dislike. He knew many artists, all of whom had studied long and hard to achieve whatever success they had. Each of them strove to broaden and deepen their creativity.

Tanya had long wanted to be thought of as an artist. But instead of studying, she began to slop paint onto canvases and call them "abstract paintings." She had been doing this for several months when a friend of

Frank's pointed out to him a full-page ad for one of Tanya's paintings in a high-end artists' magazine.

"This is absurd," Frank had sputtered when shown the ad. "She's not an artist; she's a paint splatterer. An untrained baboon can do what she does."

Tanya's proclivity to gain notice by the easiest path possible had always irked Frank. This new escapade especially angered him. It flew in the face of what he considered fit behavior; and it affronted what he had ingested long ago from his parents: that any worthwhile achievement is only accomplished by long, patient, hard work.

The surge of antagonism toward Tanya had distracted Frank. A lull in guests appearing at the front door allowed him to nurture his resentment of this woman whom he could not extricate from his life.

Frank contemplated wandering into the rooms where the party was swirling, eating, drinking, and chattering, but a gentle tap on his shoulder made him turn around.

"Ah, my friend, presiding over a fete, I see." It was Christopher Fermoyle.

"Yes, yes…something like that," Frank responded, limply shaking his friend's hand.

"I can see that you're distracted with care, Francis, or perhaps antagonism toward one or more of your guests, which would explain your serious and frowning look, as well as your preoccupied dimness."

Frank smiled. A surge of warmth came over him for his friend. He hoped fervently that Christopher Fermoyle, with his acutely sensitive judgments, his wit, and his baroque conversation, would be his friend forever.

"I guess it's a combination of things. First of all, I don't like cocktail parties and only did this one because I owe a lot of people dinner. And, then, to cap it off, Tanya Devereaux just came in."

"Francis, Francis, you are troubled about many things. You need to prune your life, restore it to simplicity, and get rid of those in your life with whom you're not compatible…like Tanya Devereaux."

"Easier said than done, my friend. Both Paula and I have difficulty ending relationships with people with whom we no longer want to maintain friendships."

"I understand the kindly proclivities of both of you, Francis, but the results are that you have become dyspeptic and annoyed, and you realize that you can't do anything about the source of your annoyance. And this all goes on ad infinitum."

"I know you're right, but I've got to focus on how to go from agreeing with you to making it a reality in my life."

"Yes, much like the process of getting through life—choices, decisions, implementation."

"I lack your ability to run my life as intellectually as you do, Christopher. Even someone like Tanya, whom I despise, I can't eliminate. She's been in our lives for years, and neither of us seems to be able to get rid of her."

"And that's what is going to continue to chip away at your lives. But let's not dwell on this. I'll go in and get a drink and see who's here."

As Christopher walked into the dining room, a few of the early arrivals had begun to leave. Frank shook hands with them, kissed a couple of the women, and bid them farewell. "Thanks so much for coming," he recited to each as they thanked him for the invitation.

There was no one at the front door, and Frank thought it was probably time for him to mingle with his guests. Before he could leave his station, however, Alden Capellini walked up to him, holding a Campari and soda in his hand.

"I thought I'd track you down and chat, if you have a moment," he said.

"Sure. It's become quiet out here. What's happened to your date?"

"Oh, she found a couple of guys she knows. She's chatting with them."

"Is it serious?" Frank asked, hoping for a negative response.

"No, I don't think so. I met her at a party at the Burlingame Country Club. She's pretty and vivacious and fun to be with, but I don't think she's my life companion...for whatever part of life one gets a companion."

"Still lamenting your ex-wife?" Frank inquired, smiling at the good news.

"I thought it would be 'until death do us part,' but I guess she didn't think so. Maybe I miss being married more than I miss her. I don't know. It's strange being single again."

"You'll have to take my word for it, but time will end the strangeness and you'll vaguely remember the time when you were married to her. But it helps to replace her with someone who is truly 'till death do us part' and with whom you can be happy with until death separates you."

"Easier said than done," Alden responded with a sad face. "As you know, I'm no Casanova, and trying to figure out how to predict the future as to a mate is almost impossible."

"Alden, you're bright, successful, and good-looking. That's a start for attracting women."

"But how do you know that someone is the sort you want for a lifetime soul-mate? What is it that women want?"

"If I knew the answer to that question, not only would I be as well-regarded as Plato or Aristotle, but I'd be a multi-billionaire."

Alden smiled. Frank looked about him to see whether any guests were arriving or leaving. From the other rooms he could hear the hubbub of the party, the noise and laughter surging and ebbing. Frank was pleased to be sequestered in the front hall with Alden.

"You know, Alden, there is no easy answer to your conundrum. I suspect that a lot of women are going to come on to you, and you're going to be receptive. You're vulnerable at this point in your life. You're lonely. And you're probably horny.

"Some women will look on you as a meal ticket or as someone who will provide them with a social position. Somehow or other you've got to filter these out, no matter how good-looking, sexy, or personable they may be. Don't get into a deep relationship with someone not suitable who's going to wear you down to provide a wedding ring.

"Sorry to bend your ear this way with probably unwanted advice."

"Hey, Frank, you're doing me a big favor. I appreciate you taking me in hand like this. Most of my friends just tell me how lucky I am to be single. 'Get laid a lot,' they tell me. But I still can't get out of my mind a question I keep asking myself: Why did my wife leave me?"

Frank looked at Alden's sad, quizzical face. He felt sorry for him. It would be tough moving on while he was still puzzling about why his wife had left him. "Look, Alden, you may find an answer to this someday, or you may not. And I doubt that torturing yourself trying to find an answer is going to do much good for you.

"A lot of people—both men and women—are never satisfied with their lives. They live in fantasy worlds. If they can change this thing—whether a spouse, a job, or a lifestyle—life will be better. They act on this change, and, guess what, their lives don't become better.

"I think you just got sideswiped in one of those situations. Your wife's leaving you had nothing to do with any deficiencies in you. There is no doubt in my mind that her leaving you had everything to do with her inability to find contentment and happiness in her own life."

Frank couldn't believe his long preachment to Alden Capellini while his party was swirling just a short distance from where he and Alden were dealing with such weighty matters. He felt as if he were making love with a woman in a bathroom during an immense party.

"Thanks for the pep talk, Frank," Alden said. "You're always wonderful to talk to. Our conversations always raise my spirits."

"You'll be over this thing pretty soon. Just don't make any hasty decisions as to Ms. Right."

"I'll have you look over each one I'm dating," Alden declared, laughing. "If you don't approve I'll drop them."

"I think that's a hell of an idea. It will mean that you'll have a second opinion...very effective in avoiding mistakes."

"It's a deal. And now I think I'll grab my date and get out of your hair. If I don't see Paula before I leave, please give her my love. And, thanks for your candor and encouragement, Frank. I appreciate it."

"That's what friends are for. Thanks for coming."

Alden wandered off to search for his date, and Frank followed him, planning to move among his guests and fulfill his duties as host.

Across the room stood a woman who appeared as exotic as a South American bird. She stood talking intensely to someone Frank didn't recognize, but there was no mistaking the woman—Allegra Nero. Paula must have sneaked her onto the guest list, Frank thought. He involuntarily shuddered with distaste.

Allegra Nero had captured Paula's imagination from the time Paula had volunteered for the Helpers of the Unfortunate Women, a shelter for unmarried, pregnant women. Allegra was the executive director. She had taken over an almost moribund organization that had been started by two nuns some decades before and had poured her manic energy into the institution.

Her love of the retail industry and her passion for fine clothes led her to begin a large store that sold second-hand items of top quality. Proceeds from the store helped to fund Helpers of the Unfortunate Women. Among the inventory was designer clothing with minute imperfections donated by high-end stores and couturiers. Allegra would appropriate each donation that she thought would be more seemly in her own closet.

Bazaars, auctions, and other fundraisers helped raise the operating funds for the organization; Allegra helped herself to a substantial salary and a healthy expense account.

Despite "doing good while doing well," Allegra Nero had acquired a saintly reputation, the "Mother Teresa of San Francisco." And, aside from her passion for fine clothes and accouterments and her care for her finely cultivated reputation for saintliness, Allegra loved the social swirl. Each day she attended some lunch and each evening some social gathering to benefit a charity.

Allegra's photo, with the massive glasses she traditionally wore, appeared frequently in the *Chronicle* and in the various publications that showcased San Francisco society.

What annoyed Frank most about Allegra was her basic hypocrisy. For the past several years there had been no Helpers of the Unfortunate Women, except in name. From the earliest years when Allegra had taken over the organization, she had bought real estate, until the organization owned six homes, housing about twenty-five pregnant women. Then, a few years ago, there were no more unmarried, pregnant women in the homes of the Helpers of the Unfortunate Women.

Allegra claimed that there was no longer any stigma about being pregnant and unmarried, and the girls were not coming to the homes. If this were true, she could have transformed the homes into shelters for abused women or some other like purpose. But, the truth was that Allegra had had her fill of helping the unfortunate. Even though all the day-to-day work was done by paid staff or by volunteers, she no longer wanted to be bothered with the travails of others. As each pregnant woman delivered, decided what to do with her baby, and then left the guidance of the Helpers, she was not replaced. The homes were spruced up and rented, which, in addition to the continuing income from the store, bazaars, auctions, and other fundraisers, supplied the Helpers of the Unfortunate Women with a substantial annual income.

As a charitable organization the Helpers had to distribute this income, which Allegra did as if it had originated in her own foundation, and only after her own substantial salary and expense account had been paid. The fine couture continued to grace her closets, the saintly reputation was maintained, and the substantial salary continued to be paid—even though no purposeful charitable enterprise existed—and for this Frank despised Allegra Nero.

Frank moved quickly to avoid being seen by Allegra. As he turned around he found himself face to face with Jack and Cynthia Sherman.

"Hello, sport," Jack said instantly. "You look like you were about to flee from your own party."

"Hi, Frank," Cynthia added. Frank always wondered what was behind the Mona Lisa smile.

"Hi, guys," Frank responded. He felt off center, surprised. "How did you get in without my seeing you?"

"You were deeply engaged in conversation that we walked by. We didn't want to interrupt you." Jack was wearing one of his sardonic smiles—a look that Frank could remember all the way back to St. Aloysius days.

"I know...serious conversations are banned from cocktail parties, but I just couldn't help myself," Frank said.

"Hey, we're always happy to have a serious conversation with you, Frank, any time or any place, but we never see you anymore," Cynthia Sherman looked archly at Frank.

"Yeah, I don't know where my time goes. Even though I've begun the retirement process..."

Jack suddenly looked serious. "I didn't know you've retired."

"Well, I didn't put an ad in the newspaper," Frank continued. "I told the firm that I'm cutting back, and that I'd be out completely in five years." Frank was puzzled by Jack's response to his news.

Jack's seriousness now turned to the sardonic. "I can't believe you've decided to stop chasing the buck," he said, a smirk on his face.

"I can't say I was 'chasing the buck,'" Frank countered, annoyed. "We call it 'work.'"

"For you it was 'chasing the buck,'" Jack retorted laughing.

There was something behind Jack's humor, Frank felt. How had the two of them ever become friends? he wondered. And why did they bother to stay friends?

Cynthia broke the uncomfortable silence that had ensued. "Whatever it's called, congratulations, Frank, on beginning the retirement process. You're going to have great fun."

Frank gave her a grateful smile. "Thanks, Cynthia. Yeah, I think so. I've worked all my life...time to let go. And I've got a lot of interests I'd like to have more time to pursue."

Jack retreated from whatever had triggered his mockery and held out his hand to Frank. "Congratulations, old man. You're going to have the time of your life."

Where did Jack get these expressions "sport," "old man"? Frank wondered. He sounded like someone from a Ronald Coleman movie.

"We're off, Frank."

"Hello, Jack...Cynthia."

Frank wheeled around to see Chris and Monica Martini. They had gathered their coats and were on their way out.

"Nice party," Chris said without much enthusiasm. "Thanks for having us."

"Thanks so much for coming," Frank said. "You know these cocktail parties..."

"Oh, it was fun," Monica said. Her embarrassment stopped him from going on. "We saw a lot of people we know...and a lot of people we hadn't seen for a while. It was great catching up."

One could always count on Monica to say the right thing, to make one feel good about the moment.

"You're terrific, Monica," Frank said, smiling. "You were probably bored to tears, but, as always, you put a good face on it."

"Oh, no, it was..." Chris put a hand in front of his wife's mouth, gently took her arm, and guided her toward the front door. Chris and Frank waved to each other as Monica started to giggle.

Frank felt he was in a momentary oasis in the party. He looked at his watch...8:30. Presumably the last of the staggered invitees had come, and soon the entire group would depart. Frank would be relieved.

Frank noticed Christopher Fermoyle speaking to Dick Lambert and Dick Mahoney. The wives of the two Dicks had wisely removed themselves to where the conversation would be less intellectual and less replete with reminiscences of their school days. Frank decided to join the men.

"Ah, Francis, how nice of you to join us," Christopher Fermoyle interrupted an intense declamation to his school friends when Frank came up. "Have you finished presiding over the social event of the year? I see it's thinning out."

"Alas, no, I have to 'preside' to the bitter end."

"Well, at least we have you for a few moments."

"Thanks, Frank," Dick Mahoney interjected. "Occasions like this give us an opportunity to get together. It seems as if we do less and less of getting together as we get older."

"That's the paradox of getting older, if you'll pardon my philosophical sidebar," said Dick Lambert. "Here we are, old friends who saw each other every day when we were in school, frequently when we were starting our families and careers, and then less frequently. And...now that we're pretty much in retirement and have the time and leisure to do so, we see even less of each other. And it's not that we don't like each other or don't have anything to say to each other."

"Not a pretty picture," Frank mused. "It seems as if we see each other only at funerals or at big, impersonal events like this."

"Now, Francis, don't denigrate your own soiree," Christopher interjected, a sly grin on his face. "You have truly gathered San Francisco's beau monde."

"Sorry, Christopher," Frank rejoined. "It seemed like a good idea at the time."

"Frank, I'm so sorry we're so late."

Frank turned around to see a breathless, beaming Jessica. Behind her stood a young man with steel-rim glasses whom he had seen visiting Jessica in the office once or twice.

"That's all right, Jessica. I'm just glad you could make it," Frank said, wondering why his secretary looked so excited.

"Frank, you remember my friend, Ken Walden, don't you?" Frank nodded and held out his hand.

"Well, he's not just my friend anymore. Ken proposed tonight." Jessica was almost squealing. Ken smiled.

"Jess, what great news…how terrific for the two of you!" Frank pumped Jessica's fiancé's hand. "Congratulations, Ken, you're getting a wonderful gal."

Frank pulled Jessica to him and gave her a hug and a kiss. "Best wishes, Sweetheart. I know the two of you will be very happy." He looked around. "You've got to tell Paula. She's here somewhere."

"We'll track her down," Jessica responded, holding both Frank's and her fiancé's hands. "Now that you're leaving the office I'll have someone else to take care of."

Frank smiled and looked his secretary straight in the face. "And if you do half as good a job with him as you did with me, he's going to be a very happy man."

Jessica giggled and Ken smiled broadly. Frank felt as if he were a numinous god, presiding over this young couple's happiness.

"I didn't mean to disturb your conversation, Frank. We'll find Paula."

"Do grab me before you leave," Frank enjoined, as the couple began to thread their way between the guests.

Frank's close friends to whom he had been speaking when Jessica and her newly minted fiancé had come up had disappeared. Coming toward him was Barbara Kingman, whom he hadn't seen come in.

"Barbara, how very nice of you to come," Frank greeted her, shaking her hand.

"Are you kidding? How very nice of you to invite me. I've loved meeting your friends. And I'm so pleased to be asked to the house of a fellow alumnus."

"Shall we do the school song now or later?" Frank grinned.

"Oh, we can wait until later," Barbara answered.

"How's the law these days?" Frank politely inquired. He didn't know Barbara very well, but had liked her when they had met, so he decided to invite her to the party.

Barbara Kingman frowned. "Oh, you would bring that up. Actually, not so good. Well, I mean, the practice of law is okay, but the firm is another matter. I'm sure you know the story. Some of the big producers are demanding a bigger share in the profits. They're threatening to leave if they don't get them. It's tearing the firm apart, and I don't think it's going to make it."

Frank knew the situation well. He had watched as three or four law firms—firms where he himself had friends—dissolve amid recriminations and litigation as oversized egos destroyed the firm.

"I'm saddened to hear that," he told Barbara. "Any chance of your getting out before the blood-letting starts? I know several attorneys I could put you in touch with."

"Thanks, Frank, but the bloodshed has already started. I'm committed to helping keep the firm intact."

The buzz from the party was waning, and as Frank spoke to Barbara the remaining guests began to stream toward the door. Seeing Frank in conversation with Barbara, departing guests waved at him and mouthed, "Thanks for inviting us." He could see Paula shaking hands and saying goodbye to the remaining guests.

"Oh, Frank, I'm sorry," a startled Barbara said. "I didn't mean to keep you from saying goodbye to your guests...and I need to go, too."

"It's always a pleasure to see you and talk with you, Barbara. I hope we see each other again soon."

Barbara headed for the front door, where there was a claque of guests saying goodbye to Paula. He decided not to join them. Instead he peered into the kitchen and dining room, where the caterers were cleaning up and putting things away. He thanked them for the usual excellent job and realized that he and Paula would be munching the leftover hors d'oeuvres for days to come.

Frank was suddenly tired. He realized that he felt cranky and out-of-sorts.

He always hated cocktail parties and here he had given one. While he'd had the opportunity for some decent conversations, mostly it was superficial snippets of talk. He had barely seen most of his guests, much less talked with them.

His disgruntlement with the evening was aggravated by the vague unease in his stomach. Can't be that I ate or drank too much, Frank thought. I barely ate or drank a thing.

"Well, my dear, that's all she wrote." Paula had said the final farewell and joined Frank in the dining room. "The party is over."

"Thank God," Frank retorted. "That's the last cocktail party I'm ever going to give. We're going to stick to small dinner parties in the future."

"That's fine with me. But I think this party went well."

"It was okay, I guess. But I'm dead tired and I'm not feeling well. There's something wrong in my stomach. I'm going to go upstairs, get some Pepto-Bismol, and go to bed."

"You do look a little pale. Why don't you go upstairs and tuck in? I'll be up as soon as I close up down here."

Frank smiled at Paula's penchant for making certain that everything was put away and the house was neat as a pin before going to bed. Nothing could pry her from a final inspection and making certain that everything was to her satisfaction.

"Good night, Sweetie. Don't stay up all night being a neat-nik."

CHAPTER 26

Harry Zonich had been a waiter at Sam's for forty years. He knew the five men at the table well, had waited on them for years. He cracked a joke as he took their orders, but they responded with only the faintest glimmer of a polite smile. Something must be up, he thought. No more jokes.

"I still can't believe it," remarked a somber Chris Martini when Harry had walked away. "He looked the picture of health at the party he gave a few months ago. I've seen him since, and I never got a sense that he had cancer."

"How do you think I feel?" Terry Donohue looked stricken. "I'm his doctor. And I didn't have a clue until he came in and complained of abdominal pain. I also noticed that he was considerably thinner than the last time I'd seen him, which hadn't been that long before. I sent him for some tests, and, when I got the report, I began shaking. I thought it was a mistake and had him re-tested. But there was no mistake."

"My God, this is so quick," blurted out Dick Mahoney. "What has it been—four months—since you diagnosed it?"

"Just about," Donahue responded. "Maybe a little longer."

"He's going to be missed," Dick Lambert said, morosely shaking his head from side to side.

Harry came to the table and silently poured water at the five places, picking up that something was troubling them.

"He was always pleased that there was no cancer on either side of his family." Chris Martini managed a wan smile. "And, now, poof, he's got pancreatic cancer."

"And here's a guy who came in every year for a physical," Terry Donohue reflected. "Every year he was checked from head to toe. And between last year and this he's been given a death sentence."

"Was there any chance for treatment when you discovered it?" inquired Dick Lambert.

Donohue was silent for several seconds, looking down at his plate. "None. It was Stage Four. It was too late for surgery, and he didn't want radiation or chemotherapy. Smart...it wouldn't have done him any good. When we went over the prognosis and the possible treatments, he said to me, 'God is calling me, and I don't want to keep Him waiting. Just see to it that I'm comfortable...whatever you have to do.' And so I've arranged that he is to be given as much medication as he needs to dull the pain."

Christopher Fermoyle had kept silent during the conversation. The look of haughty, cynical amiability that generally sat on his features was gone. It was replaced by a contemplative sadness.

"I'm sure he'll be offering up his pain for the souls in purgatory," he intoned.

Four heads turned toward him. "My gosh, I haven't heard that expression since high school," Dick Mahoney was smiling.

"It's time you heard it again," said Fermoyle. "It's an important idea, and I'm sure it's very much on Francis's mind."

"I'm just surprised that he won't see us," declared Dick Lambert. "I'm still shocked from getting his letter, telling me that he was dying from pancreatic cancer, thanking me for many years of friendship and saying goodbye."

"Yeah, and saying that none of us were to see him, but that we should remember him from the time each of us first met him to the last time we saw him." Chris Martini seemed quite amazed by his friend's injunction.

"I keep thinking that I'll drop by the hospital and see him," said Dick Lambert, "but I just can't bring myself to do it."

Terry Donahue cleared his throat. "Better you should keep to that resolution. He's skin and bones and heavily medicated most of the time. I see him every day with his oncologist. It won't be long."

"I feel as if something very, very important is going out of our lives," Dick Mahoney declared.

"It is...most definitely." Christopher Fermoyle's eyes had misted. "He was at the center of a community of friends who have known each other intimately for half a century. He was the glue that held us together. We were no longer a group of individuals who went to school together, but a group of friends who continued their friendships for all of this time. It was Francis Molinari who continuously welded us together. His leaving us is a major loss in our lives."

The friends looked at Fermoyle in surprise. They had never witnessed such passion and emotion from Christopher. He always seemed so detached and above the fray. Their looks seemed to indicate that if Christopher Fermoyle could become so passionate, then, indeed, Frank Molinari's impending death must be a cosmic event.

It was Dick Lambert who broke the silence. "This is not the first death —even though Frank's not dead yet—of a close friend I've experienced, but it certainly is the toughest. Frank had a special place in my life."

No one nodded or agreed, but everyone sensed that Lambert's feeling was shared by all.

"For virtually all of our lives we know about the inevitability of death... and we experience it from time to time...grandparents, parents, aunts and uncles, the occasional contemporary, but somehow each time is different." Dick Lambert was gnawing on the subject of the imminent end of his friend.

"So, Christopher, why did you bring up the subject of Frank's probably offering up his pain for the souls in purgatory?" Dick Mahoney asked, wishing to deflect Dick Lambert from pursuing his train of thought.

"All of us went to Catholic schools at a time when the concept of the Mystical Body of Christ was flourishing," Fermoyle answered. "We were taught that we were all responsible, through our sacrifices, to lessen the time of punishment in purgatory for sins committed on earth. And we were made responsible for saving souls throughout the world. ...Remember the money given for 'pagan babies'?...and we were all to help the poor and the suffering on earth.

"Well, most of us forgot about such things. They weren't part of our lives. But not Frank. One caught glimpses every once in a while that these ideas were still part of his mental and emotional furniture. Such occasions surprised me. I used to think they were part of his whimsy, but then I realized that they were part of him."

"Well, you know Frank. He had lots of quirky ideas, and this..." Chris Martini interjected.

"Quirky? Yes, Frank had quirky ideas...we all do. But this was no quirky idea. A couple times he told me that the greatest failure of his life was not to have done more to help the poor and suffering, that he had concentrated too much on the demands of raising his family and those of his career."

"I think we all can say that," said Dick Lambert. "But none of us did anything about it when we could."

"I am well aware of our deficiencies," Fermoyle blurted out, somewhat impatiently, "and I'm aware of Frank's, as well. What I'm saying is that, of all of us, he ingested the ideal, kept it before him, and, even if he failed to do what he thought he should be doing he measured himself against the ideal."

"Not to put too fine a point on it," said Terry Donohue, "but isn't this all a little archaic? Whoever talks about pagan babies any more? Hell, the Church is only half-heartedly doing any missionary work. And there are all sorts of Catholic theologians who state that purgatory is a myth."

Fermoyle flushed. "Who gives a good God-damn what a bunch of lily-livered theologians proclaim? And why would the Church's current failure to adhere to the gospel injunction to evangelize become something to guide us?

"What we believed many years ago, and what Frank continued to believe, was that there was an interdependency among all, living and dead...a mystical bond, if you will.

"Despite that it's fallen in disuse in my life, I still think it's a magnificent structure and a brilliant concept: that we're all responsible for each other, living and dead."

There was quiet. Each person at the table was wrapped in a cocoon of thought that centered around Frank Molinari's impending death, mixed with Christopher Fermoyle's theological lucubrations, but most intensely concerned with their own sense of mortality.

Harry came to the table and poured each a glass from a bottle of Calera chardonnay that he had set on the table. Another waiter brought their plates of food: two orders of sand dabs, two of petrale, and a Frank's Salad for Dick Mahoney.

In unison, the quintet took a sip of their wine and began to eat their lunch. It seemed as if they were exhausted by their conversation and by the sad burden of a dear friend about to die. Each was cognizant that his primary concern was not the fact that Frank Molinari would soon die, but the recognition that he also would die.

Dick Lambert broke the silence. "I feel as if I need some closure with Frank. How about we all go see him and say goodbye?""

"I don't think that would be a good idea," interposed Terry Donohue. "He gave specific orders that he have no visitors. He has said his goodbyes to his children. Only Paula is allowed to visit him."

"How is she doing with all this?" Dick Lambert inquired.

"I saw her a couple days ago," Chris Martini declared. "She seems very sad, but she's putting up a good front...for Frank and the kids.

"She said something very moving when I saw her. She said 'Chris, I am going to lose my playmate.'"

"Yeah, they've been very close. Their marriage was really an example of the song's message, 'Love is better the second time around.' They were very much in love and continued to do a lot of things together." It was Dick Mahoney who made the assessment.

"I think Paula will do fine," expressed Chris Martini. "She has a strong, level-headed temperament. She's very close to a couple of the kids. And she's got a lot of interests."

"Still, it's going to be a big adjustment...losing Frank, and just as he's about to retire," added Dick Lambert. "They were both looking forward to doing a lot of traveling."

"Yeah, well, you know...these plans we make...you never know if they're going to work out." Chris Martini glumly threw out. "Live for today. Right?"

"Don't become banal," growled Christopher Fermoyle. "This is not a time for absurd statements."

There was silence again. No one wished to respond to Fermoyle's statement, fearful that they would trigger a tirade from their grieving friend.

Around them at Sam's swirled pleasantries, serious business conversations, animated exchanges between friends. No one seemed to notice the somber quintet at the table in the middle of the restaurant. No one knew that these five men were lamenting the near end of one of their beloved companions. Each of those in the restaurant was intent on the present moment in his or her life, the enjoyment of the food and beverage, the relishing of the companions with whom they were sharing their meal, intent on having a good time.

There was no such effervescence at the table where five men in their sixties attempted to deal with the imminent death of their dear friend whose terminal illness had served to bring their own mortality into focus.

"I wonder what plans he's made for his funeral," asked Dick Lambert.

"Why don't you wait to find out when he has died?" Christopher Fermoyle spat out, rage and contempt etched on his face. Ever since they had met, Fermoyle and Lambert had been friends mostly because others expected it rather than a camaraderie they themselves shared. For decades their submerged dislike for each other had come out in calculated "digs" often disguised as humor, or as criticisms to their mutual friends.

"And why don't you shut the fuck up?" retorted a flushed Dick Lambert. "I can ask any question I like without having to listen to you pitch a fit."

Fermoyle was about to retort when Dick Mahoney interposed. "All right, guys, let's cut it out. We're all depressed and on edge. It doesn't help for us to lash out at each other. Come on, Dick, Christopher, kiss and make up."

Each man addressed mumbled something while looking down at his plate, and the crisis passed.

Chris Martini joined Dick Mahoney in his peacekeeping efforts. "I think all of us should keep in close contact with Paula and Frank's kids. My God, Pamela's my god-daughter, and I haven't spoken to her since I heard about Frank."

The other four gloomily nodded. Each felt a vague discomfort about contacting Frank's wife and children at such a time.

"Has anyone spoken to Claudia?" Terry Donohue asked.

"Yeah, I have," Chris Martini answered. "I bumped into her the other day while we were shopping at Cal-Mart. She was really upset. She and Frank have become pretty close in recent years. But she was also indignant that Frank is only allowing Paula to visit him."

"That sounds like her." Dick Mahoney smiled. "She always wants to be in the middle of a crisis, whether it's medical or psychological. But...she's got a good heart."

"It's amazing that after their tempestuous marriage that they should become such good friends," Chris Martini observed.

"Time burns out old hurts and allows good memories to shine forth," Christopher Fermoyle said, in a flat, almost hollow, voice. "They shared some very good times, they share children, they are both somewhat zany. I think they've buried the hurts and the disappointments that marked their marriage."

As often had happened in the past, Fermoyle's philosophical observations were met with silence. It generally took his friends some time to absorb his thoughts, to digest them sufficiently for conversation.

"It's been amusing to see them come together during the past few years," Chris Martini added. "They're almost like an old married couple. Even Paula finds it funny...and certainly doesn't mind."

Sam's was half empty. The noon lunch crowd had departed. Those who remained were finishing a late lunch or had no duties to rush back to, like the five friends at the table in the middle of the restaurant.

Harry Zonich was eying the table. They were the last to be sitting in his station, and he wanted to finish his shift. They certainly don't look very happy, he thought.

He walked up to the table. "Gentlemen, can I get you anything else?"

"No thanks, Harry. Just the check, please." Christopher Fermoyle realized that Harry wanted to leave.

The waiter handed Fermoyle the check. He waved away his friends' proffered cash and credit cards. "This is on me," he proclaimed. "You can buy me drinks after the funeral." With that he waved the check and his credit card at their waiter.

Almost immediately Harry Zonich brought back the credit slip. Fermoyle signed it, took his credit card, and said to the waiter, "Sorry, we kept you so long, Harry. We won't be needing anything else. We'll be here for a few more minutes, and then we'll be going."

"No problem, Mr. Fermoyle. It's always a pleasure to serve you all. I'll be going, but if you need anything else, tell Charlie over there."

Fermoyle nodded and Harry left. None of the friends spoke, each preoccupied with his own thoughts.

Dick Lambert broke the silence. "Well, I don't think there's much more to say...or to do. We should probably be going."

"Yeah," added Chris Martini, "all that's going to happen if we stay is that we're going to become even more morose."

"You know what I can't figure out?" said Dick Mahoney "is why Frank has cut off visitors. He was always so gregarious, eager to be with us...with his children. I thought he'd want to have us around him, chatting about our lives together...he pontificating on life."

Terry Donohue got up from his place at the table and looked at his friend. "Dick, if you could see Frank, you'd know why he doesn't want to see anyone. I've never thought of Frank as vain, but this cancer has ravaged him. He doesn't want anyone to see him in this condition.

"And, then, there's something else. Every time I drop by to see how he's doing, he seems distracted. He doesn't seem to have any interest in the past or the present. He knows he's going to die very soon, and it seems that he's engaged in some titanic struggle to come to grips with the end. It's a personal struggle. I don't think he wants any distractions."

There was no response to Donohue's analysis. Each of the friends got up, thanked Christopher Fermoyle for lunch, and solemnly said goodbye to the others. Each was aware that possibly the next time they would see one another would be at the wake for Francis Molinari.

They filed out of Sam's into the pale but shimmering winter sunshine in San Francisco. The unpleasant glare caused a couple of them to put on dark glasses.

The five men shook hands and silently departed for their next destination. Christopher Fermoyle walked up Bush Street to Grant Avenue, pausing momentarily, deep in thought, and walked deliberately north along the tourist shops that characterize that part of Chinatown.

Fermoyle crossed California Street and walked into the red brick church that stood at the corner. Old St. Mary's Church had been built in the mid-1850s as San Francisco's first Roman Catholic cathedral. Twice it had been ravaged by fire; twice it had been rebuilt.

A handful of old men and women were rapt in prayer as Fermoyle entered the quiet church. There is always something distinctive in entering a Catholic church, he thought: the quiet, the serenity, the smell of polished wood, the red glow of the sanctuary light, the sense that the structure is open to anyone who wishes to pray.

It had been a long time since he had just dropped into a church to pray. He often went to daily mass—and he always went to mass on Sundays—but it had been some time since he had knelt in a church when there wasn't a liturgy.

Fermoyle slipped into a pew, knelt, and, with his head in his hands, began to whisper some prayers. No one knelt near him, but if someone had, he or she would have noticed water trickling from between his fingers.

CHAPTER 27

Frank blinked at the sterile brightness of his hospital room. He had spent only two nights in the hospital in his life (aside from a stint when he was a small boy and his tonsils had been taken out), and now he had been at St. Francis Hospital for a week. He hated hospitals, and the past several days had not changed his mind.

Frank looked around. Paula must have gone out, he thought. Despite his urging her to go home and rest, she had sat in his room day and night. No nurse or doctor was prodding him, thank God. But there were the tubes that were in him and, he believed, would be appended to his anatomy until he died—which wouldn't be long.

The pancreatic cancer diagnosis had shocked him. He immediately surrendered his final responsibilities at Blakesley and Montgomery and spent his time putting his affairs in order. He realized that no treatment would alleviate the rather short sentence of death and had asked Terry only that he be made as comfortable as possible in his last days.

When he first heard the news, Frank was determined not to tell Paula, his children, or his friends. Paula had been surprised at his sudden decision to retire fully from Blakesley and Montgomery, but she had not pressed him on it. Neither his children nor his friends had questioned him about that decision.

But, after about three months, his increasing weakness and the mounting pain forced him to tell Paula. He proposed a weekend in Mendocino, and they stayed at the Heritage House, where they had spent many a relaxed and rejuvenating weekend.

Paula was devastated. He had told her the news while sitting on the porch of their unit, watching a splendid sunset over the Pacific Ocean after polishing off a bottle of Pol Rogier champagne.

She had cried and lamented, and he had tenderly held her. He mused that no matter what happened to him after he died, he would miss her. She had been his rock, his anchor, and the love of his life.

A half hour went by before her tears stopped; but he could see the sadness etched in her swollen face. He had become matter-of-fact: he told her that he had composed about ten letters for her guidance; that she would be well taken care of financially; how she was to dispose of his personal items, giving her directions for his funeral. He had tried to think of everything, but, if she needed additional advice, he told her, she should convene a gathering of the selected handful of his friends.

There had been a possibility of making love that night, as much as he would have liked to, but they lay holding each other, awake most of the night, Paula occasionally crying softly.

Frank was puzzled about how he should tell his family and his friends. He didn't want them hanging around with doleful countenances and sorrowful thoughts.

He came up with what he considered a solution—eccentric, perhaps, but what he considered most conforming with his desires. He waited until increasing weakness and pain convinced him that he would soon become incapacitated. Then he arranged a series of dinner parties with each of his children and their families. The dinners had been set up on four successive days. And during each of these evenings he told them how much he loved them, and, without sounding too maudlin, asked their forgiveness for his deficiencies as a parent, father-in-law, or grandparent. They seemed somewhat puzzled, but did not pursue his peculiar behavior.

After the last dinner, shortly after he realized that he would shortly be confined to a hospice or a hospital, he wrote to them, telling them of his condition and asking them to honor his wish that they not visit him.

Of course, Paula received calls of protest, but they all honored his wish.

Frank did the same with his friends: he had individual lunches with his closest friends, and, without divulging his illness, conveyed to each one how important that friendship had been. After the last lunch, he wrote letters of farewell with an injunction not to visit him.

Once again, Paula received calls protesting not being able to see him "one last time," but each friend had acquiesced to his wish.

Frank was desirous of sharing these last days of his life only with Paula. He didn't want to be distracted by the well-meaning conversation of family and friends, but wanted to concentrate on the inevitable end of his life. He

een a number of such moments in his life; milestones along a
always determined would be a "large" life. Well, sometimes
other times it hadn't.

n wrong to have wished to live life "on the edge"? It hadn't
as to exclude his working hard and obtaining and enjoying
s of life—a fine home, nice cars, books and art, trips—but
been less conventional than those of many people he had
hat never took a risk, never dwelt on ideas, lives committed
e"—golf, tennis, and skiing.

ll behind him now. It was too late to take up golf...or to
ss missionary. What he had been, he had been.

he was troubled by whether this had been enough. Should
ve given more of his time, energy, and worldly goods to the
ouls of this earth—those suffering from injustice, the poor,
ld he have been an activist for their causes and given more
ir misery?

nk realized, too late to have done anything differently. But
ack of involvement would be held against him in the next
him. For most of his life Frank had told himself that at
would cease to seek his own and his family's advantages and
dedicate his life to the service of others less fortunate than
oment never came...and it would not come now.

again shifted his body on the bed, trying to rid himself of
e thoughts. A portrait gallery of people in his life suddenly
h his mind's eye: his parents, his grandparents, his siblings,
is youth, teachers, neighbors, those he had met in school,
ers he had met in his decades of working, the hundreds he
ed socially, some of whom had remained in his life and the
n't.

scope stopped at the figure of one Nick Simonides, and Frank
barrassed. Nick had been very generous and supportive of
difficult time in his life. They had been friends. Then, for
n, Frank had not held up his end of the friendship. There
argument or any disagreement. Perhaps he had been busy
ome too complicated, and he no longer communicated with
ad turned into months and months into years. After some
uld no longer find Nick. It had been a source of sorrow to
..and now a flush of embarrassment came over him as he
worked to piece together what his life had meant.

Shortly after Frank sent letters to children and friends, his pain became unbearable, and he was admitted to St. Francis Hospital, where the apparatus to make comfortable a dying man awaited him. Punctured with tubes, he lay on his back, his mind mildly disordered, but suffused with a drug-induced pleasantness, awaiting death.

Frank had asked for a clock that ticked. He now listened to its sounds, punctuating the quiet hospital room. "Tick-tock, tick-tock, you'll soon be dead," it seemed to say. Sunshine slashed through the partly closed drapes in his room, giving it a mellow light. Somewhere, off in the distance he heard muted voices, the click of heels on linoleum, but then there was silence.

Frank didn't fear death, but he was mildly apprehensive. He had done all he could to arrange for his affairs to be in order. He couldn't recall any loose ends. But images and memories flooded his mind, unbidden, in chaotic fashion. Despite Frank's efforts to review his life in some rational fashion, what was transpiring was an incoherent series of memories that dashed through his mind.

There he was on Strawberry Hill in Golden Gate Park, some distance off the path, lying on the ground "making out" with Annette Hillman, putting his hand up her blouse, undoing her brassiere, and touching her breasts. He was a freshman in college, he seemed to recall, and felt a sense of guilt afterward.

Almost as if some mad cinematographer had spliced together scenes from many documentaries, the next image flashed back many years earlier, when his father had taken him fishing. His father had told him to stay put while he went downstream. So Frank stuck his pole in the ground, pulled out a book he had hidden in his jacket, and began to read. About an hour later his father, unheard by Frank, came upon him reading. He had been upset that Frank didn't share his love for fishing.

Another image followed, one from an even earlier period. He was very excited that his mother was taking him and his brother one Sunday afternoon to see a movie featuring Uncle Remus—he couldn't remember the name of the movie—but his brother had come down with a cold and had a fever. Frank felt that if he made his brother drink glass after glass of cold water his fever would go away. When this remedy didn't work and his mother announced that they wouldn't be going to the movies, and Frank felt a bitter disappointment.

Where were these memories coming from, fragments of his life from decades before? Insignificant bits and pieces. Where had they been retained? What did they matter? Why were they coming up now in this ceaseless kaleidoscope?

Frank tried to return to a more focused approach to his life. What did his being born and living for seventy years mean? It all seemed to be so haphazard. His parents had met, married, and conceived him. He had been much loved by his family, although he was brought up in strict circumstances and without much emotional nurturing.

All of his life he had tried to be someone outstanding. But in the end, he felt defeated. His life had turned out to be much like others'. His first marriage had been a failure; his second a success. He'd achieved some financial success but had not been a great financier or industrialist. He hadn't written any great books or made any great discoveries. He'd had no political triumphs, nor had he led a life of abnegation for the sake of others.

So, what did his life add up to? Like others, he had met, married, and procreated. He had worked for a living, successfully enough for him to lead an upper-middle-class life; but certainly he hadn't had a remarkable career. He loved to read, had various interests and hobbies, contributed to various philanthropic causes; but, he realized, he had lived a rather unremarkable life. Could it have been different?

That was all his morphine-filled body could handle. It was back to the monkey-mind of successive memories. There he was, now, seducing Dorothy Neufeld, a voluptuous secretary at Blakesley and Montgomery, on the couch in her apartment. He had been married to Claudia for five years and had become increasingly unhappy in the marriage. His lust for Dorothy surmounted his sense of guilt and his marriage vows.

Then he drifted back to his childhood, when for some obscure reason he had urinated out of his bedroom window. His father discovered this misdeed, cut some branches from a bush in the garden, and thrashed him with them, leaving giant welts on his back and rear-end. Not a happy memory.

And there he was walking on the beach along San Francisco's Great Highway one night shortly after his separation from Claudia, feeling bereft, as if his entire world was sinking, depressed about his failed marriage and about no longer being a daily presence in the lives of his children. In the midst of this "dark night of the soul," listening to the pounding of the waves, he had an epiphany: his life would work out, he would again find

love, and his torments would cease. And splendid insight into the essence of his bei Molinari, stripped of the accidents of hi him for many years.

But now he was grappling with a simil to turn off the rapid cinematic images of l troubling thoughts. He began to fret w to God. Would God admit him into Par had always believed in an eternal life, bu commitment? Was there a possibility tha further consciousness? Only a dark void

In time he would be forgotten. His frier would have only blurred memories of h only a name on the genealogical list. Was into a future of oblivion?

No, Frank forced himself to affirm, t lives with Heaven and bad lives with He what about Purgatory? Was there such a

Frank tossed on his hospital bed, b because of the tubes stuck in his body. De pain. He knew that the increasing amo into his body were keeping the pain in sense of nausea that swept over him.

He relished being by himself. He had have his children or his friends visit him same to Paula, but it distressed him to on her face as she sat by his bedside.

A door opened, and he closed his one of the floor nurses making her rou equipment connected to him.

The door opened and closed again, a eyes.

He stared at the ceiling, enjoying the it gave him not to be distracted from v now his mind flickered onto a scene fr at St. Aloysius, when he had won an or proud he had been: and how pleased an was in the audience.

There ha life that he i it had been Had he been so radi the good th it had certa known: live to a "good That wa become a se Once mo he perhaps marginalize the sick? Sh to alleviate It was, F whether this world troub some point would inste he. But that Frank on his trouble rushed throu friends from clients and c had encount many who h The kaleid felt acutely him during whatever rea hadn't been or life had be Nick. Weeks years, Frank him for year remembered this shameful failure to remain a friend to someone who had been a benefactor.

Movie scenes from when he was a boy began to flicker through his mind. He had always loved the movies, oftentimes going twice a week in the 1940s. There was a scene from a Technicolor film, showing someone trying to impress a girl by diving into a lake from a tree and being rescued by a rival for the girl's affections. He couldn't remember the name of the movie...not that it mattered.

And, then, like a portrait gallery, came the faces of those stars and starlets who punctuated his erotic fantasies for probably two decades: Piper Laurie; Kim Novak, whose sensual elegance in *Vertigo* had haunted him for years; Barbara Rush in *The Young Philadelphians*; Sandra Dee in *A Summer Place*; Ali McGraw in *Goodbye, Columbus*.

What was it about these celluloid cuties that stayed with him for so many years? Did that happen to others? Does it still happen? Will the images of Jennifer Lopez, Cameron Diaz, and Julia Roberts stay with today's teenagers for decades to come?

These faces that had peppered his pre-pubescent, teenage, and early manhood years now gave way to a long-forgotten incident from the late 1960s. He was driving to an investment conference at Del Monte Lodge in Pebble Beach. He had decided to drive through the Santa Cruz Mountains over Highway 17. At one point he noticed that an attractive young woman, probably in her twenties, was driving alongside him. As he turned his head to look at her, she smiled and waved. Frank smiled and waved back, and then turned his eyes back to the road.

Soon, he noticed that her car—a snappy sports car—remained exactly parallel his. When he again looked over, she once more smiled and motioned him to pull over to the side of the road. Frank was puzzled, but slowed down and pulled over. The young lady skidded to a stop immediately behind him, and got out of her car. Frank looked at her quizzically and wondered if she were having car trouble.

"Hi, my name is Jackie," she said. "I saw you in your car and thought, 'What a cute guy he is. I'd like to get to know him better.'"

They were standing at a small clearing by the road, the tall trees of the Santa Cruz Mountains surrounding them. Frank was startled by her declaration.

"Ah, sure...ah," he stumbled, not certain of her meaning.

For the last few years Frank had watched the eruption of sexual freedom in the San Francisco Bay Area, part of the youth revolution that had been dubbed "the hippie counter-culture." It had excited and intrigued him, but he was not part of that culture. Married with children and a responsible position with an investment firm, Frank had not acted on the sexual opportunities that had engulfed northern California, and, seemingly, the country.

"Why don't we step behind those trees and get to know each other?" Jackie offered in an archway.

Frank could only bring himself to smile and be led by the hand through a screen of trees into a small, grassy clearing. He felt desire and lust surge through his body...and a disbelief that this was happening to him.

"I felt horny driving," she explained, "and I saw you and said to myself, 'Why not?'"

"Oh...I see," said Frank, while she pulled him down on her on the grassy clearing.

They began to kiss passionately, and soon they began to explore each other's anatomies. Clothes were shed and soon the two were soon naked, writhing on the warm grass. Frank's excitement at this unusual event caused him to orgasm prematurely, and he lay panting and spent.

"That was great," she said. "I hate to fuck and run, but I'm late for an appointment. Have a good weekend."

Frank didn't know how to respond, but watched her quickly assemble and put on her clothes. She smiled and waved as she left, and Frank was able to stutter, "Y—you have a good weekend, too."

And, now, Frank's imagination began to be a phantasmagoria of images: so many and so rapidly did they flicker across his mind that he couldn't process them. He felt restless and disconnected.

Frank became conscious of a lassitude in his arms and legs—even in his torso. It was as if he were somehow being separated from his body. He tried desperately to move his arms and legs, but his commands were not obeyed. The sensation felt strange and frightening.

Then it occurred to him: Is this it? Am I about to die?

The thought stunned him. He knew when he entered the hospital that he would die there, but that realization had seemed abstract. Now, he felt, he was confronting the reality.

"Sacred Heart of Jesus, have mercy on me," he muttered. I've got to do something, he thought. "Oh, Blessed Virgin Mary, intercede for me with your Son," he whispered.

He began to speak out the shards and fragments of prayers and intercessions he had learned as a boy, quickly, desperately.

The white hospital room began to fade from his vision, and the reality around him was replaced by a black void in which he felt himself in a free fall, unable to hold onto anything.

This is it, Frank thought. I hope this all works out.

* * * * * * * * * * * *

ABOUT THE AUTHOR

 Charles A. Fracchia is a native San Franciscan. He received a BA in history from the University of San Francisco, an MA in history from San Francisco State University, an MLS from the University of California at Berkeley, and an MA in theology from the Graduate Theological Union in Berkeley.

Fracchia spent 20 years in the investment banking and investment advisory business and 35 years as an academic, teaching at San Francisco State University, City College of San Francisco, and the University of San Francisco.

He is the author of 15 books; *Palimsest* is his first book of fiction. He is a Fellow of the California Historical Society and the Founder and President Emeritus of the San Francisco Museum and Historical Society.

Fracchi was one of the founders of *Rolling Stone* magazine.